Isabeau

Isabeau

A Novel of
Queen Isabella
and Sir Roger Mortimer

N. GEMINI SASSON

cader idris
press

For Reini and Mitchell -

Dreams are meant to be lived.

PROLOGUE

Isabella:

Boulogne, France — January, 1308

THE FIRST TIME I saw Edward II of England was on our wedding day in the cathedral of Our Lady of Boulogne. He was twenty-three, a king newly come to his throne. I was not yet thirteen—a girl on the lip of womanhood: nervous, excited, and awestricken by my tall and slender groom. Far too curious to pretend coyness, I stole quick glances at him as we stood before the altar. Faint winter sunlight penetrated the vaulted expanse from high lancet windows and fell about him in a silver haze. The ivory satin of his tunic reflected the smoothness of his complexion and the jewels on his cloak glittered like the bright blue of his Plantagenet eyes.

I was the only daughter of Philip IV of France and, of all the kings in Christendom, Edward had been chosen for me. For years, I had waited for this day, dreamed of it, planned for it.

All morning my damsels had fussed over me, like bees humming about freshly bloomed clover: arranging my pale, silken hair beneath my gold caul with delicate care, plucking my brows into precise arches and

1

rubbing my skin with rose-scented oil until it glistened. They dressed me in a gown of gold and brightest blue, to match my hair and eyes. Next, they hung a mantle of red lined with yellow sindon over my shoulders and secured it with a brooch encircled with sapphires and rubies. Then, with tears of joy, they hugged me and told me I was the fairest woman in all of France and any man who was not struck dumb by my beauty was certainly blind.

Not once during the ceremony did Edward look at me.

I stared intently at him, certain he would sense my tacit plea for attention and glimpse my way, but he kept his eyes fixed on the bishop, a look of sleepy boredom dulling his countenance. As the hour wore on, a chill seeped beneath my skin and gripped my bones. Frigid sweat dampened my chemise. I clasped the edges of my mantle and drew it closer to my shivering body. One of the pins that held the tightly wound plaits of my hair in place dug into my scalp. The beautiful coronet studded with amethysts, emeralds and pearls that I had donned so gleefully that morning began to feel like a jagged band of iron clamped across my forehead. I wiggled numb toes. My shoes were pinching my feet and my back ached from standing so dreadfully long.

Edward gazed up at the web of vaulting ribs that sprung from the fluted columns. He shifted on his feet. Yawned. And sighed.

When the bishop gave his final blessing, Edward's cold kiss barely grazed my lips. He stuck his elbow out stiffly, flinching as I curled my fingers around his arm. We started forward down the central aisle of the nave, our steps mismatched. His stride was long and hurried, mine hindered by the long train of my gown. While a thousand eyes appraised us, I forced myself to match his pace and pressed the corners of my mouth into a false smile.

At our wedding feast, he leaned close and whispered, "You needn't wear your dread so plainly. You are . . . how should I say this—not yet ripe for the picking. There will be time, later, for that." He attempted a half-smile of apology, but it looked to me more like a sneer of disdain.

We spoke no more that day. I fell asleep alone in my bed that night, thankful that he had kept his word and not come, but bewildered as to why he had paid so little attention to me, his new bride. Had I been thrust upon him against his wishes? Did he love another? Did the sight of me so repulse him that he could not bear my presence? Whatever the matter, I vowed to learn how to become a good wife and queen to him. It was my duty.

I was still young then . . . and naïve. I had so much to learn.

THIRTEEN DAYS LATER, BENEATH a lowering sky, we disembarked at Dover, England. There, I discovered the cause for my husband's distraction. Piers de Gaveston stood on the dock swathed in velvets and furs, waving a kerchief high in the air. Edward sprang across the plank, took Gaveston into his arms and showered him with kisses. Then, he showed him a trunk filled with gifts—gifts which only the week before had been given to Edward by my father. With a flourish of praise for serving as Keeper of the Realm in his absence, Edward draped a gilt chain around Gaveston's neck, from which hung a lion of gold, each foot balanced on a shimmering pearl and its eyes set with two fiery rubies. If my father were to hear of this, it would be cause enough for war.

"That was meant for you," I reminded him meekly as I approached. The weathered boards creaked beneath my feet and a cold sea wind nudged me toward the edge of the dock. My damsels were still aboard ship to oversee the unloading of my trousseau, but my brother, Charles, who had followed close behind, came abreast of me. I stood firm and pulled the hood of my favorite red, ermine-lined mantle up over my head.

Edward's laughter broke off. The hint of a scowl twisted his mouth. "What did you say?"

I moved closer and raised my chin, trying to sound more confident than I actually was. I thought it only fair to warn him. "Those gifts—the jewels, the brooches and chains—they were given to you by my father. You cannot give them away like that. He would not approve."

He scoffed and shook his head dismissively at me. "They're mine now. I'll do with them as I please." Then, he threw an arm about Gaveston's shoulder and together they walked away, laughing at jokes only they understood. Like an impertinent child, I had been dismissed. My chest burned with indignation.

Charles clasped my hand and said lowly, "If you ever need my help, Isabeau, you only need ask."

I squeezed his fingers and tried to smile, but could not. Was it because my cheeks were too stiff from the cold, or because some dread had seeped into my heart and begun to blacken it like a frost that withers still green leaves?

Although only a year older, Charles had always been protective of me; however, the time for that would soon end. I had a husband now, a new home, new life. "But Charles, my coronation is in less than a fortnight and after that you'll be gone. Who knows when we will ever see each other again? What help could you possibly be, so far away?"

"Come now, our father is King of France—and you ask what I can do?" He touched my face, his thumb stroking my cheek lightly. "Remember, I'm only as far as a letter. Already he neglects you, dear sister. I will not have it so."

Neglect? That seemed too harsh a word. But had I not just done worse? In speaking my mind, I had made a poor start of our marriage. If there was ever to be some measure of affinity between us clearly it would have to begin with me. "Perhaps, perhaps I have made too much of too small a thing?"

With a sigh, Charles kissed me on the forehead and offered his elbow. "Oh, Isabeau, are you truly such an innocent?"

A sharp voice cut above the roar of the sea wind. At the door of the aftcastle on the ship, my damsel Juliana clucked at a pair of pages as they carelessly hoisted a trunk filled with my gowns onto their meager shoulders. Beside her, Marie shivered within her cloak, her wide eyes darting shyly from one pale English face to another. I lowered my voice as I tucked my arm into my brother's. "You mock me, Charles. Please don't. It's only that . . . well, that there is so much Edward and I have yet to learn about each other. This Gaveston is an old friend, I hear. They were overjoyed to see each other. Surely, that is all?"

A bemused grin tilted the corners of his too delicate mouth. "You think you can change him, do you? That your marriage will get nothing but better? I wish you luck, then. Luck and a long streak of tolerance."

We turned and walked toward the carriage that would carry me first to Dover Castle to refresh overnight, and then off to the Palace of Westminster for my crowning. Tufts of white drifted across my vision and I blinked. Snow tumbled down, melting as it touched the earth. I looked out over the somber, glassy surface of the harbor to one side and then far up at the imposing castle of Dover, its stout, gray walls shouldering a joyless sky. With Charles' help, I climbed inside the carriage. Draping a fur across my lap, I peered out the back as my trousseau was loaded onto wagons to the rear.

Luck, as it turned out, I did not have. Tolerance? Too much for my own good, I dare admit.

Some things, some people—as I was to learn—they do not change, no matter how much we wish them to. We are foolish to even hope they might.

And to hope in vain is to live in despair.

PART I:

You know the King is so suspicious
As, if he hear I have but talked with you,
Mine honor will be called in question;
And therefore, gentle Mortimer, be gone.

Isabella
from Christopher Marlowe's *Edward II*

1

Isabella:

Tower of London — September, 1312

I HEAVED MY UNWIELDY bulk upward, my legs cramping with fire. Pressure constricted my ribs, as though someone had clamped a set of irons around my middle and meant to squeeze the life from me. A surge of bile splashed at the back of my throat. I gritted my teeth, swallowing it back, and leaned against the cool, stone wall of the staircase. After a few strained breaths, my knees wobbling, I forced myself up the last few steps. When I reached the landing, I pressed a hand to my gown to blot away the sweat pouring down my breastbone.

The staircase of St. Thomas's Tower was not any steeper than it had been just a few months before. I had simply grown fatter. Fat with child.

At just past seventeen years, I was vainly conscious of my size. Two months yet to go and my belly was as broad as a merchant's ship. If set out to sea, I would most assuredly sink to the bottom however, not float. This morning, I could not put on my own slippers without Juliana's help. And my seamstress had yet to stitch together a gown that flattered my bloated figure in any way, no matter how ornate or colorful. If this—this discomfort—was what it meant to be a woman and bring babes into the world, I would gladly have returned to my own childhood and dallied there interminably, giddy in my irresponsible innocence.

Within the first month of Edward's visits to my bed earlier this year, I had awoken violently ill, unable to hold down my morning bread and wine. The episodes of vomiting were a fair exchange for the reprieve they brought, for Edward had carried out the act of bedding me with no more tenderness than a yearling ram would give a ewe in season. It was a marvel he ever got around to the business at all. For a time, I was convinced I would die not only childless, but a virgin as well.

Standing before the door to the king's apartments, I nodded to the lone guard, his mouth carved in the lines of a permanent scowl. With a jerking bow, he swung it open. I squinted in expectation of a flood of sunlight, but the shutters were drawn. Instead, a thin haze veiled my vision. Wood smoke stung my eyes. Blinking, I focused on the limp figure some ten paces away. Edward, chin to chest, sat slumped in a chair by the hearth, his hands dangling down and his knuckles nearly scraping the floor. The rough shadows of unshaven whiskers darkened his cheeks. Blotches of spilled wine dappled his pale blue tunic.

He had been this way since that odious day in June: heavyhearted and listless. Not even the prospect of an heir had served to uplift his spirits in that time.

"Come closer," he uttered thinly, his only movement a quick shifting of his pupils.

My footsteps echoed in the desolate expanse. The walls were bare of coverings. Even the tables and other furnishings had been removed—all but the carved oaken throne upon which Edward had not sat for three months—as if to discourage visitors or activity of any kind.

"Into the light," he drawled.

There was little light to be found in that musty, suffocating room. The fire in the hearth had faded to sputtering embers and an early autumn draft fanned the smoke into every corner, tainting the air with the smell of ashes. I walked closer, into a knife of light where the sun stabbed through a crack in the shutters. He flipped a hand up to stay me.

"Turn around."

Slowly, so as not to lose my balance, I turned in a circle, holding my breath while he studied me like a prize cow in calf.

"You need to eat more," he said. "You'll starve the child."

Letting out a burst of air, I faced him. "Of course, my lord. I shall. The morning sickness has finally abated." A lie. It had not passed at all. But there was no purpose in arguing with him. He only wanted a healthy child, an heir . . . as any man would.

With a sound that was half whimper, half groan, Edward leaned forward to rest his elbows on his knees. As he drew forward the hand furthest from me, a glint of gold caught my eye. In his palm he clutched the jeweled lion pendant, the chain swinging freely from the open end of his fist. A sheen of sweat glistened on his blanched cheeks as he tilted his head to look at my belly from a different angle—like a robin would cock its head at a worm. "I pray this one is not a girl."

"Daughters can bring strong alliances," I countered defensively.

He scoffed. "Like you? I suppose, but little good that has done me lately. Where was France when they mur—" The thought died on his tongue with a shudder. Slouching back against his chair again, he turned his face toward the dying flames and brought the lion pendant to his chest, laying it over his heart.

Even now, months later, he still could not say his name aloud. Not anymore. He had only spoken it one time since then—on the day he learned of Piers de Gaveston's death.

For too many years, Gaveston had mocked authority. Twice, he was banished from the realm. Twice, Edward wooed his barons and proffered promises until they relented and Gaveston was recalled. Then a third time, Gaveston was sent into exile, warned never to return. But return he did. This time, however, the barons were implacable. Edward and Gaveston had fled from London, only to be pursued and besieged by the king's own cousin Thomas, Earl of Lancaster. In the end, Gaveston gave himself up, sure he would receive a fair trial and reunite with Edward once more.

One month later, in the dark of night and stripped of his clothing, Gaveston was executed on Blacklow Hill with a blunt axe. It was said that he was wearing the lion pendant and chain and that Edward demanded its return when told of the murder. Now he clove to it like a starving man to his last loaf of bread.

"Lancaster should be brought to account for his crime," I said, attempting to offer some compassion. But I stopped short of saying Lancaster should die for it. The question still stood of just how involved he had been in the cursory execution. Besides, bloodshed never ended bloodshed. It only perpetuated more of it.

Edward sniffed. "When our son is born, England will rejoice. And I will hold the upper hand. Because the more boys you can give me, my queen, the further from the throne my murdering cousin Lancaster will be." Eyes clamped shut, he threw the back of his head against the chair. The veins in his neck throbbed blue against the scarlet rising along his throat. He slammed a fist against his thigh. "Red-handed, perfidious, donkey-swiving miscreant! May his testicles shrivel and turn to stone. He gave his word to Pembroke." His eyes flew open and he jabbed a finger at me, punctuating each vitriolic syllable. "Gave . . . his . . . word!"

There would be retaliation. I had no doubt of that. But now was not the time. Better to let him simmer in despondency until his head had cooled. At least let him wait until our child was born. Already it was becoming clear that my duty would go far beyond bearing royal English progeny; my duty—unspoken though it may be—would be to bear influence upon my inconstant husband, upon whose unfit head the crown had fallen.

As if cued by my thoughts, the ache in my back fanned upward. The floor tipped beneath me. I spread my arms to steady myself and looked about the room for another chair, but there was only a low foot stool next to a rolled up tapestry at the far end of the room. The murals spanning the walls were obscured in smoky darkness, the figures adorning them now taking on the ghastly shapes of the eternally condemned struggling to escape the torments of hell. A chill rippled from my tailbone up my spine and I braced my shoulders against it to stop my whole body from trembling.

I could not remain in this dank, comfortless room for much longer without crumpling into a weary heap. With stiff fingers, I kneaded at my lower back to emphasize my condition. "My lord, I leave for Windsor in two days. If you will allow me to take my leave now, I need to oversee the packing of my things. Otherwise, Juliana and Patrice will want to take my whole wardrobe, most of which will do me no good. As you know, I will not be back in London for some time—not until my churching at Westminster."

Rigid now, he molded himself to the chair frame. His fingernails clawed the length of his thigh, snagging the cloth of his hose. The pendant was still clutched in his other hand. His lips went taut, then began to twitch, as though he fought back tears.

I ran my hands down my sides, from breasts to hips, to remind him not only of the future, but to distract him from past horrors.

"Edward," he muttered. "We will call him Edward."

I had expected nothing else. Of course he would name the child after himself. "You will attend the birth, I trust?"

The last log in the fire cracked, then crumbled into a pile of flickering ashes. "If it is safe for me to leave London . . ." He brushed his fingers toward the door. "Go. I shall provide you with a sizeable armed escort. To keep you safe."

In our more than four years together, it was the closest thing to genuine concern that had ever graced his lips. I uttered a perfunctory word of thanks, gathered up the ponderous weight of my skirts and dipped at the knee. As I took my first steps to leave, a knock rattled the door in its frame. I halted partway across the room, braving a look back. Edward peered at me through tearful, slit eyes.

"Were you expecting someone, my lord? I can send them away, if—"

"People come and go at all hours," he sniveled. "The sooner they state their business, the sooner I can be rid of them."

With a nod, I went to the door and opened it. The musky scent of horse hide and leather wafted in. Behind the guard stood a nobleman, hands clasped behind him. His clothes had the wrinkled and smudged look of one who has ridden long and with purpose. At his right shoulder, a circular silver brooch secured his hooded riding cloak. On his left side, the scabbard of his sword dangled beneath the cloak's embroidered hem. Black hanks of hair, knotted by the wind, hid his downcast eyes.

"Sir Roger Mortimer, my lady," the guard said lowly, as if he were reluctant to disturb Edward yet again, "to seek an audience with the king."

Slowly, Mortimer looked up, his dark eyes lingering for a moment on the mound of my pregnancy. My fingers groped the air for a mantle to cover myself, but with a flush of embarrassment I remembered I had none. I retreated behind the door—as if I could hide there, suddenly invisible.

"What? Is Death at my door, come for *me* now?" Edward jested. "Who is it?"

"Sir Roger Mortimer."

"So soon from Ireland? The devil indeed has wings, eh? Send him in. I have rotten work to be done in Gascony."

"Gascony?" I echoed, my hand upon the door, stalling. "But I thought Ireland and Scotland—"

"Ireland, Scotland . . . the whole mad *world* is against me. Why not Gascony, too? Even the pope chides me. Anyway, it's Mortimer's kin who are quarreling now—and they're costing me in fines levied by your father. So I'll set Mortimer to task. Now please." He waved a hand in the air expansively.

Tugging the door fully open, I took a step back.

"My lady." Mortimer bowed, his mouth spreading into a broad smile as he met my eyes again. "Your condition, if I may say, suits you exceedingly well. My own wife, Joan, is at Ludlow this very moment, due our eighth child."

Eighth? He was barely in his mid twenties and his wife the same age. The poor woman. I could hardly imagine bearing a child of Edward's every year for the next eight years. But then, Roger Mortimer was not at all like Edward.

"If it is a girl," he said, "I will ask that she name her Isabella, in hopes she will grow to be as beautiful as you."

Heat ignited in my breast and flared upward from my neck to my face. Unable to hold his gaze, I spoke at my shoes in a voice no bigger than a small child's. "I-I have no objection. It is a common enough name."

I scurried down the stairs, too quickly for good sense. When I reached the bottom, dizzy and breathless, I sank down to rest on the last stair. The chill of the stones seeped through the cloth of my gown and into my hips. I drew my knees in close and curled both arms around my extended belly, aware of an odd sensation. Not pain, but a stirring. Movement. Slight perhaps, but certain.

If it is a boy, let him become a greater man than his father.
I prayed:

"Hail Mary, full of grace,
God is with thee.
Of all women, thou art most blessed
And blessed be the fruit of thy womb . . ."

This time the babe kicked hard, just beneath my ribs. I pressed a hand there, overcome with wonder as I felt his strong limbs push against my palm.

THE DAY THAT YOUNG Edward—or so I would come to call him—was born at Windsor, the nursemaid, Ida, swore she saw a lone golden eagle soaring above the Round Tower, as if it were heralding some extraordinary event. My damsel Patrice argued it was merely a buzzard eyeing the bloated corpse of an old stable cat that had strayed onto the roof to die. But superstitious Ida could not be convinced otherwise. She believed it was an omen that there would be a great war in the young prince's lifetime. But when is the world ever without some terrible strife between or within kingdoms?

I did not see the eagle—only the strange, blue-veined protrusion of my stomach, looking to my vain, seventeen-year old self like a tumor that did not belong there. For me, the birthing was easier than it was for most women. It did not go on long. I had awoken in the night with a sense of urgency, my middle contracting. While Ida fetched the midwife, I paced the floor, chatting with Patrice to pass the time and stopping occasionally as a shiver rippled through me. When the midwife came, she made me lie down, spread my legs apart in a rather vulgar pose and exclaimed that the baby's head was already crowning. It was almost as though I were watching someone else give birth to him. Afterwards, my astonishment gave way to a wave of exhaustion, but I do not remember any pain. I remember more the tickling of pride, like I had indeed done something out of the ordinary. The midwife placed the small, wailing babe in the crook of my elbow. Immediately, he looked at me and quieted, as if he knew my face already and that sanctuary would always be within my arms.

2

Roger Mortimer:

Berwick — June, 1314

T HE DUTIES OF A king's liegeman are too often unwanted, unending and thankless.

For years in Ireland I, Roger Mortimer, had fought against small chiefs who called themselves 'kings' and brought them all down. Then, just as a lull had settled there, King Edward sent me to play peacemaker among my petty kin in Gascony. I had barely set foot in Ireland again when another summons was flung at me—to join the king on campaign in Scotland to relieve Stirling Castle. Did he not think for a moment to better prepare himself against the Bruce?

Bannockburn. Thousands upon thousands of Englishmen lay dead there now. Yet I had survived.

For this.

Two carrion crows eyed us from the distant parapets of the towers that flanked Berwick's gate. My gaze drifted to the walls surrounding the city. How many batterings had those walls seen? The scars were still there from Longshanks' assault, almost twenty years ago. Inside now huddled his successor: Edward II, King of England.

This Edward was nothing like his father.

I pulled in a breath and held it. My lungs burned. The air was still hot with the scent of blood, even though the battlefield was many days and miles behind us.

"Come, Maltravers," I said to my companion beside me. His horse flicked its ears, reluctant to go on. Eight years ago on Whitsunday, Sir John Maltravers and I had taken our vows of knighthood at Westminster. He was now less half of the last two fingers of his left hand. His reminder of Bannockburn. Not yet healed, he kept them wrapped in strips of cloth that were brown and stiff with dried blood.

I shifted in my saddle, my arms and legs flaming sore. The ride to Berwick had been long and hard. The sun so searing hot it felt as though my flesh might melt from my bones. Sweat pooled in the creases of my clothing. I licked at dry lips, making them sting.

With his good hand, Maltravers yanked at the reins of the extra horse we had been given. Flies swarmed around the canvas-wrapped lump draped over its back. The corpse was beginning to stink. Perhaps it would have been better had I not survived the battle. Or been ransomed instead. Anything but this.

Bloody Christ, I had not asked to do this. It would earn me no favors.

I pricked my horse's flanks with my spurs and we rode up to Berwick's gate.

To bring the king a token of his defeat.

AN HOUR PASSED BEFORE Maltravers and I were given entrance to the town. Another hour before we were taken to the castle. All the while, flies assaulted us in great swarms of agitation. We paused on the steps to the main door of the great hall. There, an old woman gave us water from a ladle dipped in a leaky bucket. I guzzled it down, doubled over as a pain ripped through my belly and turned my head aside to vomit. My insides cleansed, I dragged my hand across my mouth and straightened. I fought the urge to turn and go back the way I had come, but I had a duty to complete. I owed my life to it, however disagreeable.

Like a lion's yawning jaws, the doors opened. Maltravers and I were led inside. I probed the sack I carried for a lump. Still there. Several knights, scowls visible even across the distance, leered at us from the dais at the hall's end. In his high-backed chair in the middle, the king slumped. I forced myself forward. I still felt the aches of battle, sharp as knives, especially the sword blow I had taken to my left shoulder. My mail had saved me. The Scotsman who struck me had lost his arm for the offense. I had not bothered to finish killing him, merciful as that might have been. There was too much going on around me and he was going to die anyway.

Maltravers staggered like a drunk under the weight slung over his shoulder. His knee banged against the leg of an overturned bench and he spit out a curse under his breath. The tables and benches that lined either side of the hall were in disarray. Toppled cups lay atop the tables; puddles of spilt ale beneath. Rotting fruit littered the floor. My eyes lingered on a half eaten chicken. When had I last eaten? I could not recall. I reached out my hand, thinking to sample the meat, but the fetid smell wafting from beside me made me retch.

"I thought you were dead, Sir Roger," King Edward drawled.

Before the dais, I halted Maltravers with my hand and set the sack down at my feet, eager to be rid of it. "Is that how you would prefer me, sire?"

"Not at all," he muttered absently, his gaze fixed on Maltraver's burden. "Too many are dead already." Tears rushed to his eyes. He clenched both fists and threw his head back so hard it thunked against the back of his chair. Then he gulped air and spoke again, his voice cracking with sorrow. "You were with the Earl of Pembroke at . . . at Bannockburn, were you not? He is in Carlisle, I was told. Why, then, are you here?"

"We were followed by the Scots, my lord. I turned and fought, so that Pembroke could escape. My horse, a good one, was piked. I lost my sword as I went down. I had no choice but to give myself up. When they learned who I was, they took me to their king, the Bruce. He was at the little church of St. Ninian's, praying over the body of this his fallen kinsman—and yours. He released me so that I might bring the body to you. That, sire, is why I am here." I motioned Maltravers forward.

As he neared the king, Maltravers dragged his feet. In relief, he exhaled heavily and lowered the great weight from his shoulder. He laid it out full length on the step below the king's chair and backed away, his head down so that he would not meet the king's eyes and his maimed hand hidden behind his leg.

"Robert the Bruce," I began, "said to tell you, my king, that he grieves, as well, and that your nephew was a good and courageous man." I peeled away the cloth covering the face. Despite a cursory embalming by the monks of Cambus Kenneth Abbey, the sweet odor of decay invaded the air. I held my breath and looked down at the bloodless, wizened face. He had died young. And foolishly—thinking he could take the Bruce single-handedly. "Gilbert de Clare, Earl of Gloucester."

The group of men who stood to the side of the dais murmured. I recognized only a few of them. With so many great lords dead or captured there were bound to be new faces surrounding the king, all plying for their fortunes.

Edward took one glance, shivered and clamped his eyes shut. "Cover his face, Hugh. Cover it!" The Scottish monks had taken great pains to sew up the skin over the cleft in his skull near Gilbert's left temple. That was where the Bruce's axe head had been imbedded. But it was Gilbert's body being dragged across open ground by his frightened horse that had torn a hunk of flesh from that side of his head. The mending had left his features ghoulishly distorted, his mouth stretched taut to one side. Edward sniveled. "That grotesque . . . *thing* . . . is *not* my beloved Gilbert." His voice dissipated like mist scattered by the wind. "He always wore a smile. Always."

The younger man beside him obliged. He paused to study the face before carefully laying the cloth back over it. "It is him, my lord king," he said in a detached, languorous voice.

I recognized him then as Hugh Despenser the Younger. He had been with the king at Stirling's gate. His wife was Eleanor de Clare, Gilbert's sister. I had seen him at court only a handful of times, as he dangled expectantly on the fringes like a hound waiting for scraps to fall from the table. It appeared he had found the abandoned foxhole and burrowed himself under the king's armpit recently.

With a shudder, Edward opened his eyes, wept red and dry, and gave Despenser a doleful look.

Despenser moved up the steps of the dais and knelt before the king. He touched a hand lightly to his knee. "He was a loyal kinsman, a kind friend to you. His loss is a heavy blow to many. Eleanor will shed many tears when she hears of it."

His words were too contrived, his tone too hollow to have been in earnest.

Edward laid his hand on top of Hugh's. He shook his head for a long time until his lower lip began to quiver. "Was it not enough, what happened? This, too? He was so dear to me. So very, very dear. My brother, I often called him."

"A pity he never had children, my lord."

No heirs. And Hugh Despenser married to one of his sisters, who would undoubtedly inherit Gilbert's numerous holdings, including an earldom. What a convenience that Despenser now stood close enough to mop the king's tears away.

Edward nodded and then cocked his head to one side. "Bruce—he expects something for this . . . morbid gesture?" He scoffed into his hand. "I'll not call that bastard 'king', ever."

"He did not ask that, not yet." I reached inside the sack at my feet and revealed its contents. "But he sends this: The Great Seal."

Edward's eyes bulged. The Great Seal bore his likeness and without its imprint in wax no royal document was valid. He gestured at Despenser to retrieve it. Once in his hands he turned it over, inspecting it carefully to confirm its authenticity. Then he clenched it so hard his knuckles went white. "What does he want for it?"

"His wife, sisters and daughter back, my lord. And Bishop Wishart of Glasgow."

"Wishart? The shriveled old turd is blind and deaf."

"Then it will do little harm to release him. He says, also, once you send them back to Scotland, he will free the Earl of Hereford and other lords."

"So why did he let *you* go?"

He would have doubted me had I been his own brother. "To bring you this message."

"Phhh . . ." Listless, Edward wilted into his chair again. "I need time to think. To seek counsel."

"As you wish, my lord king. In the meanwhile, shall I carry the Earl of Gloucester's remains back to one of his sisters, so he may be properly buried?" Inwardly, I revolted against the prospect of traveling so far south with a putrid corpse in the blazing height of summer, but it seemed the proper thing to do. Besides, I did not want to stay here and watch King Edward wallow in self-pity. I would return to court when he had regained his senses, or else I would go back to Ireland and earn his regard there. Meanwhile, I had a wife to get home to.

Edward traced his jawline with a fingertip. "Yes, do that."

"Which sister, my lord?"

He waved a hand in the air. "Eleanor. Take him to Lady Eleanor in . . . in . . ."

"Gloucester," Despenser answered for him. "Do you wish me to go along as well, my king? To settle his estates?"

"No." Edward clasped Despenser's hand fiercely, as if the thought of him leaving was too much to bear. "No, Hugh, stay. I will need your guidance on these ludicrous demands. But first, we shall go on to London. Oh, London . . . dear God, I do not want to go there at all. But we cannot stay here. Not in Berwick. Even York is too close. If we are pursued one more step with a pack of Scottish dogs on our heels . . ." He stopped himself and flipped a hand toward the door. "Go, Sir Roger. At once. Have a Mass said in Gilbert's name for me."

I bent to retrieve the empty sack at my feet, but before I could turn to go, the king said, "Gilbert's father-in-law, Ralph de Monthermer. What became of him?"

I hesitated to answer. He would not like the truth. Sooner or later, though, he would hear it. "Taken by the Scots, my lord."

"For ransom? Part of the exchange for the Seal?"

"No, my lord. The Bruce gave him his freedom. Some sort of repayment for a past favor, as I understood. I do not know the story behind it, but Monthermer chose to stay as his guest . . . for now."

Edward jerked his face away and snarled. "Traitors, everywhere."

He narrowed his eyes at me, as if he were still suspicious as to why I had been spared by the Scots. I hardly knew. Nothing more than luck, I supposed. Bad luck, at this point.

He skimmed the Great Seal upwards over his throat and the whiskers of his chin, until it came to rest on his lips. He kissed it before he returned it to his lap. "Then I thank you, Sir Roger, for your loyalty. And your service. You have done well by me in Ireland. I do not forget such things."

I bowed to him and went from his presence. Maltravers hoisted the reeking bundle back onto his shoulder and followed.

To have a king's gratitude was a good thing. But kings were fickle creatures. Especially this one. I did not want to offend him, although that was a hard thing not to do.

To offend a king is to court death.

Wigmore – July, 1314

IN GLOUCESTER, I GAVE Gilbert de Clare's body over to his sister. She fell to her knees and wept while she clung to my shins. I hardly knew the earl well enough to share in her grief, or Lady Eleanor enough to comfort her.

On the road north of Hereford, I paid Sir John Maltravers with the money that Lady Eleanor had given me for my labors and dismissed him.

He wanted to go home, he said. So I let him, but I told him also when the time came for me to go to Ireland, I would need him.

It was well past nightfall when I arrived at Wigmore. Not wanting to be assailed by an exuberant flock of children, for I was too spent to endure their attentions, I hushed the porter and crept up the stairs. I turned the latch to our chamber door and nudged it open.

Joan stood by the open window, vigilant. Moonlight outlined the pleasing roundness of her hips through the edges of a white nightshift. My weariness was swept away in a rush of longing for her.

She glanced over her shoulder at me, nothing more than passing irritation in her voice. "So, did you come home merely to dispel rumors of your death—or is there some other reason?"

"I've come home to be with my wife." I barred the door behind me.

"For longer this time, I hope."

"How else," I said, "is a man to advance himself at court when it is his sword that is his strength? It has won me the king's gratitude several times over."

"And the king's gratitude is more important to you than your wife's company?"

I let the matter go. Too often our reunions had been callous ones, tainted with misunderstanding. This first night, at least, I wanted to be pleasurable for us both.

As she turned sideways to fetch me a cup of wine, I noticed the slight fullness of her belly in the haze of the moon's silvery glow. How long since I had lain with her? Four months? No, five. And only eight since our last child was born.

I walked past her, took the cup she held out for me, and eased onto the bed. While I gulped down the wine, Joan knelt at my feet and tugged off my boots. I must have stunk like a cow shut up in the byre too long. Despite my rankness, she kneaded at the arches of my feet, my calves, my thighs.

"Your uncle is here from Chirk," she said. "He heard of the king's defeat at Bannockburn and hoped . . . knew you would be home soon.

Although, we heard nothing until the Earl of Pembroke passed through. Shall I fetch your uncle now?"

"In the morning."

"How was your journey home?" Her question was a courtesy, the same one she posed every time upon my return.

I leaned back, caught her by the wrists and pulled her hard against my chest. Her breath caught. "Let us not talk of it. I would rather have you." I rolled her over beside me and ran my calloused palm over the curving mound of her middle. "Is it safe?"

"Has that ever stopped you before?" She looked up at the ceiling.

It was not an answer, but it was not denial, either. Beyond our bed, sometimes even in it, we were strangers to one another. Even after so many years.

I tried to lighten her mood, teasing, "Have we room here at Wigmore for an eighth? Do I need to build another wing?"

"It will be our ninth, Roger." She wriggled free of my hold and slipped from the bed.

I propped myself up on an elbow to gaze at her. "Will it? Well then, tomorrow I shall have to reacquaint myself with them all. They forget their father so quickly."

"It is not the children who forget."

In invitation, I pushed the corner of the bedcovers away. "After this one, let us work on the tenth, and the eleventh, and the . . ."

As she lifted her nightshift from one shoulder and then the other to let her breasts spill out, I forgot what I was saying. I went to her, peeled her shift downward so it rested on her hips, and kissed her neck. Instinctively, I pressed against her body, the growing heat in my loins seeking to be quenched within her. She turned her head aside and a thin sigh escaped her throat.

Had I cared to listen, I might have heard it for what it was—a sigh of indifference.

THE NEXT MORNING I awoke late. Joan's side of the bed was long since cold, the indent of her body smoothed over by fastidious hands. She was probably with the children somewhere already or going over records with the steward. I had not told her I could be sent back to Ireland at any time, should the Scots cause trouble there. When the time came for me to go, I would insist that she come with me, even though I expected her to protest profusely over the conditions there. At least she would not be able to complain of my absence.

Wearing only my breeches, I rose, stretched my arms and went to the washbasin Joan had left out for me. I dipped the washcloth in and began to scrub. Every time I wrung the cloth the water turned browner and cloudier, until I could not see the bottom of the blessed bowl. Indolent servants. Or had Joan shooed them all away to let me sleep?

"Gladys? Clementina?" I grabbed a dry shirt and buried my face in it. There was a faint knock on the door and a long creak as it swung open. "Fetch me more water."

"Fetch your own."

I turned to see my uncle, Lord Roger Mortimer of Chirk, in the doorway, propped up by a carved walking staff. He hobbled across the room and tapped me on the knee with his stick.

"I waited up half the night, do you know? Going to tell me about it? The whole thing?" He leaned into the gnarled staff, rotated his weight on it and gimped over to a chair, where he plopped down in anticipation of a story. He pounded the staff on the floor to punctuate each sentence. "I want details. Who fought well. Who died. Who lived. Who's being held for ransom. All that."

"Tales of battle are better told over a cask of wine and late at night."

He grumbled in disappointment. "What took you so long to find your way home? Pembroke came this way over a week ago. Said he lost you after the battle and had not heard from you. For shame, you should have seen your poor wife. She assumed you were dead. We all did."

"How unfaithful of you all." I gave up on getting clean water and put on the shirt I had dried my face on. Next, I went in search of a fresh pair of hose. As she always did, Joan had lain everything out for me on top of the chest at the end of our bed. "The king has another sycophant, Uncle."

His white feathered eyebrows leapt upward. "Who?"

"Hugh Despenser the Younger. His brother-in-law, Gilbert de Clare, was killed at Bannockburn. I think he covets his earldom."

"Gloucester dead? That will set things on end." He hunched forward, scenting scandal. "Is Despenser anything like Piers de Gaveston?"

The king had pandered to the impertinent Gaveston, a man of humble Gascon origins, by granting him the earldom of Cornwall. Rumors about the king and Gaveston had abounded, until the Gascon's murder ended speculation. "No, this is no roistering boyhood friend of the king's, to be spoiled with sparkling jewels and fancy clothes. No, he is . . . different."

"Hah, I don't doubt, given his stock. Watch him carefully, but from a distance."

I hitched my shoulders in a half-shrug. "What do you mean? Do you know something of this Hugh the Younger?"

"Him? Barely anything. But I know his family. I know the oath his father once made to your father."

"Tell. What oath?" I fastened the cord on my hose.

"That he would kill him."

"Come now. I have never heard such a story. Did father slight the elder Despenser somehow? Steal his cows? Hunt on his lands? Sleep with his mistress?"

"You take it too lightly. I warn you not to. This Hugh the Younger— *your* grandfather killed *his* grandfather at the Battle of Evesham."

"Evesham?" I scoffed. "Evesham was fifty years ago, Uncle. My grandfather fought for Longshanks then. Saved his life—it was you who told me so. Surely King Edward will know of that?"

"Hmph, a Plantagenet's memory is not that long. But Despensers . . . they do not forget." He slammed his stick down hard once, emphatic. "*Watch him.*"

I belted my tunic and sat down on the chest. "I am more concerned for the king than for myself."

He replied with a visceral grunt.

"Despenser and I are on the same side—unlike our grandfathers."

"For now. But be careful. If you offend the king's favorite, you offend the king. Edward has hardly forgotten what they did to Gaveston." He drew a kerchief from his sleeve and wiped his nose. "Now, tell me about Bannockburn."

"Later, I told you." I slipped my shoes on and went to the door. "I'm going to go find my wife. Have a look at my children." And count them again.

3

Isabella:

Tower of London — August, 1321

ONCE, LONG AGO, I dreamt of a happy marriage. But how quickly that dream had been quashed. First, Gaveston had owned Edward's attentions. Now it was Hugh Despenser upon whom he lavished titles and treasures. Whenever I spoke up, I was chided by Edward, spurned even— as if he resented my presence altogether. Yet time after time, when things were at their worst and there was nowhere else to turn, it was me Edward called upon. Me, who salvaged the shattered bits of his life and pieced them together like shards of pottery into a mosaic. My one reward for enduring such perpetual misery had been my children, four of them. Four joyful blessings that gave some purpose to this misery of a marriage.

Beyond the Salt Tower, dawn's first blush showed against a brightening sky. Armed sentries peered sleepily down at us from their posts along the walls of the outer ward. To the west, a pair of guards clutching poleaxes glanced through the open gate behind them. The groan of a winch rumbled in the morning silence. Iron scraped stone in a drawn-out screech as the portcullis of the Middle Tower went up.

Puffy-eyed and yawning, my nursemaid Ida cradled a tiny bundle in the crescent of her plump arms. I peeled back the edge of the blanket to gaze upon my little Joanna's pink face. She wriggled a hand free to grasp my thumb, a bubble of spittle forming around her tiny mouth. When I smiled down at her, she cooed, bursting the bubble, and laughed. If only I could know such happiness, too.

"My lady?" Aymer de Valence, the Earl of Pembroke, cleared his throat in a signal of impatience and swept a hand toward the waiting carriage, which was surrounded by a mounted guard of three dozen fully armed men. Impatient hooves tapped on the cobbles. Bits jangled. Pembroke had returned from Paris only a week ago, having just wed my cousin Marie, a daughter of the Count of Saint Pol. Although he was nearly two decades my senior, I regarded Pembroke as a dear friend, but I sorely regretted that he was being tossed into the lion's den of disorder that was Edward's court so soon upon his return. By evening, we would arrive in Westminster. Worse than leaving my youngest child behind, who was barely now a month old, I dreaded the purpose of this journey.

Reluctantly, I tugged my thumb free of my daughter's grasp. Her forehead puckered like a grape that has shriveled under the sun's rays. Red fists flailing, she stretched her lips taut across toothless gums. An ear-splitting wail emanated from bottomless lungs.

"You'll come back soon, my lady?" Ida rocked her arms gently to soothe the babe. When that did not seem to work, she bounced on her heels, making her too heavy bosom jiggle inside her unbelted gown. There was a fleeting moment of peace as Joanna inhaled, but too soon another demonic howl ensued.

"Take the babe outside for fresh air as often as you can,"—I stepped back, guilt weighing down my heart like a sack of stones—"but shield her face from the sun so that her cheeks do not blister. When you're walking in the garden with Ella, watch that there are no bees about. She likes to sniff the roses before looking. It was most traumatic when she was stung inside her nose last month. She could not breathe properly for two days because of the swelling. Take care, too, that she does not prick a finger. She'd sooner smear the blood on her clean skirts as she would complain of a throbbing finger. As for John, do *not* allow him within sight of Young Edward's new pony. That, if nothing else, is imperative. He wants to do everything exactly as his brother does, but he cannot understand that he's more likely to get trampled than anything. He'll sulk and wield his temper, but do not be swayed, Ida. Do not. Let him cry himself to sleep, if you must. I'll not come back to find my second oldest lying broken in bed."

Ida harrumphed at me. "My lady, you know I do not let them fool with danger. Never. Or say cross words, or eat with dirty hands or forget their prayers. None of that. I'll see that Young Edward is awake for his lessons, too, and does not pester his tutor with requests for stories about battles." She cocked her chin out, her pride evident.

"My lady, please." Pembroke came up behind me and hooked an arm about my waist to shepherd me toward the carriage.

I stole one last glance over my shoulder at Ida and my daughter, then climbed inside and scooted along the cushioned bench seat. On the opposite bench, my damsels Patrice and Marie leaned against one another, already dozing.

Pembroke appeared at the rear of the carriage and undid the ties of the curtains. Before he let them fall, he held them aside for a moment, concern furrowed between his Spaniard-black brows.

"Thank you, my queen, for obliging my request. I know you are not long out of childbed, but this is dire. The Marcher lords have surrounded London and will not scatter until their demands are met. The king *must* come to his senses. The past, unfortunately, seems to be repeating itself and if so . . ." He shook his head of close-shorn dark hair and let out a long sigh. "If so, there will be bloody days ahead. Worse, I fear, than before."

He disappeared then, leaving me in near darkness to contemplate his warning. The carriage jolted forward and soon we were rumbling along over the cobbles as London stirred sluggishly to life around us. I groped for the stray cushion at my feet and wedged it behind my back to ease the jarring.

If I could not convince Edward to exile Hugh Despenser and make amends with his barons, blood would rain down upon England until we were all bathed in it.

Already it was worse than before.

Westminster — August, 1321

EDWARD MARCHED THE LENGTH of the King's Chamber of Westminster Palace. The long toes of his leather soles slapped the tiles like the rhythmic threshing of a flail. Twenty-five paces. Head down, hands clasped behind him. He halted beside the vast canopied state bed, gazed up at the metal bosses studding the panels of the ceiling, then spun around to face me.

I stood moored in the doorway, Pembroke behind me. It would be dangerous to approach the king or speak before judging his mood—that much I knew. Too far from me to see his countenance clearly, I dipped my head in a bow and waited.

A warm breeze stirred the hairs that had pulled loose from beneath the brim of my coif, tickling my cheeks. Tall windows lined the long wall across from me where Robert Winchelsey, the Archbishop of Canterbury, stood. Jewels, a hand-width apart, trimmed his brocaded red chasuble. Piled in folds around his neck, his amice was adorned with quatrefoils formed from gold braids. He smiled serenely at me and tipped his head so far I thought his miter would topple from it.

When I looked again, Edward had grabbed at one of the dense green curtains hanging down from the canopy above the throne. He buried his face in the heavy cloth for a moment, then yanked hard before letting go. The frame of the canopy rattled, but held. Hands outstretched, he rushed toward us. "Have you any idea how they have betrayed me?"

I shook my head, feigning ignorance. During the time that I had been awaiting Joanna's birth at the Tower, I had insisted on hearing the news from across England. Patrice had fed me every detail. Edward's un-bounded patronage of the younger Hugh Despenser had fostered wide-spread dissent among the Marcher Lords. Rebellion loomed. Had he heeded the signs—any of dozens—it could have all been averted. But Edward was beyond obstinate. He was blind with devotion to Despenser, just as he had been with Gaveston—and that had ended miserably.

Edward stomped to a halt before me, his face contorted, as if he were wracked with anguish. "Not only have they burned and ravaged Hugh's lands, but they've taken up with Lancaster. God in Heaven—Lancaster!"

Eyes downcast, the archbishop's shoulders sagged, as though he had long since given up trying to persuade the king to hear reason.

Pembroke stepped past me into a slanted beam of reddish sunlight. "It was said that the Mortimers sent Lord Badlesmere to meet with Lancaster in Pontefract. If Lancaster joins them, their might and power will be far beyond anything we can muster. I beg of you, sire, this is not the time to resist. Remember your coronation oath. Hear the barons out. Grant their request to banish Despenser. Then promise pardons in full. If you shut your ears to their pleas, you stand to lose more than your king-dom."

"I *know* what I stand to lose, Aymer," Edward snapped. "I will lose him either way, it seems. Already I have lost the power my birthright has afforded me."

"Then you understand that you must put your own preservation above all others? To ignore that is to perish, sire. Where is Lord Despens-er now?"

Edward's eyes flew wide, like those of a rabbit caught in the snare, knowing there is no escape—no sense left in struggling, else the string will tighten. His hands, now hanging limp at his sides, began to tremble vio-lently. "Leave us."

"Sire?" Pembroke's feathery black brows twitched.

Edward's voice bore the ragged edge of strain. "I trust you brought my queen here for a purpose?" He straightened his spine, although his mask of authority fooled no one. "Both of you—leave us. Now. I wish to speak with the queen. Alone."

"As you wish, my lord." Pembroke inclined his head toward the door. Archbishop Winchelsey took his cue and followed him from the room.

The moment the door banged shut behind them, Edward dashed to the middle window and clambered over the window seat. The buttons of his tight-fitting sleeves clacked against the window pane as he pressed his face to it to survey outside. A muffled voice hailed him from below. He scrambled backward. Then, darting a suspicious glance around the chamber, he went to stand in the very center. He beckoned me with a curled finger.

"Trust no one," he whispered as I neared him. "Not the nobles, not the servants . . . Not even the clerics."

"Do you at least trust me?" I laced my fingers together beneath the slight bulge of my still overstretched belly. The creation of four children between us, I hoped, had at least forged some measure of confidence.

Blue eyes narrowed, he cocked his head. "Who do you think asked for you? Did you think it was all Pembroke's doing? The archbishop's? Fie!" He spun away to face the window, arms crossed. "I recalled Mortimer from Ireland again, thinking he would defend me. After all I have done for him, making him Lord Lieutenant there. And what did he do when I asked his help? He joined the wolves in their hunt. I am like the orphaned lamb bleating in their midst, as they circle around me, fangs gnashing."

Shaking his head slowly, he drifted toward the end of the chamber. His voice grew not more distant, but louder with vehemence. "They all want to tell me what to do. To control me. *Me*. Who is king, I say? Oh, so many of them think they ought to be. That they could do better. I trust none of that writhing pile of worms who call themselves 'lords'. Nor the crows closest, who squawk in my ears and try to scatter the rest whilst they pick at my very eyes to blind me. Who, I ask you, was meant to sit *here*?" With a deft twirl, he landed on the cushioned throne, sitting tall and defiant. "*Who* was born to rule England?"

"You were," I said, approaching him, "Edward of Caernarvon. And your son after you." I knelt beside him, my skirts bunching around me in a sea of pale green satin. Gentle and soothing, I laid my hand over his forearm. Again, I must turn his mind to lighter things, away from the anger and the darkness. "Only yesterday Young Edward asked when you might take him hawking. He has tired of his peregrine and fancies the gyrfalcon you keep at King's Langley. Do you remember the one?"

He blinked, as if in momentary confusion. "The one I had brought from Norway?"

"That one, yes."

"The best birds are from Norway."

"He knows, which is why I think he covets it so much."

"It is a tercel, not a hen, and far too much for him yet."

"Perhaps, but he is always dreaming of bigger things. He pretends his new pony is a great warhorse, a Flemish one, and goes about all day with a wooden sword tucked in his belt."

The barest hint of a smile crept over his mouth. His sight drifted to the mural high up on the wall above the nearest door—the one which the earl and archbishop had departed through. There, the slight figure of David hurled a stone from his sling at the raging Goliath. "One day, my son will fight my battles for me."

My husband was no warrior. Certainly no general of battles. Bannockburn had been testament to that. To speculate that his oldest son would be a more apt leader than him was no strain to the imagination. That prospect, however, was many years ahead and of no use to him now. Thus, it was my duty to serve as his peacemaker—to calm the waters that he had stirred. I stroked my husband's arm until he met my gaze. "First, you must make peace, so you can keep your crown. Then, when it is your son's time to wear it, he will not have to fight for it."

He squirmed with uncertainty. "It is always a fight for power. Always."

"You know what you must do?"

His jaw twitched. A tear slid down his cheek, then dripped onto his silk tunic. Dully, he nodded. "Have I any choice? I must send my dear Hugh away." Then, he gripped the arms of the throne until his knuckles turned white. "Tell Pembroke to gather the barons in the morning again. I will present the soft of my belly—give them the banishment they clamor for."

In truth, I had expected more resistance from him. Perhaps his willfulness had already been spent. Or perhaps he had indeed learned from the past. Whatever the reason, I embraced the result. Finally, Edward was learning the art of compromise, as well as the consequences of his selfishness.

He rubbed a sleeve across his face. "Our daughter, Joanna—how is she?"

"Bright, beautiful, spirited. She favors you." I told him that because it pleased him, not because it was true.

"A pilgrimage to Canterbury is in order, to give thanks. Once things are settled."

I stood, my legs tingling from knees to toes as the blood returned to them, and rearranged my wrinkled skirts. "Gladly will I go. We have much to be thankful for."

"Perhaps for you, 'tis so." He folded his hands in his lap and sighed in defeat.

As I made my way across the floor, I overheard Edward mumble above the rustle of my skirt's fabric: "I am no man's chattel. I swear on my life . . . there will be requital."

With that utterance, any hope I might have held—for lasting peace, for my children's future—crumbled into a dust so fine that even the slightest whisper of civil war would blow it away without a trace.

Leeds Castle – October, 1321

TWO SWANS, WING TO wing, their bills tucked to their downy breasts, floated across the lake encircling Leeds Castle. The ripples of their wake broke the mirrored surface in a broadening fan. A bank of white rolled across my view, obscuring the limewashed walls beyond and the helmeted figures that watched us from the crenels of the uppermost towers. Even the sun, climbing toward its pinnacle now, had not chased away the morning mist.

While I had gone to Canterbury and knelt before the shrine of Thomas Becket a week past, Edward had ridden out to the Isle of Thanet—where he met Hugh Despenser. I know this not because he admitted it, but because he went with such haste and purpose that it left me no doubt. While he made to return to London, he ordered me to come here to Leeds Castle, "To befriend and forgive," he had written. And so I came, even though the pretense of my visit was as flaccid as a wet rope. I considered it a diplomatic gesture, if nothing more. This morning, however, I had awoken with my bowels churning. The day, I feared, would not end well. My breath hung trapped in a cloud before me in the damp air. Draping the reins of my gray palfrey across the horn of my saddle, I called my newest squire to me. Arnaud de Mone parted from the rest of my guard, some thirty armed men, and came to stand before me.

"You sent word ahead as soon as we left Canterbury, requesting lodging for us?"

He nodded. Pearlescent beads of moisture shimmered among the golden ringlets of his hair. Although young—and temptingly beautiful—he had, in a very short span, proven himself devoted. "I did, my lady."

"And just now—you asked that we be permitted entrance?"

"I did."

"And what was Lord Badlesmere's reply? They have had ample time to prepare for our arrival. Why have they kept us waiting?"

"Lord Badlesmere is not inside, my queen."

"Then who refuses us?"

"Lady Badlesmere. She says that her husband gave the fortress into her care with firm orders that no one, for any reason, was to be permitted entrance."

"But I am not *no* one!" I protested impulsively. How dare she?

Indeed, I traveled with armed guards, but that was only a precaution. I had not come here to take possession of the fortress, but to engender harmony. That had been clear in my message. Why must even the simplest of good intentions be suspect? Edward had given in to strict demands. Pardons had been issued. The peace may have yet been a fragile one, but it was peace. Trust first had to be a matter of practice before it could become belief. This . . . this disobedience threatened that very premise to the core. If she would not do it willingly, then Lady Badlesmere would need to be forced to open up her home. "Go back to the gate. Tell her that her queen *demands* entrance and lodging."

Arnaud moved a foot, hesitating. "If . . . if she refuses?"

My mare twitched her ears, as if she, too, awaited my response. "We go back to London. This will be dealt with later." By Edward—who would not likely find it in him to be lenient this time.

He dipped his head in a nod and trotted away. With a detachment of two dozen soldiers, he rode across the narrow bridge of land connecting the mainland to the island on which Leeds Castle sat and up to the gate. A guard appeared at a crenel atop the gatehouse. Arnaud shouted my orders. I could not make out the guard's reply, but it had the terse ring of a warning. Arnaud stood his ground and repeated my demands. The guard disappeared.

A moment later, one of my mounted soldiers behind him snapped back in his saddle, an arrow protruding from his chest. Clutching at the shaft, he uprighted himself. Blood poured between his fingers. He swayed, then slumped to the side, his other hand still entwined in the reins. As the wounded man tumbled to the ground, his horse wheeled around, feeling the sudden yank of its bit. Unable to scramble free, the man threw an arm over his head. But too late. An iron-shod hoof circled through the air and cracked squarely against his skull, shattering it like an eggshell beneath the blow of a hammer.

I gaped in horror, barely able to comprehend what I had just seen.

Then, the air hissed. Arrows sailed above the breaking mist, arced downward and plunged into flesh. Two horses went down, pinning their riders. Another man fell from his mount, eyes wide in death. His party trapped on the narrow tongue of land, Arnaud flailed an arm, signaling retreat. But even as they turned to go without ever having put up a fight, another volley of arrows sang their requiem. The causeway was too narrow to allow them to all flee at once. Corpses clogged the way.

I could not move or speak. A dozen dead or wounded lay scattered before the gate and along the land bridge. One man staggered to his feet and took two steps before he was struck through the neck. Another behind him, his way blocked, leapt into the water, desperate to escape. His head bobbed above the surface, then flew back as an arrow pierced his cheek. Blood sprayed around him. With a drawn-out gurgle, he slipped below, crimson bubbles marking the spot where he had last drawn air.

Trumpeting in alarm, the swans beat their wings and arose in a cloud of white above the silver-dark water. Sleek necks stretched out before them, they ascended, going higher, higher. Above the pandemonium unfolding in the mist. Away from the massacre.

The remaining men cleared the causeway and rounded the lake with a rumble of shouts. When Arnaud came to me, he said nothing, but grabbed my reins and led me away.

My heart thudded in my throat. Hooves clattered around me. Taunts rang out from the castle.

The moans of the dying fell away behind me. But I could not look back.

It had begun.

4

Roger Mortimer:

Kingston-upon-Thames — October, 1321

T HE RIVER THAMES FLOWED by in ageless indolence. A young boy, adrift on the current in a battered old rowing boat, rested his oars in his lap. In open-mouthed awe, he stared up at the long column of eight thousand fighting men moving along the road. My men. Many had fought with me in Ireland. Others lived on my lands or those of neighboring Marcher lords. They had all seen the consequences of Edward's indulgences on Despenser. With every footfall and plodding hoof they stirred up swirls of dust. Several men stared back menacingly at the boy. He flipped his oars down into the water and pulled away as fast as he could.

We had not yet crossed to Kingston-upon-Thames on our way from Oxford to Leeds Castle when the banner of Aymer Valence, the Earl of Pembroke, appeared at the bridge over the river. I reined my horse and signaled the column behind me to stop.

"Who is it?" My uncle, Roger of Chirk, squinted into the angled morning rays of a late October sun. The creases around his eyes deepened with shadows. Beside him, Lord Bartholomew de Badlesmere stiffened and readjusted his dented helmet with a finger to his noseguard. He was Edward's Royal Steward and the reason we had been plunged into this latest mire. He was also my kinsman by marriage. My eldest son, Edmund, had been married to his daughter, Elizabeth, for some years now, although at eight the girl was not yet old enough to join my son's house-hold. Of late, Bartholomew likely regretted the union, for it placed him squarely at odds with the king.

I shaded my eyes with a bare hand. Plates of armor caught the sun's reflection in scattered bursts. Pennons fluttered atop lances in the cool breeze. The earl's small contingent clattered over the stone bridge. "Pembroke, but he hasn't more than fifty men with him."

My uncle snorted. "So, the king sends Pembroke to do his talking for him. At least he picked the right man."

Bartholomew touched the hilt of his sword. His jaw quivered. "Is there hope yet, d'you think?"

"I'll not grasp at hope until I hear what the earl has to say." I spurred my horse forward and my personal guard fell in behind me. My uncle let out a sharp curse as he struggled to catch up before I reached the earl, who was now across the bridge and coming up the road.

My uncle huffed as he came abreast of me and strained to stay in his saddle. "Do you believe me—what I said about Despenser long ago?"

I gave him a sidelong glance. He jounced hard in his saddle, but rather than a grimace he threw me a smug smile. I leered back at him. "Your gloating is of no help at the moment. But yes, I do. I should have believed you when you first warned me about Despenser. And I should have believed what you said about the king. But what good would that have done, Uncle?" I lowered my voice as the earl slowed his horse and prepared to dismount beneath a grove of oaks on the north side of the road. "In the end, we're all forced to choose sides anyway. And if we don't, the king will somehow make us, won't he?" I leaned back and jerked so hard on the reins that my horse arched his neck and spun in a half circle before coming to a stop.

I dropped to the ground and felt the weight of my armor with the impact.

"Good day, Earl Pembroke!" I called with feigned enthusiasm. I swept my mail coif from my head, tossed it to a squire behind me and reached a hand toward the earl in greeting.

He clasped my hand firmly and drew me to him in an embrace. His head barely came to my shoulder, but he was broad of girth. Each of his thighs was as stout as a Yule log. As reputation had it, he was not a man one wanted to face in the jousts. "A good morning it is, my lords."

When he stepped away, his eyes, dark as a Moor's, were grim with foreboding. His gaze swept toward Bartholomew. The strained smile that crossed his mouth was not one of goodwill, I guessed.

"King Edward is still besieging Leeds?" I said.

My uncle sidled up to me, his breathing still ragged. He acknowledged the earl with a stiff bow.

Pembroke nodded at each of us in turn. "He is. Lady Badlesmere will not surrender the fortress."

Bartholomew clambered down from his saddle and stretched his hands forward, imploring. "M-my wife," he sputtered, unable to hide the desperation in his voice, "she did not understand my orders. She did not know the queen was merely returning from a pilgrimage. Please, she meant no harm."

"Perhaps," Pembroke impugned dryly, "she should have advised her archers not to aim so accurately."

I silenced Bartholomew with a glare. "Earl Pembroke, let us not waste breath arguing over what is already done. We come, at the lady's request, to relieve the siege. However,"—I summoned a smile as diplomatic and genial as I could, given the circumstances—"this can be easily resolved with words alone. There need be no more blood shed."

"You would do well, Sir Roger, to go back to Wigmore and stay there awhile."

I glanced over my shoulder at the sizable army my uncle and I had brought with us. "There are more coming."

Pembroke was too levelheaded, and well-informed, to be swayed by my threat. "Who? Lancaster? Forgive me, but whatever promises he may have made to any of you, he won't hold."

It was true. Lancaster had proven unreliable more than once. What's more, he detested Badlesmere and made no secret of it.

My uncle shook his finger in the air and limped intrusively close to Pembroke. Without his stick to lean on, he was noticeably lame. "Aymer, we're old friends, are we not? Fought together in Scotland how many times? You were there when I tumbled from my horse and shattered my hip. It has never been good since." He clamped a hand lightly on Pembroke's upper arm and gave him a stern look. "We know each other too well to dance around this. So, let us leap to the truth, shall we? It was well out of Queen Isabella's way to stop at Leeds Castle. And she approached, not with a mere retinue of damsels, but an armed force. All this less than two weeks after Edward and Despenser met at the Isle of Thanet?" My uncle had his sources, too. "Oh yes, we heard of that. How bloody coincidental. I say the queen was an instrument of their devices, not a passing pilgrim who became the victim of the Lord or Lady Badlesmere's mistrust. We both know that."

Pembroke's lips tightened beneath his coarse, black mustache. He was not a man to betray his own emotions, but there were subtle signs he was not at ease representing the king in this. He looked away for a moment and selected his words with care. "I did not come to hear complaints and speculations, Lord Roger. Do you think any of us want this?"

"I think King Edward takes cruel delight in it," my uncle retorted. "My son's daughter-in-law Elizabeth is in there. Other children, as well. Surely the king has not resorted to holding women and children as captives in their own homes?"

Bartholomew blanched. This encounter, undoubtedly, was doing nothing to lift his hopes.

"Go back, all of you," Pembroke urged with a trace of kindness. "Understand what I say. For the mercy of God, I'm trying to spare your lives. If you march on Leeds, you'll be outnumbered, you'll be defeated, and your little Elizabeth won't have a father-in-law or a father, let alone a home. Norfolk and Kent have joined the siege. Even the Earl of Surrey. They number some twenty-five thousand. By now maybe more, with Arundel's men. I do not exaggerate, my lords. If you believe me a liar, come count them yourself."

The words fell heavy and foreboding in my ears. Many of those he spoke of had stood with us only weeks ago. Now they flocked around the king like birds during a lean winter to peck at crumbs. My uncle and I exchanged a swift glance.

"A moment, my lord," I said to the earl. I drew my uncle across the road where we could not be overheard. I put my lips close to his ear. "We must negotiate."

"No."

I gripped his arm. "We cannot argue in front of Pembroke. He knows we are fewer in numbers. I beg you, let me handle this."

His wrinkled lips contorted in a sneer. "I want full pardons, for all of us. Nothing less."

I nodded and we rejoined the earl. "My lord," I began, "we shall withdraw our army, disband it and return to our lands." At that, my uncle glared at me so murderously I thought he might silence me with the butt of his sword across my jaw. But he clamped his yellowed teeth shut and allowed me to go on. "In return, the king shall break the siege and grant the inhabitants of Leeds their freedom in exchange for possession of the fortress."

Bartholomew did not raise his eyes from the ground.

"Furthermore," I continued, "our grievances shall be heard out in parliament and no actions taken against us beforehand."

Pembroke turned toward his horse. "I will do what I can to convince the king."

"No, you *will* convince the king. It will be done. You are the only one, my lord, who can."

He stifled a smirk and paused with one hand resting against his saddle. "As I said, I will do what I can."

44

We all clasped hands in agreement and mounted our horses. Pembroke sped off with devilish purpose. Badlesmere galloped back to our ranks for safety. But my uncle and I lingered on the riverbank.

Uncle Roger shook his head in disbelief. "Return to our lands? Disband? What sort of swine manure was that? Have you lost your wits?"

"Hardly. We will collect our allies and go north—to meet with Lancaster in Pontefract. As for Leeds, we can do nothing there. We'll have to trust that Pembroke can work his miracles on the king. By the time King Edward learns where we are and who we are with, Badlesmere will be back with his children."

But I held little faith in that.

Bridgnorth — December, 1321

LEEDS SURRENDERED TO THE king. Mercy, however, was not forthcoming. They hung twelve of the garrison from its walls as a warning. Lady Badlesmere and her children, including Elizabeth, went to the Tower. As prisoners of the king.

In Pontefract, we secured Lancaster's promise to join us, then swiftly returned to the Marches to secure our holdings. Edward, bloated with confidence, advanced up the Thames from Leeds. He halted in Gloucester long enough to gorge himself at Christmas supper and take wicked amusement in a few more hangings.

In haste, we withdrew west of the Severn, secured the bridge at Worcester against the royal army and pressed north to wait for Lancaster.

How easily Lancaster had sworn to stand with us. How easily he soon forgot.

Rain turned to sleet. Sleet to snow. The hills gleamed like polished marble beneath an iron sky. The valleys lay eerily still and the towns barren as folk fled before us. All the while Edward's army stalked us like the specter of death from the other side of the Severn.

We had no time to stop and warm our bodies before a fire. Our bellies roared with hunger. Yet every day we pushed on, our fingers stiff and frozen, our feet swinging like dead stumps from the ends of our legs. My horse began to lag and soon he developed a rattle in his chest. I left him tied to a post at the gate of a farmer's pen and hoped he might live to serve another, but knew he probably would not. Men went off to piss and never came back or disappeared into the darkness while others fought for sleep beneath tattered cloaks. Each day we waited for word of Lancaster. Each day none came. Just as the winter sun became veiled behind high clouds, our hopes grew ever dimmer.

I looked southward into a coal black sky smeared with amber flames. Smoke rose in twisting spires from the town of Bridgnorth and drifted on a brisk, cold wind to sting my nostrils. Earlier that night, we had launched a surprise attack across the bridge. Edward, unfortunately, recovered quickly enough to prevent a complete routing. Before my men fled back west across the bridge, they touched torch to thatch. The damp thatch was slow to spark, but once it did, billows of thick smoke poured into the streets, creating confusion amongst the king's ranks.

A growl of contempt rumbled deep in my uncle's throat. "So what did this buy us? One more day? A few hours?" A streak of soot ran from the right side of his forehead to the edge of his mail coif, making him look like some old beggar who had been digging in the ashes for bones. "What do you suppose the king was thinking," he mused, rubbing at his sagging jowls, "when he told me to secure Wales against you?"

"That it would come to something like this. He gambled, his luck against ours. And if Lancaster does not arrive on the morrow, the king will win."

My uncle gulped down ale and handed me the flask. "If Thomas of Lancaster could keep his blessed word, we'd be warm and dry right now. Spineless bastard."

I had no desire to banter over the obvious. Lancaster should have arrived days ago. He had broken his promise. It was not the first time. Even Pembroke had warned us that the earl was all bombast and bluster. I emptied the flask and let it drop to the ground. Had I a dozen casks, I would have drained them dry, too.

"To think," my uncle lamented, "our bliss lasted all of two months before King Edward lashed out like a teased and tethered dog. Longshanks was a horrid tyrant, but he honored loyalty and let no one rule him. His son is a limp kitten who wants to be stroked and suckle himself to sleep."

I said nothing. Once, I had been high in the king's favor; now, I was a hunted rebel. I sank to my haunches and cradled my throbbing head in my hands.

"What now, nephew? We can't go west. The Welsh will slaughter us like lame cattle before they allow the king that pleasure."

The taunts of Edward's archers carried from across the bridge. Arrows hissed back and forth in the darkness, some landing astray, some piercing flesh. I pressed my fingers over my ears to deaden the screams of a dying man and spoke at the ground. "We must keep going north, then."

"Humph. Lancaster's not so stupid as to rush his own death."

I raised my eyes. "Joan is pregnant again. She may have had the child by now, for all I know."

"An even dozen, will it be?" He gave me his hand to pull me up. "How many years is your Edmund now? Nineteen?"

I nodded dully, feeling the faint buzz of ale, and stood. Together we began the walk back to camp. Ice crackled beneath our boots. "We quarreled the last time I saw her—bitterly."

"Over what?"

"Everything. She complains incessantly—whether I come or go, whose side I take, what I have done or not done. Nothing I do pleases her."

"It is you who complains. You're ungrateful if you don't realize what she's given you and I'm not talking of inheritances. Your daughters will build you more alliances by whom they wed than any other bargains you might strike. And your sons will sire Mortimers by the score to carry on your name."

I almost told him after what happened to the young Elizabeth

Badlesmere, no man would marry his daughter to a Mortimer traitor. Instead, I held my tongue and told a passing squire to spread the order to break camp. We would leave enough men to hold the bridge and march again, through the night. Our numbers were compromised, but it gained nothing to stay and we could not leave our backs unprotected.

"To Shrewsbury?" my uncle asked.

"Yes." Beyond Shrewsbury, the Severn snaked back westward and if we did not cross the river and race north to find Lancaster, then we would be trapped interminably between the Welsh and the royal army.

"What there?"

"Either we are met with a miracle when Lancaster arrives as our savior . . . or we throw ourselves at Edward's fickle mercy."

In horror of the thought, he sucked his chin to his neck. "No. How can we?"

"What else can we do? Fight? It would be suicide. I want to see my children again, Uncle. I want to go home someday. It is the only way. The *only* way."

"And what of Lancaster? Why should we grovel at Edward's feet while he roams free? The king will take our lands. Put us in chains."

"Better that, Uncle, than hang with him."

The corners of his mouth plunged and he rattled his hoary head at me. "This year I turned sixty, Roger. And this is what is to become of me? I am too old to be shut up. Too damn old." He turned his face from me and walked away.

In the darkness, I heard the short, indrawn breaths of a man weeping to himself, hopeless and exhausted. A man who had no more years of his life to waste on pursuits as futile as trying to correct a lawless king.

5

Roger Mortimer:

Shrewsbury – January, 1322

TRODDEN IN SPIRIT AND road-weary, we did not make it to Shrewsbury ahead of the king. Like fish in a net being hauled into the boat, we were trapped, bounded on three sides by the River Severn. It was only a brief matter of time before a royal detachment would cross the river somewhere behind us or a band of screaming Welshmen would fly down at us from the mountains.

Across the river, the king's army, insouciant, warm and well fed, sprawled around Shrewsbury. The smoke from their fires, infused with the aroma of cooked meat, drifted to us on an icy January wind, reminding us constantly that starvation was only ever a few days away. Provisions were running short. Already rations had been halved. We had ceased to forage. The local farms had been wrung stone-dry. We had butchered every cow, pig and chicken within two days' ride. The abbeys had bolted their doors against us, shouting the message that if we wanted any more from them we would have to burn them out. I considered it, but my uncle was a more reverent man than I. Each day I cinched my belt a little tighter, as I succumbed to the same, irritable languor that was slowly devouring my men and turning them against one another like starving dogs in a pit.

When we left Bridgnorth, skulking away in the darkness, I thought we would gain enough lead to get across the bridge at Shrewsbury before Edward ever took sight of us. But illness struck too many of my men along the way. Already they were weak from hunger and exhaustion. We did not march to Shrewsbury; we crawled. There, we came upon our dread—the king's army not only holding the bridge to Shrewsbury, but encamped along the near bank. Had Edward wanted to, he could have sprung on us like a cat pounces on a cornered mouse.

Why kill the prey, though, when he could play with it a while? Supplied with provisions from Shrewsbury, the king was more than willing, and able, to starve us into submission. I could either send my men to a quick and bloody end or condemn them to a long, slow death at winter's cruel whim. If, however, my uncle and I gave ourselves up, our men could all go home.

Edward demanded our complete submission. We were not in a position to bargain. Edward knew it. I knew it. My uncle, however, did not. He again requested full pardons. Edward refused.

For a long, wearisome week, I argued with my uncle, but he would not give in to the king. He was all stubbornness and no sense, even as he grew weaker day by day. The winter cold had gripped him hard. His skin was as white as the snow capping the mountains. The circles around his eyes were the deep blue of an evening sky. His lungs and throat were choked with phlegm. In the mornings he coughed so hard it sounded as though he might expel his innards. Between spells, he wheezed like a sickly child. I feared that if I did not deliver him to rudimentary comfort, he would die from his own obstinacy.

My uncle's tent next to mine, I lay awake, unable to sleep. A dozen arguments swirled in my mind: why I should still hold my ground against the king, why I should give in, why I should fight . . . and above the muddle of questions, my uncle's bellowed protests echoed in my head. I heard then his hacking cough, followed by hoarse retching through the canvas walls. Defeated, I sat up, hunched forward, and tugged the blanket up around my aching shoulders. My elbows on my knees, I buried my head in my hands.

Edmund stirred beneath his covers. "Uncle Roger—how is he?"

I looked toward my son through the veil of night, his face only a vague outline of black against a field of darkest gray. "He will not last, I fear."

There was a long silence. Edmund sniffed and I heard him rub his nose with a sleeve. "Perhaps he doesn't want to." He flopped over and within minutes his chest rose and fell in the steady rhythm of peaceful slumber.

Half the night or more I stared at my son, wrapped tight in his thin cocoon. I did not ponder on what he might think of me. I did not want to know. Hours went by before I came back to Edmund's simple observation about his great-uncle. If my uncle died before he was forced to give himself up, then he would have won one small victory. He would die never having given in to a tyrant.

Come morning, I would bend to my uncle, sense or no, and let him keep his pride. We would go back south, find somewhere to make our stand, and pray to God winter did not kill us before the king's army did. If we could hold out until spring, perhaps old allies would return to defend us. Perhaps angels would swoop from the sky and strike the king dead with bolts of lightning. A man could dream . . .

Restless, I rose at first light, even though I heard nothing but the rumbling snores of my uncle. I trudged out into the camp and wandered along the narrow rows between the tents. It was so quiet it looked as though the plague had struck. Had the king attacked early that morning, he would have butchered us beneath our blankets. Frost shimmered on the cloaks of soldiers as they lay on the ground. Even in their sleep, some shivered. I pounded my gloved palms together to bring the blood to my stiff fingers. With care, I picked my way between dozing men and poked at a dying fire with my sword. A charred pot lay overturned beside the fire, traces of burnt bean pottage crusted along the rim. Beside it was an empty cask, still smelling of ale. I jabbed at the logs, turning them over in the white ash, until I found the glowing embers. But when I looked about for more firewood, there was none to be had. I sank down, my sword resting in my lap, and stretched my hands toward the faltering flames.

Across from me, a man writhed beneath layers of muddied wool, rolled to his knees and stood. My companion Sir John Maltravers. Eyes still shut, he swayed from side to side and scratched at his crotch, yawning. He opened one eye just wide enough to locate the struggling little fire and fumbled beneath his tunic to slide a hand into his breeches.

My sword blade hovered above the dying flames. I raised it to his widening eyes. "Piss on my fire, Maltravers, and I'll make a eunuch of you."

At the sound of my voice, Maltravers blinked to clear the sleep from his eyes. Muttering an apology, he yanked his hand free, retreated backward, and stumbled over the cask. He fell with a thunderous thud. In lighter times I would have mocked him for his clumsiness, but I was still in a bad temper from my sleepless night. He gave a rough moan and rolled to his side, clutching the back of his head. I started toward him to offer a hand, but something, a sound in the distance, made me turn around.

Hooves pounded against frozen earth. A mounted messenger came down the row at an easy canter, searching left and right. He slowed as he saw me and brought his horse to a halt. "Where can I find Sir Roger of Wigmore or Lord Roger of Chirk?" he said.

I shoved the end of my sword blade into the rock hard ground and rested both hands on the crossguard. "That depends. Who are you?"

His fair eyebrows lifted. "Simon de Beresford."

"And whose man are you, Simon de Beresford?"

He gave me a skeptical look. His pale blue eyes had the cold, hard look of steel. "I am Lord Pembroke's squire."

"Then I am Sir Roger."

He tipped his chin up as a sly grin flickered across his mouth. "Ah then, I have, at times, had my purse filled by your uncle when he had need of information. My Lord Pembroke sends me to tell you that he has news of the Earl of Lancaster that should interest you."

"Go on."

"He has proof that the earl is in league with the Scots."

That should have come as no surprise to anyone, least of all a man as well-informed as Pembroke. "And the king knows of this?"

Simon nodded his head of silver-fair hair.

"What proof?"

"If you answer this, Earl Pembroke will tell you himself." From beneath his padded tunic, he produced a letter and extended it to me.

As soon as the letter left his hands, he turned his horse and started away.

"Stop!" I called. "Were you not told to wait for a reply?"

"You are to be the reply, my lord!" he shouted over his shoulder. "Or not."

He kicked his mount hard in the flanks and galloped away. I skimmed the letter once. Then, I read it more slowly. I snatched up my sword and slammed it back into its scabbard. "Christ's blood," I mumbled to myself, but Maltravers heard me.

He got up on one knee, still rubbing at his skull. "What? The king on his way? Is there to be a fight?"

"Not today, no. But if I'm not returned by this time tomorrow, put yourselves as far from the king as you can."

I raced to my uncle's tent, thrust the flap aside and found him still snoring like a bear under his heap of furs. I nudged him in the small of his back with my boot.

"Unless you've got food or drink," he grumbled, "go the hell away."

I smacked the top of his white head with the letter. He thrashed an arm at me in refusal. Unwilling to abandon the warmth of his little cave, he clutched his covers tighter.

"Sit up, old toad," I ordered firmly. "You'll want to hear this:

53

"My Lords,

King Edward waits at Shrewsbury to hear you out. Twice he granted you time to consider his offer and extended you his grace. Twice you gave no reply. There can be no more delays. King Edward was prepared to march against you this very day. I convinced him to forego spilling the blood of Englishmen and to seek a peaceful end, as our Lord Christ would wish of him. If you submit willingly to him, in person and before nightfall, he will grant you your lives and your freedom. I shall wait at the bridge until you come and I will escort you both personally to an audience with the king. You have this on my solemn word.

Aymer de Valence, Earl of Pembroke,
Given at Shrewsbury, 22ⁿᵈ of January, 1322"

My uncle propped himself up on an elbow and blew a thick stream of snot from his nose. "What of it?"

"Pembroke kept his word. He did as he said he would. I trust him more than any man."

"Trust him all you like. I don't trust the king. And Pembroke is the king's man. That puts him in bad company."

"Simon de Beresford. Do you know the name?"

The muscles in his jaw tensed. He looked at me with narrowed eyes. "If I do?"

"He was the messenger who brought the letter. How is it he can be in Pembroke's ranks and your pay at the same time?"

With a groan, he struggled to his feet. He kept his furs wrapped about him so the chill would not invade his bones. "What else did he tell you?"

"Tell me first—is Beresford your spy?"

He nodded. "What did he say?"

"He told me Lancaster has allied himself with the Scots. Pembroke has proof of it. The king knows. Do you know what that means for us? Lancaster will not leave the north, because he knows there is an axe waiting for his neck here. He will never come to our aid. Never."

Almost meekly, he proposed, "What of Adam Orleton, the Bishop of Hereford? He promised men . . . and money."

"And sent both, but it was not enough. We are on our own now, Uncle. Alone. We cannot win in battle and we cannot run. So we can die on this ground . . . or we can go to Shrewsbury and take our chances. I'll wager my life on Pembroke's honesty over dying slowly of hunger."

He shook his head and spoke softly into his beard. "You say these things because you are desperate."

"And you are not?"

Instead of the quarreling I had grown so accustomed to, he shed his furs, summoned his squire and told him to saddle his horse for him and bring him some ale, if any could be found. He did not want to meet the king, he said, without having one last drink while he was still a free man.

"You believe Pembroke, then?" I asked.

"Not in these circumstances, no."

"Then why are you going?"

He rounded on me, his face crimson with fury. "Because I know Simon speaks the truth!" As if he had to restrain from striking me, he clenched his fists before him. He gathered several deep breaths to calm himself before he went on. Finally, he stepped close and raised a crooked finger to poke me in the breastbone. His breath reeked of staleness. "We must denounce Lancaster. Turn our backs on him, as he did us."

So, he believed a spy and not me. Well enough, I thought. We would go to Shrewsbury, each for our own reasons.

While I paced, my uncle bustled about madly. He called for a pot of scalding water, although what he got was melted snow, and washed his face clean. With a frayed twig, he scrubbed at his teeth until his gums bled. All the while, he carped at his young page for being slack and getting in his way. When he had finished grooming, his body squire helped to dress him in full mail. Next, the squire fastened on his poleyns, greaves and arm plates and then belted on his sword. When my uncle's ale was poured, the squire went out to see to the saddling of his horse. Only then did my uncle pause in his frenzy to rest. I had not seen him so vigorous in months. But as he held his cup, I could see his hands trembling with weakness and the fear stark in his sunken eyes.

As much as he sometimes aggravated me, his recalcitrance had always been a part of his very sinew. To see it gone from him . . . I found it hard to look upon him thus. I needed to leave. There were matters that required attention and not enough hours to do them all. "You wish to go later—in the afternoon?"

"I wish—" A cough tore through his words. He let the cup fall from his grasp with a clatter and braced his hands on his knees until the fit had passed. Before he straightened, he spat at his feet and drew a shaking hand across his mouth. His words were raspy, his tone wistful. "I wish to get it bloody over with. After this, I'm going to go back to Chirk—that is if the king keeps his word. That is where I'll stay, until I die." He laughed dryly. "If I make it so far."

I nodded, understanding that he had at last abandoned his stubborn pride and yielded to reason. Hastily, I backed out through the flap. A pair of light hands grabbed my shoulders and spun me around. Edmund. I passed him the letter.

He did not take even a moment to think it over. "I'm coming with you."

"You're to stay here," I told him flatly.

Word had spread rapidly. The camp buzzed with preparations: the honing of blades, the packing of supplies, the strapping of armor and the fitting of bowstrings on their staves.

"Why?" He threw a sweeping glance around him at our diminishing army of rebels. We both knew that they were as much preparing for a fight, as they were preparing to run. "Lord Badlesmere is my father-in-law. I've as many marks against me as you, if not more. I'd rather go to the king and pray for mercy than have him come after me. If he's in a forgiving mood, as Pembroke says, it's best we all take advantage of it, don't you think?"

"Go to Picardy. Find your brother Geoffrey there."

"Run and leave Elizabeth to languish in the Tower? What would that say of me?"

The gnawing feeling in my gut told me not to let him come, but there was a raw truth to his argument. I pushed past him to find Maltravers.

SNOW WAS FALLING IN huge, wet chunks when we went to meet Pembroke at the south end of the bridge. On the floodplain of the Severn, the king's soldiers flanked us on both sides. I knew as we rode between them toward the earl there was no turning back. My bones jarred with every stride of my mount and the stiffness of my muscles plagued me. Even so, my blood coursed with alertness, as if I were marching to battle to fight for my life. In a way, I was. Only it would be words, not weapons, I would fight with.

I held a flat palm up to Pembroke as we halted our horses. "You said you had proof against Lancaster."

"I do," he said.

"What proof?"

"A letter intercepted near Pontefract. Written to the Bruce. Lancaster signed it as 'King Arthur'."

My uncle spat and planted a fist on his hip. "I could call myself 'Merlin' if I wanted to. What sort of proof is that?"

"Proof enough," Pembroke said.

"And where is this proof?" I asked. "Do you have it with you now?"

"I do not." Pembroke's left eyebrow crept upward. He tilted his head back. "The king does."

My uncle had nothing to say to that. True or not—and in likelihood, it was—if Edward believed it, he would be bent on getting his revenge on Lancaster for betraying him with the Scots. With the king's anger focused on Thomas of Lancaster, we were the lesser of two evils.

Pembroke swore on his honor the king would grant us pardons, although they would not come without cost: heavy fines, the loss of lands, and the stripping of high titles. It was a sore point with my uncle that almost sent him back to our camp, but I convinced him that in time Edward could be reminded of Mortimer loyalty and our influence among Marcher lords. I do not think he believed me. He simply had no more will to argue.

I rode beside the Earl of Pembroke, with Edmund and Uncle Roger behind us, over the bridge and into Shrewsbury. Twenty of the king's soldiers escorted us through the slushy streets of the town, up the icy hill and to the castle gates. There, only after we gave up our weapons, were we led beneath the portcullis onto the castle grounds. King Edward stood waiting in the outer bailey for us. Next to him were many of those who had lately abandoned us: Arundel and Surrey among them, as well as the king's brother, Thomas, Earl of Norfolk.

My uncle, Edmund and I tumbled down from our mounts and sank to our knees without taking a step. In a casual manner, Pembroke also dismounted and went forward to bow before the king.

"Well done, Lord Pembroke," Edward trilled. A gleeful smile lit his face. "Well done." An ermine-lined cloak swung from his shoulders and dragged the snowy ground as he circled us in triumph.

His head still bowed, Pembroke announced, "Lord Roger of Chirk, Sir Roger of Wigmore and his son, Edmund Mortimer come to offer their—"

"I know why you went to fetch them," Edward snapped. "They wouldn't be here otherwise."

Pembroke raised his chin, a slight look of bafflement clouding his brow. "Perhaps you wish to hear it from them, my lord king?"

"They can say whatever they want. They can sacrifice themselves to the Virgin Mary, for all I care. It doesn't change what they have done. It is treasonous. And treason is unpardonable."

Deep in the pit of my stomach, a knot drew tighter by the moment. I felt my uncle's hot gaze turn on me.

"You promised you would procure our pardons," I said aside to

Pembroke.

"He tried," Edward said, his lips curving into a sardonic smile as he stepped before me tauntingly, "valiantly. But I am not of a humor to grant any of late. Besides, *you* said you would go home, lay down your arms, and send your men away. That is not at all what you did. Instead, you continued to plot rebellion against me with the Earl of Lancaster."

I chose not to argue with him over what constituted 'rebellion'. Instead, I remembered my uncle's words and played our acquiescence against Lancaster's intractability. "Sire, Lancaster is not here. We are. And we disavow him and humbly submit to you. My uncle and I admit our wrong. We will do as you bid. Surely that begs some leniency?" It took every bit of my will to speak such terrible untruths, but if outright supplication was not enough for King Edward, nothing was.

With a gloved hand he brushed the snow from the red Plantagenet lions adorning the front of his surcoat. "A trifle, perhaps. Only a trifle. Pembroke was not altogether wrong in what he told you, although he took tremendous liberties with it. I was merely musing aloud when I spoke it. I will let you live—today. But you're to be put away until it is decided what to do with you. I cannot run the risk of your cohorts clumping around you and whispering of insurrection again. Treason is a poison to kings, and a king is the beating heart of a kingdom. So I will keep you where it is safest. For me. For England." He paused and cut Pembroke a cunning glance. "In the Tower."

Pembroke's countenance hardened. His arms stiffened and his fingers, slowly, curled into fists of stone. He understood the implication as well as I did. The Tower of London was where traitors awaited their deaths. I knew by his look that he had not known of this. The king had conceded to him merely to lure us into giving up. He had betrayed Pembroke as well as us.

With a flick of the king's fingers, a swarm of guards rushed forward and began to strip us of our armor and mail. My uncle flailed his arms and cursed Edward, but the king walked away without a backward glance. His retinue of new bloods trailed after him up the steps to the great hall.

There they would raise their wine goblets, exhilarated by their conquest of the rebels, and sing honeyed phrases to the glory of King Edward while they drank themselves beneath the tables.

We never saw the inside of Shrewsbury Castle, never stepped within its warmth or were offered a meal to silence our rumbling bellies. Our hands were tied with rope that smelled of damp hay and manure. Like livestock loaded up for market, we were shoved onto the bed of a wagon and taken away.

A single falsehood had robbed us of our freedom. Meanwhile, Edward was free to do as he pleased. Not a lord was left in England who would dare defy him.

6

Roger Mortimer:

Tower of London — February, 1322

T HE ROPE THAT BOUND my hands together burned raw into my flesh. My wrists had been chafed bloody on the first day, the cords drawn so tight that my fingers went numb. I dared not turn or stretch my hands even slightly to try to relieve the discomfort. If I developed an infection, they would gladly let me rot to death.

The slumbering countryside rolled by in a blur; the dull gray of a winter sky blending with the mud-brown of earth. A dense mantle of smoke lay still and suffocating above the rooftops of the towns. Deep, bone-biting cold enveloped the land, sinking its teeth into exposed flesh. Every tree limb and grass stem was covered in a pearly frost. Small rivers had frozen into ribbons of ice. Had I been a free man, instead of a prisoner mired in gloom, I might have seen some beauty in it.

I wedged my fingers between my knees to warm them. The wagon that my uncle, Edmund and I were being transported in rattled incessantly. I drifted between half-sleep and hazy wakefulness. In my more lucid hours, I searched the faces of passing strangers. I hoped beyond hope that some old ally would come to our rescue. But no one afforded us more than a glance of mockery. Most dared not look at all with the king's livery surrounding us.

I hungered. Hurt. Slept hardly at all. Lost count of the number of days we were on the road, even though it must have been no more than a week. Always, day slipped into night without distinction.

Suddenly, the right front wheel plummeted into a hole. My head banged against the back plank of the driver's seat and my teeth came down sharply on my tongue. Before I could recover from the jolt, the wagon bounced upward. My chin snapped forward onto my chest. A blow of pain hammered through the back of my head and down my neck. I thought the axel might break and we would be tumbled into the roadway to be crushed by the hooves of the guards' horses, but the wagon wobbled unstoppably on.

I looked around only to discover it was night again. Somehow, I had slept. To my left, still as a dog lazing by the hearth, my son Edmund lay flat on his back. Blankly, he gazed up at the stars through a rare break in the clouds. Since leaving Shrewsbury he had not spoken at all. Rather than flee to Picardy, where his younger brother Geoffrey served in the household of Joan's relatives, the de Fiennes, Edmund had chosen to stay and fight beside me. But it had not been much of a fight for him thus far. At Bridgnorth I would not even allow him to take part in the assault across the bridge. I had wanted to keep him safe. At Shrewsbury, I had delivered him straight into Edward's hands. Now this. A bleak end to a life barely begun.

Except for Edmund and Geoffrey, the rest of my children were at Wigmore with Joan. King Edward would have sent a small army there by now. I might never know what had become of them, or the child Joan was expecting. I would not be there to give it a name.

"There are things," I whispered to Edmund, "that I never had a chance to tell you, to teach you."

He turned his face toward me, his lips drawn tight with dread, only long enough so I could glimpse the quenched hope behind his eyes.

"Fight only when forced to," I went on, "and when you do, let others take the advance. Never lower your shield until the one you are fighting has spent himself. A knight must not waste himself with rash—"

The wagon driver threw a look at me over his shoulder and growled a warning. I went quiet, the oppressive silence tightening like a rope around my throat. Soon, the monotonous rumble of the wheels lulled the driver into a stupor, but by then Edmund had closed his eyes. Whether he truly slept or was merely shutting me out, I did not know.

On my right, my uncle lay curled on his side away from me, his face averted so that he, too, would not meet my eyes. He blamed me. Still. He would rather have rushed to his own slaughter at Shrewsbury than bend his knee to the king and be dragged away like a common thief to meet an ignominious end on the Tower Green.

"It was not Pembroke who failed us," I muttered at the back of Uncle Roger's head, risking a beating from our guards. "He tried to influence the—"

"You're a fool!" he spat.

I looked down at my lap. "If Lancaster had—"

"Fool!" he repeated. He drew his head deep into his shoulders like a badger retreating into its burrow. His entire body was coiled so tight with anger one touch more might have unraveled him altogether.

The driver and closest mounted guard laughed. Probably, they figured my uncle's shunning of me was punishment enough.

In my uncle's eyes, I deserved no forgiveness.

I gazed at Edmund's face, ashen as a funeral effigy. So young. And I, although not old, already had much to look back on. But, what more did I have to live for? Children I rarely saw? A wife who did not love me? Not those things, no. I had been a rich and powerful man, thousands at my command, heady with my victories in battle. Efficient in office as the King's Lieutenant of Ireland. A man on the verge of an earldom. *If not for the all-encompassing greed of Hugh Despenser.* Had I died in battle at Shrewsbury fighting for all I had gained, then it was Despenser who would have won, without even being there. With the resistance to Edward's tyranny dissolved, it was only a matter of time before he beckoned Despenser back to England. I could not stop that from happening now. Not bound and bleeding in the back of a wagon. Not locked up in the Tower as the king's prisoner. Not swinging dead from a traitor's rope.

But if I lived—and lived long enough—one day, I could have my revenge.

I COULD TELL WE had arrived at the city's edge simply by the power of its nauseating stench. Our wagon rumbled into London at the darkest hour of night. The timing of our arrival was well planned. The streets were hushed and vacant. Only the occasional yowling of a cat in season or the alert yap of a dog sliced through the dead air.

When we entered the city at Ludgate, a surly guard dismounted, clambered into the wagon bed and one by one covered each of us with a moth-eaten, mildewed blanket. Out of habit, for I had always hated London and avoided it at all costs, I muttered about the odor and swiftly felt the toe of his boot to my gut.

"Quiet, bastard traitor!"

I was not spoken to again until we reached the inner bailey of the Tower of London. There, they snatched the blanket away and pitched me sideways from the wagon. My elbow and chest slammed against the cobbles. Air was sucked from my lungs. Before I could draw breath, Edmund landed across my legs, tumbled over, and banged his head on the stones. He gritted his teeth to keep from crying out, but a long hiss of pain escaped his mouth. I choked and sputtered as I fought to breathe. Then I saw another shadow wobbling above me. There was an irascible grunt, followed by a spit and a curse.

They hurled my uncle from the wagon. My torso broke his fall; only he did not land with the lithe reactions of my son, but the dead weight of an old man stiff in the joints. I tried to inhale, but his weight crushed me. My lungs would not expand. Down low my ribs burned with pain, as though someone had plunged a flaming poker into me.

"Get . . . off," I gasped.

They hoisted him to his feet and began to drag him away.

I tucked my right elbow beneath me to roll over, but the pain burst through me again. With my hands still bound, I could not push myself up with either of them. The scrape of fading footsteps urged me to try again. I lifted my other shoulder and turned my head enough to see, in the silver etchings of a winter night, my uncle being escorted toward one of the tower doors. A virulent sneer tore from his lips.

"May you rot in hell!" he shouted at me. His crackling voice echoed off the high walls like the shattering of glass. They shoved him headlong through the doorway. He cursed again. The door slammed shut. Then . . . the sound of a beating. His profane oaths were muffled by fist blows, until at last they faded to heavy sobs and drawn-out whimpers.

On his knees, Edmund shook his head. Slowly, he turned his face toward me. A trickle of blood traced its way from the indent of his temple to the ridge of his cheekbone. "He did not mean it," he said barely above a whisper.

At that, one of the guards seized him by the back of his shirt, yanked him to his feet and slammed a fist into his belly. "Keep your mouth shut, you hear?"

Edmund crumpled against the wagon, his eyes squeezed tight in pain. Before he could recover, they hooked their hands beneath each of his arms and were taking him away, too. Had I any breath to spare, I would have called after him. With stoic courage, Edmund lifted his head, picked up his feet, and kept silent so they would not give him the same pummeling they had given his great uncle. He was escorted to the same door, but when it was opened there was neither sight nor sound of my uncle. Edmund dodged to the side to avoid being slammed into the doorway as they jostled him through.

Vaguely, I was aware of the clop of hooves, the wagon rattling away over the stones, a barking of orders, the groaning of a gate, and the slow murmur of deep voices from behind me.

"—the Lanthorn Tower. There is a room for him there. Mind you, no one is to speak to him."

Measured footsteps approached me from behind. I felt a pair of hands lift me carefully up until I was sitting. I winced involuntarily.

A man in full mail and wearing the king's red and gold stepped around me and sank to his haunches. His balding head, bare of coif or helmet, was fringed with close shorn chestnut locks and streaked with the first white hairs of middle age. "A bit bruised, aren't you?" He began to probe about my head with lightly jabbing fingers and worked his way down my neck and shoulders. When he came to my last two ribs on the right, I clenched my jaw, but there was a little groan deep inside my throat he must have heard, for he drew his hands away and stood. "Take him away. And see to his injuries. 'Tis the king who says whether he lives or dies, and when, not us."

Silently, I thanked him for that grace, however morbid.

A SHAFT OF WHITE daylight broke through the single window of my room. I stretched my arms outward, only to feel the pain clamp around my ribcage. It had worsened through the night, but I had been so grateful for a mattress and a blanket, despites the lumps and fleas, that I went dead with sleep minutes after lying down. Besides a real bed, I had been given a room with a chair, although its cushion was flat and its red cloth frayed, and a cracked chamber pot. Slowly, I pushed my blanket away and eased my feet onto the floor. I curled my fingers into loose fists and unrolled them one by one. The scabs on my wrists were puckering. I turned my arms over. No fresh blood. No sign of infection. I draped the blanket over my cramped shoulders and hobbled across the room in six small pain-riddled strides. Winter wind leaked around the leaded panes of the recessed window. My view was of the waterfront and the Thames itself. I guessed from my height above the river that I was housed on the uppermost floor.

I heard a scraping sound and looked over my shoulder. But it was only a mouse, scurrying from under the bed into a tiny hole between the stones at floor level. I leaned back against the cold, rough wall and gazed out at the world beyond. A world to which I no longer belonged. Below, fishing boats slipped downriver on their way out to open sea. Merchants' barges slogged past them against the current. One maneuvered into a wharf to unload sacks of grain. The sun beamed bright over London, alive with activity, but I felt only the icy fingers of winter slip beneath my tunic to steal the warmth from my flesh and the pain sharp in every rattled bone and bruised muscle.

At intervals, I heard dampened voices through the thickness of the door. Mostly, there was only silence and the faint clack of boot heels from the sentries along the walls connecting the towers. Finally, the latch turned. Hinges squeaked. The door opened. A guard shuffled in, flashed me a look of contempt, and flung a hunk of bread and a cup of drink on the floor next to the door. Had I remarked on how he had spilt half the drink in his carelessness, I would have gotten a rude welcome from him. He backed out. Two others behind him parted, but instead of one of them reaching to close the door, another stepped between them and entered. It was the man who had given the orders to send me here last night. He gestured for the guards to close the door.

"I take it you know who I am?" I grinned facetiously. "Sir Roger Mortimer, England's greatest traitor, did they tell you? Some might argue that. Myself for one. But I wager you're an important man in these ranks to have been granted the honor of looking after me. What is your name, good sir?"

He crossed his arms. The lines of his face were firmly set to show he afforded me no sympathy. "Gerard d'Alspaye, Sub-lieutenant of the Tower. I came to see if you needed a physician?"

"I am to live after all, then?" But even as I asked it, I feared the only purpose in keeping me alive was to put me on trial. A trial with the sentence already written. When he gave no reply, I plied him further. "How many years have you been in the king's service?"

"All of it. And ten years under his father before that."

"Well then, you deserve the honor. Although it may not be for long. If Edward has his way I'll be headless ere springtime." I went to the chair and eased my aching body onto it. If I stood any longer, my legs would give way. "So, where have you put my uncle and son?"

Impervious to my attempts to learn more, he repeated himself. "Do you need a physician?"

"Do I look broken?" I answered peevishly. I looked toward the window, quite sure I would be spending many days, months perhaps, alone like this as I awaited my fate. "Send your physician to my uncle. He is old and ill."

D'Alspaye nodded and turned to go.

"Lieutenant," I called, still not looking at him, "is there anything you *can* tell me?"

"Only that it is a pity to see you here . . . my lord."

Then I heard his knock on the door, the sliding of the outer bar, and his footsteps fading away. I sighed and regarded my meager meal. The mouse froze momentarily, a morsel of bread clenched between its tiny claws. Its whiskers twitched in frantic indecision. We studied each other closely. At length, it scampered away.

I rose, kicked the cup against the door and lay down in my cold, hard bed.

NEVER AGAIN DID I see the guards that had escorted us from Shrewsbury to London. Those that kept watch over me daily were less violent men, but more impressionable. They had heard of my exploits in Ireland. I told them how I tamed the Irish and brought law to the land. I told them of Bannockburn, a tale that needed no embellishment. Shortly after that, Gerard d'Alspaye came and asked me to tell it again. He poured us both cups of ale and sat down on my decrepit chair, listening with the rapt attention of a young boy who sits at his father's knee and dreams of being a knight. When I was done telling my story, he gave me news of the outside world: Lancaster had been brought to battle by Andrew Harclay, the Earl of Carlisle, at Boroughbridge. He was captured the next day and taken to Pontefract. His end came as quickly as Edward—and the recently returned Hugh Despenser—could get there.

Had I known that they would lop off Thomas of Lancaster's red-faced head in a fit of revenge for trying to make peace with the Scots . . . I would have swum to Ireland before laying down my arms. Great lords by the dozens were sent to their deaths, including the meek Bartholomew de Badlesmere, who was taken to Canterbury and hanged. Every day, I expected them to come and escort me to the scaffolding. Yet days stretched miserably into weeks with no word of what was to become of me.

While I languished, Edward marched into Scotland. I wondered how he would fare there, failure that he always was at war.

I might have gone mad, shut up in the Tower with the rodents, muttering to myself. A likely outcome. No doubt many a man had, as he picked at putrid scabs and retched his guts dry from hunger. Had I more faith in God's plan than my own, I would have turned monkish and welcomed my death. But I was not so certain that heaven awaited me. Souls bound for heaven ought to be pure and repentant and full of forgiveness.

I was not.

For every night that I lay my head down on my pillow crawling with lice, I dreamed of revenge. It was the only joy I had.

7

Isabella:

Tynemouth Priory — October, 1322

E DWARD SAID HE WOULD come. He told me to wait for him and when he did not come I thought surely he would send someone to bring me to his side. Yet the days crawled by like years and there I waited, praying to the dusty bones of a trifling saint, far from the places I had come to know as home, far from my beloved children.

Once, he had abandoned me in York. He would again, I feared—this time in a remote, holy place, as if God and His saints would guard me.

I raised my face to the new light. Three silver-yellow fingers reached through the tall, lancet windows on the eastern wall of Tynemouth Priory. They crept silently across the length of the nave, stretching moment by moment, illuminating the dusky tiles of the floor and the spindly columns that aspired heavenward, until at last they brushed my face. I blinked at the intrusion and shifted on the velvet cushions beneath my knees until the prickling sensation in my feet lessened and the steady pulse of blood returned.

ISABEAU

I folded my hands to pray, the beads of my rosary bunched between my palms; but prayers did not pass my lips or fill my mind. Instead, a thousand screaming visions battled in my head. Terrible and haunting. Visions of Scottish hobelars with their swords high above their heads; of arrows hissing and twanging, leaving bodies sprawled in bloody puddles; of people stumbling from burning homes, their crying children clutched in their arms; of women being brutally raped. Visions of war. Nightmares of the daylight hours.

I had seen the aftermath with my own eyes. Heard the tales. I wished not to live it.

Inside the priory church there was no rote chanting of monks, no shifting of the congregation on weary knees, nothing but the pregnant stillness of dawn. The ominous silence—the nothingness of it—only blew breath into my grotesque visions.

Kneeling next to me, my damsel Patrice drew her hand from the folds of her skirt and touched me on the forearm. Her touch gave me solace, as only the closeness of a friend could.

Sensing a shadow, I looked again toward the windows. Outside, a cloud must have scuttled across the sun, for its darkness fell upon me and I shivered deep in my bones. Patrice fumbled with the clasp on her mantle to give it to me, but I shook my head, foregoing the gesture.

"Shall I fetch your mantle, then? With the fur lining?" Patrice kept her voice low, mindful of the sanctity of our surroundings. "Tell me what you need, anything at all, and I'll bring it."

I curled my fingers around Patrice's and squeezed. *An army—can you bring me that?* I wanted to say.

In search of further guidance, I glanced toward the tomb where the bones of St. Oswin were enshrined. "What I need . . . what *we* need, Patrice, is a swift miracle."

Edward despised war, but the events of the previous year—a rebellion led by the Mortimers and soon afterwards the Earl of Lancaster's furtive dealings with the Scots—had driven him to invade Scotland in order to quell his uneasy barons. He had made it unchallenged this summer as far as Edinburgh, ravaging the abbey at Holyrood before turning back. On his way southward, vexed by the elusive Robert the Bruce, he had set fire to Melrose Abbey as a token of his passing. When his soldiers soaked the ground with the blood of monks he did nothing to intervene.

I had been awaiting his return at Tynemouth Priory near Newcastle ever since then, as I had been told to do. But Edward had not come yet. He was riding on instead to Rievaulx, where he was to meet up with Hugh Despenser, leaving the Earl of Richmond to cover his back.

As if her words were a secret better left unspoken, Patrice leaned closer and whispered, "The Scots won't come this far into England . . . will they?"

Patrice knew how to draw men's eyes to her with a modest glance or feed their arrogance by feigning interest in all they said or did, but she did not understand men's entanglements in war or politics, or their reluctance to do without either. I smiled nervously and drew my childhood friend closer. "Robert the Bruce would be a fool to cross the River Tyne while an entire English army stands before him."

But I had spoken the words only to allay her fears. Many times, the Scots had raided this far into England. That constant annoyance had been the crux of the Earl Thomas of Lancaster's argument with Edward. So rather than give his cousin Lancaster what he needed—men and money, because in truth Edward had none to spare, or a treaty of peace with the Scots—Edward had simply taken off his head out of spite, thus ending the disagreement.

Skeptical, Patrice tilted her head at me. "But after what the king did at Holyrood and Melrose?"

Indeed I doubted the Bruce would let it go unpunished. Edward was ignorant to even think he might.

"If they come this way," I said, "*if* they do, Tynemouth's walls will keep them out."

"But for how long?"

Not long enough, I feared.

"The king will send someone to us," I said, trying to convince myself.

I could only pray that the 'someone' would not be Hugh Despenser.

Far behind us, the main door of the nave groaned. A sharp autumn draft blew across the distance, chilling me to the bone. Patrice glanced over her shoulder and immediately tucked her chin to her chest.

"Arnaud," she breathed, the blush rising from her breast to her neck and then flaming her cheeks.

I dropped my arm from her shoulder. "Perhaps he wishes to see you . . . alone."

"Not *here*," she objected too quickly.

I winked at her. "As you choose, but I would advise you to find somewhere besides the storeroom. You reeked of onions last evening. This," I said, looking around, "would seem a more suiting place to tempt your lover into a proposal. You're twenty-seven, Patrice. An old maid. Put this one off and you'll have no one calling but haggard old widowers with curled toenails who want you to rub their yellow feet at night and fetch them the chamber pot in the morning. You're daft if you don't ensnare de Mone. Shall I speak to him of my concern for your 'honor'?" Sincere, I narrowed my eyes at her.

Arnaud's steps rang closer, slowing as he neared. Patrice hushed me with a glare and a clenched jaw.

The toe of Arnaud's boot scraped the stone tiles as he halted and clicked his heels into place. When that brought no reply, he cleared his throat roughly.

I jabbed Patrice teasingly with an elbow. "Will you see what it is my squire wants? I'm deep in prayer and wish not to be disturbed." My lips pressed together, I stifled a laugh at her embarrassment and pretended to resume my prayers. Between barely parted lashes, my chin tilted toward my shoulder for a better view, I watched them, intrigued.

Slowly, Patrice rose, turned, and met the clear blue eyes of Arnaud de Mone. So much was shared in the fleeting look between them that the poignancy of it struck a pang of jealousy in me. Even before Arnaud, men had always desired her, pursued her and she had played with them like a sailor plays at dice to pass the time. But unlike the others, she had not grown bored with him. Rather, she had been the one doing the pursuing. When he first arrived at court on the tail of his knighted uncle, every female at court had learned his name, the place of his birth and his family lineage by his first day's end. But it was only Patrice he saw. His eyes followed her everywhere, even though for a whole month he could not summon the courage to speak to her. Proving more of a challenge than she was accustomed to, she threw herself wholeheartedly into the pursuit. Two more months passed before he kissed her and two after that before he could no longer deny himself of her.

Before his lips even parted to speak, Patrice must have recalled clearly the sweet tenor of his voice and the words he had spoken recently, for her fingers drifted up to her ear and paused there. For a moment it was obvious that she forgot me, forgot where she was and that only a day and a half had passed since she had been in Arnaud's arms.

"M'lady," he uttered, his gaze locked on Patrice's form, both of them visibly flushed. Then with a hard shake of his head, he bowed and thrust a letter into Patrice's hands. "For Queen Isabella. From my lord king."

The letter rustled in Patrice's outstretched hand. She stared at it as though he had given her a poisoned dagger.

I willed myself to stand, but my knees were locked, legs numb, the blood draining from my head in a shockingly cold rush.

"Read it," I uttered.

Patrice shrank into her shoulders. The tight, black ringlets at the back of her head disappeared into her mantle. She could read, although not well, and the king's scrawling, she had once remarked, looked more like the fingernail scratches of an angry child on frosty glass than the letters of a learned man. After so many years of severity leveled at him by the Lords Ordainers, King Edward was too suspicious to entrust letters addressed to me to the scribing of a secretary. But more than the awkwardness of having to decipher the king's writing, I knew Patrice was as reluctant to reveal the news that might be there as I was to hear it. She retreated, shaking her head.

Sensing her discomfort, Arnaud stepped closer to her. "May I?"

ISABEAU

The letter relinquished gladly into his hands, Arnaud broke the seal. He squinted, twisted his mouth up tight and read, fumbling along at intervals where the words were crowded illegibly together:

"Our Dear Consort,

At present, we are unable to send aid to you, our beloved consort. My dearest and most . . . most trusted cousin, the Earl of Richmond, after a long and courageous battle, was taken at Byland Moor by the wicked and traitorous Robert the Bruce. We are deeply . . . deeply concerned for our kinsman. As soon as circumstances permit, we will demand his release and if need be offer . . . monies for his ransom. We fear, however, the price will be impossible, if only to taunt us.

We have taken flight from Rievaulx Abbey by way of Bridlington and at last found refuge at York, where we await you. You are commanded to take ship posthaste. My councilors advise that the . . . Scottish traitors may be aware of your location and will ride on Tynemouth—we pray not before this letter reaches you.

May the Holy Spirit bless and keep you.
Edwardus Rex
16th day of October, 1322"

I forced myself to my feet, plucked the letter from Arnaud's unsuspecting hands and reread it. When I raised my eyes again, my voice began shakily, but with each word it grew in volume and spite. "Take ship? I have no ships. He provided me with none, saying I would not likely need them! How am I to take ship to him if he is in York *forty miles from shore?!*"

"My lady, I believe he means," Arnaud began gently, trying to insert calm into the crisis, "for you to make land to the east at—"

"I *know* what he means!" I stomped my foot. White pain shot up from my heel through my calf, but it was lost in the red fury that consumed me. I had requested . . . *begged* for a sufficient escort to see me safely back to London and for weeks I had been given nothing but excuses. "What this means is the Scots are somewhere between here and York—that we are cut off from any relief force and left to fend for ourselves. What this means is the Bruce has once more outwitted our king. The Scots will plunder their merry way home until there is not a cow left between York and Carlisle and—"

The Scots. We were doomed indeed if we expected them to turn away or spare their arrows because we claimed sanctuary here. I scooped up the hem of my gown and took four quick steps toward the door, then whirled about. "Arnaud, where were they last reported?"

"The Scots? Richmond."

"On the road to Durham?"

"I don't know. They could be aiming for Cumberland."

If such was true, it would gain us precious time, however small. I breathed deeply, gathering myself inwardly. Clearly, we could not rely on others. Certainly not Edward. Our only surety was in ourselves.

THAT EVENING PATRICE FOUND me seated on a pillow in the arched window seat of my apartments. Loose strands of hair dangled down over my forehead. Even as I glanced toward the door, I did not brush them away. I was too fraught with worry to bother.

"Come," I bid to Patrice, scooting a pillow across to her. "Sit with me."

Patrice sat down and took my hand.

"So cold," she remarked, scrunching her eyebrows with concern.

"It was warmer yesterday. The storm has brought a terrible chill with it. Winter is not far, I fear. It always makes me feel as if my bones might snap." I returned my gaze to the window. Rain pattered steadily against it, smearing the gray of the nearly night sky into the black of the sea.

We had grown up together in Paris, born only a month apart. That aside, we could not have been more unlike. My hair, once as pale as yellow primroses, had mellowed to a tawny hue. I was slight, despite having given birth to four children—my prominent collarbone and angular elbows apparent even beneath the thick layers of my brocaded gown. Patrice was dark-haired, dark-eyed, and everything about her was invitingly round: the swirling ringlets of coal black hair; the attentive curve of her brow; the healthy plumpness of her cheeks; a bosom so full and firm she looked the part of perpetual wet nurse. Had I not loved her so much I would have envied her for her looks alone.

I was the daughter of a king: Philip IV of France. Both my father and mother were dead now, along with my two oldest brothers, Louis and Philip, who had both ruled in succession. My brother Charles, childless and only a year older than myself, was now King of France.

For these past fourteen years, I had been queen to Edward II of England and done more to preserve this kingdom than any man shall ever know. Fourteen years, mostly unhappy if not for my children to give me some purpose and Patrice to absorb my sorrows.

Patrice began to get up. "Let me tend the fire and bring you your furs."

I held her hand firm. "In a moment. Please, I need someone to . . . to talk to."

"You've been up since before prime. You're weary. In need of rest. When the ships are ready you'll—"

"It will be days, maybe, before we can sail. Even when we do, in these rough seas we'll be crammed into the dark hull of some merchant ship like mice drowning in a barrel of rainwater—nowhere to go, nothing to do but tread water and pray it stops."

"Oh, Isabeau, must you always worry so?"

Isabeau. I smiled faintly at the childhood endearment. Even now, with disaster looming dark like a thunderstorm on the horizon, it was a sweet sound in my ears—one that I never heard come from English lips.

"Yes, I must," I admitted. "I cannot help it. Storms like this, this time of year—they can last for days. And while we wait for it to pass, the Scots have not stopped to dry themselves beneath a roof somewhere. They are still riding. Hard. Fast. If they know I am here . . . well, we dare not ride from here without an army of our own, do we? No, we have to wait. Wait for the sea to relent and the skies to break. Wait and hope."

Sometimes it seemed that had been my whole life: waiting. Waiting for something to happen. Waiting for Edward to come to his senses. Waiting for things to get better by some miracle.

Patrice had been with me at York barely three years ago when the Black Douglas, leader of the Bruce's lightly armed horsemen, the hobe-lars, had ripped through Yorkshire, raiding town after town, burning farm after farm, to divert the English army from their siege at Berwick. If not for the rash bravery of Archbishop Melton of York, who clashed with Douglas at Myton, though it amounted to a massacre of English monks and burgesses, we might have fallen into Scottish hands then. The selfless act bought us enough time to escape by horse. But on our way south, we witnessed the terror that Scotsmen left in their wake. The memory stirred the sharp taste of smoke in my throat and visions of bloodied bodies piled three high in carts.

"I remember, too." I brushed my fingertips against Patrice's cheek, and then laid my head upon her shoulder. "I used to wonder what would have befallen us if . . . if we had given ourselves up to the Scots then." I thought I felt a shudder run through Patrice's body, but I realized it was me. "They say that when the Bruce held Ralph de Monthermer prisoner, the stepfather of Gilbert de Clare, after Bannockburn that they went hawking together whenever the weather was good and feasted together daily. His nephew, Thomas Randolph, who betrayed him, was granted every comfort and kept in his constant company until Randolph was won over by his charm. Can the Bruce be so bad a man, then? Certainly there is kindness to him, despite his reputation in battle."

"I have heard he is fine to look upon," Patrice mused.

"And that he had a dozen mistresses while his wife was being held captive in England." I had meant it to shock her, but I believe she thought it somewhat alluring. "I know not, Patrice, how long we can hold here against the Scots or how many lives I can give up trying to save my own. I only know it should not have come to this. If we stay, if too many die . . . I will have to surrender the fortress. But they do not come to take a monastery. They come for a queen. And if they ask a ransom for me, Edward will balk at it. He will stall in negotiations. He cares not what happens here, to me. But I do. Not for myself so much, though. I cannot be without my children, Patrice. Cannot."

We sat close for a while, saying nothing, our fears absorbed by the sound of the rain as it drummed against the window. Finally, the deep rumble of thunder shook Patrice from her trance. She crossed the room to the hearth, jabbed at the logs with a poker and busied herself sweeping ashes, even though it was not her duty to clean. Then, she took my furs from the bulging chest at the foot of the bed.

"You will see the children again soon. You will," she promised as she draped a deep pelt of fox fur over my shoulders.

"I pray so. If not for them, I would as soon wait here and give myself over to the Scots than throw myself to the mercy of the sea."

8

Isabella:

Tynemouth Priory — October, 1322

TYNEMOUTH WAS BOTH MONASTERY and royal residence. On two sides its buildings were enclosed by a stout wall, one side was further defended by a deep ditch and the other by sheer sea cliffs. It would have seemed a likely place to discourage any foe's assault, but the Bruce and his men, I knew, had conquered higher walls and crossed wider ditches than these. Thomas Randolph, the Earl of Moray, had taken Edinburgh by scrambling up the craggy, forbidding face of the mountain-high rock on which it sat. Sir James Douglas had scaled Berwick's walls with his crude rope ladders, even as archers let loose their arrows into the darkness around him. In comparison to those fortresses, Tynemouth was an anthill. A siege would have been a mere formality: a grace before the slaughter. I thanked Our Lord for having given me the sense to leave my children behind: Young Edward at Windsor and the others—John, Eleanor and Joanna—at Langley.

I had to leave Tynemouth. I had to return to them. I could not leave them with only Edward as a parent. They would fare better as orphans.

Three days more it rained. On the fourth day after receiving the letter from Edward, there was only a thin, dreary mist coming down. The clouds broke, gathered, and broke again, all before midmorning.

I leaned upon the parapet of the seaward wall of Tynemouth, my fur-lined mantle bunched tightly to my chest against a breath-stealing wind that muffled even the incessant cries of the kittiwakes. Occasionally, the gulls took flight from the cliffs—rippling clouds of gray-white against a shining dark sea. They beat their wings to go higher, only to retreat in ex-haustion and huddle once more upon the broken cliffs. I thought I saw a pair of gannets dive from the clouds and slice into the water, but they were far away and the whitecaps were everywhere. Even further out, a thick bank of slow-moving clouds muted the union of sky and sea, but whether it was a new storm building or the last of an old one was imposs-ible to tell. Westward, the land swelled up in a blend of moss-color and straw beneath a sky of slate. Somewhere there, the Tyne cleaved the undu-lating hills and a road traversed its length.

The sea wind nipped at the back of my neck as I looked once more in that direction. A shaft of sunlight gilded the waves and I smiled to see a broad break in the clouds. If we were going to leave Tynemouth, it would have to be soon or else the next riders to come sweeping along the west-ern road could very well be Scottish hobelars. Trusting in the sentries, I gave up my vigil on the wall and went inside.

I was in the gatehouse, meeting with the garrison's captain, when Lady Eleanor de Clare found me. My lady-in-waiting swooped at the waist and, before receiving acknowledgment, burst out, "My lady, the Scots have turned eastward from Haltwhistle and are following the Tyne."

Perturbed, I paused in my instructions to the captain and gazed at Eleanor. She was Edward's niece and the wife of Hugh Despenser—that alone made her less than loved in my heart. Even more, Eleanor had been placed in my household without my consent. I would just as soon not have Despenser's bedfellow, however occasional she might have been in that manner to him, hovering about. I might as well have had my mouth pressed to Despenser's own ear.

"When?"

Eleanor shrugged. "The scout said they may be as far as Hexham by now."

Hexham was roughly a day's ride. Outwardly, I did not waver at the news, but within I felt the rain's dampness on my skin, felt it seeping through my flesh and into my bones.

"My lady . . ." Eleanor began, her voice thinning to a mewl, "if we do not do something, they will—"

"As I was telling the captain: The ship has already been loaded with provisions. But for my personal guard, the garrison will stay and defend the castle until we are safely away. If the winds allow, we'll go as far down the coast as we can."

Immediately, I set about issuing orders. No task, I had learned, was ever accomplished by pondering on it overlong. By noon we departed Tynemouth, our cloaks wrapped tight about us as we descended the steep and winding path toward the shoreline where our ship awaited.

Beyond the cliffs where the Benedictine priory sat, a rising wind lashed at the blue-black sea, churning the waves into foamy peaks. Against the ragged shoreline, the raging waves crashed in sprays of white. Then, broken and hushed, they retreated seaward in defeat. At the northern edge of the horizon, the sky had already begun to darken again.

I looked once more toward the priory, wondering if I should order us back to wait until tomorrow, but with a glance Patrice banished my thoughts. She did not want to relive York, nor did I.

My men-at-arms lifted the small rowing boat from behind a sand dune and carried it forward on their shoulders. I waited on shore while they rowed my damsels out in twos and threes to board the ship. The youngest of my damsels, Cecilia de Leygrave who was fifteen, hovered at my elbow, already blanched in complexion.

"You do not like to sail, Cecilia?" I asked cautiously.

Tremulous, she cast her brown eyes toward the lowering horizon. "Oh, I have not sailed much. Once before maybe. I was little then, so I don't remember much of it. But I do not like storms, my lady. I do not like being wet or cold or standing out in the lightning. Ida told me once about her cousin who was struck by lightning—there was nothing left of him but a pile of ashes in his boots and the ring from his finger. And I have heard there are monsters in the sea that follow ships. That they especially follow ships with women on them."

It was strange to see the usually witty and tittering Cecilia so terror-stricken. I hung an arm over her shaking shoulders and forced a laugh. "Was it Ida who told you about the sea monsters who devour women? She is full of silly stories. Well, I have never seen a sea monster, nor have I ever known anyone who has. It is simply a tavern tale told by old sailors to make themselves sound braver than they are. So you needn't worry about monsters, Cecilia. They don't exist. Besides, I have hired the best sailors and the fastest ship north of London. We will arrive somewhere safe sooner than you know."

But I stretched the truth. The ship I had commissioned for our rescue was one that had recently been blown back by storms. A sodden and battered crew had crudely mended its sails, sliced by the gale. The hull had received a hasty caulking of moss and a spotty daubing of pitch. Its seaworthiness was highly suspect, but taking ship was no surer a fated death than remaining at Tynemouth.

She pressed her fingertips together in a hasty prayer. "I am to be betrothed to a squire from Oxford. A good man, I'm told. He sent me this." She splayed the fingers of her left hand and wiggled them to show a ring of tarnished silver set with a milky blue stone. A pretty bauble, it was nothing of great value. To her, however, it was a treasure.

"Very beautiful." I leaned close to peer at it. "So you have not met?"

She twisted the ring on her finger. Then, deciding it was loose, she switched it to another finger. "No, but he writes. I have one of the monks read them to me. It is . . . embarrassing sometimes, what he says, to hear a holy man say it. But he sounds most kind."

Two soldiers each extended a hand to help us into the little rowing boat that reeked of fish. "A very important trait for a husband to have.

You will be happy." I hooked my arm through hers and together we walked into the foamy rush of cold waves that wrapped about our feet. The boat rocked as we each stepped into it. We plunked down on a rowing thwart in the front and the two soldiers took the back, leaving the oarsman in the middle. I hugged Cecilia close. As I did so, I saw, far to the south and high up at the edge of the cliffs . . . a line of horsemen, armed. Their silhouettes cut stark and ominous against a gray veiling of clouds. The tips of their spears jabbed at the sky as they rode hard and fast along the thin lip of earth.

The oarsman pulled hard, grunting, and we slipped away from shore. My heart tumbled in fear with each jerk of the oars. Most of my damsels, including Patrice and Juliana, had already boarded the broad-bellied merchant ship that would take us down the coast to safety, but three others still waited on shore for the rowing boat to return for them.

Cecilia bit fiercely at her lip as we lurched toward the bobbing ship, each wave knocking our tiny boat back almost as far as the oarsman could manage to advance.

"He will be in York, waiting for me." Her voice was barely a whisper above the roar of waves around us. Rain began to fall suddenly, heavily, stabbing at my shoulders and back. Cecilia crouched down before me and tucked her head tight against my bosom to keep the rain out of her eyes.

I did not think to ask what her betrothed's name was, so fixed was my attention on the horsemen now leaning back in their saddles to plunge rapidly down the steep trail toward the shore. "Do not worry, Cecilia. The brunt of the storm is to the north. Away from us."

But there was a closer fate to the south, closing fast. The last of my damsels were quaking in a tight huddle at the edge of an angry sea. A remnant of my guard, four men, waited with them. A small garrison had remained at the priory, thinking that if anyone came to attack, they would approach by the road to the west. Lightning cracked overhead. One of the soldiers glanced up at the cliffs. In the flickering light, sword blades glinted. I could now make out the round, studded shields affixed to their forearms—the targes of Scots. And at the lead a man with wild black tresses that fell to his shoulders. With his sword thrust out before him, he raised himself up out of his stirrups and closed on those below like a demon of the night.

The garrison soldier let out a cry to stand in defense. The black-haired Scotsman cocked his arm back and leaned out hard to the side. His blade slashed through the darkness and severed the man's bare neck. The soldier who had given the warning was forever silenced. His head bounced in front of the terrified clutch of women and rolled to the water's edge. The man's torso swayed until a gust of wind finally pushed it over.

Above the crash of thunder, I could not hear the screams that followed.

They were now three men against thirty. Through the deluge, I saw the rest of the hobelars swoop down upon the English soldiers, who did not last a minute under the onslaught of weapons, valiant though they were. Before we reached the ship, their bodies lay strewn over the sand, the rain washing red rivers of blood into a turbid black sea.

And then I saw my women being plucked up by the Scotsmen like half-empty sacks of grain and slung across their horses' withers.

The black-haired Scotsman galloped his horse out into the stormy sea, stopping only when the waves crashed so forcefully against his horse's chest that the beast refused to go any further. Our eyes met across the bleary distance and I knew, without being told, who the dark-haired one was: the Black Douglas.

For a moment, my heart faltered. I felt our little boat struggle and pitch back toward shore as the oarsman tired, but with a fit of energy he leaned hard into the oars once again. With a few strokes more we were there and being pulled into the ship. Cecilia, still in my protective embrace, saw none of the swift massacre or the man who had led it.

We were no more than a few hours out when the winds began to beat like the fists of undeniable death at our ship.

Rain lashed cold and heavy. The sail was taken down while the keel heaved high above jagged waves. The ship did not hold its mending. The mast groaned against the hammering of the wind. There was no bargaining to be had. The sea would exact its price for passage. One which was dear. The storms were no more merciful than the Scots had been.

It was almost a week before we stumbled, less several of my household, into York.

9

Isabella:

York — October, 1322

T EARS OF AGONY BLINDED me as I crossed the floor of the king's chamber at York. The muscles in my back were drawn into a fiery knot so tight I could not raise my arms above the level of my shoulders. My throat had been scraped raw by the wind. Since setting foot upon land at Scarborough two days past, I had not changed my gown nor combed my hair. My musty cloak was splattered with mud and torn in two places at the hem. Heads had turned at my appearance in the main hall a short while ago. The gawking, however, was not due to the surprise of my sudden arrival, for I had sent no heralds ahead of me, but because everyone had to study me, disheveled as I was, to confirm that it actually was me and not my ghost.

I pressed the back of my hand to my forehead and felt the burn of a slight fever, but dismissed it as anger. I had silenced the porter with a glare and refused the help of servants when I entered the King's Tower. I had but one purpose in mind; I meant to confront my husband. He had more than failed me. He had put my life in peril in order to save his own.

Edward was immersed up to his midriff in a tub of steaming water, his back to the door. At the drag of my weary steps, he twisted to look over his shoulder. His mouth gaped. Quickly, he donned a smile, although the tight curve of his lips only accentuated the shock revealed in his eyes.

"Ah, dear wife," Edward began nervously, "I see you've arrived whole. And sooner than I expected. You sailed then? To Scarborough?"

Jankin, Edward's red-haired servant, gave a cursory bob toward me and rinsed away the traces of soap on his master's back. On a stool beside the tub, leaning lazily with one elbow upon its rim, sat Hugh Despenser: the barnacle affixed to the ship's hull. Despenser did not stand or so much as nod his head in acknowledgment. He glared at me mildly, as if bothered by the interruption. When he was banished to the continent last year, I had thought myself forever rid of the louse. But my reprieve had been short-lived. As soon as the Mortimers and Lancaster had been taken care of, Edward had summoned him home.

As I halted, the blood drained from my head too quickly and I felt my knees nearly fold beneath me. I swooned forward and caught myself on the bedpost. Leaning against it, I tried to swallow before I spoke, but even that hurt. The words came out thin and cracked, as if spoken by an old woman somewhere in the distance. "We were flung ashore like limp ship rats."

"But the ride was uneventful from there, I trust? The Scots are long gone by now and—"

"They were well beyond Hexham when we left," I interrupted, my voice gaining strength.

Edward tugged at his neatly trimmed beard and chuckled in amusement, as if I were a child conjuring up falsehoods. "Hexham? I doubt. They could not have made it that far. More likely headed toward the Kielder Gap at the border. Going home." Daintily, Jankin held a towel in front of him. Edward rose immodestly from his bathwater, arms extended so that Jankin could pat him dry. "You were quite safe, I assure you. We seeded the entire countryside about Rievaulx with the rumor that you were there with us—even that you fled from there in a nun's habit. If they thought you were in Tynemouth, they did not come to that conclusion until much later. Although I had heard that Bruce eventually sent . . . oh, who was it? Not Randolph or de la Haye. Help me, Hugh. Who was the bastard?"

"James Douglas," Despenser answered, stifling a yawn.

"Yes, Bruce sent his man Douglas after you. But by the time they figured out—"

"I saw him," I uttered. The blood, now bubbling with rage, had returned to my head. I dug my fingernails into the bedpost.

"Who?"

"Douglas. I saw Douglas as we were leaving Tynemouth."

"Truly? But does it matter now? You're here."

"Four of my guard were killed. Three of my damsels carried away by Scots."

He glared at me. "*You* are here. If not for the rumors that bought you time . . . days, it would have been you on your way to Scotland."

"You did not mention all those things in your letter to me—that they knew where I was."

Edward exchanged an innocent, yet almost rehearsed, glance with Despenser. "I told you—they didn't. Not for certain. Besides, I wrote you in haste. Some of it I didn't know until later. Your forgiveness?"

He said the words with no more regret than if he had spilled a cup of wine.

While Edward stepped from the tub and began to dress, I bit back my words with such effort that the ache in my jaw pounded, reverberating in my skull like a hammer striking iron. My bones burned with exhaustion. My nose ran over my chafed upper lip. More than anything, I wanted to sink back onto the bed behind me and let sleep overtake me, but I had been wronged, terribly . . . purposefully. Through a cold rain I had ridden from Scarborough, accompanied only by a handful of sea-lashed guards and a few of my ladies who I knew wished not to be without a roof overhead and a fire in the hearth after our catastrophic voyage. Still, I had been wronged. Wronged by Hugh Despenser who sought to dominate Edward's attentions at any cost—even my life.

Ignoring the leech at his side, I watched Edward going about his nightly ritual—his wet hair being combed back off his face by Jankin, his skin oiled and perfumed—until I could say the next words without accusing him of murder outright.

"Cecilia de Leygrave drowned at sea. She was only fifteen. Newly betrothed." Her betrothed was somewhere here in York, waiting for her.

At the name, Edward paused Jankin with the flat of his palm. He pursed his lips thoughtfully. "Cecilia, Cecilia . . . Ah, yes. The daughter of my old nurse, Alice?"

A rhetorical question, he followed it with an even more succinct one. "How?"

I stared at Edward in disbelief. *How? How can the obvious so baffle you? You drove us to take ship in a storm and now Cecilia . . . beautiful, young Cecilia is dead. Only by God's abundant grace are we not all lying open-eyed and empty-mouthed at the bottom of the sea.* My eyes shifted from my husband's blank countenance to that of Hugh Despenser's, who remained smugly observant, despite my scrutiny.

As I recounted the tale, my voice was now more dead than angry. "She had gone above to look for a trinket . . . a ring, given to her by her betrothed. She could not find it and I called for her to come back below. She started across the deck, was knocked off her feet as the ship rolled, then was helped up by one of the sailors. She almost made it. Almost . . . I reached out for her. But a wave came, knocked me back down into the hull. It . . . the same wave, it must have carried Cecilia over the side. I heard her scream, on and on . . . I could not tell the roar of the ocean from her cries."

How utterly helpless I had felt as it had happened. Patrice and I had held each other, sitting in salty water, shivering violently. Yet while those around us huddled together, sniveling and terrified, the ship heaving with the wild pitch of the waves and the rain stabbing at the deck above, I had taken someone's hand, whose I know not, and said a prayer aloud:

"Hail Mary, full of grace,
God is with thee . . ."

By the time I uttered '*Amen*', Cecilia's screams were no more.

Like a cross, the king held his arms out as Jankin draped a mid-length nightshirt of crisp, snow-white linen over his head. "How horrible. It was quick, at least."

"*It was not,*" I growled.

Abruptly, Despenser altered the conversation. "My wife—Eleanor?"

"Somewhere," I snapped. I grabbed at the lining of my cloak and twisted it into a knot between my cold-cramped fingers. I was shivering even though I felt as though I were standing next to a roaring fire, but in Edward's bedchamber there was only a brazier alit by the tub.

Hugh gave a nonchalant nod. "Tell her I'm glad she is here and well."

But he did not ask to see her and I most certainly did not offer to send her. My jaws clamped as tight as a clamshell, I decided it was best to leave. My thoughts were too clouded with rage, my body too beaten to launch into what was sure to prove a long and terrible argument if I began it. Besides, Edward would be too emboldened with Despenser at his side. Tomorrow, when Despenser was elsewhere and I had renewed myself, I would speak to Edward alone. Speak to him about all this and about Despenser and his part in it.

I let go of the bedpost and began to retreat toward the door, but it felt as though my shoes were weighted down by ingots of lead.

Before I could place my hand on the latch, Edward called out. "Wife, dearest . . ." Such words always sounded forced when they came from his lips, as if he was never quite sure how to address me. It was seldom that he called me by name and when he did it was usually either in anger or condescension. "We shall take our supper here, Hugh and I. There is a meeting of the council tomorrow morning. There will be scathing words, accusation, blame, that sort of unwelcome stuff. Bruce has our Great Seal . . . again . . ." He slipped on a fur-lined pelisse to finish out his attire, lifted his shoulders alternately and then tugged at the cuff of each sleeve until their length matched. ". . . and our kinsman, Richmond. He has not yet named his price for their return. He will delay it to keep the upper hand. Ah . . ." He stole a swift glance at the window nearest, noting darkness. "Later than I thought. In the afternoon, then? Sleep well."

I wanted to spew my rage at him, but the longer I stood before him, the more I realized the futility of it. It did me no good to hold on to it.

My husband had taken no concern for my anguish. None. He did not inquire of my health or that of my ladies, whether I was tired after my arduous ride or even hungry enough to share a meal with him. No embrace, no kiss upon the cheek. He spoke to me as if I had only been out of his sight for a few moments. It had been four months.

DURING THE STORM AT sea, Edward's letter delivered to me at Tyne-mouth had been soaked to a pulp. Even though the words had been washed away, I remembered every one of them—each stroke of ink seared into my mind as permanently as the burn of a branding iron. On the ride inland, numbed by a dank, late autumn wind, I had asked myself over and over if somehow I had misread it, made too much of too little a thing. And over and over when I answered, it was that I had not.

I did not see Edward the next day as I intended, for when I tried to rise from bed a fever flamed through my body and my neck was so stiff I could barely move my head without feeling as though someone had a knife to my throat. For three days I drifted in and out of a fitful sleep. Being confined to bed was always the worst of all things for me, for it gave me time to worry about my children, to stew in anger and then to alternately doubt myself . . . and to relive the horrific voyage from Tynemouth to Scarborough.

In the nightmares that came again and again it was always night, it rained endlessly and the floodwaters rose until the world was a sea and only the topmost towers of the tallest castles stood above hellish waters. I crouched upon a parapet, soaked through, watching dead and bloated bodies float past. At last I saw a boat, a little rowing boat with a man in it with one oar. The boat drifted sleepily toward me, but for a long time I could not see who was in it because of the rain and the darkness, until at last it was close enough that I could almost reach it. The man was Despenser. I recoiled at first, and then knowing I would die otherwise, I reached out my hand and leaned from my shrinking island of stone. Despenser gave an arrogant laugh, slammed his oar against the stones on which I stood to thrust his vessel from me and then plunged the oar into the water and pulled away. I opened my mouth to cry out, but rain filled it, choking me.

I awoke in a frigid sweat. Patrice was there to dab at my forehead with a damp cloth.

By the fourth day the fever had broken and I was eager to get on my feet, but Patrice scolded me and once even pushed me back down and threatened to call Ida if I did not stay put. I complied, not because I feared Ida's mothering, old hen that she was, but because it felt as though I might fall over if I actually stood up.

"Has he called?" I said hoarsely to Patrice. There was only a small lump left in my throat and for the first time in days I felt a twinge of hunger.

Patrice shrugged, at first not understanding what I was asking, and gave me a sip of water. "The king?"

"Yes."

She pressed her lips together, trying to conjure a politic response, but in the end all she could manage was a simple shake of her head and a light hand upon my forearm. "Do you feel better today?"

"I do. But I must look an awful sight."

She smiled in amusement. "You should have seen yourself a few days ago. Not at all pretty. Rumors were amuck that a changeling had taken your place."

Soon I was as restless as a child confined to the indoors for too long a winter. I still meant to go to Edward, to speak to him, but the number of days gone by and the fever had lessened my determination to go to war with him.

On the fifth evening after our arrival at York, as my ladies prepared a bath for me, old Ida raked a comb through my twisted mess of hair with her knobby fingers. Marie offered me a cup of hot water sweetened with honey and licorice to rid me of a tickling cough. Sorting through my bed-clothes, Patrice offered a litany of comment on how each of them did or did not follow the latest fashions, until I finally told her what I needed was whatever was the most comfortable.

"Did I not tell you to stay at Scarborough awhile?" Ida scolded gruff-ly. With each stroke of the comb she yanked harder. "You must have figured I told you to stay put just because I don't like to get wet. You are a stubborn one. When I was a child, my older sister went out in a cold rain one night to meet with her sweetheart. Caught the ague, she did. Died from it. Just as well, though. My father would have whipped the life from her anyway. The boy . . . well, let me say that he did what he pleased and they—"

I winced as she jerked at a lock of hair so fiercely my eyes watered. She paused in her lecture only long enough to apologize and pat me on the head, or rather grumble and thump me on my head. Then she went back to work unknotting the tangles, her words twisting together in a waspish buzz that I had long ago learned to tolerate. I seldom asked her advice, although she often gave it. I pressed my fingertips to my temples. Without me needing to tell her to do so, Ida set aside the comb and went to prepare my bath.

As I waited, I closed my eyes, trying to rest. As ever though, my lids had no sooner drawn shut than my thoughts carried me elsewhere like the rush of a river in full spate—churning over things I could not change, searching for things I could.

For the sake of peace, I told myself, *let this go. Don't anger him, Isabella. Don't.*

Marie beckoned me quietly. She sprinkled the bathwater with cha-momile and orange peel, tested it with her fingers, and then dipped her knee to indicate it was ready. I shed my robe and slipped in, letting its warmth seep into my flesh. Slowly, my aches melted away.

Soon, my children would surround me and I would take them in my arms. I would say to Young Edward how tall and strong he looked and to John, who would ask a hundred questions in the first breath, how much he had grown before I told him about Cecilia. My daughter Eleanor, sweet Ella who adored flattery, I would tell her how bright and beautiful were her eyes. And Joanna, the babe . . . I would kiss her tiny forehead and tell her over and over how very much I missed her.

When the bathwater began to cool, Marie dressed me in a clean velvet robe and turned down my coverings. But first, Ida plaited my hair loosely to dry so that it dangled down my back like a woven rope. One by one, they drifted away to their sleeping places in adjoining chambers, until only Eleanor and Patrice remained.

Poor Eleanor. She had only half a husband, as well. Yet never so much as a frown when he spoke ill of her before others. Had she not been so abrasive she might have been worthy of pity.

Not until Eleanor spoke, did I realize I had been staring at her.

"Do you need anything else, my lady?" Several strands of her hair peaked from beneath her crooked barbette. Like all the de Clare women, she had brought a fat inheritance to her marriage. When Gilbert de Clare, the Earl of Gloucester, was killed at Bannockburn, his earldom was eventually divided amongst his three sisters, whose husbands all suddenly became very wealthy, Despenser being one of them.

I blinked at her. "Oh no, nothing. Only a good night's rest, perhaps. You as well, Eleanor."

Patrice closed the door softly behind Eleanor and cocked her head at me, a question framed by her pouting lips.

"Tomorrow," I told her, "I will speak to him."

I slid beneath my down coverings and turned toward the single window of my small bedchamber. Before Patrice blew out the candles, I saw a glimmering of frost on the inside of the window.

Winter had come to York.

10

Isabella:

York — November, 1322

YORK WAS ABUZZ WITH English barons for the upcoming session of parliament like flies on rotting fruit. Robert the Bruce had made his demands in exchange for the Great Seal, but there was no talk of ransom for Edward's cousin, the Earl of Richmond. It seemed the Bruce wished to keep him as a pawn, although I am certain he would have preferred me. Without his cousin, however, Edward was deprived of one more ally and his enemies were increasing by the day—not across the border, but inside it.

The roads leading to York lay like trampled brown ribbons over threadbare white linen. It was not yet December, but a light snow had fallen for three days straight and turned the roads to quagmires. At first, the snowflakes melted as they tumbled to earth. In time, however, the snow began to cool the ground and pile upon itself until the hills of York-shire gleamed like pearls beneath feathery clouds. I would not have liked to travel over such a mess, but from the top of King's Tower it was a

96

hauntingly beautiful sight.

At midmorning, before going to the king's chambers, I took a light meal of a pear spiced with cinnamon and some bread sopped in wine. The day before, Edward had turned me away, saying he would send for me later. He never did. I would not let him avoid me again.

The pair of guards flanking the door barred my entrance.

"Stand aside," I said.

"The king is in an important meeting," the first guard replied. The second guard, less resolute, looked down at his feet.

"No more important than the one he is to have with me. Let me pass." I tried to move past, but was greeted by the glimmering edge of a poleax.

"I will tell him you called," he grudgingly offered.

I placed a finger upon the heavy bottom of the poleax blade and traced its edge down to where it attached to the pole. "Then you will be too late." And I wrapped my fingers around the haft and slammed it down on his foot. He yelped and hopped back like a wounded wolf cub. The second guard chortled and gave me a mirthful wink as I slipped by.

To my immense relief, the only member of the council in Edward's presence was Aymer de Valence, the Earl of Pembroke. Edward stood by the window, one hand propped on his angular, jutting hip, while the fingernails of the other raked at his scant beard.

Pembroke rose from his chair, swept low in a bow and then came toward me, hands outstretched. "My queen, I hear you had a rough voyage from Tynemouth. I have already sent my condolences to Cecilia's family. So very young, she was."

He reached for my hand and bent to kiss it. I clasped both of his hands and gave them a firm squeeze. His coal-black eyes glinted with compassion. Then he stood on tiptoe to kiss me gently on the cheek. When he stepped back, for he was very short, I could see the part in his hair, still black except for a feathering of silver at the temples. A shrewd negotiator, he had dampened Lancaster's fiery temper countless times, sparing Edward waves of rebellion.

"The days will be somber without her. But thank you for your kindness, my lord."

"Her mother?"

"Still in Scarborough," I told him, "grief-stricken. And not well enough to travel, as it is."

"Ah, but you are better now?"

"Much," I imparted with the flicker of a smile, "although I miss the children terribly." I clung to the earl's hands for comfort, but too soon he gave me a parting embrace and words of farewell, saying that he was overdue to write to his wife.

Then . . . I was alone with Edward.

I bent my knee to him, hoping that the gesture would elicit a small greeting. Instead, he spread his fingers over the cold glass and squinted as he peered at the snowy world outside. "They leap at every opportunity to claw at my soul. They blame me for Byland Moor, thankless traitors. Even those who were loyal have turned on me—like fighting curs in a pit. Pembroke, as well. I was not even there. Richmond was. He should rot in Scotland for it, I say."

Edward was not at Byland Moor because he had run from there to be with Despenser.

"Cruel words," I said, "for one who has always stood by you, my lord."

He spun sharply on his heel. "You, too?"

"I did not mean it like—"

"How did you then? You are just like the rest of them, always blaming me. Worse, maybe. You do not cloak your criticisms in policy. You come to murder my character in person. Have at it, then."

He spread his arms wide in a sacrifice of himself, but I refrained; I had arguments other than those that parliament had been pursuing with him.

"I came to ask why my husband did not call on me during my illness, but I can see that you were deeply engrossed in important matters. Pembroke has said something in particular to upset you?"

He softened at the sympathy. "In particular, no. In general, yes. Even he thinks I should honor peace with Scotland. My father would have struck him for even letting such absurdities pass over his tongue. Pembroke treats me like an ignorant child."

I took a window seat while he paced angrily. Finally, he stopped before me and gestured toward the door. "If that is all, you may leave now. I have . . . others . . . to discuss matters with."

I had no doubt that 'others' meant solely Hugh Despenser. I looked at him squarely. "You should not have abandoned me at Tynemouth as you did. Our lives were in danger. You could have sent word ahead for us to come here when you crossed the border. You waited. Why?"

He snorted. "Abandoned you? Your life was never in danger." He added a snarl to his defense. "We went over this yesterday."

"Five days ago, Edward. I have been ill and bedridden for five days, yet you never once inquired of me. Never came to my side. Not once. Had you not a few minutes for the mother of your children?"

"Parliament does not grant cessations for visits to the sickly. Now do not correct me. The matter is dead."

"Because you say? I say otherwise."

"And I say I have more important things to attend to than your unceasing, abysmal whining. Good God, woman, remove your pointed tongue from my ear. It bleeds. And be gone. Back to your gaggle of women. Talk to them of your never-ending troubles. Perhaps they will care . . . or at least pretend to."

"Was it so long ago that you used to speak to me of your troubles, Edward? Did it not soothe you when I listened as you railed against Lancaster, Mortimer and Badlesmere?" I had given so much of myself, believing it was what he needed—comfort enough to put him in a better mood and grant him a clearer outlook. But it had not been enough and I was only beginning to understand why . . . or who. I stood to face him. "What has so come between us that you cannot give a care as to where I am or whether I live or die? How have I fallen in your eyes? No, no, spare me that. I know. You know. And there is nothing I can say or do that is right anymore. Not as long as . . . as he . . .”

I had to stop myself before I leapt from the precipice. I turned for the door.

“*He?*!” Edward shouted. He stomped at me, grabbed my arm and yanked me around so fast I might have fallen had he not had a hold of me. “Bloody God, wife. Say his name. Say it. Say it! Who is *he?*”

“Despenser,” I gulped. The sound of his name in my mouth made me want to vomit. “Despenser is between us. Despenser has taken my place.” When I said it, at last, I saw it in my head. I saw them—together.

His fingers pinched my arm until I felt a blood blister forming. I could not raise my eyes to meet his. “What? You would deny a king the one advisor who dares speak the truth to him? The only friend who would defend him to the death? How does that put him between us?”

I shook my head. “Those things do not. You know . . . what I mean.”

“No, I don’t. Say your mind, wife. How?” His hands flew up and pressed smartly against my cheekbones, forcing me to look at him. He leaned close, his breath hot upon my face. “How has he put you away from me in any way you have not managed to do yourself? *How* has he taken your place?”

I tried to shake my head again, but he locked his palms tighter against my face. His fingernails pricked at my temples. As he dug them deeper the words shot out of my mouth with a force of resentment I could not halt had it meant saving all the souls on earth. “*In our bed.*”

I whimpered as he pinched my face tighter. Why had I said it? Why? I had never found them together, not in that way. But . . . there were so many pieces that fit so perfectly together. So many times that I had seen Edward kiss Despenser upon the cheek and how it lingered and how he had whispered into his ear and a smile of affection played upon Despenser’s lips. I had heard more—of late meetings, followed by early ones when Despenser was never seen to leave his chambers, long hunting trips, occasions when neither of them could be found. A royal household was always abuzz with gossip. The private moments of the king were no exception.

Edward laughed wickedly. He let go of me. Still laughing, he slapped me hard.

I had half turned my face away before his palm struck me. But the blow thrust me back a step. The burn of it brought tears to my eyes. I blinked them away before I met his wrathful gaze again.

He pulled in three sharp breaths, the anger in him boiling over with each gasp. "Your women have poisoned your head with too many lies. And now you are wracked with delusions. I am of a mind to replace every one of them. Consider it a purging of evil forces that you arrived here less a few. Be as a good wife should. Say only kind things of your husband, will you? It is a sin to lie, Isabella. And treason to lie about your king."

Treason? Was that what he called the truth?

"No, Edward." I taunted him to strike me again, hoping he would draw blood so I could outwardly bear some evidence of his mistreatment of me. "It is you who lie, even to yourself."

I hardly cared any more what he thought of me. I hoped he never wanted me near him again. Nothing would have pleased me more. By him, God had given me four fine children. Giving my body to Edward for the purpose of bearing them—hardly for his pleasure, but wholly for his own arrogant posterity—had been a vile deed for us both. For years I believed the fault of not making my husband love me was entirely mine. The task, however, was impossible from the outset. At best, I had indifference from him. The worst always happened when I believed he could ever care, when I hoped . . .

Edward swept his arm across the table and overturned a full flagon of wine. He yanked the tapestries from the wall, toppled unlit candles, sent a bowl of apples rolling and flailed maps and documents onto the floor.

It was a show meant to put fright into me, but after a few minutes of his tirade I realized Edward was too cowardly to become violent with me. They said he shied from battle because the sight of blood made him queasy. I believed it. He could not even beat his wife properly. He uttered no curses or threats, but kept his eyes from me as he kicked at a chair and hurled the same candlestick for the fourth time. He did not even see me leave.

Head down, I rushed through the corridor and bumped into someone's chest.

"In a hurry?"

Hugh Despenser. In his eyes was a look of disgust one might make having stepped in a pile of cow dung. A look that he gave everyone near enough to him to draw his attention. Everyone except for Edward.

I felt a sting along the back of my hand. The jewels studding the front of his shirt had scraped it and a fine red line of blood sprang forth. I pulled my hand into my sleeve and brushed past him without a word. I had turned two corners and was halfway down a flight of stairs before I stopped. By now Edward was telling Despenser of my jealous rant. But why was Despenser with him again?

In a minute I was back at Edward's door. I stood slightly to one side of it and listened through the crack where Despenser had left it ajar. He had obviously dismissed the guards—the same ones who had not budged for me.

"Your day has not gone well, I see." Despenser stepped over the mess of parchments littering the floor. "I daresay Pembroke did not make this mess. Was there a riot here just now?"

"The she-wolf, dear Hugh." Edward's voice still vibrated with umbrage. "Come to put her fangs to my throat."

My hand was upon the door, nudging it further, my eye to the crack. I saw them standing but a few feet apart, the morning light from the window falling in a silver haze between them.

Despenser closed the gap with a step, reached out and gently touched Edward on the shoulder, then the cheek. "Dear Edward, do not let her trouble you."

Edward tilted his head and the glint of a tear showed in his eyes. Had he but turned to look, he would have seen me in the doorway. Yet he saw nothing but Despenser before him.

"She spoke of us. Accused us of . . . of being . . ." his voice fell to a whisper, "intimate."

"Let her. It is jealousy, nothing more." Despenser took Edward's face in both hands. Edward's mouth parted and Despenser leaned to him. Lightly then, he kissed him on the forehead and drew Edward's head against his shoulder in comfort. As Edward's face turned toward the door, I shrank away, my heart hammering against my breastbone, my breath trapped in my throat.

There was a long silence. I should have gone then. I should never have listened. What I heard next cast a quiet terror upon my heart.

"If she ever threatens you, Edward . . . if she tells anyone what she thinks she knows, remember—you can always remind her of her place. You brought me back from exile more than once, dissolved the Lords Ordainers and when Lancaster conspired against you, you stuck his head on a pike and had his body divided up into fours. *You* have the power, Edward, not her. You are king. King by birth. By divine decree. Anointed and crowned. *King*. Never forget."

If Despenser had declared me a threat to their imagined harmony, I shuddered to think what contrivance might come of it.

Just as I leaned from the door to take my first step away, I heard Despenser, loud and bold, as if he wanted me to hear, as if he knew I was there:

"Whatever she loves most, take it from her. Lands? That will leave her powerless. Finer things, money? It will leave her wanting." He gave a sinister laugh. "Her children?"

Edward paused as the thought sunk in. "Yes, her children," he echoed with a whimper. "Her children."

And the crying of the king was muffled on the shoulder of the one who ruled England. The one who had taken my place.

As I hurried away, I heard the sliding of the bar across Edward's door.

THE SLASHES OF INK blurred before me in the pale light of a single candle.

I squeezed my eyes shut, then pressed them open as wide as I could and dipped my quill once more into the inkhorn on my writing table. There came a knock at my door. My heart faltered.

"Who is there?"

"Patrice," came a hissing whisper.

My heart resumed its pace and I went to the door.

"Where have you been?" I asked her as I pulled her in. "Midnight was hours ago."

She gave a mirthful wink. "May I say only that I was with Arnaud? I was reluctant to leave him, even for you." She sauntered over toward the table, swishing her skirts back and forth in the clenches of her two hands as she hummed. "I have decided to marry him. Although if my mother were still alive, she would not approve. He is too poor, but he has promise, don't you think?"

There was an intimation cloaked behind her question—that I would in some way bestow favors upon him, but given what I had overhead earlier that night, it was unlikely I would be in a position to do so anytime soon. I evaded Patrice's question with another one. "He's asked you to be his wife then?"

She frowned. "No, not yet. Not quite. But he will, soon."

"Not quite?" I felt a lecturing was timely. "Patrice, you stay with him half the night then think he will want to marry you? Why should he, given that?"

"He will if he thinks—" She craned her neck to look past me, then started toward the writing table with curious determination. "What is that, Isabeau?"

I stepped between her and the table.

Patrice arched an eyebrow at me. "Who is it to?"

"My brother."

"Hmm, it must be an important, *secret* letter to be up at such an hour writing it."

"Not secret, no. But important, yes."

"And you want me to make certain it is sent?" Proudly, she lifted her head. Great men such as bishops and earls were set on high by such simple correspondences. Or ruined. Hers could be the hand that delivered the nudge.

"This letter I will give to Lady Eleanor a week from now."

She smirked in annoyance. "Then you could not have waited until morning to call on me?"

"For you, there is another letter. It must be sent immediately— without anyone knowing of it. I wish for Charles to receive it first." I went to my bed, dropped to my knees and drew a leather bag from beneath it. I tugged the cord on its mouth tighter and then handed it to her. "Give it to Arnaud. Go to him now. He is to go at once to Scarborough where he will give it to Lady Juliana . . . if she lives. She will know what to do with it."

Juliana had been among those seized by the coughing fits, although hers had been the least. Her husband had served as my messenger to France all these years.

Patrice was slow to take the pouch. "You wish Arnaud to come straight back then?"

"Of course. I need him. And clearly, you can barely do without him for a day. The ride to Scarborough is not long. He will be back before week's end."

"Then I will wish him Godspeed," she conceded. She must have thought my trust indicated I favored her lover. Perhaps she believed a knighthood would follow?

All I could have given him then was my thanks. Soon I would have nothing at all to give.

Our Dearest Brother,

Charles, I ask your forgiveness that I do not write on happier terms, but all has gone from bad to worse once more. I fear Lord Hugh Despenser will take my children from me. I am in peril, as are your nieces and nephews, your own blood, whom I know you love even

105

from a distance.

    Despenser's greed and cruelty are notorious. Good and loyal men who had the courage to defy him will die if I cannot convince Edward to cease this bloodshed. He will never concede to your demands for homage while Despenser counsels him otherwise. If Despenser is not removed from his side, England will surely fall into ruin.

    Send word that you will help me and I will do whatever you say. Or if you wish to keep my name clear of blame, do what you will and I will know when it is done. Only, help me, in whatever way you can.

    Our Lord bless and keep you . . . and keep us from war.

Your Dearest Isabeau

11

Roger Mortimer:

Tower of London — Summer, 1322

SEVEN RAVENS ALIGHTED ON the battlements of the Salt Tower. In the afternoons, they surveyed the Thames from their windswept perches, their crescent, blue-black wings stretched to warm themselves in the sun's rays. At night, they roosted there. During last winter's bitter cold, they had huddled wing to wing with beaks tucked against their glossy breasts. Whenever the sentries ambled past, the birds would burst upward in a confusion of black, their bellicose caws slicing the air. When I rose at dawn that summer morning and went to my window to look out at the world, as I did every day, there were seven arrayed in the same place on the battlements, black as Dominican friars. Always seven.

My uncle and I were taken in shackles to Westminster Hall to stand trial. Seven black-robed men were perched in their chairs on the dais at the far end of the high columned hall. Among them was Hamo de Chigwell, London's mayor. A hundred barons stood before their benches on both sides of the hall, condescending in their silence. Chins forward, we shuffled past them. Our chains clunked as they dragged on the floor. Some of those who stared at us were the very same barons who had complained in private repeatedly about the king's misrule; yet they had never taken a stand against it. They all knew what the outcome of the day would be. And they had all come to regale in their own fortune as my uncle and I marched to our doom. I was too numb of mind to fume with the contempt I should have felt toward them. Loathing is a lost cause for those soon to die.

We were given seats on two separate benches, each at an angle so we could see the judges and each other. It was the only time since we arrived at the Tower a few months ago that I ever saw my uncle. We were not permitted to speak to one another that day. Even so, my uncle did not afford me the slightest glance. He kept his face turned askance, his expression impassive. His gnarled fingers kneaded at his thighs like a kitchen maid's at dough. Whenever he stopped rubbing his legs, his hands trembled. His body had wasted in the five months since we were parted. Blue-veined skin hung loose on his skeleton like an ill-fitting rag. The pugnacious old man who had ridden at the head of an army with me, from Wigmore to Kingston and back to Shrewsbury not so long ago, looked as though he could barely sit upright on his bench, let alone a saddle.

The charge was treason. We had waged war on the king, they said, and therefore were his enemies. We were told to stand side by side in the middle of the hall. One by one, the seven judges gave their verdicts. Seven times, the word 'guilty' was pronounced. The sentence: to be hanged and quartered.

I wanted them to take me then and finish it. But as my uncle and I stood next to each other, Chigwell opened a letter from the king and read it aloud. All our possessions had been confiscated and either sold or redistributed to those loyal to the king. Our close kin had been taken into custody and everyone suspected of taking part in the rebellion had been tried and punished. Lastly, our sentences were commuted—to life in the Tower.

I was stunned. I heard the words and yet I could not comprehend them. Why had we been spared when a dozen other lords had met their deaths? Had Pembroke intervened on our behalf?

Suddenly, my uncle went limp and collapsed to his knees. I stooped to grab him by the arm before he fell forward onto the floor, but guards had already rushed forward. They wrenched me away from him and shoved me toward the back of the hall. I twisted around and tried to look over my shoulder, but the chains tangled around my feet and I stumbled several steps before I went down.

I lay on the smooth, cool flagstones. The murmurs of the barons washed over me like the cool rush of an ebbing tide. Then, I mustered my dignity and drew my knees up beneath me. I waited for the guards to clamp hold of my arms and drag me to the outer door, but no one laid a hand on me. The barons' voices faded to hushed whispers. Curious, I raised my head.

Before me stood Lord Hugh Despenser the Younger. Only a week ago I had been informed by Gerard that Despenser had been proclaimed the Earl of Gloucester—a prize he had coveted since Gilbert de Clare's death at Bannockburn. At his shoulder stood his glowering father, Hugh the Elder, now known as the Earl of Winchester.

The younger Despenser was dressed in finest green velvet, with a chain of gold dangling across his chest. In his feathered cap were glittering jewels that caught the light streaming in through the high windows. "You may thank God in your prayers tonight," he exhorted, his mouth drawn downward in contempt, "that you yet draw breath. It seems the queen took pity on your plight and begged for your life to be spared. She is a poor judge. To me, you are worse than worthless. You are a bane on England. An ulcer. A plague that infects all around it. If I had my way, you would have been disemboweled, castrated and beheaded when you showed your face at Shrewsbury."

What stake does Queen Isabella have in my life?

Slowly, I stood. My foot throbbed where the chain had whipped across it. I let my weight gently down on that foot, not altogether certain it was not broken. I looked at him boldly, as if he were the condemned man and not me. "Perhaps, someday . . . I will have the pleasure of watching your head roll from the block, instead. Arrogance deceives those who are afflicted by it, Lord Despenser. I vow it will be your death. If I can, in some way, hurry it along,"—I took a tender step, seizing my exit before the guards could force it on me—"I will."

With an arrogant smirk, Despenser stepped aside, as if he deigned my monition unworthy of reply. Then a guard shoved me forward and I heard Despenser and his father laughing.

As they escorted me back to the Tower, a terrible grief welled up inside me. Although I had been given my life back, for reasons I could not comprehend, somehow I knew . . . I would not see my uncle again.

Tower of London – March, 1323

OUTSIDE THE SUN WAS high and bright, promising a final end to winter's bleak skies and the damnable draft that cut across my room whenever the wind was fierce. From my window, I could not see to the west or north where newcomers to the Tower would pass. Perhaps that had been the notion behind putting me where I was. A punishment, of sorts. But I took what pleasure I could find in it and allowed my mind to wander beyond the walls and to places and days far, far away.

The outer bar scraped across its iron brackets. The door opened halfway and Lieutenant Gerard d'Alspaye peered around its edge.

"Gerard?" I broke from my place of vigil to welcome my keeper and unlikely friend. "Don't linger by the door there. Do come in." I scooted an oak barrel that served as my table between my chair and a lopsided stool I had recently acquired, thanks to the thievery of one of my guards. "I promised you another game of chess. You've become quite good at it since I taught you when I first came here. Relentless, almost. You may beat me yet. Perhaps this will be your day?"

He shook his head in regret. "Not today, my lord."

I forced a laugh. Gerard was a man of few words and scarce humor, but he had become invaluable to me. From him I had learned of the battle at Boroughbridge, Lancaster's swift trial and execution, Edward's latest botched campaign in Scotland and Queen Isabella's narrow escape from the ravaging Black Douglas. I relied on our daily discussions over a chess-board, and the rare cup of small ale. "Tired of losing, Gerard? Shall I throw the game this once, just for you?"

Again, he shook his head. "Someone to see you, my lord." He backed away from the door.

A black-robed friar with his hood pulled up over his head shuffled in. They sometimes sent holy men to me, assuming I might want to shrive myself of past sins. But even if I had felt the need, I did not trust any men, secular or spiritual, remotely in the employ of the king. I might have thought nothing of the unprompted visit, except this was a friar I had not seen before. And either he was a very poor and lowly friar, or not one at all, judging by his oversized sandals and frock. In his arms, he bore a loose bundle of clothing. He dipped his head as he walked past and began to lay the clothing out on the bed in meticulous piles. Four tunics: two brown, one scarlet, one gray. A tabard of reddish brown. A hood. Three pairs of leggings. A pair of leather shoes, barely worn.

"Where did you get my things?" I ran my fingers over the cloth of the tabard.

"My lord purchased them," he said, peeling his hood back to reveal a close-cropped shock of pale hair and stark blue eyes. "He thought you might need them."

There was something strangely familiar about him, a flicker of memory, and yet I could not place him. I looked to the door, expecting to see Gerard there, but he had gone and the door was closed. "Tell me—who is your lord?"

"The Earl of Pembroke." A surreptitious smile broke the tight lines of his mouth. "Although, I have at times served your uncle, as well."

"Simon de Beresford," I recalled aloud, remembering with a pang of regret the day my uncle and I rode over the bridge to Shrewsbury to kneel before the king and lost everything: our inheritances, our family, our freedom. "Have you any word from my uncle?"

He snapped out the last tunic and laid it on top of the others. "What would you expect to hear? He suffers the same circumstances as you, my lord."

"Is he well?"

"Well enough . . ." He turned away, his voice taking on a low growl. "For a man of his years imprisoned in the Tower."

"Ah, he still thinks it was Pembroke who deceived us?"

Simon squinted one glassy blue eye. "He said nothing of the earl. We did not speak long. But he did send you a message."

"Go on."

"He said that although he may not live to see it done, he could forgive you should you make right on your many mistakes."

Mistakes? Was everything my fault in his eyes?

"I hardly see how I can correct anything," I said.

The scrape of footsteps sounded from beyond the door. He glanced toward it, flipped his hood back over his head and stepped away, until he was nearly at the far wall. His voice was but a raspy whisper emanating from the dark shadows beneath his hood. "You may yet be able to. Fortunes change. Sometimes swiftly."

I circled the room, pausing by the door to listen. Confident no one eavesdropped, I approached him. "Speak plainly. What do you mean?"

"Many who fought with you against the king and Lord Despenser were killed to forever silence them. But many more remain. Among the nobility. The clergy. In high places, some. Abroad, even."

His words were an enigma to me. Edward's summary executions of his opponents had been so complete I would have thought all opposition totally annihilated. Yet my uncle and I had been spared the same fate. "Who? Pembroke?"

He shook his head slowly beneath his cowl. "Others. The earl is too close to the king."

And too loyal to him. "Can you not say who?"

"You will learn, in time. For now, despair not."

I was hardly in despair. That had passed long ago. I was skeptical of a spy who delivered cryptic messages. Skeptical of old allies who had turned their faces from me in shame at my trial. Too much did not make sense. "So what am I to do? Anything?"

"I leave London in the morning. Lieutenant d'Alspaye will bring you pen and parchment. I will carry messages for you. Be warned, though— the fewer the better."

"And will you bring replies?" I could not refrain from sarcasm. If any of my letters were intercepted and they could even remotely be construed as treasonous, King Edward would have in his hands the perfect reason to hang me from the highest scaffolding he could find. Perhaps this was all concocted to entrap me? But if that was true, why so elaborate a ruse? A year had gone by in which time he could have sent me to my death.

I went to the window and looked toward the Salt Tower. Instead of the ravens, sparrows flitted from the merlons to the wall walk, chattering like young maids enthralled with gossip.

Could Edward be using me to ferret out more of his enemies? Again, why bother, unless there was some clear threat to his hold on power? Or on Despenser's life . . .

I rubbed at the scruff on my chin and neck. A letter to Joan would seem innocuous enough—a husband longing for his spouse. Sweet Jesus, I had not thought of her for weeks. I hardly missed her querulous company, but I had at times ached to have her willing body beneath mine.

"Can you get a letter to my wife?" I went closer to him, hoping I could catch a glimpse of his countenance beneath the overhang of his dark cowl and judge the depth of his deception.

Simon nodded. "I can get a letter to the Pope, if you so wish."

With his fingertips he tapped at the sleeve of one of my garments. There was something inside it, a long lump. A roll of parchment? I approached the bed and reached for it.

The bar of the door moaned as someone slid it back. Simon grabbed me by the shoulders and slammed me to my knees.

Before I could recover from the bolt of pain, he placed both hands on my head and began to utter unintelligible words, which I determined to be mangled Latin.

The door opened. Two guards entered, followed by Gerard.

"Please, accept this charity," Simon said, sweeping his arm above the clothing. "What you do not need can be sent to the poor." He waved a hand in the sign of the cross before me. "God be with you."

Without a backward glance, he left. Gerard followed him.

I remained on my knees with my head bowed, clasped my hands together, and turned toward the bed, as if to pray. One of the guards darted out and quickly back in, bearing a wooden platter with a cold bowl of beans in a fish broth, a heel of bread to sop it with and a cup of watered ale. No use in complaining of the fare. It was sustenance.

I thanked him, as I always did, rose and placed the platter on top of the barrel. Despite my leer, the guard sauntered over toward the bed to peruse the clothing covetously. I drew my tottering stool up close to my makeshift table and sat. Watching him from the corner of my eye, I brought the bowl to my lips and tipped it up. Beans and flakes of fish nearly gagged me as I consumed it greedily. There would not be another meal until the vesper bells rang. I spit out fish bones and suspect chunks onto the floor for the mice to steal. I wiped the bowl clean with the stale bread and washed my mouth out with a guzzle of ale. The guard leaned over the pile of leggings.

"Done," I announced with impatience.

Startled, he straightened and blinked at me.

"You may take it away now," I said to urge his departure. I stood, the platter between my outstretched hands. "Ask Lieutenant d'Alspaye if he will bring me the implements later with which to shave. I feel as though I'm sprouting a forest on my chin."

He gave a grunt, which I took to be an affirmative.

After he was gone, I let a few minutes lapse before I pulled the letter from the leggings. Before I opened it, my heart bounded. It bore the wax imprint of my fifteen-year old son Geoffrey's seal: a swan taking flight. A seal I had presented him with upon his departure from Wigmore.

The handwriting . . . was unmistakably his.

Dearest Father,

I pray this finds you in good spirits. I have often wondered how you fare through these long, dark days. It should please you to know I am well. My cousins here in Picardy have been unduly kind, although Grandmother ails. Our kinsfolk are sympathetic with your plight and wish you to know they will give whatever help they can arrange. I hear there are many lords who have fled England and taken refuge in the courts of Hainault and France, where they are welcomed. King Charles, however, is on poor terms with our King Edward. There is talk of war.

We may yet, one day, see each other again. I have hope.

God protect you,
Geoffrey de Mortimer

I rolled the letter up tightly and crammed it into the crack at the bottom of the wall from where the mice came and went.

Simon spoke the truth then. I had not been abandoned. There were those who yet sought to bring an end to Despenser's grasping avarice and Edward's oppression.

I sat down on my stool in the middle of the room. Motes of dust swirled on a beam of sunlight that fell at a long, low angle from window to floor. I had not noticed the warmth of the day before then. I let it seep into me as my mind filled with uplifting visions of the many terrible ways I might make my enemies suffer for their offenses.

A day that might yet dawn.

12

Isabella:

Tower of London — June, 1323

CHARLES' LAST LETTER HAD been given to me discreetly by Juliana only five days earlier:

Our Very Dear Sister,

> *Grant me only time. Such things should not be done in haste. I know you have convinced your king to spare the life of his fallen liegeman, Sir Roger Mortimer. Nonetheless, a traitor's fate is still that of death, whether slow or sudden. You will go to this knight, bargain for his service in return for his freedom. Should he agree, you are to tell him his release will be arranged in secret. He will come to Paris. Here, he will learn his role.*
>
> *First though, beseech the assistance of Bishop Orleton. He is an old ally of this Mortimer, from what I have heard, and as you have often said a loyal friend of yours. This will put you further from*

116

suspicion.

    I shall send more details by word of mouth soon to both you and the bishop. Letters are too easily intercepted. The proof they bear too condemning.

    The glory of France and the friendship of England are foremost in my mind. You and the children are always in my heart.

Our Lord God keep you,
Charles

The correspondence had made the sea crossing in a simple carved hatbox, folded and sewn tightly into the lining of a small, white silk pillow at its bottom. Within the hour, I had dispatched a messenger to summon the Bishop of Hereford, Adam Orleton.

I was standing alone at the back of the Chapel of St. John's in the White Tower, counting the number of courses in the stones—nine high in the columns, eight in the arches above—when I heard him enter.

"My queen." Bishop Orleton swept through the doorway of the chapel and received me into his arms with tender familiarity. Early summer sunlight flooded in through the arched windows in the upper-story of the chapel. Despite his fifty years, the flesh around his eyes barely creased as he squinted. Tiny beads of sweat dampened his forehead and trickled over his temples and cheeks, giving a saintly glow to his long, narrow face.

"Your grace." I returned the embrace, closed the door gently but firmly behind us, and took his arm. "You are two days overdue."

He surveyed the shadows as we walked the short length of the nave side by side. Our footsteps echoed against the bulging columns, every stone immutable, every window beaming with celestial light, every floor tile bearing the wear and worry of the footsteps of all the kings and queens since the time of William the Conqueror. We stopped before the altar and he touched his fingertips to his head and chest, making the sign of the cross in reverence and devotion. Then, he stilled his breath to listen for the rustle of intruders.

"We're alone," I assured him.

He turned to me, the corners of his mouth drawn downward in concern. "I wish I could plead it was nothing but church business which caused my delay."

I knelt before the altar. "We must be quick. Tell me—is there unrest in the Welsh Marches?"

"Unrest? Not outright. But it will soon come to that." Orleton moved to stand before me. "Despenser cowed his own sister-in-law, Elizabeth de Clare, into handing over Usk to him in exchange for Gower, although I have no doubt he will have it back in short time. With the abolishment of the Ordinances and the forfeiture of Mortimer's lands, given enough time, Despenser will be lord of Chirk, as well as Berkeley, Usk and Gower—and every rock, puddle and blade of grass between Chester and Bristol."

Whatever Despenser wants, Despenser shall have.

I folded my hands, pretending to pray, and bowed my head. "What of Scotland? Did Pembroke succeed?"

"The truce has been agreed to by now. Thirteen years. Despenser himself even had a hand in it."

"Despenser? I heard he was in the north, but . . . why would Despenser attach his name to a treaty with Robert the Bruce?"

"I think even he has finally realized the war against the Scots cannot be won."

No, not while this Edward sits upon the throne.

"Even more shocking," Orleton added, "is that Bruce signed the treaty 'as King of Scots'."

I gasped. "Truly? And still Edward agreed to it?"

He nodded. That alone was unimaginable. If the barons of England were ashamed to lose to the Scots, they would have Edward's murder on their minds now. Pensive, I tapped my fingertips together. "But there must be some further motive to it. Some plan. Thirteen years is an eternity."

"An arbitrary number."

"An unlucky one. Could they be weighing war with France? Charles wants Edward to pay homage for Gascony. Edward is loath to do it. He would sooner fling his army unprepared and ill-led upon the shores of France than go there and prostrate himself before my brother."

"My lady . . ." Orleton touched the soft veil covering the crown of my head. The gentle pressure of his fingertips drove the meaning of his words deeper. "I doubt the king wants a war with France any more than you do."

"But it would unite his barons behind him. He needs that now more than ever. France is ever the enemy here, no matter who rules or what happens. When England's fortune turns ill, blame France for it and the world takes order. Does it matter what it costs me if it serves him?"

"Hmm, I'll not argue that, but still, if he could not manage Scotland, then he'll not take on France."

" 'Should not' and 'will not' are different matters. Think of whom we are speaking about."

"Agreed, agreed. But as for Despenser, you and I could postulate on his motives until we are both dust blown away by the wind. The man is led by nothing more than the whimsy attached to his greed. The king spoils him like a child with an unbearable temper."

What I cherished about Adam of Orleton was not his piety or his power within the Church, but his candor. The bishop himself knew the danger in his directness and Edward resented him for it, accurate though it often was. Unlike my husband, however, I was neither so vain nor shortsighted that I could not take advice from someone who knew the answers when I did not.

I bit at my lip, trying hard to draw conclusions where there were too few clues. "Then Harclay gave up his life for naught. Where is the sense in it, your grace? Where?"

"I know not, my child. I only know there are many things these days I do not understand. Probably, I never will. Nothing causes me surprise any more. Least of all Lord Despenser. Kings have let favorites run the kingdom before when they had not the head for it themselves, but never in so careless a manner and certainly not to their own ruin. God is our one true constant in this world. Place your trust in Him, my child." Orleton bent slightly forward and let his fingers slip to my shoulders. "But why did you ask me here? Not for gossip, nor a simple blessing, I venture."

"Indeed not, dear bishop. I need your promise of help to . . ." I faltered, uncertain of how to say something so utterly important, yet so simple.

"To what?"

I lowered my voice to a whisper. "To save a life."

His gaze was penetrating, perplexed. "Whose?"

"That of Sir Roger Mortimer."

His hands fell away from my shoulders. A lengthy silence bespoke his reluctance. He turned his head away. "I am a man of the Church. Not everything is within my power."

Defiant, I stood to challenge his momentary cowardice. "But much is. Court and Church have been brothers since the word of Christ became known to man. Both meddle in the other's business."

"Sometimes to their mutual detriment. I remind you of King Henry and Thomas Becket. Power breeds distrust. My lady, this is . . . an unusual request. Not the sort I am accustomed to granting. I fear, if I am to guess—which you leave me to do—you go against your husband's wishes . . . or worse."

I dropped my chin like a little girl chided by her father. Then I raised my eyes and looked straight at him. "A marriage does not make two persons of one mind. I would not ask if this . . . if this did not . . ." I needed the bishop on my side more than strategically. I needed his sympathy. I needed him as my champion. Not even a prelate could harden his heart to a woman who had been wronged. With a lingering sigh, I began. "I cannot tell you how it is with him. How long I have tried to be dutiful—complacent in the marriage bed, nurturing in motherhood, in public agreeable . . . but in private I cannot bend to his blind arrogance forever. There are things you do not know of. Things I dare not give breath to.

Things I leave to Our Lord to levy His judgment upon."

"If the details are too difficult, then—"

"You are not my confessor, but they do concern the king . . . and Hugh Despenser."

"In what nature?"

"The rumors, about them—they are not rumors. Believe what you hear. Believe more than you hear. I will not burden you with full divulgence. That has already fallen on my brother's shoulders."

"And what does he say?"

"That he shall help relieve us of Despenser. If we can free Mortimer, Charles will help him do just that."

"Mortimer agreed to this?"

"He will. I have no doubt."

"What makes you think he will not try to bring down Edward as well? Charles will only incite him."

Naïve though it was, I had not thought so far as that. "I do not know." It was the truth. I did not know what the end to all of this would be. I only knew the bond between Edward and Despenser must be forever broken, whatever the cost. "Promise me your help—or it will not be war with France we will need to worry about, but war with our own."

The bishop studied me hard. Any other ecclesiast might have lectured me on the importance of a wife's obedience, but Bishop Orleton perceived an opportunity even he could not deny.

He took both my hands in his. "You have my promise."

13

Isabella:

Tower of London — June, 1323

THE VIRGIN LIGHT OF morning had not yet broken when I stole up the steps of the Lanthorn Tower, one hand on the outer wall to guide me along, one holding up the hem of my skirt to keep from tripping in the darkness. Each footfall was carefully placed in silence, unhurried, even though my heart, which felt as though it was somewhere in my ears, raced wildly. I wore the garb of a servant: a wrinkled kirtle of gray linen and a plain white veil. Anyone who saw me would not have recognized me from a distance in the night; however, should a guard pass by, I kept my chin down so that the edge of my veil dangled over my face.

I followed in the shadow of Gerard d'Alspaye, who held a lantern before him. Behind me trailed Arnaud, who had earned my undying trust since Tynemouth, carrying a dozen letters as far as Hereford and returning with as many. He never inquired about their contents and never failed to travel swiftly. I had brought him along to stand sentry, for it would only take one pair of spying eyes to ruin what had been so painstakingly laid out.

At the door to the prisoner's cell, Gerard muttered an order to a slant-eyed guard propped against his pike. The guard hobbled the few short steps to the door, dragging one leg. He drew out his clanking keys to let us in and passed a torch to Gerard in exchange for the lantern. Arnaud brushed past the guard, touched the hilt of his sword to indicate he was now in charge and banished him with a glare.

Before I went by Arnaud, my eyes lingered a moment on him, to remind him secrecy still meant everything. He nodded his understanding and closed the door softly behind me.

Awoken by the jangle of keys, Sir Roger Mortimer raised himself on his elbows. His moth-tattered blanket fell to his midriff, revealing a bare chest. He squinted at the flush of torchlight boring into his sensitive eyes. "Blessed Body of Christ . . . not so close. What hour is it?"

"Just before dawn, my lord," Gerard replied. He rammed the torch into a sconce by the door. I sought out the darkest shadows of the room and went there, more to give myself time to look upon him than to hide from him.

"Ah, Gerard. A familiar voice. But is that good or bad, given the hour? Last they roused me at this time of day was to hurl me from this louse-infested piss hole to my trial at Westminster." Mortimer scratched at the dark scruff on his chin, nudged his blanket away and groped for his shirt, then pulled it over his head. Yawning, he put his feet on the floor and rubbed at his eyes. A smile, charming and playful, graced his lips as he stood. "Who is that with you, Gerard? A nun to see to my spiritual needs? Are they going to hang me on the Green today?"

I stepped into the light. "On the contrary, Sir Roger, I come to spare you that fate."

Mortimer hesitated long before belief crept into his eyes. Finally, he went down on his knees before me. Even so, he held my gaze, appearing as curious to hear more, as he was doubtful he had heard me right at all. When the shock of my words had finally passed, Mortimer shot a questioning glance at Gerard. But the lieutenant, who had befriended him while at the same time keeping an oath of secrecy to me, deferred to me and stepped into the shadows.

"Then you come to tell me what I already know, my lady? That I'm to stay here until old age takes me?" Mortimer asked, a derisive grin on his lips. "Good, then. I have become quite accustomed to the place. I know every inch of it in the darkness. Why yesterday I accidentally stepped on a spider. I mourned its passing. Surely King Edward, even so long after our little squabble, would never deprive me of such familiarities?"

I gave him my hand. He took it lightly and bent his head. The heat of his breath brushed over my knuckles. Blood surged from my heart throughout my body. Before he placed a kiss upon it, I pulled my hand back and hid it in my skirt, blotting away his sweat to remove any trace of his touch.

"Despenser plots your death," I told him abruptly. "He means to see you dead before summer is out."

He eyed me with skepticism. "On what authority did you learn of this 'plot'?"

"A high enough one."

"God?" he prompted cynically. Even shut away and powerless, Mortimer wanted to know who schemed against him.

"The Earl of Pembroke, through his wife. Rather than argue with Despenser, he shared the information discreetly." Although no surprise, the news had hurried plans along. Thankfully, Orleton had already set his devices in motion.

"Then it is so." Mortimer sank back on his haunches and tilted his head. "I thought myself dead long ago. I suppose I should be thankful for the warning, but you see, I'm at quite a disadvantage. They've spared me the shackles, let me keep my head, but I have nowhere to run, nothing with which to fight but my own fists. So, my queen, I do hope there's more to this than my being given time to reflect on my life before an assassin cuts my throat. Or will it be poison in my broth?"

I circled him within the tight confines of the cell. It was easier to stare at the back of his head than meet his gaze straight on and had always been thus for me when near him, even when I was a newly arrived bride and barely a woman.

"I do indeed come to give you time to think about your future, Sir Roger. My brother, King Charles, has agreed to receive you at his court."

"Paris?" Mortimer spun on his knees, catching my hand as I moved by. "I . . . I don't quite follow. You arranged this on my behalf? Why?"

The warmth of his fingers singed my flesh, but this time I did not pull my hand away. "You were wronged—like Lancaster, like Harclay. England has been drowning in its own blood. I'll have no more spilled."

"Why did you plead for my life?" he asked abruptly.

I did not answer. Indeed, I had begged Edward to spare Mortimer's life, reminding him it was Mortimer who had wrested Ireland from the Scots, Mortimer who had stood by him while others, even at times his own brothers, vacillated in their loyalties like grass bends one way and then another in a blustery wind, praising him in one breath and condemning him in the next.

"Your eldest sons are—"

"My wife, Joan? What of her?"

A spark of envy kindled within my breast. "At Hampshire for now, with your youngest son, John. She was never in any great danger. I have made certain that the allowance for her care has been increased. I sent her some of my gowns, as well. As for your sons: Edmund is here, of course. Your son, Roger, is under heavy guard at Windsor. Your daughters have been dispatched to various nunneries. Your mother—"

"Joan—she was expecting another child when I left her last." There was a desperate longing in his voice, but I could not tell if it was because he longed for his wife, or that he regretted never having seen his youngest child.

"A girl, healthy. She named her Blanche."

"After her sister."

As he held my hand, I told him more about his sons and daughters, at least those I knew of, for there were twelve in all, and where they were being kept.

"I must ask you to make a choice, Sir Roger . . . take a risk, rather. I can offer you your freedom, but it will put the safety of your family in jeopardy. If the gamble is too great, say so and I will withdraw my offer."

"Ah, I see. This clemency comes from you alone. Done in secret. And the price is the peril of those I love." He gave up my hand. "What choice do I have? Any? If I refuse my own freedom, fair queen, I will most certainly die . . . and then so will they. Oddly, it's not death I dread so much, as the waiting for it. The boredom of not knowing what is going on beyond these walls—that alone can drive a man mad. The helplessness . . . the solitude . . ."

He withdrew into himself for a moment, deeply. I touched his shoulder. "Gentle sir, I wish I could guarantee you their safety, but I put even myself at risk by being here."

Feebly, he nodded, as some bleak realization took hold of him. "If you set me free I swear I shall make the trouble very worth your while." He met my eyes with a stark sincerity and vulnerability that could have convinced me of anything at that moment. "If my murder is imminent, then refusing you for my family's safety would indeed be thoughtless, wouldn't it? My enemies may have deemed me rash in the past, but never a fool. Only . . . how is my freedom to be delivered? And when?"

"Be patient, Sir Roger. You have allies. Many. Besides, already you have received and sent messages from here. I am well aware of that. So is Lord Despenser. Your letter to the Abbot of Wigmore was intercepted, which is perhaps why Despenser sees an urgent need to end your life. Care must be taken. In the meanwhile, Bishop Orleton of Hereford often inquires of you. I shall ask him to say a prayer for your wellbeing."

At that, Mortimer gave the first hint of a smile, understanding my tiny clue that the bishop was involved. "A prayer, yes. But tell me—why this boon?"

"You were loyal to Edward for many years. In his anger, he has forgotten."

"And you defend him even now? You contradict yourself."

"And you speak too boldly, my lord."

126

"Ah, I do. I daresay that is why I am here. I should take a lesson in humility from you. But, may I ask one thing? Tell me—how shall I return the favor?"

"Charles will speak further with you when you arrive in Paris."

"You cannot tell me?"

"Even if I knew, it would be best not to say."

The sound of a mouse scratching came from behind Mortimer, but he took no notice. He rubbed at the stubble on his cheeks with his knuckles. "So, I am to agree without knowing what it is I owe you?"

"You're an honorable man. I'm a fair woman. My brother is reasonable, as well. Think on it."

"If I inform the king you were here . . . that you made me an offer?"

"You won't. Besides, it would spare you nothing. Despenser would still have you killed for ravaging his lands and threatening his power."

"They were not *his* lands."

"I know that. We all do." Everyone except Hugh Despenser. And Edward.

Sensing that too much time had passed and I should stay no longer, I took a step back. "Forget that I was ever here. When you find your way to Paris, say it was by chance. Remember—Edward would have never sent you here of his own volition. He has failed only in his judgment of whose advice he follows. Despenser is to blame for your plight . . . and for England's misery."

"Yours as well?"

I could have launched into a tirade about my hatred of Hugh Despenser, but I answered him merely with a doleful look. Already, we were beginning to understand each other.

Gerard stood aside and took the torch from its sconce, even though it would leave the room in darkness and no daylight yet pierced the narrow window of Mortimer's cell.

Before I reached the door, I heard a single word: "Yellow."

I stopped short and cast a quizzical glance over my shoulder.

Mortimer's face, his unshaven chin resting on his chest, was dark with shadows. As he raised his head, I could see only the bare outline of his strong nose and lips, the firm ridge of his brow. His eyes met mine. This time I did not look away.

"On your wedding day. I was there, did you know? It was long before we Mortimers fell from favor. A face in the crowd to you, perhaps. You didn't know me then. Ah, but I remember. You wore a gown of yellow to match your hair. The day was bright, though January, and your hair shone, even beneath your veil. The trim was blue. Darker than your eyes, but not nearly so brilliant."

Hardly aware I was doing so, my hand drifted up to touch a stray strand of hair. "I . . . I was only a girl then. You remember more than I." And differently. He saw a young bride beginning a new life. I saw a groom . . . who saw me not at all.

"You were radiant. And frightened nearly to tears."

So he did know. Had I been so poor at hiding it? "A long time ago. I didn't know what it would be like—" *As Edward's queen. I did not know.* Hastily, I added, "What it would be like in England."

"Not at all like you envisioned. Nor what you deserved." His words faded to a dreamy whisper. "Shall I see you in Paris?"

"No. I have not been there for years."

Although I would have given up anything then to go there and leave Edward and England behind. Anything, except for my children. So I thought.

14

Roger Mortimer:

Tower of London — August, 1323

A MASON'S CHISEL PINGED on stone, fracturing the silence of the night. I sat up in bed, my heartbeat quickening. Slowly, I turned my head, trying to locate its source. From behind me, metal rasped at mortar. I crept to my cell door and listened. Only the snores of a sleeping guard. I went to my window. A watchman was slumped against the wall of the battlements, dozing soundly. Beyond the wall walk and the Salt Tower, nothing else stirred. Not even the ravens on the merlons. They were not there.

I slid my bed over the floor planks and away from the wall. Bending down, I probed with my fingers and detected the first fine crack between the stones. I searched the dimly lit confines of my room frantically for some crude tool to hurry the work along, but there was nothing that could have served. And so I watched and waited, keen to the alarm of guards' voices or the scuff of boots.

So it was true. Soon, I would be free, just as Queen Isabella had promised. Almost four months had gone by since she stood before me like a dewy angel in the darkness, beguiling and beautiful. At that moment, I thought God had indeed smiled on me. But why would such a heavenly creature cast favor on a troublesome rebel like me when she herself stood to lose so much? A pity I might never have the chance to thank her. An even greater pity that I would not come to know her better.

Finally, one of the stones groaned as it was pulled from the other side. I strained to push it free with my fingers. It was half way out when it became wedged at an angle against the other stones. I tried to rock it from side to side, but it would not budge. From the other side of the wall, something hammered at it, like the butt end of a weapon striking its base. Suddenly, the blows stopped. A long pause followed. I crouched nearer. Then, the scraping and pinging started anew.

At last the stone moved again. I pried my fingers into the mouse hole beside it to gain leverage and with the other hand maneuvered it until the block slid away, pinching two of my fingers in the crevice. As I wrenched my throbbing fingers loose, I bit back a howl of pain. Candlelight flickered through the dark hole. Cautiously, I peered into it. The outline of a familiar face greeted my eyes.

"That's one," Gerard huffed. "The rest will come easier, my lord."

"Hurry," I whispered back.

He disappeared. I heard the low murmur of another voice. When Gerard reappeared he slid a length of heavy metal through the hole: a crowbar. "With your help."

I chipped at mortar and swept the dust and jagged flakes aside by hand. Twice, I stopped to listen at the door, but all was as strangely dead as before. Another block fell away, and another, each one loosening more easily. Gathering an armful of my clothes, I arranged them lengthwise beneath my blanket. Not entirely convincing, but if anyone glanced over it in the darkness they might assume I was still asleep there. When the hole was barely big enough, I put the bed back in place and crawled under it. Arms before me, I wriggled forward. Sharp stones scraped at my shoulders and caught on the cloth of my shirt, tearing it. When my torso had cleared the opening, I dragged my hips and legs through.

Arnaud de Mone hauled me to my feet. We were in the adjacent room, lit by a single candle. The room, much like the one I had inhabited for a year and a half, appeared as though it were used for nothing more than the storage of spare furniture.

A haze of dust billowed from my shirt as I pounded at it. "I gather you could not get the keys to the door?"

"The castle's lieutenant keeps them on his person," Gerard said, "and since there is more than one lock on the door, we would have made far more noise trying to get you out that way. Besides, this room is closer to the kitchen."

"The kitchen?"

Gerard lifted the lid of a chest and tossed me the clothes of a kitchen servant, drenched with the smell of grease and rotting refuse.

"There are men," Arnaud explained, "waiting on the far side of the Thames with horses to take you to Portchester. Then on to the Isle of Wight. There, you'll find a boat which will take you across to France."

I smiled as I rubbed at the stains on my borrowed tunic. So Orleton had held true on his promises. King Charles, as well. Perhaps my days of being betrayed had at last come to an end? I thumped Arnaud on the arm. "You're coming, I trust?"

Ignoring my question, he handed me a belt with a sheathed long knife attached. He knelt down and shoved the bottom stone back into place.

I helped him with the rest, but he bore the brunt of the work with easy strength. My muscles had withered from imposed idleness. If the ride to Portchester did not break my back in two, I would consider myself fortunate. "I'll make it worth your while once we get to Picardy, Arnaud."

He checked his sword with the heel of his hand and motioned me to the door. With a puff, he blew out the candle. "I'll come, but not because of the money."

My eyes adjusted to the dim glow of starlight coming in through the single small window. Although grateful for Arnaud's company, I sensed he was not coming along out of pure loyalty to me. "Why else?"

"Later, my lord."

Carefully, Gerard lifted the bar of the door. He stuck his head into the corridor, and then hitched a shoulder at us.

I snagged Arnaud by the sleeve. "We're going to get my uncle and son now."

He shook his head. "No time."

I leapt forward and blocked Gerard's way, my arm across the door. I pulled it shut. "We cannot leave without them."

They exchanged a swift look, but the shadows veiled their faces and I could not read the meaning that passed between them.

"We were told," Gerard said blandly, "to get you out of here. Not anyone else."

In one sudden, twisting motion, I grabbed Gerard by his jerkin and slammed him up against the wall. The side of his head glanced a sconce. He winced sharply.

"They staked their lives alongside mine," I growled. My fingers dug deep into his padded jerkin. A shining bead of blood trickled down his cheek.

"My lord, please." Arnaud laid a hand on my arm pleadingly. "There is no time . . . no way to get to them. Your uncle is housed in the White Tower. Your son on the far side of the grounds from here. We cannot risk that distance. Too many doors, too many walls between here and there. We must get beyond the outer curtain, quickly. Every minute that we—"

"No! We *don't* leave without them."

"There is no time," he repeated with calm restraint. The rest of his words came more hurriedly. "There was a feast tonight. The cook put a sleeping potion in the ale. The entire garrison is sleeping soundly, but any one of them could awaken at any moment. We've already used too much time. We may not get more. If we try to rescue your uncle and son, we would put all our lives in peril. We cannot save them if we're dead."

And I would not be able to save them from France.

I let go of Gerard and pulled my hands down over my face, gathering my senses. How could I go without them and reason it was the right thing to do? Yet how could I risk even more than I already did? I circled the room, my mind spinning, even as time slipped dangerously away. I knew my uncle would more than despise me for abandoning him.

No, even if it was possible to free him, the old goat would not want my help. He would curse and turn his back on me. But my son, Edmund . . .

Too many doors, too many walls between here and there.

At the window I paused and leaned on its ledge to look down into the seemingly empty outer ward below. I had no view to the inner ward, but I remembered the gaping expanse of the Tower Green.

There is no time . . . no way to get to them.

No, if I risked saving my son and my uncle, then England's woes would forever be upon me. It simply couldn't be done.

"From whom did you take your orders for this night?" I asked Arnaud.

"Bishop Orleton."

"And the queen?"

"She will not learn of it until morning."

When everyone else would.

"Then let us hope," I said, pushing away from the window and crossing the room, "she hears Roger Mortimer is nowhere to be found. Gerard, lead the way."

Arnaud fell in behind me and we slipped out into the corridor, around the corner—stopping often to listen above the creaking of the floorboards beneath our weight—and crept, step by step, down the tightly winding stairway of the Lanthorn Tower. We came to a landing where Gerard halted. Torches flamed brightly in their sconces on either side of the door. Gerard knocked twice, waited, and knocked twice again. A fine, ragged line of dried blood marked the near side of his face.

The latch clicked and the door, slowly, swung open without a sound.

A black cat darted out with a silver fish's tail dangling from its mouth. From where I stood, I saw only a wall with pigs' carcasses on hooks and strings of onions hung along its length.

Gerard entered the kitchen cautiously. "Do you have the ropes, Dicken?"

A tall, hunch-shouldered man appeared, mumbling. The fire in the cooking hearth had burnt out hours ago, but torches threw ample light throughout the spacious, high-ceilinged chamber. One table was strewn with dirty pots, another with the remnants of the night's meal: a bowl of eggshells, baskets of leeks and cabbages, scattered apple peels. Casks of ale were stacked along another wall.

Arnaud and I stepped beneath the low lintel of the door, closing it behind us. Dicken shuffled over to a row of barrels and lifted the lid from one. He stooped over it and plunged his huge hands inside. With a careless heave, he hurled a coil of rope, reeking of salted fish, at Gerard's feet. The hook tied to its end clanked on the stones.

Gerard lifted the coil over his head and slipped an arm through it. Then he dug beneath his jerkin and produced a pouch. "More than you asked for." It jingled as he tossed it to the cook, who snatched it out of midair with surprising reflexes.

Dicken untied the pouch and ogled the treasure within. Then he tucked its bulge beneath his apron, went to the hearth and ducked beneath its broad, stone arch. He fumbled above his head and the knotted tail of another rope dropped down. He emerged wearing a scowl.

Ignoring him, Gerard scooped up a pile of ashes and smeared them on his forehead and cheeks, avoiding the still seeping gash.

While Gerard grasped the rope above his head and scrambled up, Dicken went about cleaning up his tables, brushing the waste into a bowl at his hip. I passed by him, grabbed a strip of dried dough and heard a low rumble in his throat. Although I stepped wide of him, he leered at me.

"Best hurry," he warned. "One arrow in your chest and you'll drop dead as a goose." He chortled to himself as he flung a spray of almond shells onto the floor with a sweep of his hairy arm, missing his bowl entirely.

I tossed the dough onto the floor. Before the hearth, Arnaud and I swiped our hands through the ash pile and darkened our faces. I went up next. With each pull, I slid my feet further up the rope, squeezed it between my feet for leverage and raised myself up again. The rope burned between my legs. My arms shook with the effort, my shoulders tightened. Halfway up, the sides of the chimney narrowing, my grip weakened. I paused, bearing my weight in my legs, until they, too, began to tremble. Lying on my flea-infested mattress and staring up at the ceiling for so many months, I had become an invalid. I reached above my head to grasp the rope again with cramped fingers, but my palms were slick. From below, Arnaud tugged at the rope. My fingers slipped down the rope, its fibers searing my palms. I locked my arms and caught myself with a jerk. I swallowed back my heart like a stone. Sweat poured down my neck and chest.

"All right up there?" Arnaud asked.

This was no time to yield to infirmity. No time to lament that I was neither as young and strong as Arnaud nor as agile as Gerard. I looked up to see Gerard's shadow black against the scattered stars above. I clamped my hands around the rope above me and pulled with all my will. The blackened stones closed in around me, pinching my shoulders. Several heaves later, Gerard reached down, clasped my hand and pulled me over the lip of the chimney. The first thing I saw was a sleeping watchman lying stretched out next to the stairway door, oblivious to our furtive activity.

Before I could flex my fingers freely, Arnaud had scrambled up and was standing beside me. Gerard drew up the rope from the chimney and then lifted the hook. As he arranged the bundle in his arms, the hook spilled from within the tangle. It fell with a clatter at his feet. We all froze. The watchman let out a snort and flopped over onto his side.

Carefully, Gerard plucked up the hook, hunched down and shuffled over to a crenel on the eastern side of the tower's roof. There, he hooked the chimney rope. The other was still slung over his shoulder for later use. On his stomach, he inched out over the brink of the battlement wall. He studied both inner and outer wards before he let the rope down.

135

One at a time again, we plummeted down. I cursed silently at the burning trail the rope left on the inside of my thighs and my arms. On our bellies then, we began to crawl along the wall walk toward the Salt Tower. Partway across, Arnaud grabbed my ankle. I glanced back to see him jabbing a finger to our left. I hissed at Gerard to stop and raised myself up on my elbows.

A shadow floated across the inner ward—a woman, her skirts flowing behind her, her hood pulled up to conceal her face. She caught the rail of the stairs to the White Tower and flung herself up them two at a time. She had not quite reached the top landing before the door, when she faltered, sank down and crumpled into a quivering heap. Gerard motioned me forward and I followed to the other tower. We pressed ourselves into the corner between the last merlon and the door.

Still in the same place, Arnaud stared across the dark distance at the woman slumped on the steps as if he recognized her. I waited, but he did not move. Finally, I plucked up a loose stone chip and tossed it at him to capture his attention.

Instead, the woman's head snapped up and she sprang to her feet, her hand fluttering up to touch her neck. She peeled back her hood and gazed in our direction. Arnaud flattened himself. Gerard and I pressed our backs deeper into the shadowed corner. The woman remained in that pose for an unbearably long time, as though frozen in place. It was some minutes later before she sank back down, pulled her knees into her chest and laid her head on them.

Arnaud slithered forward. When he reached us I chastened him with a harsh glare. Gerard dropped the second rope over the wall into the outer ward and went down. As I descended, I realized we had one more wall to climb and no other rope with which to do so. Trusting in Gerard, I had not dallied to interrogate him on details. I dropped to my feet with a dull thud. My aching legs nearly gave way from exhaustion. I clenched my knees to steady myself, but my hands had been rubbed raw with the last descent and so I leaned back against the wall to rest. Arnaud landed silently after me, alert and upright. He cocked his head and gripped my arm.

Voices reached our ears. It was difficult to tell if they came from somewhere within the Tower grounds or outside it. We huddled in the corner at the tower's base. The voices grew louder, clearer.

Two men staggered through the gate between the Salt and Lanthorn Towers: members of the Tower garrison. One of them stumbled forward and went down on his knees. He swayed and fell onto his side, even as the other sentry scolded him.

"Stephen, ah, bloody hell . . ." The second man kicked his companion in the buttocks. "Get up, you steaming lump of horse—"

Stephen vomited. He was too drunk to lift his head from his own puke. His companion hovered over him, muttering insults and poking him with the bottom of his pike.

Gerard turned to me. "You're drunk," he said. Then to Arnaud, "Bring him. Follow me."

Arnaud hooked me by the arm and whipped me out from the shadows. We headed directly toward the two men. As we neared them, the sentry who was still on his feet looked up in alarm. Upon recognizing Gerard, he straightened. Arnaud yanked me along gruffly.

"You're not fit to do your duty, Tom," Gerard remarked. "Get out of here."

"B-b-but I . . . I . . ." Tom, fighting a yawn, lifted a shaking finger toward the outer gate. "I . . . I know we're late, but we—"

"We? You're one swallow from being as far gone as him. And this one—" He hooked a thumb over his shoulder at me— "is going in the stocks. Caught him in the pantry swiving a laundress. By the sounds of her, she was not entirely willing."

"Begging for more, she was" I drawled. "Can't a man—"

Arnaud rammed an elbow hard into my gut. I threw my head back to gulp for air. My knees folded under me. Arnaud pulled my arm over his shoulder and braced his feet wide to hold me up.

His jaw jutting out in authority, Gerard said to Tom, "Get him out of the way. Then go. Report to me at noon."

Tom nodded so hard he tottered forward a step before gaining his balance. Clumsily, he grabbed the unconscious Stephen by both hands and dragged him along in stops and starts until he reached the shadowed recesses of the inner gate from which they had come. There he sank down exhausted next to Stephen, leaned back against the wall and closed his eyes. His head bobbed twice, unable to fight the sleeping remedy that had so insidiously incapacitated the rest of the garrison. Drool dripped from his chin.

Gerard strolled toward the outer gate. I stumbled along at Arnaud's side in feigned drunkenness, wondering who else might thwart our plans. As we entered the archway to the outer gate, Arnaud released my arm. There was no one there. The sentries who should have waited for their relief, had either abandoned their post prematurely in impatience or staggered off drunk and succumbed to a deep slumber like all the others. Arnaud and I unbarred the door and slipped through to find the portcullis raised just high enough to squeeze under. Our steps quickening with each stride, we crossed the short bridge over the moat to the river's edge. Tucked against the marshy embankment was a small rowing boat. We skidded down to the river and Gerard and I stepped inside. Arnaud pushed us away before leaping in and taking up the oars.

"Who was the woman?" I asked him.

"Does it matter?"

"I imagine it does to you. Who is she to you?"

He paused momentarily in the rhythm of his strokes. "She will do better without me."

Somewhere past the nearest corner of the Tower walls, a frenzied dog barked in alarm at the sound of our voices. The high-pitched screech of an old woman followed. Arnaud pulled harder and we skimmed across the Thames, angling further east as the current swept us along. The dog yipped in agony. I heard a splash and looked back to the end of the wharf where the hag stood silent and alone.

I dipped my hands over the side of the boat, scooped up a handful of water and splashed my face to remove the soot. The sky had lightened to steel gray and a faint glow of pink washed the horizon to the east. On the far bank, I could barely discern the outlines of several horses attended by four men. As we came closer, I could see one of them was Simon de Beresford.

We climbed out of the boat and scrambled up the bank. Simon handed me the reins to a well-muscled sorrel. "We'll stop a few miles beyond Greenwich for food and a change of clothing," he said. "Tomorrow, you sail for France."

"And you?"

"Staying. Someone needs to be your eyes and ears here."

I placed a foot in the stirrup and pitched myself up onto the saddle. My arms and legs still burned. Simon sprang onto his mount and dug his spurs into its flanks. He bolted off on the road to Greenwich, and I followed him.

To freedom.

15

Isabella:

Tower of London — August, 1323

T HE FEAST OF ST. Peter ad Vincula began in vulgar revelry. St. Peter
was the patron saint of the Tower of London and every year on the
first day of August the garrison embraced the occasion by gorging themselves on roasted pig, meat pies, smoked fishes and tarts and saturating
themselves with ale and cider. By nightfall, the horrible bellowing of
drunken, bloated men-at-arms was loud enough to topple the outer walls.

My ladies and I stayed far from the uproar. We sat in a circle in the
solar, with the wavering glow of the hearth dancing in our midst, as I read
aloud the *lais* of Marie de France. Long before I had finished, Patrice
slipped away. Juliana and Marie shared a knowing look and we all expected a breathy recount of some stolen tryst with Arnaud come morning.
The rest of us, not so lucky to have a trembling lover awaiting us, took to
bed far sooner than was our custom.

Usually, the drinking and shouting went on all night and faded away
only in the small hours before dawn. But a hush came on oddly early that

evening—well before midnight. I lay awake in my canopied bed, listening to an ominous silence that had crept over the whole of the Tower.

I drifted between thought and dream, my heart and mind racing uncontrollably. With each passing hour I grew more and more exhausted. Once, thinking I heard some faint, but distinct, blunted clank of metal on stone from somewhere outside, I stumbled from my bed to gaze into the darkness from my window. I searched the towers, the walls, the courtyard below, but all was shades of gray. My eyes wearied from the strain. I held my breath to listen. Nothing. I straggled back to bed and burrowed beneath the twisted sheets.

A voice . . . I went and looked again. A shadow on the outer wall? Had it moved? I stared harder. Again nothing.

I imagine things. Voices. Shapes. Sounds in the night.

Finally, I gave up and returned to my bed, wondering what might have happened elsewhere, if anything had at all, and if this was the night Mortimer would be freed. For my own protection, Charles and Orleton had withheld the details from me. I only knew that it *would* happen, not when or how. Even so, Edward would need very little to accuse me of treason; he trusted no one but Despenser. I had taken great care to burn every letter. Yet if even one had fallen into Hugh Despenser's hands . . . whether I was a queen or not, he would be the first to loop the rope around my neck and rollick with laughter as I dangled like a rag doll on a string. It was doubtful Edward would grant me even the same grace he had given to Roger Mortimer. My begging for Mortimer's life and then having a hand in this—double betrayal.

My gaze leapt from the drooping gold cloth above my bed to the square of starlight slanting down from my window and back again. Just outside my door I heard footsteps. I sat up in my bed, clutching my blanket to my chest as if it were a shield. For minutes I stared at the door, certain of my ears. But when the door finally crept open, it was only Patrice, coming to bed. She was quickly into her nightclothes and faster asleep. Nothing more happened. No one shouted out in the night to arrest the queen for plotting to free a rebel.

I waited in anguish for morning to come and the news it would bring. It was a miracle my tossing and turning did not awaken Patrice. But every time I looked toward the trundle bed where she slept, she was nothing but a long lump beneath her covers.

The light of morning was yet weak when Patrice roused me.

She pinched my upper arm in the circle of her fingers and hovered over me. Disheveled hair sprung from the sides of her head like a bristly halo, indicating that she, too, had been awoken abruptly.

"Lady Eleanor is here, my lady," she imparted. "She needs to see you at once, she says."

My middle went tight. "I am hardly awake, Patrice. Tell her to come back after I have eaten. Have the bells even rung for prime yet?"

A deep line of worry cut between Patrice's eyebrows. "I think she will knock down the door if you make her wait too long. She is disturbed. Says it is urgent."

"Did she say why?"

She whispered, "Sir Roger Mortimer is gone."

"Gone?"

"Not in his cell. Missing."

I told Patrice to allow me a few minutes and instructed her to have Ida lay out my clothes. In truth though, I needed the time to reassure myself that I had nothing to fear. Time to think of and rehearse what words I would say. Eleanor would tell me the news; I would react appropriately, order a full search, and pray it was unsuccessful.

I was barely out of my nightclothes when Lady Eleanor entered my bedchamber wringing her hands so fitfully I thought she might pull her own fingers off.

In only my kirtle, I placed myself on my stool near the window while Patrice brought me a selection of lightweight over-kirtles, suitable for a summer day's warmth. Meanwhile, Ida began unplaiting my hair and raking her fingers through the strands before pulling a silver comb through it.

"Lady Eleanor," I began, keeping my voice level, "is it true that they could not find Sir Roger Mortimer in his cell this morning?"

She bit at her lip so hard I expected to see blood streaming down her chin. "Yes, my lady, it is true."

"Mercy," Ida muttered, resting her comb. "I never liked being here. Even less now. Full of ghosts, it is. Saw one myself in Flint Tower week before last and Dicken the cook—"

"Ida!"

"—swears he hears the voice of—"

"Enough, Ida!" She was superstitious to excess and obsessed with the spirits of the dead. Although I did not allow such talk she managed to insert it at every opportunity. I returned my attention to Lady Eleanor. "And they have not found him elsewhere yet? Perhaps someone moved him to a different cell?"

"No, my lady. When they moved the bed on which he slept, they found a hole in the wall behind it. Big enough for a man to fit through."

Ida yanked at my hair. I grabbed at her wrist to halt her. I stood, my hair falling free down my back. "A hole? How does a prisoner hack at stones and move them without anyone hearing? Do things like that not make enough sound for someone outside his door to hear?" I grew stern in my tone, working the words out between clenched jaws as if trying to contain my anger. "Was there not a guard there? How can this happen?"

Eleanor flinched. "I do not know, my lady."

"Find out!" I blustered. Quivering, Eleanor shrank from me and even Patrice and Ida held their breath. "And when you have an adequate answer come back and tell me how it is that the most important prisoner in all of England suddenly disappears without anyone knowing about it. The king will be outraged when he learns of this. Outraged! When he finds out who is responsible for this mess he will have their heads!"

I turned sharply on my heel and flung myself back down on my stool. Eleanor scurried away, muttering a stream of worries under her breath and pulling at her fingers. Ida commenced combing my hair, this time with more purpose, and at my indication Patrice laid out a gown of yellow and blue upon the bed while returning the rest to the wardrobe. I smiled as I gazed out the window and felt the morning light wash over my face.

Deception was never a trait I aspired to, but I could learn it well enough. Edward would never be wise to me because he thought me too timid, too guileless.

Mortimer was free.

And I had determined the future of England in a handful of letters.

IDA BEGGED THAT WE leave for Windsor at once, but I remained in my apartments that day, issuing orders for a thorough search, dispatching messages and receiving frequent reports, most of little substance. I took a light dinner in my chamber, Patrice seated across the small table from me. Sweat trickled down my neck and breastbone and collected in the small hollow at the bottom of my ribs. I pressed a hand to my garment to blot it. A stifling August wind blasted through an open window near our table like the fire-air expelled from a smith's bellows.

Patrice, who had been unusually quiet all morning, sat staring blankly at her white rolls while flies dotted their surface.

"A game of tables?" I said to break the silence. "I promise not to play too wickedly. Or I had a few books sent from my library at Beverly— romances, in French. Remember, as girls, how we used to sneak those away and read them in the chapel, pretending they were missals? We *could* say a few prayers, for real, in the chapel, if you—"

"No. Not today."

I glanced around the room and, seeing that the others were busy elsewhere, pressed her to speak. "You returned in the middle of the night and have nothing to say? I would think you would be hurrying to the chapel to offer a confession of some kind."

She let out a sigh, laden with worry. "Where should I begin?"

I pushed aside my food and leaned across the table. "What do you know of Mortimer's escape?"

She pressed the point of her knife into a roll, disturbing the flies. "There were two guards outside his cell—asleep."

"Drunk?"

"Drunk indeed." She nodded knowingly. "With a potion."

"How? In the ale?"

"Possibly. Or baked into the custard. No one knows for certain. Just that the whole garrison, everyone who ate or drank in the hall last night, fell dead asleep."

"So that is why—"

"No one would have heard a thing." She laid her knife down and stared out the window again, her brows drawn together.

"Then someone has been planning this, someone inside . . ." I was unsure how much to reveal. I yearned to tell Patrice what little I knew, but I did not want her involved.

"Arnaud," she said almost in a whimper.

"What of Arnaud? You were supposed to meet him last night—at least that is what we all assumed when you left without a word. Did you?" I grabbed her hand, imploring her to look at me, but she continued to gaze out at the cloudless sky. "Patrice, what happened with Arnaud?"

It looked as though she might burst into tears, but she startled when Ida's voice boomed from an adjoining room as she chastised Marie for being sloppy over some menial task. When Ida's tongue-lashing finally ceased and the two women moved off, Patrice began with pained reluctance.

"I was to meet Arnaud in a storeroom of the Wardrobe Tower. He was late, but rather than worry—for he *always* comes—I busied myself inhaling the spices. I had my finger dipped in a jar of cinnamon when he finally arrived. But he told me very suddenly that he is contemplating devoting himself to the Church, because . . . because he feels he has sinned terribly. That he must serve his penance."

I went around the table to stand behind her and stroked her back consolingly. "How can he say such a thing? He is far from the first man to . . ." I did not need to say what they had been doing or give her pause to think he was running away from her. "You could not change his mind?"

"He spoke of going to Rievaulx to live with the monks there . . . join-

145

ing the Cistercian Order, eventually—I have heard there were Templars in his family. He had an uncle, dead now, I think, who was an abbot with them. I don't know. I stopped listening, truthfully. His words all ran together. I did not remember them until later. All I knew was that, that . . . that he would not look at me. The more he talked, the more I felt as though . . ." She shook her head emphatically. "I was going to tell him, going to . . ." She slid from my hold and, cradling herself pitifully in her arms, sank to the floor by the window. "Tell him I was carrying his child."

"Oh." I sat down in her chair, facing her. I could hardly say I was surprised. In actuality, I had expected it for some time. "And did you?"

"I had no chance. Before I could say it, he told me he was leaving . . . to go on pilgrimage to Santiago de Compostela. After that, he would be studying for the priesthood. That it was what his father had always wanted. What he wanted."

"But Patrice . . . you must tell him."

"I cannot. It is too late. Done."

"What do you mean? Because he is gone? I'll send for him. He cannot have gotten as far as any of the ports by now. He'll do what is—"

"No, no, noooo . . . I've ruined it." She shoved her face into her hands to contain her pain. Frail words leaked through the cracks between her fingers. "I told you—it is too late. Done. There will be no child."

"I don't understand. What do you mean?"

With a shaking hand, she reached into the side of her overkirtle and pulled out a leather purse the size of her fist. From it, she drew a tiny flask. "Mathilda, the cook's wife, she knows of herbal remedies such as this that will end a pregnancy. I went to her last night . . . asked her for it. She said after a while, I would only feel a little ill, that I would have some pains, small ones, sleep heavily, and it would be over with." She began to rock back and forth, like people do when they are mourning the death of a loved one.

If Mathilda knew how to induce a miscarriage, then perhaps she knew how to make men sleep so hard nothing would rouse them. And if not Mathilda, then her husband Dicken, the cook.

I grabbed the flask from Patrice and looked inside, but it was empty and had only the faint, but distinctive odor of wild carrots. "Oh, Patrice, why did you do this?"

"Because, I wanted no part of him. Besides . . . he lied to me. He was *not* going on a pilgrimage." She gritted her teeth in anger. Her fingernails dug into her skirts so deeply they must have pierced her flesh beneath. "I saw him again afterwards. After I left Mathilda. After I had already taken the remedy. I passed through the inner ward on my way here. I was feeling nothing yet—no pains, nothing but emptiness. I wanted to sit a while, to think. Then I saw him atop the wall. There was a rope. They went down, to the other side. Disappeared."

"They? Who was with him?"

"Two men. Nothing but shadows against the moonlight. I could not tell who. But this morning, I spoke to Juliana. Along with Sir Roger Mortimer, Gerard d'Alspaye is also missing, as well as Arnaud. And no one knew anything of Arnaud leaving on a pilgrimage or taking vows."

I joined Patrice on the floor and held her, as sorry for the child she would soon lose, as I was that Arnaud had deceived her. I, too, had trusted in him, had relied on him, and now he had disappeared with Roger Mortimer and was on his way to France. To me, though, it made some sense that on any of his missions to carry a message to Bishop Orleton, he might have been convinced to take part in the scheme. Orleton would have recognized him for his courage and loyalty and made use of it. I only wished that somehow I might have known and so been able to spare Patrice this private agony.

But I could not tell her. If she knew anything, it would only endanger her. Some day she would find out everything. Not now, though. Not now.

By the time Ida came back into the room to see if we were done with our meal, Patrice was doubled up on her side and crying because of the pain shooting through her belly. I summoned my physician and told him in confidence that she might be miscarrying a child, but I said nothing of the flask and its contents. She bled heavily and although it weakened her, the pains soon began to fade and she slept the rest of the day.

WHILE I WATCHED OVER Patrice, more details arrived in scattered bits. All gates had been closed and every room searched. A thorough scouring of the premises revealed a rope dangling from the wall near the Salt Tower to the outer ward. Most likely, the garrison soldiers, nursing headaches from too much ale and the disorienting effects of the potion, had walked past it more than once before noticing it. Another rope was discovered, this one on the roof of the Lanthorn Tower. The door of the south-eastern gate was found unbarred, indicating that Mortimer had indeed gained his freedom. How he got so far was a mystery. Some said that he was kin to the devil and had used magic. Others swore he had had help from within.

How right they were no one knew.

Eventually, there were reports of a boat being rowed across the Thames at a peculiar hour and horses waiting on the far shore. After that, the trail went completely dead. Messengers were sent with haste to the king at Kirkham. Edward dispatched soldiers to those places he thought Mortimer would be most inclined to go: to the Marches, further on to Wales and also to Dover. Ships were searched, letters read, suspects inter-rogated. For weeks they went on looking and yet no evidence of Mortimer was ever found.

Across Wales and England, fortresses were reinforced and readied for attack, for Edward feared a fresh rebellion. Tournaments were sus-pended because they might give Mortimer's rebels a place to gather in arms. But it was all in vain. There was no trace of Sir Roger Mortimer. None at all. He had vanished into the night.

Every day the tales grew. Some said Mortimer had drowned in the Thames, while others said that he was a changeling and had simply walked away from the Tower and from London in the shape of another person or an animal. One old woman babbled about a three-legged dog that dove from the wharf and swam the river before rising on the opposite bank as a man. She was later discovered to have thrown her own dog into the water, trying to drown it when it bit her after being beaten.

For me, it all provided a private kind of amusement. For Edward, however, it incited an obvious panic in him—so much, I think he even feared the people of London might oppose him, and so he kept from there for a very, very long time. I stayed, despite Ida's loathing of the place. I did not want to suffer Edward's moods.

If Edward ever learned of my doings, he would indeed know I had betrayed him. But there is a worse betrayal than keeping secrets from someone. It is a sickening sort of betrayal to me, beyond my comprehension and upbringing.

I did not have to witness Edward's infidelity with my own eyes to know that he had engaged in it with Despenser and likely Piers Gaveston before him. The heart knows, sometimes, what the eyes cannot see. Edward could never give me his love because it had been reserved long ago for one such as Hugh Despenser. Despenser, who hated me. Despenser, who would do me harm at any cost.

I would have preferred that Edward frequent a brothel than be with Hugh Despenser. I might have forgiven him then, for whores have no ambitions. Despenser, however, did.

16

Roger Mortimer:

Paris — December, 1323

T HE FIRST TIME KING Charles summoned me to the Palace de la Cité in Paris, I expected more ceremony upon my arrival. Not a tournament, nor even a feast. But something . . . less casual than what I was greeted with.

King Charles of France was reclined in a green cushioned chair, his silk-shod feet stretched out before him while a courtier strummed at a lute. A red-haired young woman sat in Charles' lap and trailed a teasing finger over his lips. In the corner behind the enamored pair, a clutch of pretty women in high-waisted gowns and jeweled chaplets tittered behind their hands. Around them hovered a dozen men, finely primped in their velvets and feathers. I wondered for a moment if I had not happened upon a Persian brothel. As I strode across the room, Charles finally noticed me and banished the object of his flirtation with a whisper. She pouted her fleshy lips and slipped from his lap, stopping at his side long enough to place a kiss behind his ear.

"Sir Roger Mortimer." He held one hand out, palm open. In moments, a servant placed a goblet in his grasp and filled it with wine. "How do you find Picardy these days?"

I bowed. "Comfortable, sire."

"Bearable, you mean?" He took a sip of wine and ran his tongue around his mouth.

"No, I mean comfortable—in a rustic, uncomplicated sense."

Sniffing his drink, he cast his eyes upward. "Ah, boring."

"One could call it that."

For a moment, his attention drifted to the music as he inclined his head and tapped his fingers on his leg. Suddenly, his eyes narrowed and he waved me into a chair adjacent to his. "So, your son, Geoffrey—can I rely on him, now that he has been sworn to me?"

In early summer, Joan's mother had died, leaving her Picardy estates to Geoffrey. When I arrived on the continent Geoffrey had been at the French court, paying fealty to his new lord, King Charles. But there was far more to the question than what he had asked. I gave him an equally vague reply. "As much as one can rely on a boy of fifteen years."

Without breaking his gaze on me he called for one of his courtiers. "Bertrand." He crooked his finger to beckon the man closer. "When we are seated in the hall for supper, will you see to it the lovely Colette is not in my direct sight? I have a hard time keeping my eyes from her, but the Count of Evreux and his wife will be in attendance this evening. Considering they have a daughter available for marriage, I would prefer they believe me as celibate as any monk."

Bertrand nodded, but before he could scurry off, Charles added, "Leave us. Everyone."

With that curt command, the room cleared.

"And you?" Charles said bluntly when the door closed behind the last person. "To whom do you give your loyalty?"

"I no longer hold lands in England. I place my loyalty where it best serves me."

"Which is not with King Edward?"

"Which is with no one, for now."

"Ah, but we have a common enemy?"

"One could say so."

Emptying his cup, Charles rose and placed it on a small table. Then he poured wine into another goblet and handed it to me. "And what do you say?"

In one thirsty gulp, I drained my goblet. There was more to his question than the obvious. He twisted words, leading. I suspected he sought something more than my gratitude. I saw no reason to withhold that, or to evade the point of this meeting. Queen Isabella had told me that when I came to Paris, I would learn what was expected of me in return for my freedom. If Charles would only spit it out, I would have my answer.

"What is it, precisely, that you want from me?"

"Your cooperation. Your expertise." Charles slipped into his chair, stretched his legs and touched his fingertips together. "Your influence."

Amused, I scoffed. "And who is it that I, a vagabond, could possibly influence?"

"You have followers. Men who would throw themselves before the ancient legions of Rome at your merest bidding. I know many of their names already. Some have made their appearances at my court. Their grievances are common knowledge. Shall I read you the list of names, as a reminder?"

"I'm hardly as powerful as you suggest, but even so, what good are faithful friends when they have no more means to exact revenge than I?" For months now, I had been drifting without purpose. The scraps handed me by my wife's relatives hardly amounted to an extravagant life. How was I to gather an army of followers and pay them?

"You will get what you need, Sir Roger, but you will have to beg for it."

"Should I start with you, sire? On my knees?" I leaned back in my chair, mirroring his posture to show I had no intention of going down before him.

The first hint of a smile broke over his mouth. "No, no need. My sister has already vouched for you. Besides, you are neither desperate nor groveling. Nor am I, Sir Roger. Consider what I am about to propose to you, but do so with care . . . and commitment, should you agree to it. Our desires are not mutually exclusive. You want your revenge on Edward and this Hugh Despenser. I want something as well."

"Your proposition, then?"

"Edward holds lordships in Gascony and elsewhere, which makes me his overlord. As long as he acknowledges that, there can be peace between our kingdoms. However, he does not seem to want to drag himself from England. If, eventually, he will not, then I need you to remove Hugh Despenser from his company. My dear sister is much aggrieved over his constant presence at her husband's side. A leech, I think she once called him."

"You would go to war against England?"

"Me? Oh, no, no. I'm trying to avoid that. But a recognized traitor such as yourself, plus a growing number of other disaffected English knights . . . with a little help, you could all regain what has been taken from you and make Edward bend to your will."

"*Civil* war, then?"

"Strong words. I would be more inclined to say . . . hmm, 'a forced proposal'. But you have done it before," he leaned forward, "which is why I chose you."

"Yes, and although it began well, it ended very badly. Despenser has returned, greedier than ever . . . and England has never been worse off."

"Ah, well, perhaps there is something to be learned in all that, Sir Roger. Perhaps simply demanding the removal of Edward's favorite was not enough. Perhaps you would need to be a little more, as I said, forceful this time? More . . . permanent."

"Meaning?"

"Merely a thought. Let it mean whatever you like." He slouched back again, running his glittering ringed fingers over his chin and down his throat. "Tomorrow I ride to Vincennes. My cousin, Philip of Valois, is to meet me there. He has persuaded me to go wolf-hunting, *par force*. A

153

rather complicated affair that involves dragging a horse's bloody carcass through the woods the night before and then tethering live quarry to lure the wolves to a feeding spot. It can go on for days, but a thrill if we succeed. I have chosen from the best of my running-hounds to give chase, but it will be Philip's mastiffs that bring it down. If they do, he'll claim the prize for himself and boast of it until this time next year. You will join us?"

So, I would have to play at sport to gain his favor. A small price to pay to get what I wanted. "If you'll forgive my inexperience. I admit I've never hunted wolf before. You'll not relegate me to blowing a horn, I hope?"

"If you are so brave, Sir Roger, you may thrust the spear into the wolf's heart."

"Nothing would satisfy me more, sire."

THAT NIGHT I SUPPED at the high table of the King of France. The next day I went with Charles to Vincennes. There, I met not only his pompous cousin, Philip of Valois, but Philip's sister Jeanne, who was married to Count William of Hainault—a very, *very* rich man.

I hardly cared about stirring up wolves to kill when there was money for the asking and alliances to be snatched at.

At dawn the next morning, the bait was set out. In a clearing, an iron stake had been driven into the ground. Chained to the stake was a half-grown lamb.

The morning mist drifted and broke. I crouched nearby in deep mud, the stink of horse blood strong. The far-away baying of hounds rolled through the wooded valley. I stood, wrapped my cold-cramped fingers tight around the haft of my hunting spear and held my breath to listen. A twig snapped. Then, a lanky wolf padded through the gray tangle of trees. The wretched thing looked near to starving. Nose quivering, it stopped to lick at blood-soaked earth. Slowly, it raised its head and fixed its yellow eyes on the bleating lamb. The beast lifted a paw and coiled back on its haunches, preparing to spring.

I drew the spear back, planted my foot and heaved.

The wolf jerked sideways and turned its head just as the spear tore through its chest.

That night Philip of Valois drank as heavily as if he had killed the wolf himself. Charles was pleased he had not. More valuable to me than a scrap of wolf pelt was the invitation I procured from the Countess Jeanne to come to Valenciennes in Hainault.

I cannot say I missed England, but I would go back there one day. When the time was right.

17

Isabella:

Kenilworth – Christmas, 1323

I FIRST LEARNED OF Mortimer's whereabouts almost two months after his disappearance. Bishop Orleton informed me Mortimer was in Picardy among relatives. Although I yearned to know more, I dared not ask. Ever reticent, Charles made no mention of Mortimer or his plans for him in his letters. Rather, he renewed his demands that Edward come personally to France to pay homage for Gascony. Urged by parliament to settle matters promptly, Edward at first agreed to go. But within the week he postponed his departure until the following year, saying there was too much unrest in England for him to leave it. In truth, it was Despenser he did not want to leave.

In parliament, Despenser accused Bishop Orleton of aiding Mortimer. There was almost a riot on the floor. Evidence was merely hearsay, but since Orleton could not provide proof of his innocence and no one was willing to openly defy Despenser, Orleton was taken into custody. To protect me, the good bishop had kept our secret. Edward wrote to the

Pope and demanded Orleton be removed from his bishopric. But when the Pope would not comply, Edward begrudgingly released the bishop—although his every word and deed were scrutinized.

If suspicion alone implied guilt, I wondered what would become of me in time.

For Christmas, the children and I joined Edward at Kenilworth. At the Twelfth Night feast, I took my seat next to my husband at the high table. On the other side of him sat Despenser. All night Edward leaned away from me and whispered to Despenser, who laughed behind his hand.

The trumpets sounded as servants carried out three great platters bearing a boar's head with gilded tusks and two peacocks with their feathers pretentiously displayed. All around me, wine and merriment overflowed, but I observed it all as if I were watching from outside through a glass window.

Young Edward and some of the older children broke off into a game of Blind Man's Bluff. Little Joanna began to fuss at her nursemaid's knee and I quickly took her onto my lap, welcoming the distraction. I wound an errant curl from her temple around my fingertip and hummed to her. Her stubby fingers slid into her mouth. She went limp with sleep in my arms. I kissed the crown of her head and waved her nursemaid away. With Joanna's head on my shoulder, I settled back in my chair.

Suddenly, a shiver ran up my spine. I stiffened and then turned to look at Edward. He leered at me with a hatred so black I quailed. If I could have placed a finger upon his heart, I would have lost it to frostbite.

I looked away. He suspected me. He must have. In place of Mortimer, he would cram me in that tiny, lightless hole and tell my children lies upon lies about me. They would not forget me, at first . . . but they would be kept from me and the months would blur into years until I was but an echo of the past to them.

Joanna stretched and yawned. Her eyelashes fluttered. She poked a finger at the corners of my mouth, trying to push my lips up into a smile, and then she kissed me wetly on the cheek. I drew her tightly to my breast.

"I love you, my little one," I whispered.

She threw her arms about my neck and hugged me as fiercely as any three-year old could.

When Ella escaped Ida's watchful eye and pulled her big brother John onto the floor, they pretended to take part in a ring dance. I tried to forget about Edward. Tried to forget about Orleton and Mortimer. About Despenser. I concentrated on my children, so giddy with merriment and mischief that they clutched at their bellies and bumped into those around them because they had lost their place in the dance.

Then, the fiddler laid down his instrument and the music ended. Everyone clapped and drifted away . . . and I could still feel the cut of Edward's stare like a cold blade drawn down the side of my face.

During the fortnight we were at Kenilworth, Edward never once spoke directly to me. We were never together except for when public events demanded it. Countless times, though, Despenser was next to him, his lips as close to the king's ear as any lover's. To see Hugh Despenser stroll haughtily about Kenilworth, trimmed in the plushest furs and the brightest jewels, issuing orders at the slightest whim, anyone could have mistaken him for the king had they not known otherwise.

By winter of the following year, Charles' patience had been exhausted. He threatened to seize Gascony. Again, Edward stalled. He sent the Earl of Pembroke to France in a furious attempt to remedy matters. I held the greatest of hope in the earl. He was the one man remaining in Edward's confidence who bore a level head on his shoulders. But Pembroke had barely set foot upon French soil when the hand of God struck him down. My hope withered with the untimely news.

In June, wearied of the stalemate, Charles sent men to take Gascony by force. Edward's great blunder was to appoint his youngest half-brother Edmund, the Earl of Kent, as Lieutenant of operations there. Eventually, Kent's campaign eroded into such a debacle he conceded to a truce that, in effect, left the duchy in Charles' hands entirely.

Although it had not been declared, England and France were already at war. And in my husband's eyes, I was the enemy.

Langley, June, 1324

As THE MONTHS PASSED, Edward imposed ever-increasing restrictions on me, ordering me where he wanted me to go, forbidding me to travel without his permission. The following summer, he confined me to Langley to stay with the children while parliament, scrambling for another course of action after Kent's failure in France, convened at Westminster. The result was that I was also stripped of my lands, along with the income they provided. My allowance, with which I paid my household staff and personal expenses, was reduced to one-tenth of my former income.

Not so long ago, it seemed, while Young Edward was still a plump babe suckling at the breast of his wet nurse, Edward and I had summered at Langley. Sprawling above the banks of the wandering River Glade, Langley is a grand manor, with its hall hung with shields of green, gold and blue. We held a feast there that Whitsuntide. I can still recall the blur of tumblers, the riotous laughter, and the rounds of song. Edward and I hunted and hawked the days away and in the evenings we battled each other at chess. We stayed on for weeks. Our family was just beginning. Our future glimmered with promise at last.

But just as summer is brief, so was our joy. Unlike summer though, it was never to come again.

On a glorious June morning, almost a year after Mortimer's escape, Young Edward and I rode out from Langley into the countryside. Two of my favorite bitch hounds and a gangly pup loped alongside us. Occasionally, the two older dogs stopped to investigate a smell and invariably the pup would turn the diversion into a game of play-quarreling, which usually earned him a quick nip to the muzzle. He soon learned to curb his roughness and sink to his belly whenever either of the other two so much as lifted a lip at him.

Of course, we were accompanied by guards—Despenser's men—but

Young Edward and I made sport of galloping in spurts through hidden trails in the woods and over deep ditches, trying like mad to lose them. Eventually, they slackened in their diligence, letting us ride on ahead, so long as they could keep us in their sights.

We eased our mounts to a walk as we went eastward along a shallow stream. The dogs padded through the water to cool their feet. We stopped to let the horses drink and just as the guards caught up with us, two of them dismounting to dip their hands in the stream, all three dogs lifted their heads, sniffed the air and bolted up the far bank.

"Hares," my son whispered. He slapped his horse on the rump and kicked its flanks hard. I rode after him, although I was not nearly so skilled a rider. The guards by then had tired of chasing us, but they struggled back onto their mounts and followed from a comfortable distance.

My son flew over the sea of green like an osprey diving at an angle toward a school of fish. Every now and then a dog's tail flicked above the top of the grass or a head bobbed up in an arc as the dog reached out in full stride, but the longer the chase went on, the less I saw of them and the further and further ahead Young Edward went. It was some minutes later, over a mile perhaps, before the prince reined his horse to a halt. By the time I caught up with him, the bitches had a half-grown hare trapped between them and were letting the pup have it.

Gleaming white teeth bared, the young dog lunged. Without a sound it sunk its fangs deep into the thin flesh of the animal, raised it up in its eager mouth and gave a hard, sharp shake. The little creature's head snapped to the side and its body went limp.

"Did you see that, Mother? He'll make a fine hunter. Oh, I'd have ten of him if I could. Such a nose. And keen eyes. And girls," he said to the two bitches, who panted and hung their jaws low to the ground as they eyed the blood bubbling from the nose of the tiny corpse, "well done. Well done, indeed!"

"Rather young for such a conquest, isn't he?"

"Six months, maybe," Young Edward beamed. "Not half grown."

"He has promise, though?"

"Promise you call it? Brilliance, I say."

"Like you. Beyond his years."

He slipped down from his horse, thumped the pup on the top of his gray, wiry head, and grinned. The pup laid the prize at his feet and the two bitches stalked closer, licking their lips, but awaiting their master's approval. "I have done nothing half as amazing as him."

"But you shall do many great things. It was easy to see in you long ago."

"You only say that because I'll be King of England one day."

I looked back over my shoulder. The guards were still a long way away. All the same, I kept my voice low. "And King of France, perhaps."

He shrugged. "My uncle is King of France."

"Yes, but he has no heir yet."

For a while, he seemed not to understand, but finally, his mouth broke into a smile. "Then I am his heir? Has it been proclaimed? Has he made a promise to you?"

"No, not yet. But I would say you are the favored one. I have done my utmost to sow the idea in his mind, Young Edward. I think he is receptive to it, but it will take time. He has been searching for a new bride, without luck so far. Sooner or later he will have to give it hard consideration."

Young Edward toed the blood-wet hare with his boot, then kicked it toward the bitches, which at once ripped its small belly open and gnashed at its entrails. The pup got none of the prize. "France and England? Can a man be king of both? How?"

"Not any man, no. But one who is favored by God, loved by those he leads, a brilliant man . . . yes. He could be king of both. You could."

I anticipated the skeptical look of a boy and a shrug of his shoulders again. Instead, he lifted his chin and nodded, as if they were words he had waited and hoped . . . no, expected to hear.

"I could," he said.

Tower of London – October, 1324

BY SUMMER'S END, I left Langley with my children and household and
returned to the Tower of London. At the king's summons, Lord Edward
sat at his father's side for the remainder of parliament. It was not an
unusual request for the king to expect his heir to attend, given his thirteen
years, but every parting from any of my children filled me with terror, for
I always feared that I might never see them again.

After supper one evening, Ella and I strolled through the cook's herb
gardens near the kitchen. Clouds had loomed above all day, but never
delivered on their threat. The damp air carried the first distinct chill of
autumn. Ella tugged me along the paths, stopping to smell every herb and
ask its name. For her it was the current fascination, but next week she
would be in the stables and the week after that in the kennels, pestering
the grooms or the kennel keeper for each animal's name and what it had
eaten that day.

"Fennel," I said, as she poked a finger at its feathery leaves.

"That one? And that one? What is that?" She gestured so rapidly I
could barely follow her.

"Lavender. Sage. Borage, I think."

"That one?"

"I don't know, dear. You must ask the cook the next time you are in
the kitchen." The cook, however, was no longer Mathilda's husband,
Dicken. While awaiting his trial in the dungeons after Mortimer's escape
last year, Dicken had taken suddenly and violently ill. The guards claimed
the food had been bad—rank lamb stew left on the table too long before
being scooped up and sent off to feed the prisoners. But no one else had
gotten sick from it. Most likely, Dicken had been poisoned by someone
who feared he might talk. Mathilda, whom I later learned possessed an
endless wealth of knowledge about the properties of herbs, had been mys-
teriously snatched away one night. Perhaps she had been the one who had
drugged the drink? Little matter and better I did not know.

"They are all for eating?"

"Some are for strewing on the floors, so we cannot smell the garde-robe."

She wrinkled her nose at that. Then, distracted once again by the tidy rows of plants at her feet, she stripped some of the faded lavender from its stem to inhale. A smile opened up her face and she giggled. But it was not the lavender that tickled her nose in pleasure. She waved and I turned to look behind me.

"Edmund?" I said, not expecting to see the Earl of Kent in England again so soon.

He rushed at me with such suddenness that as Ella scurried forth to greet her uncle, I grabbed her hand and pulled her to me. She churned her neck to look up at me in confusion.

Breathless, Kent dropped to his knees before me. "Sister, there is something I must tell you."

"Should you not be in Westminster, Edmund? Or have you only now arrived?"

"I was there." He looked up at me with those same pale eyes as Edward's, only his were not so cold and harsh. "I came straightaway, to tell you, so you would have time to prepare. To get away."

"Away? Edmund, what do you mean? Has this something to do with why I was told to come here?"

"Everything, Isabella." Standing, he cast a glance over each shoulder and lowered his voice. His fingers twitched. "Men-at-arms will arrive here in the morning—Despenser's men. Your French servants, all of them, are to be banished. At least that was the talk when I slipped away, which was not easily done. Oh, Edward had much to say. He gave me quite a scathing lecture about my failures—as if he could do any better." He turned his face aside, fighting a snarl. "He hasn't, you know. Not once. Not really. The French come at you in deep columns, and as wide as the horizon, with row upon row of mounted knights in their shining armor. I was hardly sent with enough soldiers to take on the likes of that . . . or enough money to pay for what I did have. How was I supposed to—"

"Edmund, they will discover your absence soon. They will wonder

163

why you are gone and when they find out . . . What will you tell them?"

He scoffed nervously. "Nothing. I can be at Kennington Palace by nightfall. I won't run and I *won't* hide. If they wish to hang me for failure, they will find me wherever I go. And when they do, I shall say, truthfully, that I had tired of their persecution."

So, Kent thought his own life forfeit if he offended Despenser and if it was to be then he might as well spare me the same fate.

"Where is my eldest son?" I had no more time for Kent's self-pity, however grateful I may have been to him. I had to think, to act.

"Still with Edward." With a sad tilt of his head, he reached out to touch Ella on the arm, but she yanked it away from him. Her reaction startled him. Suddenly, he grabbed my hand and squeezed it so hard I felt the bones of my fingers crushed against one another. "Isabella, the children . . . they are to be taken from you. Lord Despenser argued before parliament that there was too much danger of spying from the French in our midst. He rallied the barons to agreement, although they did not need much convincing. They all fear Charles' intentions. Fear he will take us to war however he can. That he does not mean to return Gascony and will only make more and more demands of Edward. And before that rumble had died away, someone stood up and cried out that the king's heirs were not safe and that they should be put into English hands so—"

"Meaning out of mine?"

So, it had come to this at last. I marveled that it had taken so long. And all because Hugh Despenser whispered his every direction into Edward's ear. Edward, who could not think for himself. Edward, who neither wished nor cared to be king . . . who should *not* be king.

Kent released my hand. His chin fell to his chest. "I am ashamed to say it, but yes."

I gathered Ella into my arms and lifted her up. She was almost too big for me to hold like this anymore. The scent of lavender drifted on the air as she buried her cheek against my neck.

What does he think I will do to them?

Ella whimpered and wriggled against my ribs, making me realize I was holding her much too tightly. I pressed my cheek against her tangle of hair and stroked her small back.

My oldest son was at his father's side. The request for his attendance at parliament had been nothing more than a ruse. And I had fallen so easily for it, believing the boy would be intermittently learning procedure and battling boredom, while pompous old men droned on like bees hovering about their hive. Being yet a child, he would sit obediently by and say nothing. They would inure him with their own mistrustful thoughts and blind prejudices.

This had gone beyond reason. I had no power to hold over Edward, no force with which to defy anyone. What choice did I have, but to take my children and run?

18

Isabella:

Windsor – October, 1324

A WHITE FOG LAY suspended over the river as my barge sliced its thickness. It was two days past Michaelmas, October now, and the trees clustered along the banks of the Thames had just begun to yellow. I pulled a fur-lined mantle over little Joanna as she lay sleeping, her head in John's lap. Ella, holding my hand, her eyes closed, leaned against me and yawned.

With my three youngest children and Ida, I had left London by barge during the night. We slipped past Westminster where Despenser had been conducting his own parliament, past Sheen and Kingston, until at last Windsor appeared around a bend, rising above the mist hugging the river-banks like Mt. Olympus above the clouds of heaven. As I gazed up through the curling fog at a high window in the Round Tower, I thought I saw a figure looking out from there. But it was far away and the fog had thickened. By the time we broke through the mist near the bank and I could see more clearly, there was nothing there.

166

Beneath the feathery, drooping branches of a giant willow, the children and I left the barge and climbed into a carriage that had been awaiting our arrival for the short ride from the river to the castle. As nervous as a goose with her goslings, Ida unfastened the curtain ties at either end of the carriage to conceal us. I had brought along but four of my personal guards. Too large a party would only draw more attention. The rest had been sent late yesterday to accompany my French damsels, who were given no time to gather their belongings or say farewells. They were to meet me at Windsor and from there we would go north, or south or west, somewhere other than London, although how far or to where I did not yet know. Somehow I would get word to Charles, find a ship, and leave England, keeping my children and friends with me.

Joanna slept soundly in Ida's lap, while Ella and John clambered to the front and peeked out between the curtains. The houses along the road that wound up toward the castle were too familiar to invite my curiosity. I sought out a cushion toward the middle of the carriage, propped it against the side and leaned back. Since leaving London, I had not slept at all and could not keep my eyes open—not even when the carriage paused before passing through the main gate. Soon, it lurched forward again, the wheels rumbling noisily over the cobbled path along the perimeter of the lower ward.

Strong midmorning light invaded the musty confines of the carriage as little Ella parted the curtains. I peeked through my eyelashes to see John leaning inquisitively forward for a look. But as he pressed his full weight into his sister's shoulder for a better view, Ella mewled like a crushed kitten. Her whine, however, was drowned out by shouts from outside.

"Stop there!" someone bellowed from in front of us. A coarse reply came from my guards riding alongside.

The rumble of men's voices. The creak of weapons being drawn. The clatter of hooves. Horses snorting.

We slammed to a halt. John threw himself backward and cringed in the corner atop a scattered heap of cushions. "They're here," he whimpered. "*He* is here. *Motherrr?*"

The sounds—gruff words hurled back and forth, a truncated rumble of defiance, somewhere a scuffle, a single clang, a muffled thud—they all came one after another so quickly it was impossible to tell what was going on. Finally, there was an extended silence. A silence interrupted only by my own heartbeat and the rapid, indrawn breaths of Ella as she grappled at her brother's sleeve and buried her face in the cushions.

"Ida, Ida," I whispered, grabbing her knee, "look. Tell me who it is." My other hand crept up to cover my heart. *Do not say it is Despenser. Do not.*

Gently, she nudged Joanna from her lap, but she had not even stood to look out when a voice greeted us with the chill of January hoarfrost.

"Ah, Queen Isabella, welcome," Hugh Despenser called out. He tossed one of the rear curtains up over the covering's frame and climbed inside. Upon seeing the three youngest children within, his lips spread into a wicked smirk of triumph. Then he stuck his hand out for me to take. "Please, let me help you."

John snarled like a cornered dog, but Despenser gave him no regard. Despenser was staring at me, commanding me almost, with those ghostly pale eyes of his.

"Why are you here?" I demanded. "Parliament is still—"

"Still shouting back and forth, I would imagine. When I left they were squabbling over the building of ships—or perhaps it was bridges. I don't know. A dreadful bore. Anyway, my business there was done. I always make certain it is addressed first. Last night, when it was learned you left London of a sudden, the king requested I find you. It wasn't difficult. Barges move so slowly. And one seldom sees one so richly decorated as yours on the Thames. Besides, there are only so many places along the river fit for a queen. Once we found your French servants, I knew you would be along shortly. The king will be pleased to know you are all fine."

Ella scooted to me and tucked herself beneath my arm. I stared at Despenser's outstretched hand and tilted my head back to look down my nose at him. "I would have sent word. It has not been my custom to seek my husband's permission every time I wish to move about."

"Naturally." He cocked his head to one side. "But then, with the situation in Gascony, these are not ordinary times. The whereabouts of his children are highly important. So you can understand why the king . . . shall we say, why the king was overcome with consternation when he arrived at the Tower last night to find them gone?"

This was not right. In fact, it was terribly wrong. Why had my personal guards not been able to stop him, or at the least warn us? When Ella retreated again to the front of the carriage and peeled back a corner of the curtain, the answer was there in the ward—all fifty of them. Despenser's guards outnumbered my own more than ten to one. They stood with swords drawn, facing my guards down, who by then had been ordered down from their mounts, herded into a clump and forced to their knees. My men had not bothered to unsheathe their own blades, for on the walls above archers stood poised with their arrows nocked and ready.

"What is this?" I asked. This could not be happening. Not now. Not here. Had Kent somehow led them here? Or prompted me to flee in order to give Despenser cause to apprehend me and charge me with some crime against the king? All I could think of was to shout out at the driver to take us away, anywhere, quickly, but I was not even sure if he was still there. Even if he was, there would be an arrow aimed at his head.

Despenser's gloating grin twisted into a sneer. He must have sensed the scream of terror rising in my throat, for he stepped further into the carriage and stuck his hand in my face, wiggling his fingers. "Do come out, my lady. Surely you are tired from your nightlong journey?"

"I'll go nowhere with you, Lord Despenser."

"Of course not." He drew his hand back, smug. "And I have no plans to take you anywhere, personally. You see, I did not come for you . . . although, you *will* be sent back to London." He swooped across Ida's torso and snatched up groggy little Joanna. She flopped in his grasp like a limp kitten as he went to the back and leapt down.

A scream tore from my chest. I lunged at him, my fingers instinctively curled like claws. Joanna startled and awoke with a jerk. My nails slashed at Despenser's bare cheek. He plowed his elbow into my breastbone and I felt the air whoosh from my lungs. I reeled back against the seat cushion. As I gulped for breath, Ella cried out. She flailed her hands wildly as a man-at-arms wearing the Gloucester livery yanked her out the front of the carriage. In between curses, Ida hammered punches at the soldier, but her gnarled old fists tapped fecklessly against his rings of mail. He laughed at the old woman for her efforts, tossed Ella to a waiting pair of hands and then dove back inside to go after John.

But John was not so easy a target. He growled as the soldier came at him and bared his small teeth like a wolf cub. "Don't touch me! Don't touch me, you pig turd!"

As the soldier reached in to take John by the shoulders, John whipped his head sideways and bit down hard on the soldier's hand. The soldier howled hellishly.

"I am the king's son! You will not touch me!"

The soldier lifted his other hand and slapped John hard across the face. A bright purple-red mark blotched John's cheek. Instead of fighting his attacker, my son now fought tears. I kicked at the soldier's legs to divert his attention, but they were like the tree trunks of a century-old oak. Like Ida's punches, which she had since given up on and resorted to hysterical cries for help, my assault proved futile. He grabbed John by the front of his shirt and dragged him out.

I bolted after him, but just as I reached the front, someone slammed an elbow into my ribs, knocking the air from my chest. Slumping back against Ida, I gasped for breath. Outside, to the front of the carriage, there was a grunt and a thump. Before I could recover, the carriage jerked forward several feet, and then abruptly skidded to a halt again. Pain throbbing in my chest, I scrambled to the front, prepared to dive through to rescue my children. But as I pulled back on the curtain, a shadow fell across my view. Instinctively, I pulled back, my hand still holding the edge of the curtain. My driver's body lay in a heap on the ground, a gash in his throat leaking blood into the cracks between the stones.

Beyond the lifeless form, Despenser stood on the lawn of the lower ward, gloating, still holding Joanna in his arms. The shrillness of her crying annoyed him, but he would not give her up—not while I was near. He had never cared for children, not even his own.

"Why are you doing this? Why?!" I screamed at him.

"Why?" he echoed mockingly. "Why to keep them safe, my lady."

"Where are you taking them?"

The slash of his mouth tilted into a smirk again. "You need not worry. They will be well cared for."

He rolled his eyes as Joanna pattered at his chest with her tiny, balled fists and called out for me. Then he gave an order to the new driver. "Back to London straightaway. Do not stop until you arrive at the Tower. The king wishes to speak with her."

The carriage lumbered around in a wide arc to start back and half of Despenser's mounted guard encircled us, firm in their orders. A pair of riders swung close to the front and two more came to the rear. The mailed soldier nearest me flicked a fly from the rim of his shield, strapped to his forearm. Like the others, he also wore his helmet, as if they had expected more of a fight. He cleared his throat, swished the phlegm around his mouth and spat a great glob squarely in the middle of the curtain.

"Stay in there till you're told to come out," he warned.

With a terrible jolt that hurled my stomach into my throat, the carriage surged forward. The new driver did not know the horses, nor did he care to make this a comfortable ride for me. I was not about to give my surly guardian a reason to batter the life out of me, but I could at least learn a thing or two from him.

"Why?" I queried. "Have you orders to take my life if I resist?"

The only answer he gave was a throaty snort. Then he wiped at his mouth with the back of his hairy hand and fixed his gaze on the road ahead. We rumbled back beneath the raised portcullis of the same gatehouse through which we had arrived only a short while before, unsuspecting. The morning mist had broken, leaving only droplets of chilly dew on the blades of grass alongside the road paralleling the Thames.

I was too stunned to wallow in tears. I had known this day would come. I had known, known they would take the children from me when all other recourse had been exhausted. Edward would never have done these things without Despenser beside him, telling him what to do.

Ida reached across the space between the seats and tried to soothe me. Her knuckles were bleeding. "He'll do no harm to them. He would not dare."

My fingernails pricked the flesh of my palms. I opened my hands to see four crimson half-moons in each one. "Ida?" I said, looking up. "Patrice, Juliana, Marie . . . where are they? They were supposed to meet us at Windsor."

Despenser had not followed my barge. He had followed my women to Windsor. Or perhaps intercepted them before they ever got there at all.

In the span of a day, my world had shrunk to only Ida. Soon, I would sit before Edward, his judgment of me already tainted by the poison of Despenser's forked tongue.

My marriage to Edward had been intended to keep the peace between France and England. Since the very day my father had told me of it, I had accepted my role with pride and honor, later giving more of myself than Edward could ever return, always fixing the pacts and relationships he had broken without him ever acknowledging it, sometimes without him knowing. Instead, our union had pre-ordained me to this fate: an enemy by birth.

I crumpled against the side of the carriage and covered my face with my hands. Soon, they were drenched with my tears.

No, no, no, no . . . Edward would rather squander his days away hunting or quaffing ale with mummers and minstrels. Hugh . . . Hugh Despenser . . . he has done this.

Despenser ripped my children from my arms. Despenser took them away.

19

Isabella:

Tower of London – October, 1324

I DA AND I WERE given nothing to eat or drink that day except for a nearly empty flask of water, tasting of old leather, a bruised pear and a fist-sized hunk of moldy cheese when we made a short stop in sight of Westminster. I feared we might be headed there, that I would be brought before parliament on some fraudulent charge, but it was only long enough to water the horses and then we were off again toward London. I nibbled at the cheese, then gave it to Ida, who stuffed it behind a cushion. She held my hand all the way and said not a word. The fear was plain on her face, as it must have been on mine, although neither of us spoke of it.

We arrived late at night at the Tower of London. The rear curtain was flung open. I stepped out and before I could turn to wait for Ida, the horses were whipped forward, leaving me alone in darkness. My legs trembling with exhaustion, I was escorted by a mob of brutish guards, their countenances as grim as any executioner's, to the king's apartments directly above the watergate in St. Thomas's Tower.

They prodded me to the center of the room. Behind me, a hundred candles lined a long wall of windows overlooking the Thames. It felt as though I had walked into my own death chamber and at any moment a priest would float forward to utter last rites. If not for the boom of the door as the guards left, I would not have noticed them going, for all my attention was drawn to the end of the room.

I stood before my judge.

On a low dais at the end of the room where he usually gave audiences, Edward sat slumped in his tall throne. His sigh was as loud as the crashing of ocean waves upon a rocky shore.

At the king's right, on a similar, but smaller throne, sat our eldest son—Young Edward. He fidgeted, his mouth sunken in a frown, as if he no more wanted to be there than I did. No one could ever have questioned who his sire was, so striking was his resemblance to his father. But there the similarities ended.

I swayed on my feet. It must have been after midnight by then. The sun had disappeared many hours ago while I was still on the road, shut up in my carriage like a caged chicken headed to the butcher's. Edward, though, had apparently been waiting up for my return, expecting me.

On the far end of the dais sat a blind harpist, his voice hauntingly beautiful. Einion, he was called, and although I had often heard him sing, I had never heard him speak. It was as if he could not form words without music.

The Welsh harpist plucked sadly at the strings of his hand-carved instrument and sang of two lovers torn apart by their feuding fathers, only to have the young woman escape her prison and find her lover had killed himself out of hopelessness. Edward was adrift in melancholy. He liked such tales—those that ended miserably. I glanced around the room, counting candles, waiting for him to blame, accuse or interrogate me. But when the ballad ended, Edward requested a gayer tune. The change in music, however, did nothing to alter his mood.

I could tell from the way Young Edward barely held my gaze that there was confusion roiling around in his head. The last time my son and I had been reunited, not two weeks ago, he had run to my embrace and bowed his head for a kiss. Now he sat there aloof, immured by some invisible wall between us, and I wondered what lies his father might have fed to him in my absence.

At the king's left shoulder stood Walter Stapledon, the Bishop of Exeter. His rigid, blanched form resembled a statue chiseled onto the façade of a marble column. Of all England's prelates, I liked him least.

"Dear, dear Isabella." Edward clicked his rings on the arm of his chair, his voice patronizing. He yawned, showing the cavernous back of his throat, and rubbed at reddened eyes. Then he reached for his goblet, took a long sip and peered at me over the brim. By the slur of his speech, he had staved off boredom by emptying several pitchers of wine. "I return here after an arduous session at Westminster, wanting to enjoy my family, and I find you nowhere. Gone. My children vanished without a word. How utterly upsetting. And disappointing. But then, you have often disappointed me. I expect it."

He leaned forward from his velvet-padded chair, elbows on his knees, the empty goblet dangling sideways from his hand. "*What* were you thinking?"

There was little point in answering his question, so I ignored it. He would tell me anyway. Along the length of the wall behind him, a painting of a hunting scene showed three men in pursuit of a stag. Edward had commissioned the painting. The hunter poised for the kill was supposed to be Edward himself, but it bore only a faint likeness to him, being much more muscular. The second was clearly his old favorite Piers, although Edward claimed it to be one of his brothers, and the third was his nephew Gilbert de Clare, who was killed at Bannockburn.

Edward leaned back in his chair and cast his eyes toward the ceiling. The long, twig-like fingers of one hand caressed the indent of his temple. There was an ethereal sort of beauty in his delicate look and he wore a king's clothes like the adornment they were meant to be, in luminous colors that drew attention to his ashen hair and translucent eyes. But in his finery, he also gave the impression of something frail and defenseless:

the fawn needing its spots and tall grass for protection.

"Why must your brother complicate matters?" Edward's face went taut with distress. "He thinks I can run to him whenever he beckons—as if I had nothing better to do? I am the King of England. I grovel to no one. Besides, the bastard knows precisely what will happen if I leave my kingdom to kiss the hem of his robes."

Young Edward stared expressionless at his hands, pressed flat in his lap. Something had transpired between him and his father. But unlike the father, the son had learned to master his emotions, to keep his outbursts private and his troubles subdued.

"What will happen, Edward?" I said in a toneless voice. The ride from Windsor had afforded me time to think. I did not want him to read anything into my words, although doubtless he would anyway.

He kept his chin tilted up. His gaze was accusing. "You know what will happen. The moment I set foot on French soil and take the road to Paris, assassins will slip a knife into Hugh's chest."

"Then why not take Lord Despenser with you?" A stupid question, but he expected it of me. Edward more than needed him; he could not exist without him.

Edward, however, did not answer. Bishop Stapledon did.

"The king believes both their lives would be in danger, if either were to go to France."

I gave the bishop a look of defiance. "Charles would never order the taking of a life."

"Mortimer would," the king mumbled.

"You know this as fact?" I probed.

"Oh, I do." Edward lifted his goblet to his mouth, then paused, realizing it was empty, and stared into it dreamily. "You will fix this for me, Isabella. You will make amends with Charles. Write to him. Tell him . . . tell him there are rumors of rebellion at home. That my life is in danger. The children's, as well. That we have to keep them in hiding and they must be closely guarded."

I nearly bit through my own tongue at the lie. My fingernails sliced at my palms. This was more than Despenser plying for power and Edward being duped by his charm. This was Edward choosing to give him all. For so long I had seen Edward as some wretched, pining creature, gullible enough to yield to whoever flattered him and made him feel needed. Now I could see that he was weak because it was easier for him. He could not make a decision for fear of being wrong. So he would let Despenser do it all and then he would defend him to his dying breath. If Hugh Despenser stole the sun from the sky and proclaimed it was still day, Edward would concur, despite the darkness.

The king let his chair engulf him. He closed his eyes, sighing wearily, and muttered, "Your brother clutches a traitor to his breast. I cannot go to France while that slime-tongued Mortimer roams freely there."

I played the innocent. "Charles is not in league with Mortimer. There is too much at stake between England and France to—"

"Mother of God, woman!" He rolled his eyes at me like an impertinent child. "Do you think me that stupid? Of course he would not openly declare him an ally, or even give the appearance of it. He pretends that Mortimer is nowhere on the continent, when it is well known that the snake was seen slithering about your brother's court in Paris." Edward leaned to one side of his chair, smirking with some inner, amusing secret. "Come, wife, tell me what you know of this."

"Less than you, I would say. I have heard nothing more than that Mortimer escaped and was last heard to be in Picardy. Do you think I employ spies across the continent? You know as much of this as I do." What I did know I had learned from my damsels. Mere gossip. Charles had guarded me from the real details for a purpose such as this. Still, I would always harbor the fear that somehow my duplicity, however small, would be discovered. Perhaps I felt guilt not so much for what I had already done, but for what I might do, if driven to it.

At last Young Edward met my gaze and held it. Whether he believed me or not, I could not tell, but in his eyes there was the soft look of fondness. A slight tilt of his head and barely parted lips said that he understood that his father had pressed a knife to my throat.

I spoke to my son. "I know nothing of Mortimer being in Paris, if he was ever even there, or what Charles would want with him." Then I directed my words to the king. "But if you believe these rumors, I will write to Charles and advise him against such associations."

"Yes. Tell him to keep the traitor far away." Satisfied, Edward glanced over his shoulder at Stapledon, smiled nervously and then said to me, "And you will tell him the rest—why it is impossible for me to leave England now?"

I nodded.

"Ah, I knew you would. I will make an obedient wife of you yet."

How have I not been obedient? I dug my fingernails into my palms to silence my thoughts, lest I speak them.

I would be compliant, but only to a point. I could not let him believe that I would give up everything out of fear of him. "First though, you will let me go to my children and allow my servants to return to me. If you prefer me close by, Windsor is agreeable."

It was a step too far.

All I saw of him when he propelled himself from his throne were the whites of his eyes blazing yellow in the half-light. Every cord in his neck was stretched taut against the delicate skin of his neck like arrow strings stretched for the pull. His hands shot toward me. I stumbled backward, expecting him to grab me by the throat and squeeze until the last breath of life died in my chest. I should have screamed out and fought back, but like cornered quarry, I threw my arms over my face and quivered.

Moments passed. His hands never touched me. I heard only the broken rasping of his breathing. Slowly, I dropped my forearm to look. He was still standing there—his hands outstretched in a grasping gesture, his jaw jerking with unspoken oaths.

"You will do as I say!" he finally screamed at me.

His own rage seemed to have frightened him. His hands drifted downward, his mouth went slack. Edward was always the sheep, never the wolf.

"When I believe that you are as loyal and innocent as you espouse, then Is-s-sabella," he hissed, "*then* I will let you see the children, but only when and where I say. As for your pilfering, spying French rats, they are already on their way to France. Back to the ungodly shithole they came from. Where they belong. Out of my land."

I saw him for the first time then as he truly was. Not what I wanted him to be, nor believed he could be with me at his side. He was too cowardly to be a tyrant, too arrogant to admit he had not the courage or intelligence to make his own decisions. Strangely, I pitied him. But also, I feared him, for one who is so desperate for the approval of another will do anything to fill that need. He would find a way, any way, to be rid of me. Edward and I would never again be as husband and wife. We had long ago ceased to be, long before I had accepted the fact. But more than having ruined our marriage, Hugh Despenser needed to be disposed of for the good of all England. However, I was also aware that removing Despenser from Edward's side might abate England's woes only temporarily—until the next favorite-to-be cast himself to bathe in the rippling pool of Edward's tears.

Certain my life was already forfeit, that tomorrow would find me kneeling by the block, my hair shorn close to give the executioner's axe a clean neck, I lashed out in a fit of bravery born only out of desperation. "Then you will lose Gascony, Aquitaine, the Agenais . . ."

He flashed a sneer at me, and then slunk back to his chair. His head sagged between his narrow shoulders. Gradually, the slant of his lips lifted into another prancing smirk. "I may have already. But you will lose your children. Do as I say and you shall have them back. In time, I may be so kind as to return your lands, too. But my trust is no longer so easily given. Proof of your loyalty will be a long while coming, my unfaithful queen."

And proof of your humanity, Edward, will be never. The devil has possessed you, enslaved you with lust.

I turned my head aside and closed my eyes. The dulcet notes from Einion's harp encircled my numbed head, taunting me with dreams of sleep. I had been nearly two days without rest, snatching only minutes at distant intervals on the first leg of this awful journey from the Tower to

Windsor and none at all on the way back here. Exhaustion overcame me. I could stand no longer. I folded my hands together and sank to the floor.

Let him think I am complacent and fearful of him. Let him. I will find a way to overcome this.

Edward slumped heavily, finished with me, depleted in his triumph. I expected to be escorted away then, but through the lacework of my eyelashes I saw Bishop Stapledon stoop before Edward. On the back of his chasuble, embroidered in heavy gold thread, was Christ on the Crucifix. He whispered long to the king. Edward's reply came at first as a growl and then faded to an infantile mewl. His head swiveled back and forth in denial, but the bishop kept nodding and finally placed a firm hand upon the king's shoulder.

I overheard Stapledon say, "Pope John wishes to free you of your troubles."

"It is surrender," Edward grumbled.

Stapledon sighed, straightened himself, hands locked behind his back, and reasoned, "It is compromise. A way of keeping what is yours."

I braved a look at my son. His eyelids fluttered as he tried to keep them open.

Beside him, Edward writhed in his chair and kneaded at his thighs as if he were in bodily agony. "Tell her then," he conceded with a scowl.

As Bishop Stapledon turned toward me, I could see the high forehead beneath his tall miter, revealing a balding pate. "The Pope suggests that you might be helpful in negotiating terms of peace with your brother King Charles."

Charles! Charles, my hope!

He must have arranged this by communicating with the Pope on my behalf. Could it be? Yes, yes, it made some sense. Still, there had to be some trick to this, some cost to me.

I clenched my hands. "How am I to do that when I have not even the freedom to travel so far as Windsor?"

Stapledon sniffed at my insolence. "It would mean, yes, that you would need to journey to France. You would return to England as soon as the terms for a truce are arrived at."

This had everything to do with the abduction of my children—to ensure my cooperation. If I had any thoughts of fleeing England altogether, my return would be guaranteed so long as Edward hoarded my children. I had more to lose if England went to war with France than Edward did.

"You will go then?" Edward prompted in agitation. "But not immediately, mind you. There are details to work over."

I could not think fast enough. Was he *asking* me? Why not just order me? Dangle my children before me? What if I refused? I tested him.

"I don't know. I . . . I would not know how to negotiate something as critical as a truce."

Yes, let him think I have no confidence in the matter, that he is cleverer than me and I am nothing but the doting mother and obedient wife, desperate for his guidance and approval.

Stapledon replied, indicating they had already discussed this privately, "You will be informed of your role."

Told what to say and do, more likely, I thought. "But how could I possibly be of help? Why send me? Why not another? Perhaps you, your grace," I said, indicating the bishop, "would better serve? Or one of your brothers, dear husband?" I paused there to remind them of the Earl of Kent's debacle.

Edward slapped the arm of his chair. "Listen, wife! Because the Pope has bloody appointed you—that is why. I suppose he thinks your brother would be more amenable to your sniveling, accursed female presence than that of a true Englishman."

"But . . . you will come later? *I* cannot pay homage to Charles on your behalf, my lord," I said in feigned innocence. "Perhaps I do not understand the situation fully, but is that not the root of the problem?"

As if my words had scoured a festering wound with salt and vinegar, Edward flung his goblet sideways. It clattered across the floor and skidded to a halt at his bard's sandaled feet. "Damn you, man! Do you not know anything more pleasant to the ears? Next time I shall call on my kennel

181

keeper to play his fiddle. The dogs will join him in a chorus more uplifting than anything I have yet to hear from you. Now get out of here before I strangle you with your own strings!"

Einion, accustomed to Edward's shifting moods, gave a subtle bow, and tucked his instrument gently beneath his arm. Then, he felt his way along the wall until he reached the door and left.

The bishop cleared his throat. "That is a . . . a matter we have not yet resolved. There are many complexities."

Meaning Edward would never leave his dear Hugh for fear of losing him to assassins.

I glanced at my son, who looked away the moment his eyes met mine.

In the span of a day, I had been robbed of my worldly possessions, my freedom, the friends of my childhood and my children. A princess of France and Queen of England and I had nothing left—nothing but the thinnest thread of hope that somehow, by God's favor or some miracle of circumstances . . . somehow, with the help of others, I would overcome this.

20

Isabella:

Tower of London — 1324-25

THAT WINTER, IDA RETURNED to my service, but I heard nothing of Patrice, Juliana or Marie. I slept away much of the daylight hours alone in my bedchamber in the Tower of London and come nightfall, plagued by headaches, sleep eluded me. From my window, I watched clouds of thickest gray banish the sun. There was no snow that winter, only rain. A persistent, miserable rain that turned the streets of London into rivers and drove its dampness deep into every stone of every building. The roof of the Tower leaked, the cellar flooded, the hinges on the doors rusted. In his avarice, Despenser had so depleted Edward's funds there was nothing to spare for simple repairs.

For six months I waited, while letters delicately inked with diplomacy traveled from London to Paris and back again. The only letters I sent to Charles were those Edward directed me to write. Their voice was so unlike my own, I had no doubt Charles would deduce their true source.

I hoped that at Christmas the children might return to London, even if only briefly. But my fantasy faded to disillusionment when the day came and I was told they were all at Kenilworth with their father. I was not permitted to join them.

One January morning, sleet turned to ice and the sun broke through the clouds to set the world aglitter, but the spectacle did nothing to save me from my sorrow. Even as Ida ogled over the dazzling sheen of ice on the garden trees, I could not stir from my bed and hugged a pillow to my chest while a storm of tears streamed down my cheeks. Without my children, there was no wonder in the world. I only wanted time to pass. For something to happen. For an end to my despondency.

In Ida's motherly care, I felt some comfort, but she did not know my heart and thoughts like Patrice did. My days were bleak and hollow. I tried to read, but could not concentrate on the words. I worked at embroidery, but pricked my finger so often I abandoned the task. All of my normal duties had been stripped from me by Hugh Despenser and put into the hands of one of his many clerks. I was, effectively, under arrest, my every movement monitored, my every word inspected, my every habit scrutinized. Every hour of every day was a test of my faith and every endless night a challenge to my courage.

I saw Young Edward only sparingly and then always in the intrusive company of the king. I heard so little regarding the younger children that I lived in perpetual worry. John, I had been told, had been given over to Despenser's wife, Lady Eleanor. I wrote to the children, but the only response I received was one from Lady Monthermer, Despenser's sister, in whose care the girls had been placed at Pleshy. It spoke only of their lessons—not that they had grown, or whether they were well or ill, or if they asked for me.

Daily, I doubted my plans and whether I would ever see my children again.

But they had already been taken from me, as had everything else. If I had to risk surrendering my life to have them back, so be it. Pride inspired what little courage remained in me. Pride became my reason for revenge. Revenge for the confiscation of my dower lands; for the abduction of my children; the lies spread about me; the severance of any bond with my husband; the usurpation of the duties and privileges due a queen . . . revenge for the death of Thomas of Lancaster.

Revenge for my honor.

Finally, I wrote to Charles of my own accord in early February, begging haste, even though I was certain the letter would never reach him.

His reply, however, came within the fortnight.

My Dearest Isabeau,

I am overjoyed to hear that you are to come to France. It has been too long since you and I were in each other's company, although our reunion, I regret, will be more business than pleasure and undoubtedly too short. We have much to accomplish. A truce between France and England has been long in coming and a prolonged peace shall mean lasting prosperity for both our kingdoms.

My prayers for your family and friends. I await your arrival with an anxious heart.

Our Lord bless you,
Charles

I read it until the candlewick was nearly consumed, searching for some further meaning, even though I knew Charles was too shrewd to chance anything. I inspected the seal, imagining Lady Eleanor or Despenser breaking and then repairing it with meticulous skill. But the wax bond had been tight, the paper without tear or crimp.

As the candle flame sputtered and threatened darkness, I folded the letter back up. Even though I had not uncovered any signs of tampering, I was sure Edward already knew its contents. Charles had likely written directly to him at the same time. The moment my brother and I were alone, everything would begin to—

A cold draft rushed over me. Darkness engulfed the room. I thought at first a window had been blown open, but there was no breeze, no chill—only the stillness in which I could hear my own heartbeat . . . and a soft rustle from behind. Slowly, I turned toward the door.

"Who is—"

An arm grabbed me around the waist and yanked me into its deathly hold. Cold steel crushed my throat. Vile breath warmed my ear with words of loathing.

"Do not think," Despenser hissed, "that you will slip away and gain your freedom. I have your children, Isabella. Have them and will keep them for as long as need be. Now swear an oath to me, that you will do nothing so foolish as to put their lives in danger. Swear to me an oath of loyalty."

Arrogant swine. Did he think he could extort oaths of allegiance from me? His own were as flimsy as the parchment in my hands.

Words were trapped behind my tongue and nothing but a croaking sound came out of my mouth. He released just enough pressure from his blade to let me reply.

"Harm them . . ." I said, "and Edward will hang you."

He laughed softly. "No, no, I think not. I am *everything* to him: the earth on which he stands, the light of the sun and the expanse of the sky. Mortimer is the one he hates and fears. Already, two assassins sent for me by Mortimer have been executed. If any harm comes to the king's children, who do you think he will blame? His devoted servant and friend . . . or some cowardly traitor hiding far away?" He gripped my body tightly to his, so that I felt every seam of his clothing, every protruding bone and taut muscle in his body. "Such is my confidence in the king's love for me, that I think, if I wanted to, I could do just about anything—even to you. *Anything.*"

His lips brushed my neck and then I felt the wet tip of his tongue flick at my earlobe. I shuddered in repulsion. Even violating a queen was not beyond him.

"And if I cry out," I said, "what will you do? Kill me?"

"I could. If I wanted to."

"Do it then. They would more than just hang you. They would strip you bare and cut off your head, just like they did to Piers Gaveston. I would trade my life to give the world that gift."

Gradually, he lowered the blade from my throat and loosened his grip on me. "I came to remind you, Isabella, of what could happen if you mis-behave. Do as you have been instructed: make peace, gain back the land that is Edward's and return to England without a day's waste. Swear that you will and everything . . . everything will be fine."

"It is you, Lord Despenser, who ought to swear an oath to me."

He spun me around and ripped the letter possessively from my fin-gers. I could see nothing of him but the faintest outline as he darted to the door.

"Remember," he said, his voice fading with each strike of his feet, "whatever you do there, whomever you talk to . . . we will know."

I knew he was right. But it is easy to forget.

One moment we run from what we detest and perceive to do us harm, as I was doing. At other times, we cling to what we desire and love it as fiercely as if it were our last breath. Then, what we think, what we know . . . those things change. They change us, as well.

And what we envision that our lives will be—never is.

PART II:

My lord, perceive you how these rebels swell?
Soldiers, good hearts, defend your sovereign's right,
For now, even now, we march to make them stop.

Edward II,
from Christopher Marlowe's *Edward II*

21

Isabella:

Dover — March, 1325

AT DOVER, I SWORE my loyalty to my husband, promised a swift resolution and then clung to the railing, waving a kerchief, as the ship pulled away from shore on that chilly but bright March morning.

Before then, the sea had always been my tormentor, delivering me first to an ignominious fate—my new life with Edward after our marriage at Boulogne—and then further flaunting its powers when I was nearly drowned while fleeing Tynemouth. But on that day, I embraced a new love of the sea: the endless water, the froth of broken waves upon the shore, even the creak and moan of the ship's hull and the snapping of its sails.

The sun climbed higher, its light breaking from above through scattered clouds of fleece-white. I stayed on the deck, the salt air whipping through my hair like the breath of newfound freedom, the gentle heave of the waves lifting me up along with my heart. I was so enthralled with the sight of the gigantic cliffs diminishing until they were nothing but a thin

191

white line on the horizon that Stapledon's unctuous voice startled me.

"This must be difficult for you, my lady," the bishop said. Beneath his chasuble, his hands were clasped together before him. With his gaunt cheekbones and those frightful bulging eyes that followed me everywhere, he reminded me of the elongated carvings of martyred saints which flanked the transept walls of Chartres. As a child, I had attended Mass at Chartres often with my parents, but I had always left there more in fear of those skeletal saints than inspired by them. Saintliness, I had concluded, must mean starvation and misery. Stapledon always bore that same look of perpetual suffering for his faith.

"What do you mean?" I asked, half-hoping to provoke an argument with him.

A grim smile broke over his mouth like a jagged crack through stone. "Leaving your children so far behind. But, God willing, it will not take us long to settle matters with France. He is on our side."

"On England's side, you mean? Then why did God not give the Earl of Kent victory when Philip of Valois pursued him to La Réole and laid siege?" The reason, I already knew, was because Despenser had not allotted enough money for relief troops. I could hardly see where God would favor Edward's childish obstinacy and Despenser's negligence.

"Your grace," I went on, "if Edward had come to pay homage himself, as he once promised King Charles he would, then I would not have been forced to accept this task. I would never have left my children had it not been thrust upon me."

"Kings cannot abandon their kingdoms at will."

"Richard the Lion-Heart did."

"He did so in the name of God." The reddish fringe of Stapledon's hair had been trimmed so short the blustery sea wind did not stir it at all. Only the rippling of the folds of his vestments betrayed he was not the statue of a suffering saint. "But he was also taken prisoner and held for ransom, during which time Prince John tried to steal his brother's kingdom. Evil is everywhere. It surrounds us even now." His mouth tilted into a smirking slash of condescension.

He reeked of holy superiority. I made the sign of the cross over my breast. "Have we a sinner among us, your grace? Where?"

"It was an observation of mankind, my lady. I did not intend to accuse anyone."

I exhaled with a loud puff. "Ah, I feared, for a moment there was a murderer aboard. But tell me—what does keep the king at home? Is there a plot to usurp the throne from Edward? Please, if there is I—"

"I meant, my queen, that too much can go awry while a king is abroad. My lord king has his own reasons for remaining in England."

Many and good ones, I mused to myself. *His crown, for one. Despenser's life for another.*

And I . . . I have my reasons for leaving England.

If only to be rid of him, I thanked the bishop and returned to the railing. Impatient, I stared toward the southeast, waiting for France to rise magically out of the water, wishing the sight of it might erase the burden of guilt I now bore, even as I rejoiced in the breaking of my shackles. Ida and Patrice would have been a comfort, but instead of the many friends who had once been my solace, I was now surrounded by Edward's spies: Lord Cromwell, who placed himself an inch from me every moment that Stapledon was not keeping guard; William Boudon, whose paramount duty was to stingily apportion money for the maintenance of my retinue; and two highborn ladies, Alicia and Joanna—one a widowed countess and the other a cousin of Edward's. The knights that accompanied us were not of my own guard, but those who owed their station to Edward's favor. A small army of servants, most of their faces unfamiliar, also surrounded me. I would not be able to squander a single penny, sneeze or even scratch at my head without someone conveying the details of my every expenditure, the hourly state of my health and the location of my every itch back to Edward.

Ever since I had been taken at Windsor, they were always there around me. Always watching. Listening. Whispering to one another.

"A fair afternoon, is it not, m'lady?" Cromwell inquired. Beside him, a green-faced Boudon clamped both hands on the rail and swayed.

193

"For seagulls, yes," I replied, precisely as Boudon vomited into the sea. I moved further away to avoid the stink of Boudon's weak stomach and the scrutiny of Cromwell. Stapledon, apparently, had gone below deck and I found a small breath of relief in his temporary disappearance.

The clouds were gathering to the east in dark, shifting drifts of purple and red. I looked there, toward the horizon, and saw . . . France.

My home. And somewhere there—my hope.

Poissy, March, 1325

A FAVORABLE WIND HAD filled the sails and delivered us swiftly to Wissant on the northern coast of France. With my English entourage, stiff-shouldered and short of conversation as was their usual demeanor, we lodged there overnight and then made the short journey along the coastal road to Boulogne. There, while candle flames swayed in the silver light of evening, I gave copious thanks unto Our Lord for bringing me safely home at last. The altar at which I knelt was that of Our Lady of Boulogne—the very same place where I had traded my girlhood freedom for a wretched life with Edward II of England. On that occasion, it had been filled with the gaily dressed nobility of Christendom in celebration of a new beginning: a union of two great powers, the promise of peace. Now it echoed emptily within, as if this time was neither a beginning nor an end, but simply a pause, a breath before the next great event.

When I emerged from the church, I was not prepared for the warm greeting I received. News of our arrival had spread like water over a burst dam. The citizens of Boulogne poured out into the streets in droves. We stayed on for several days while knights and lords from all around came to join my escort. Finally, we began southward to Poissy, where the talks for peace would begin again.

It began to pour, heavily, hours after we left Boulogne. Although I changed cloaks frequently, the wind drove a damp chill into my bones that I could not shed. I yearned to seek shelter and wait out the weather, but I was so eager to reach Poissy I would have braved ten such storms to get there. We lodged at Montreuil the following night and the rain faded to a fine spit of a mist. I slept deeply, warmed by a crackling fire. But I awoke to another torrent of rain, which followed us all the way to Beauvais. It was then, at last, that the storm broke and a flirting sun appeared between jagged bands of gray-blue. The wind lived only long enough to chase away the dark, wet clouds, then died a thin, whispering death. Everywhere around us, there was birdsong, the bleating of newborn lambs, and the faint gurgle of water seeping into saturated earth.

I could smell the Seine long before it came into sight. It was the smell of mud and mossy rocks at the water's edge and the pungency of new spring growth in broad valleys that by summertime would be lush with grain and pasture.

At Poissy, I saw him waiting on the crest of the arched bridge that spanned the River Seine. Although my heart recognized my only remaining brother, Charles IV, King of France, my eyes gazed upon a stranger, for he looked nothing like how I remembered him. He was strongly built with flared shoulders and sculpted facial features, no longer the tall-thin boy on the cusp of manhood. We were barely more than children when we last embraced—the day he departed London shortly after my arrival in England as a hopeful bride.

He sat astride a snowy stallion, its hide flecked with dried mud and its mane the same pale gold as his hair. The day was barely warm, for it was still early springtime, but the sunlight, so bold it was almost blinding, seemed to emanate as much from him as it did from above. Behind him were hundreds upon hundreds: noblemen and women, soldiers of France, holy men from many lands. Banners of every color fluttered in a capricious breeze. Trumpets called out a greeting. Horses, startled, shook their manes and tossed their tails from side to side.

Where road met bridge, I tumbled less than gracefully from my saddle and ran the half-span of the bridge to my brother, holding my skirts nearly to the top of my shins to gain my full stride. Charles dismounted and held his arms wide, ready. But as I reached him, instead of falling into his welcome embrace, I threw myself to the ground before him and wrapped my arms about his calves, pressing my forehead to his knee.

"Charles!" I cried.

His knees unlocked, as if he thought to stoop down and hold me, but he was too much the king, even with me, to do more than get down from his horse. As I looked up at him, his pale-lashed eyes emanating compassion, he raised me gently and rested his hands upon my shoulders. I thought it was the sun glinting off his ringed fingers or the garnet-encrusted amulet dangling from a chain of gold upon his chest that made me blink uncontrollably, but it was not. Tears of joy and sorrow stung at my eyes. Joy for the love I felt in his presence. Sorrow for all I had suffered since last I saw him.

"My beloved Isabeau," he said softly, brushing the back of his fingers across my moist cheek, "welcome home." He kissed me lightly above each eye, as if to chase away my troubles with his touch. Then he pulled my head to his shoulder and held me.

"Oh, Charles," I breathed, my voice softening. "I know not where to begin. Or even how to say it, but that . . . Oh, I have waited so long to speak with you. They took everything from me. Made a prisoner of me. I could go nowhere. Had nothing . . . nothing."

"I know everything," he whispered above my ear. "So do not worry, Isabeau. You will be avenged. Edward of England will pay, dearly. I shall see to it. Already, you are free. Can you not feel it?"

I could not stop my weeping then, for as soon as I heard the word 'free' I could think of nothing but my children and how I had left them behind to gain that freedom.

As I looked back at where I had left my mount, I saw Cromwell and Boudon, their eyes wide, jaws clenched. Stapledon wedged his horse between theirs, dismounted and hurried anxiously toward me. He scuttled forward, his head bowed only slightly so that his miter did not topple off. "The queen—is she unwell?"

Charles leered at him harshly. The bishop edged backward, uttering an apology.

It was then that I felt the slight hand upon my back and heard the sweet voice familiar to my youth. "My lady, I am here." Patrice embraced me hard.

I held her at arm's length to look upon her. My heart filled with joy. "You look well. You look . . . happy."

"I am now. Half a year it has been. When I heard you were on your way, I could hardly wait to see you again."

"Oh, Patrice. I have missed you so."

In the press of onlookers behind Charles on the bridge, I saw Juliana and Marie peering on tiptoe from between the shoulders of two noblemen, their faces glowing with delight. How frightened I had been for them on the night they were taken away. I knew nothing of how they had been treated or where they had been sent.

Then, Charles swiveled on his heel and, hand held aloft, indicated for his horse to be brought forward. He issued a few curt orders, including the retrieval of my palfrey and one for Patrice. He waited until we were astride our horses to remount his own.

For all the times I had ever seen Edward riding at the head of an army or in procession, never had I seen the same look of nobility that Charles had that day. It is akin to the look that eagles have: a bearing of pride, a smoothness of motion, a certainty in every step or word. I was dazzled by the presence of my own brother, the very boy with whom I had argued and joked and tattled on as a little girl.

He edged forward, waiting for those who had gathered on the bridge in witness of our reunion to part before us. His impressive retinue, assembled in lines ten abreast with banners raised, followed behind.

Bishop Stapledon was left hugging the sidewall of the bridge while the worldly nobility of France and its power in arms passed him by without regard.

22

Isabella:

Poissy — March, 1325

LATE THAT AFTERNOON, WE arrived at the sprawling city of tents that
had sprung up along a ridgeline above the Seine. The French had
claimed the large expanse overlooking the river, leaving the English to
huddle together at the outer edge between the French and a wood tangled
with saplings and thorny brush.

We rode down the main alley of the encampment toward its center as
boisterous shouts greeted my arrival. Mud and manure squelched beneath
our horses' hooves. There, banners bearing golden fleur-de-lis on fields of
blue encircled the meeting pavilion where the peace talks were held. During the day it would have been packed full like a barrel of salted fish, and
doubtless smelling as bad. So many bodies in such a crowded area with
very little fresh water available lent itself to the sacrifice of regular bathing.

Charles raised a hand and the procession lurched to a halt. From his
saddle, he turned toward me. "I should like to invite you to sup with me,
Isabeau. There is so much to talk about: these negotiations that have gone
on for so long, my prospective marriage to the Count of Evreux's daugh-

ter"—his face lifted instantly from a look of consternation to teasing anticipation, then sunk back down to a frown—"matters in England . . ." In the fading lull of his speech, there seemed to be words that for the time being were left unsaid. He drew his shoulders up, donning a more kingly posture, as if he had momentarily forgotten his role. "I regret, however, and sadly, that my evening is full already. The Bishop of Orange arrived this morning from Avignon, just ahead of you, with letters from the Pope. Not one, but several. I find it hard to believe he could have omitted anything in the previous dozen, but I suppose I encouraged him by seeking his advice. Perhaps afterwards, I could call on you and we—"

"Oh Charles," I reached out to take his hand, even though I could barely grasp his fingertips, "you would find me dreadful company if you came then. I've hardly slept since we arrived at Boulogne. It's a marvel I haven't fallen from my saddle. Tomorrow will be a long, long day, I imagine. A quiet evening with my damsels and a full night's rest should renew me."

"Tomorrow, by the river then? We could share a supper, just the two of us."

"I should like that." I asked to be shown to my quarters, a large pavilion next to Charles' overlooking the marshy meadow. My English guardians and attendants were escorted elsewhere, in spite of their protests. They were disgruntled to learn that once in France their leash on me had, in effect, been severed.

My damsels joined me and it was very much like it had been during all our years together in England. We ate well and talked long, but soon Juliana—whose belly was just beginning to swell with evidence of another child on the way—yawned. I urged her to go to her husband and Marie, who had been stifling yawns since before supper, departed with her.

Patrice slumped onto a pile of pillows, draping the back of her hand across her forehead. "He wrote to me, not long ago. Arnaud—he is in Hainault . . . with Sir Roger Mortimer."

The last time I had heard Mortimer's name, Edward had uttered it with great contempt. Why then did the mention of him cause me to hold my breath and my heart to race? "So it was true? Arnaud helped him escape?"

She clenched her hand into a fist and brought it slowly down to her breast. "And you knew of it."

"I knew . . . that Sir Roger would find his way free, yes. But of Arnaud taking part—of that I knew nothing. Not until I saw you that day."

With a hollow laugh, she pushed herself up onto an elbow and jabbed angrily at a plate of dried herring beside her before flicking one onto the ground. "I gave up a child, all because I thought he did not want me."

I wanted to go to her, shake her, and convince her that my involvement had been small, that it certainly had nothing to do with Arnaud's disappearance, but she would not have believed me just then. When she finally spoke again, her voice carried a painful accusation. "You knew. You *knew.* You could have told me where he was going. I could have followed him."

"Patrice, no . . . I could not tell you anything. I knew little. Certainly not where he—where they would be going. Too much was at stake."

"Too much?" Deep furrows of confusion cut across her forehead. She came closer. "Who planned it then? Who planned Sir Roger's escape?"

"Charles."

"*He* plots against Edward?"

"Not directly, no. I asked his help to rid Edward of Despenser. He thinks, perhaps, Mortimer can be of use." I sat down on the woven rug before her and took both her hands in mine. They were stiff, resisting. "You understand then why I could not say anything? One word of it and I would have been accused of treason. Edward does not forgive. He does not know how. Oh Patrice, if I kept things from you, it was because I feared for my life, for my children's future, but there's no danger of that any longer. We are in France now. Safe."

Chin down, she nodded, perhaps beginning to understand, but I could tell it was not easy for her. "You are not going back then—to

England, I mean?"

I shrugged. "Not soon, but eventually. When the time is right. Forgive me, for all I have kept from you. I couldn't risk your life for my own selfish motives."

"But Isabeau," she murmured, touching her forehead to mine, "I would die before I would give up any of our secrets."

"I would never ask that of you, Patrice. Never."

From outside, I heard the clinking of cups, the loud jests, the sonorous rolls of laughter, and the ripple of a slight breeze against the walls of my pavilion. We leaned against one another, head touching head, my arm around her shoulder, comfortable in our silence.

NEAR MIDMORNING THE NEXT day, my dear cousin, Robert of Artois, greeted me outside my pavilion. He had come to escort me, along with an impressive guard of a dozen in royal French livery, to the king's meeting pavilion. Over the last few years Robert had written to me every few months and while our correspondences had been nothing but congenial exchanges, his words were always those of sincere encouragement and his love of life plain. My memories of him from childhood were sparse: he was one cousin among many, but even then he had readily sought me out to share a greeting and kiss me on the cheek. He was three years younger than me and as children I was always taller. But we were long past grown now and it surprised me that I could still look down on the top of his already balding head. As we began our walk to the meeting place, Cromwell and Boudon appeared suddenly from between a row of tents. They had been waiting there for some time, judging by the urgent length of their strides. I shuddered, knowing they had come to counsel me yet again. Robert gave me his arm for comfort.

"There is a speech they have made me rehearse," I told him lowly. "Nothing more than Edward's grievances."

"Worry not," he said, pinching the back of my hand playfully as we walked down the narrow aisles between the tents and straight past my open-mouthed English guardians. "I could beat them back with the flat of my table knife. What? You look at me as if you think I cannot fight. I rode with Philip of Valois, did you know? I tell you, though, I would rather be on the battlefield than closed up in a dark tent hurling words back and forth. If they wanted to bore their enemies into submission, they would have succeeded months ago. Indeed, I would rather scrub the garderobe clean with my fingernails than sit there listening to them another day. But I think, dear cousin, one day with you and they will fall quiet with awe. It is not often that one finds beauty and intelligence in the same body."

Then, as we stopped before the main pavilion, he kissed me lightly on each cheek and stepped back. My unwelcome shadows lurked at a distance.

A pair of French soldiers in blue bowed low and parted the entrance flaps. I was but a step within, Robert close behind, when the flaps dropped shut behind us, sending a whoosh of air past me to ruffle my skirts. A scurry of motion followed, but I could barely see for the dim light. Then shapes formed as my eyes adjusted. All had gone down on bent knee before their chairs. Grumbling, Boudon and Cromwell shuffled in, letting another momentary flood of light inside.

To my left, Charles sat rigidly on a carved throne elevated on a small dais. He wore a pelisse of brightest blue embroidered with fleurs-de-lis in golden thread and lined at the sleeves and collar with ermine. A crown aglitter with jewels sat above his pale brow and as he tilted his head in welcome the sapphire in its center flashed brilliantly. I blinked away my momentary blindness.

I took my seat opposite Charles' and one by one the great lords and bishops there came to bow before me.

My task was, on many levels, futile. I knew so. Even if I could procure peace, it would not last forever. In time, some misunderstanding would be taken as on offense. Some law disregarded, covenants forgotten. Some struggle over power or possessions would break out. There would be threats, denials, pretenses of peace, accords violated and then . . . war.

ISABEAU

Always war.

Men would rather fight with the might of their arms than reason gently with words. They preferred the clang of weapons to the scratching of a quill. The red of blood to the black of ink.

In battle, the end is decisive. Death leaves no question as to who is victorious.

23

Isabella:

Poissy – March, 1325

AFTERWARD, CHARLES AND I strolled out into the late afternoon sun. Between the encampment and the river lay a marshy plain where watchful ewes gathered with bucking spring lambs. At river's edge, budding willows reflected golden in the silty, rain-gorged waters. A shepherd rose groggily from the sea of grass, yawning, while the wiry little gray dog at his knee pricked an ear and sniffed the air.

We walked along the river's edge, the soggy ground of the floodplain making little sucking sounds around us like an infant at its mother's breast, and talked of dearer things: of my children, his betrothed Jeanne, and our long-ago childhoods. I felt at ease with Charles, but I also felt very much like a little girl under the reproachful eye of her father, always being corrected and guided.

"You know that Edward will never leave England?" I took a cup of wine a servant offered to me. A blanket was spread before us and cushions placed on it to sit upon. Servants brought forth supper in covered baskets: stuffed capons, white rolls with butter and an egg custard. "He will not leave *him*."

"I figured that long ago, dear sister." Charles took my hand and lowered me slowly so I would not spill my drink. "That may work to our advantage, I think."

As he peeked in each basket, wrinkling his nose at most of the food, I shared every detail of my past few years, complaining profusely of Edward's neglect and Despenser's cruelty.

"I believe," I told him later, leaning back upon a pile of cushions to gaze up at the sky, "there is something more between them—between Edward and Despenser."

Charles drew in a breath, the beginning of a question framing his lips.

"No," I answered, before he could ask it, "I have no proof of it." I pulled my roll apart and nibbled at it.

"Then, if you are to separate yourself from him, you must have some other justification. The denial of your children is enough. And for another, to cleave the union of man and wife—it need not be a . . ."—his eyebrows drew tightly together— "a 'physical' matter."

"I should like to think that was true, Charles. But in reality, men, kings in particular, are allowed to do as they please and everyone, including the Church, will look the other way."

"And when a woman is unfaithful, yes, she will be found out." His voice took on a bitter edge, as though memories of his first wife Blanche's infidelity must have stirred in him. "Whether you think it fair or not, Isabeau, when women follow their carnal desires with indiscretion, they jeopardize dynasties. Not so for men. But then, we are speaking now of a different kind of 'relationship' than what you are implying between your husband and his pet."

"It is only different in that there will never be bastards born of it. Does that make it any less wrong?"

He dabbed at the corners of his mouth with a linen kerchief. "When we dwell overmuch on our problems, Isabeau, we give up time trying to solve them. You have no proof, no witnesses. You may, however, very well be right about your suspicions. The question then is what are we going to do about it?"

"You will help me?"

"You are here, are you not?"

"What can you tell me of Sir Roger Mortimer?" I was abrupt. I had waited months, years to hear news of Mortimer, to see him, to speak with him again. "Has he been to see you?"

"Patience, my Isabeau. Patience." He raised his goblet to me and smiled. "And trust. I will take care of things."

But I had been patient with Edward, patient enough to shame the most devoted of the saints. Surely, at some point, patience ceased to be a virtue?

For another month the talks floundered. Charles was as stubborn as he was enigmatic. Privately he promised me much, but he would only divulge so much. I only knew that he would not endanger his standing with the papacy for me, at least not publicly. And he would guard his possessions like a famished lion standing over fallen prey.

And if I thought there was any possibility of Young Edward ever being named Charles' heir, it soon became even more remote when I met Charles' betrothed, Jeanne of Evreux. Charles had declared a short recess and together we traveled to the Palace de la Cité in Paris, where I met her.

In looks, Jeanne of Evreux was more child than woman, but very like an angel in her purity of countenance. Her hair was a pale chestnut and pulled back so tightly that it stretched her skin taut across high cheekbones. She was a mere fifteen. Charles was twice as old and at not yet thirty, Jeanne would be his third wife. Blanche, his first wife, had been imprisoned for adultery, although the marriage had not been annulled until ten years later. Charles then took a second wife, Marie, who tragically died in childbirth, as did their infant son, Louis. When my father had the Grand Master of the Templars burned at the stake, many said that a curse had been cast upon the House of Capet which had ruled France for four centuries and that the male line would end with Charles. The ill portent, so far, was holding true, for two older brothers had died before him—and neither of them old.

Despite the premonition of sorrow that I felt for the young girl who was to be Charles' bride, I also hoped the very curse that had condemned my father and brothers might prove to be my son's fortune.

Of my blood and of my body—England and France could become one.

My Very Dear Lord and Husband,

Warmest greetings from Poissy. I have met with much success. King Charles wishes to secure a lasting peace between England and France. Gascony will be returned to you, not immediately as a whole, but rather over a scheduled time. It is a small concession that will end in your favor. While largely amenable, Charles is, however, intractable over the matter of the territory surrounding Agen. He believes that some indemnity is due to him. I have warned him that his greed will only delay the process; but I also advise you, if you should permit me to do so, that some compromise is in order from both sides. A resolution is possible, but it will not happen if neither you nor Charles will give a foot of ground to gain a foot.

Also, the matter of homage remains. If you would journey to France, to Calais or Boulogne perhaps, you would be only briefly away from England. He has not said as much, but I believe Charles would more willingly agree to any demands you have regarding the territories in dispute if you would but come and be done with it.

Daily I pray for the wellbeing and happiness of my children and to see them soon again. Send them my love.

God bless and keep you,
Isabella, Queen of England

I knew, even as the ink bled black from my quill onto the golden parchment, that the mere mention of Edward coming to France—and leaving Hugh Despenser—would inspire him to seek any alternative to that unbearable thought.

24

Isabella:

Vincennes — May, 1325

"HOW SHALL I REPLY?" I asked Charles.

Charles stared out the window of my apartments at Vincennes, watching the gardener delicately snip at budding roses in the garden below. Around us, my damsels were busy putting away the dozen gowns of velvet and taffeta I had rejected before my brother's arrival. I had finally decided on a kirtle of yellow-gold and a cyclas of scarlet silk. Since my recent arrival, Charles had showered me with several gifts: cloaks with silver-gilt knots; pelicons lined in ermine and fox-fur; two cyclases edged in gold; brooches studded with sapphires and rubies; and a chaplet adorned with pearls. I never knew when another gift from him might arrive in a carved box or wrapped in folds of silk.

I waved the letter in front of him. He took it from me and studied it intently, a fine crease momentarily forming above the bridge of his slender nose.

Our Dear Consort,

    You delay too long over too little.
    As it is I who should advise you: Bring this treaty to a swift settlement. Your dalliances have cost us dearly. Our Exchequer is protesting over an extension. Parliament grows unbearably impatient. And I grow weary of excuses. Inform King Charles that we have no intention of bending over any matter, large or small. Generous concessions have already been offered. In order to hasten these mired talks and to counsel you, I am sending John de Stratford, Bishop of Winchester, and my trusted clerk William Airmyn. They have been fully informed of my wishes and my unwillingness to concede any further.
    I cannot, for now, depart from England. To do so would leave the kingdom at the mercy of those who oppose me.

Edwardus Rex,
Kent

"How shall I reply?" I repeated.

"Ah, how?" He folded the letter back up and tapped it against his cupped palm. "I am amused that he questions your competency when he has none himself."

I took the letter from him and gave it into Juliana's care. She took it into my adjoining chambers where I heard the groan of hinges and the closing of a chest lid. Soon, Marie scurried forth and held out before her a large pillow bearing two crowns. I picked the plainer of the two: a silver band bearing gold filigree and a handful of pearls across its front. Marie nodded and went off to the adjoining room in search of hairpins.

Before I could press him with the question yet one more time, Charles wandered onto another topic—that of the two newly arrived envoys from England: Bishop Stratford of Exeter and William Airmyn. Soon, Marie and Juliana returned. Carefully, they set the crown upon my head and pinned it in place.

Charles bent forward and inspected me in all my finery. "Father would be pleased, could he see you now." Then he plucked up a tiny bottle of rose water from a tray filled with more tiny bottles of colored glass. One at a time, he opened them, inhaled and passed judgment on their suitability. "This one. Lavender, I think. Or lilacs, maybe. I can hardly tell. It reminds me of . . . well, shall we say, a particularly delightful encounter?"

I dabbed a few drops on my throat to please him and because it did not matter to me whether I was dripping in roses or merely scrubbed clean.

"But again, Charles—how shall I reply? I refuse to hurry anything simply because Edward commands it. I do wonder at what I have gained so far by being here—except for my own rejuvenation," I added sulkily.

"You are not looking far enough ahead, Isabeau," he chastised. "Come along. We have guests. Important ones, I believe."

Charles gave me his arm. Outside my apartments, a flock of his courtiers parted before us and fell in behind my damsels. We went down two flights of winding stairs and walked a long corridor that passed by a row of tall glass windows, all open. A late spring breeze wafted through, carrying on it the musty smells of wood and earth. Sunlight painted patches of yellow over the bright blue woven carpet under our feet. Beyond Vincennes, I glimpsed the sprawling woodlands where the slightest fluttering of leaves among the rounded treetops stirred the forest to life.

When we came to the broad stairway that parted left and right, where it descended into the great hall, I slowed my steps, stalling. The large gathering behind us stopped at a respectful distance.

Charles traced the outline of his dimpled chin with a finger. "We will give your English king *some* of what he wants, but only a little. Not all. Then it will be done. Yes?"

I raised my eyebrows at him. "What is *some*, dear brother? He wants the Agenais. All of it."

"To train a dog, you have only to wave a piece of meat in front of it.

If the dog is hungry enough, you do not have to feed it. Understand? Therefore, we shall let him believe he has won somehow. That he will get something, eventually. A matter of language, really. The treaty . . . it will say that he will receive 'justice' regarding the Agenais and—"

"Justice? Meaning what precisely? And when?"

"Whatever he imagines it to be, dear one. He keeps your children from you and we... we shall keep the Agenais from him, for as long as needed. As for when, shall we say 'in due course'? An ambiguity. He will be momentarily confused, then angry. He will fume and grumble and whine and then . . . he will sign his name to have it done with. Then, my dear one, you can go home."

I stopped abruptly. England was *not* my home. But my children were there. And so was Despenser. How was I to resolve that terrible paradox? "I . . . I can't. I won't."

Charles pinched my cheek lightly and winked, trying to lighten my heart. "You must stay for my wedding, then. Jeanne will want you there. But please, I beg, do not poison her head with tales of wicked husbands. She is a lamb and I will have her that way on our wedding night."

"My husband will protest," I said. "Loudly."

"Then you do wish to go back?"

"No!" I said, almost too boldly, but I could not help myself. "I cannot go back to—"

He silenced me with a finger to my lips. "A thought, dear sister: What if . . . yes, what if Lord Edward paid homage to me? Would he not suffice? Then the matter of homage, at least, is resolved."

"But I thought we wanted the king to come, because only then can we remove Despenser."

"He expects that, which is why he will never come. You said so yourself. If we give him the option of sending his son in his place, he will take it to be rid of this one problem. Then, once my nephew is here . . . power turns to our favor."

"How?"

"Then it becomes perfectly clear to everyone where Edward stands.

He is not much loved by his people, is he? His son . . . is. Who do you think England would side with if you were to return with an army behind you?"

An army? I mouthed, wondering how long he had been helping to plan what amounted to an invasion.

"All those English exiles in Paris,"—Charles put a hand on my shoulder and caressed it—"did you think they were just idly passing their time here? Write to him. Propose it," he commanded with a quick flourish of his hands. "Now, our guests are probably wondering why we are standing here engaged in a private conversation in front of them. Ah, look. They have been staring at us so patiently." His countenance brightened in a look of feigned surprise. He waved at Stratford and Airmyn casually over the stair railing. "Your grace, my lord, welcome! Have you been here long? We were planning a hunt in the morning, the queen and I, and were quite caught up in the excitement."

Arm in arm, we descended the stairs into the great hall of Vincennes.

25

Isabella:

Palace de la Cité, Paris — June, 1325

T HE SUN SLIPPED BEHIND the Palace de la Cité—a stark silhouette of blue angled against a muted pink sky—as Jeanne leaned precariously from the side of the barge. Between her fingers, she crushed flower petals and one by one dropped them, watching them spin and float on the air until they landed in the river.

"Charles will wonder where we have been," she said mournfully, as if she had committed a grave sin. "We've missed supper."

"Knowing Charles, he will have waited for you." Besides, he had not let her go without a handful of dour guards. Six of them were clumped at the front of the barge sharing bawdy tales with the barge's master and its ragged crew. I found their sense of humor even more offensive than their odor.

I handed Jeanne another pale blue aster. We had spent the afternoon going first downriver, well beyond the outer reaches of Paris, to a meadow dotted with wildflowers. There, we had plucked armloads until our

214

fingernails were stained green and filled some thirty or so willow baskets with lavender, harebells and irises, taking up half the barge. The wedding was close at hand. The gown was fitted, the jewels chosen to complement it, the menu for the wedding feast planned out to the last herb and spice, the wine cellar stocked—every fine detail had been attended to.

She took the aster and stripped away its petals. "Isabella, can I ask you a question? Just one?" Her brows were so seriously drawn together that I was still contemplating when she blurted it out. "Do you love your husband, King Edward?"

Above the purl of the barge pushing through the water, the sounds of Paris slipped down from the banks of the Seine. The people there waved and shouted their greetings. My response, when it came, seemed far away, as if someone else were imparting it other than me. "Marriages are not always love matches, dear Jeanne. Sometimes it is our duty to enter into them for the sake of unity . . . and peace. To ensure the royal blood is carried on . . . To avert wars, essentially."

She plucked a sprig of lavender from a nearby basket and inhaled its essence. "Then 'no'?"

The lavender's scent made me think of Ella and the evening in London when Edmund had come to warn me they were going to take my children away. Small things reminded me of them. How I missed my children, but Edward . . . not for a moment. "No, I do not think I ever loved him, nor he me." In fact, I could not say that I truly knew what 'love' was.

"How was it . . . being with him, with a man you did not love?" The words had come out timidly, but whether out of modesty or pity I could not tell.

The act itself was always hurried, methodical, done with few words and even less touching. An act of procreation, not one of passion. I sighed, trying to expunge those black thoughts from my head. "At best—unpleasant," I admitted.

"Is it always so?"

Poor Jeanne. So innocent. No wonder Charles had plucked up this dreamy virgin and wrapped her in silk and jewels. "No, I don't believe it is. Not for everyone."

Jeanne frowned at me in sympathy. I took her hand and said, "But some are lucky, like you, yes?"

Scarlet flamed her cheeks. "I think . . . yes. If it is being able to think of no one else, that you cannot sleep, that it hurts to be apart, then yes." She opened her other hand over the water to let loose a shower of petals, but they plopped down in a clump as the barge lurched to a halt to maneuver toward the banks of the Île de la Cité.

Charles was waiting there for her—tall and golden in all his kingly glory. His arms reached for her as she came ashore, his eyes hinted at desire, and his light kiss over her ear promised rapture.

IN PARIS, THERE IS barely a blade of grass to be found. The rare weed that springs up from a crack at dawn is crushed by a thousand feet by nightfall. The main roads are of cobbles, hard on an animal's feet and harder yet on human ears as carts rumble over them incessantly. Side alleys run brown and yellow with mud and sewage, reeking of urine and waste. Houses shove against each other and totter out over the streets at the second story, choking the light from the sky. Voices, both human and inhuman, crowd the air at every hour: the shrill whinny of horses being whipped forward, the barking of shopkeepers, the harping of wives, the raucous laughter of drunken men.

But even as I noticed the diseased Paris—its squalor and apathy— I also saw again the beauty: the bridges gracefully arching over the Seine; the boats coursing up and down the river's length like water beetles skimming over pond water; the stately spaciousness of the Louvre; and the mystical solemnity of Sainte-Chapelle on the Île de la Cité, which Saint Louis had built to hold the Crown of Thorns.

It was at Saint-Chapelle that Charles and Jeanne were wed. The day began blistering hot at dawn. By noon, old women were wilting like cut flowers removed from water. Overdressed noblemen mopped the sweat from their brows and loudly groaned their misery. Jeanne's gown was violet-purple, trimmed at the collar in white velvet, and with a silver cord strung with pearls around her waist. When her veil was lifted, her small eyes glimmered with tears of joy. Even Charles smiled throughout it all, as though in this young and innocent flower he had found the bloom of hope.

They began down the aisle to the eddying peal of bells. I turned to watch them go from the chapel. The colors of Christ and all his saints streamed down on them from the high stained glass windows. Before the doors swung open to yield to the ordinary light of day, I saw a familiar figure standing in the very last row.

Roger Mortimer.

Paris roared in approval as Jeanne and Charles stepped out into the light. And he, Mortimer, disappeared into the milling crowd surrounding them as if he had never been there at all.

WHILE ONLY TWO HUNDRED were able to attend the wedding ceremony in the narrow Saint-Chapelle, four times that number must have crammed the main hall of the palace for the banquet. Servants shuffled forth with elaborately arranged dishes of food on silver platters: a meat pie covered in rows of almond slivers and shaped to look like a hedgehog, pastries painted with egg yolk and saffron so they glimmered like lumps of gold, and halved pears simmering in red wine and cinnamon. Knives pinged as the carvers sliced away at mounds of venison, lamb and beef; wooden bowls scraped across tables; pewter goblets were plopped down on the trestle boards; drinks flowing from ewers and flasks gurgled; tittering and guffaws; the pleasant hum of conversation; and low growls followed by yips of surrender as Charles' hounds, lurking beneath the tables and between the benches, lunged and battled for flung scraps and spilled sauces.

I searched the crowd for Mortimer, but with so many bodies and so much commotion it was hard to discern one face from another. People jostled elbows and bumped knees at the tables while servants swarmed around them like honey bees, bearing pitchers of wine and trays of food and carrying away the discarded samplings of the guests. Every voice joined together in a buzz of talk and laughter. The rhythm of music rose up and wrapped around it all. The din of merriment pressed out against the walls and bulged up toward the vaulted ceiling where it seemed to explode into an even greater noise.

I beckoned Patrice and whispered into her ear to seek out Mortimer. Shortly after that, she was at my shoulder, pointing to my right. Several tables away sat Sir Roger Mortimer.

"Tell him to come to me tomorrow morning. I wish to speak with him."

Patrice wove her way through the twining servants. Then, she bent her glistening, dark head of ringlets to slip my message into Mortimer's ear. He rose and lifted his goblet to me.

Robert plopped down in the empty seat next to me. Startled, I gasped, having been so absorbed in my thoughts.

"Bishop Stapledon has returned, have you heard?" He plucked a swan's feather from his cap and twirled it between his thumb and fore-finger.

I curled my fingers tight around the handle of my table knife. "When?"

"Today, hours ago, no more."

"So soon?" I carved brutally at my slab of beef, dividing it into fine ribbons, not to eat it, but to appear busy as I digested this unwelcome news. "What more do you know, Robert? Is my son with him?"

Robert traced the edge of his jaw with the feather and then trailed it down his throat before laying it to rest on the table. "Sadly, no. No sign or word of him yet. Although I think we shall soon learn whether he is to come or not. There have been rumors . . . I hear Stapledon asked—no, demanded to see you only minutes ago. Charles refused. The bishop was most displeased, I understand." He leaned forward and blew a puff of air at the feather to send it fluttering from the table and onto the floor.

Knowing Stapledon had not come to offer fawning congratulations, I excused myself from my cousin's company with a kiss and wended my way through a tangle of bodies. Charles, temporarily abandoned by his bride, stood at the edge of the open floor where the dancing was about to begin.

"I thought I should never get to speak to you today," I told him.

Charles plucked up my hand and signaled for the music to begin. "Ah, you wished to congratulate me?"

"That," I said, as we ducked through an upraised bridge of joined hands, "and to ask why Bishop Stapledon presses for an audience with me?"

"You heard he was here? I doubt it is as important as he deems it to be. I would assume he bears the treaty with King Edward's signature. But I would refuse the Pope himself today, were he to ask for my time, or yours."

"Were that true—that his appearance has to do with the treaty alone—he would have asked to talk to you, not me."

"If he has half a wit, he knows I would have said 'no'. Perhaps he wishes to consult with you first?"

"With me? He has never 'consulted' with me."

"Isabeau, forget him. Celebrate with me. The music is high. The wine is flowing. And, if God would so bless us, I'll have my son nine months from this night. Look at Jeanne. Have you ever seen anything so pure, so ripe for the picking? My life has a new beginning."

"I'm sorry, Charles. I did not mean to steal any joy from this day of yours. Only, it worries me."

Nearly breathless, we halted as he clasped my other hand and we joined the end of the tunnel. He looked past me and abruptly scowled. "Perhaps you should ask him yourself? There." He yanked me aside and spun me around.

"My lord." Stapledon wrung his hands beneath the draping folds of his vestments. He bowed, barely. "A joyful day. King Edward sends his compliments."

Nothing about his countenance conveyed a look of joy; on the contrary, he looked as if he were bearing a death sentence.

"My bride and I thank you, your grace." Charles gleamed on the surface, but his voice was terse with indignation. "You were told not to interrupt this day. You came anyway. The treaty?"

"Signed, as written."

"He agrees to send Lord Edward?"

Stapledon nodded curtly.

"Delightful! Now, if you will excuse us, your—"

"I bring a message from my king, for his queen." The bishop glared at me like a crow standing over a worm, angling its head to peck the life from a defenseless creature.

"It shall wait," Charles ordained. "This is my wedding day. I forbid any seriousness."

The request went ignored. "She is to return to England with me at once. Her business here is done."

"No!" I blurted. Charles clamped a hand on my arm, but I shook it loose. "I will not. My son, he is to come to France. I will not leave until he does."

Stapledon remained smug. "He will come later, after you have returned to England."

"My business in France is *not* done. Not until homage has been paid to my brother."

"Your husband . . . your king has decreed otherwise. Besides, he never made any such agreement to that effect."

"I will go nowhere. Nowhere!"

Charles grasped me from behind by both shoulders. My limbs shook with rage.

"My sister," Charles began, before I could bellow any further protests, "came of her own accord, on her husband's behalf, to perform *his* duties. Because he refused to come. She will remain until they are completed, if she so wishes. She'll go nowhere against her will."

The dancing had ceased. The musicians broke from their unison; the flute faded breathily away; the harp notes drifted off erratically until they stopped altogether; and the pulse of the drums died suddenly until the only sound was the lonely keening of a bow being drawn across the strings of a rebec. Even Jeanne rose from her seat at the head table and came to Charles' side to find out what was amiss.

Effused with his purpose, Stapledon glared at the fresh, young bride. "It is a woman's duty to obey her husband. Such is God's word."

"And is it not God's word," I shouted for everyone to hear, "that a man and a wife shall not be rent asunder? What has that pariah Hugh Despenser done but that?"

Charles pinched a tiny fold of skin on the inside crease of my elbow. "Isabeau!"

"I will not stay silent anymore! He will hear me. God in heaven will hear me!" I ripped myself from my brother's hold. The words emanated not from my rage, but from a truth that had gone unspoken. "Hugh Despenser has poisoned my husband's head and his heart against me. Cleaved our holy union. Threatened me, even. I have begged my husband to let go of Lord Despenser, pled with him to show me kindness, for *I* am guilty of no wrong. Yet it is because of Lord Despenser that I have been denied, not only my husband's affections, but also the company of my children. Hugh Despenser has filled my husband's ears with vile counsel—vicious words that imperil the kingdom of England and those in it. But none will speak against him for fear of falling into disfavor. So I will do it for them. England has lost its king to the egregious influence of Hugh Despenser—and I have lost my husband."

My damning words hung black and big in the air like a storm cloud that had burst and spent itself, but had not yet been ushered away by the wind. If I was relieved of having kept the truth to myself for so many years, why did I feel the urge to vomit and cleanse my throat of having spoken it?

"So be it," Stapledon proclaimed bluntly. "As King Edward no longer considers you as acting in his service, and defiant of his authority, your funds are heretofore . . . discontinued." He bowed to Charles and asked permission to leave.

Charles brushed him away with an angry sweep of his hand, then he reached for me, but I backed hurriedly away, evading him.

I spun on my heel so fast the colors in the room swirled around me dizzily. I shoved my way past the first few people, but soon they all fell back from me, leaving a wide aisle. A ripple of murmurs followed me. I did not look at the faces, did not know whether eyes stared in horror at my audacity or if chins hung low in pity of me. By the time I reached the end of the hall and the archway where the corridor began which led to the royal apartments, I was running, one hand trying to hold up skirts that were too full and heavy and the other pushing tears from my bleary eyes.

It was when I reached the first turn in the corridor, slowed and paused for breath, that I stumbled and caught myself against the wall.

Oh, what have I done now? What stupid, whining, childish thing have I done?

I curled my fingernails deep into my palms, so that their piercing would stop my tears. Holding my breath, I heard the music again and the tinkle of laughter slowly rising. I needed to stop . . . feeling and acting like a wounded little girl. I needed to summon my courage, to plan, to think, to, to . . .

"I say only my son Geoffrey had more convincing outbursts. Even so, he stopped them when he was five."

I turned to see that Roger Mortimer had followed me.

26

Roger Mortimer:

Palace de la Cité, Paris — June, 1325

Q UEEN ISABELLA STRAIGHTENED, HER breathing quick and shallow. "Are you comparing my plight, Sir Roger, to that of a child who thinks he is being sent to bed too early?"

"Not at all." I approached her cautiously, afraid she might bolt again. As I neared her, I found it hard to fight a smile. In discovering her voice, she had mislaid her dignity. "But you were full of wrath. Fiery and alive. I found it very . . . *intriguing*."

She pressed a hand to the wall and pushed herself away, as if trying to appear stronger and in control of herself. "I think you were right at first. I must have looked like a terrible child, a jealous one."

I was but a few feet from her now. "Do you always apologize for speaking your thoughts?"

"I should . . ." Blinking, she looked away. "I should learn to hold my tongue."

"You should learn that when you are right, you need not dart away like a timid fawn. You are the Queen of England. And the Bishop of Exeter is your subject, not your master. To have spoken to you like that, and on the occasion of your brother's wedding . . . why he should be stripped and flogged for it."

Her jaw twitched, as though she fought to quell her true thoughts. "Edward sent him. Gave him the orders."

I tugged at my chin, trying to pull down the corners of my mouth to keep them from creeping up into a smile, but I could not help myself and let out a small laugh.

Turning her face toward me, she arched an indignant brow. "You thought it was amusing?"

"My queen, no. I thought it was very . . . bold of you. Brave, in fact."

"Then why are you laughing?"

"I was thinking that perhaps King Edward is the one who ought to be stripped and flogged. But as soon as I thought that, the vision of it was rather . . . well, disturbing." Then, in a more serious tone, though forced, I said to her, "Your pardon, I should not speak so ill of the king."

"Why? Do you think that I am still enamored of him—or that I ever was?"

Her directness startled me. Quickly, I cast a glance behind me to confirm we were still alone. Then I leaned in so close that the wine on her breath mingled with mine, the taste of it swirling around warm and sweet in my mouth.

"Do you still wish to call me on my oath?" I uttered.

My proximity must have made her uncomfortable, for she averted her eyes, even though during the wedding feast she must have looked my way a hundred times or more.

Folding down onto one knee, I took both her hands, pressed mine flat together and slid them between hers in a gesture of loyalty. "Let me repay you for my freedom, my queen. From this day forward, I will be always at your side and I vow to forever undo the wrongs that have been done to you, to me . . . to all of England."

Charles had often hinted at his sister's misery and Edward's treatment of her was known throughout the continent. Surely, she, too, had need of an ally?

"I want my freedom," she whispered.

"From Despenser . . . or from Edward?"

"Both."

Ah, no. I was mistaken. Not bold, but desperate. Then she would be willing to risk much.

"Done." I tipped my head downward a moment so that my hair brushed her skin, as if by accident, before I looked up at her again. "Never again question yourself, my lady. I am your strength, your courage, your will. Always. In every way."

I rose, my hands still folded between hers—and it seemed she could not take her eyes from my face. In the curve where her jaw met her swanlike neck, a vein pulsed faintly, but rapidly. I lifted a hand to touch her there, when I suddenly heard slowing footsteps from behind. Taking a step back, I drew my hands to my sides and looked.

"Isabeau . . ." Her damsel's voice was but a hoarse whisper. The woman hurried toward us and threw a worried look over her shoulder. Coming our way was a small party of wedding guests, weaving and tottering drunkenly through the corridor, their guffaws broken by bits of slurred and unrecognizable song. Her damsel whipped her head back toward us. "My lady, pardon, please, but the king sent me after you. I thought you'd be elsewhere by now, though."

"What is it, Patrice?" Isabella asked.

"Bishop Stapledon has been sent on to Vincennes and told to wait," Patrice continued. "King Charles will meet with him in a week, no sooner. You, however, are to go there on the morrow; it seems the bishop has details about Lord Edward's forthcoming arrival in France that, in his haste to humiliate you, he omitted. For now, Queen Jeanne asks if you will return to the hall?" She glanced sideways at me with her dark, inquisitive eyes. "I can tell them you have retired for the evening, if you wish. A headache?"

"Cousin!" The man I recognized as Robert of Artois stumbled for-

225

ward from the group of merrymakers and swayed like a boat careening wildly on a rough sea. He hiccupped into his palm and snorted a laugh. Then, squinting at me, he puckered up his face. "Your pardon, Lord . . . Lord? Do I know you?"

"I don't believe so." I gave Isabella the slightest wink to let her know I understood the need for discretion.

"An Englishman?" Robert belched and patted his belly in relief. "Ah, better." He turned toward Isabella and cupped a hand to his mouth, as if I, two feet away, could not hear him. "Keep him from the hall, then. The English have been known to murder a cel-celebration with their s-s-sobriety." He hiccupped again.

"Indeed, they can," Isabella agreed, winking back playfully at me, her mood now considerably lighter than when I had found her. "But there is such a thing as too drunk, too, Robert. I suggest you go to bed . . . before you fall over."

"Hah!" He whirled around to face his companions, two of them leaning against each other and still nursing their wine goblets. "As you see, we are all standing, still. Simply enjoying ourselves—unlike this English mongrel." As he turned back, he reached out to slap me on the arm, but the shift in his own weight sent him toppling forward. He landed on his knees with a bruising thump. Before he could pitch forward onto his face, I hooked a hand under his arm and helped him to his feet. I gestured to Isabella's damsel to take his arm.

She guided him back to his companions and in one warbling, wobbling clump they continued on down the corridor and were halfway back to the hall when one of them remembered they had been headed in the other direction. Confusion ensued as they turned in a circle and when Robert lost his balance, lunging forward a step back the way from which they had come, they all took it as a signal of decisiveness and followed.

Patrice wrinkled her nose in amusement. "Are you coming then?" she said to Isabella. "Everyone has quite forgotten about it. The bishop was very rude. The king was incensed. He ranted for several minutes. I'm certain he will reprimand the bishop even more severely when he sees him again."

"My lady, you need not go back to the hall," I said to the queen.

She tilted her head, pondering it. Stapledon would be gone, but there would be eyes upon her, questioning. "Tell them, Patrice, if you will, I am tired, or no . . . Yes, tell them simply that I am tired and need to rest before leaving in the morning. My apologies to Jeanne. She was more beautiful than any bride I have ever seen." Patrice gave a short nod and sauntered away, stealing a glance over her shoulder as she went. Then, her jaw taut, Isabella said, "I cannot go to Vincennes alone to sit across from that ferret while he spews his righteousness at me." She turned pleading eyes on me. "Please, will you—"

"I told you—I will be at your side, always." Then I looked to make sure Patrice had turned the corner to re-enter the hall before I took up the queen's hand and kissed it lightly. "I will be there at first light. Before if you like. Call on me, anytime you desire me near. I will never be further away than the length of your shadow at noon."

Even when I drew my hand away, she was still staring at the ridge of her knuckles where my lips had brushed.

"In the morning, Sir Roger." She snatched up the hem of her flowing skirt and hurried away.

Morning could not arrive soon enough.

27

Isabella :

Palace de la Cité, Paris — June, 1325

F ROM DUSK THROUGH DARKEST night, I writhed beneath sheets that were slickened by my own sweat, taunted by a thousand thoughts, both exhilarating and disturbing. My body grew more fatigued with each lagging hour. Somewhere in the darkness, I heard Patrice's muffled footsteps as she entered the adjoining outer room and stumbled to bed. Only when quiet followed did I still myself and enter into a world that was half sleep, half waking dream, so that the hours drifted by less torturously.

I rose before dawn, dressed in comfortable clothes for riding and peered through my open window into the palace courtyard. The air was oddly lifeless, without wind or sound, as if all lay in slumber. All I could see were unmoving shapes of gray—high walls, the peaks and creases of crowded rooflines, scattered treetops—against a black draping pricked by scattered starlight. To the south, a wispy veil of clouds crept silently across the sky, dimming the heavens.

In the outer chamber adjoining mine, Patrice was stretched out like a lazing cat on her pallet, dozing heavily in a wine-induced slumber. Her wrinkled gown was twisted around her middle and bunched up past her knees, one slipper lost and one only half on. The faint light of first dawn outlined every shape in traces of silver, even Patrice's tangled curls and the downward lines of her face. I crept past her to the outer door and nudged it open.

There, with arms crossed, was Mortimer, propped sleepily against the wall. Yawning, he glanced at Patrice in vague curiosity as he entered and went to the far side of the room. As he looked out the single window there, I closed the door behind him and slid the bar back in place.

His voice was barely above a whisper. "Your English guards, upon hearing you had no more money with which to pay them, have apparently deserted you." He glided to me, silent as a fox kit stalking a vole. "If Bishop Stapledon had wanted to abduct you last night and carry you kicking and screaming back to England, he would have had an easy game of it." He eased closer, still studying Patrice who had not yet stirred from her death-sleep. "I will make sure you are looked after. My business here has afforded me friends by the dozens, mutual opponents of King Edward, if you will, who would gladly do me a favor. You've already paid me by getting me out of the Tower."

It was disconcerting to know even my guards had so readily abandoned me. But as for the rest, Cromwell and Boudon, I had expected them to leave once the treaty was signed. Already they had distanced themselves in anticipation of leaving France. But the remaining skeleton of servants I had been afforded, they had managed to hover even closer of late, to my increasing annoyance, mostly to inquire of their pay.

"Your part in this was Charles' idea," I reminded him. "Bishop Orleton saw to the details."

"But *you* had your part in it, yes?" He inclined his head toward the door of my private chambers in suggestion, as if one more wall between us and the rest of the world would guard our secrets that much better. He came closer, his gaze unbroken, and hitched a shoulder at Patrice. "Can she be trusted?"

"Patrice? More so yet than you."

Patrice mumbled and flopped over, her face now toward us. Her eyelashes fluttered. Drool trickled from the corner of her mouth and she wiped it away with the back of her hand. A few moments later, she was still again. Then a sound outside the door—footsteps passing by—set my heart aflutter. The outer door was barred, but there was no one there to warn us of visitors or to stop intruders. I hurried through my chamber door, letting him follow. Not until the door latch clicked into place did I turn around.

Mortimer's mouth curled upward in a faint grin of amusement. "I suppose I'll have to prove myself, won't I? But you've allowed me in here. We're practically alone. That says something, does it not?"

I backed a few steps away to distance myself. "You have been in Hainault a long time."

"And elsewhere." He crossed his arms and, restlessly aware of everything around him, rocked back and forth on the balls of his feet. His eyes darted from window to wall to door as he memorized his surroundings. "Too long in Picardy with my cousin and uncle, although I had the pleasure of spending time with one of my sons. Polite company, but their rustic habits inspire nothing but boredom. I've also been to Cologne, Koblenz, Toulouse, Boulogne . . ."

"And here—Paris?"

"Frequently, yes."

"Then why have I not seen you until yesterday?"

He stilled his movements and looked at me sincerely. "Because, my queen, I had pressing business—the forging of important connections, the raising of troops and funds. And all of it . . . had everything to do with you."

I gave him a sidelong glance. "Do not evade me. I need answers, Sir Roger. Charles protects me like a small child. If I am to be a part of this—and the one without whom it cannot proceed—I must know *everything*."

"Very well. Your brother told me to keep my distance until the treaty was signed. To have been anywhere near you may have jeopardized it. Is that a satisfactory answer?"

Logical, yes, but why Charles guarded the answer as if it were some great secret was a quandary.

I paced before my bed where the disheveled blankets from my sleepless night lay half-strewn upon the floor. "How will we pay these troops? How many of them? Will it be enough against the army of England? What is our plan, once we are there?"

"Ah, quite uninformed, aren't you? But far-thinking. That impresses me. To arrogantly glide over the sea and tramp upon English soil without some kind of strategy… disastrous, perhaps. Too few fighting men and we could be crushed like grapes under the press. You and I would be taken captive—not long for this world, we can be assured of that. So then how many soldiers would be enough?" He scoffed. "If I had ten thousand men and the means to fund them, I would. But men cost money. So we will make do with what we can. However, it may not take as many men as one would think.

"Rumor will feed a frenzy for us about where and when we'll arrive, leaving Edward to guess, running to and fro for nothing, wearing himself into a state of carelessness, doubting after awhile that we'll ever bother. Then, surprise and swiftness will serve us. *That* is our plan."

He gazed at me severely and, satisfied I had no protests thus far, he continued, "As for payment—my relatives and my wife's will provide some. Your brother has arranged means to allot more from his own personal treasury, but slyly done so it cannot be traced directly to him. The rest will come from the Count of Hainault."

"Mercenaries?"

"The count can 'loan' you the men, temporarily, yes. As an escort, if you wish to use that pretense. I assure you—they are the best fighting men on the continent. I would not have sought them out otherwise. The finest horses, the best arms. They are capable soldiers, disciplined. But yes, they are hired soldiers: 'mercenaries'. His brother, John of Hainault, has volunteered to lead them. But once on English soil, they will not much be welcomed without an English presence beside them. Take no offense, but for as much as you are loved by the people, you are *still* French. Your son, Lord Edward, if he were with us, why the people would flock to him like starving mice to a newly filled tithe barn. Still, he is far too young to lead an army, should any conflict arise. My lady," he said, switching abruptly from calm contemplation to fiery insistence, his lower lip drawn taut against his teeth. The glint of old battle memories sparkled from the darkness of his eyes. "I defeated the Irish pagans—with more success and certainty than any man before or since."

"By yourself? Really?" I jested, trying to lighten his mood.

He flashed a quick scowl at me. "You know what I mean. I am the one to lead your army. I did not become Lieutenant of Ireland because I knew how to please Edward privately, as Gaveston did. I was meant for it. Men heed my word. They follow my sword. They trust in me because I know my enemy and I know how to defeat them."

"I know your credentials, Sir Roger. You don't need to convince me of your abilities on the battlefield. And you need not hint at my husband's indiscretions. I'm well aware of them."

"Then we are agreed?"

"To what?"

"That I am to lead the invasion that will oust Lord Despenser and bring the king to terms."

"Were we ever in disagreement on that point, Sir Roger? You were chosen long ago by my brother. You need neither beg nor boast. We have both been slighted by Lord Despenser. You are doing this as much out of revenge as I am, so it was not some undying, chivalric desire to serve as my champion that brought you to me."

"What is a knight then, if he has no cause to serve? Perhaps that 'cause' is you, my lady? But as you wish: I'll plead no more. Let us say, that at this moment, we serve each other. Fair?"

"Fair, Sir Roger. I must wonder about the Count of Hainault, though. How is he served by any of this? He has no argument with Edward or Despenser."

"Argument, no. That is not to say he cannot be served by giving us aid."

"Come now, I know of very few who would shower a displaced queen with such great sums out of pure munificence. Hainault, at least, requires some recompense."

"That has not been entirely settled, but if you must know—and I tell you this with all delicacy—the count is interested in joining one of his daughters in marriage to one of your sons, preferably your oldest, Lord Edward. He has four fine daughters. Pleasing to look upon, healthy, well-mannered, educated."

I stopped pacing and stood with hands on hips to glare at him. "Healthy, pleasing? You talk as if they are dairy cows to be added to the herd. So you have already negotiated on my behalf then?"

He clasped his hands together before him. "I would never presume to do so. The count offered it as a means to settle a debt. Payment for a service."

"Still, you assume much. Bartering to settle a debt is a poor way to determine one's mate."

"Yet, it is done all the time. My own wife's family is very wealthy and of late, given my forced exile, I've found it a convenience."

Was that how he viewed her: a convenience . . . a commodity?

"You can decline," he said.

I nodded. "I can. Young Edward's marriage is one not lightly entered into. Once done, there is no undoing it, so whomever he decides to wed shall be not only a sound decision politically, but one that pleases him personally. Besides, you say the count's daughters are pretty? How am I to know you are even a good judge?"

"When we go to Hainault, later . . . if we do go there, you can see them with your own eyes. Besides, if I were to say the woman before me is the fairest I have ever beheld, does that not make me a proper judge?"

"Spare me your flatter—"

"An honest observation, not empty flattery, my lady. Do you always make a habit of rejecting compliments or are you truly so humble?" Until then, he had not moved from his place by the door, as if he were either guarding it or half listening for voices outside. He came near to me, stopping one slight, but chasmal step away. "Your husband is a blind and ungrateful fool—forgive me for saying it aloud. Any man who would spurn you has neither eyes nor a heart. Were you mine I would worship the sun for shedding its light upon your beauty. I would bless the night for bringing you to my bed. And I would rise each and every day and ask how I, Roger, could give you, Isabella, happiness."

His words portrayed a vision that was so vivid, so irresistible to my lonely spirit that in that moment, I was moved beyond restraint. I reached out and touched the smooth, shaven part of his cheek, trailed my finger over his ear, down his neck, the fine, ragged ridge of a battle scar slowing my fingers.

I feared he might pull away, chide me for my boldness, reject me, but he made no move other than to turn his mouth toward my open palm and warm it with his breath. My hand wandered downward, over the sweat-dampened cloth of his tunic, sensing the heat of his body beneath my fingertips.

"I do not think," I began, my voice whisper-thin as I strained to separate thought from the sensations that were overtaking me, "that you would have to ask how to do that. You would know."

You already do.

Mortimer caught my wrist in the circle of his fingers and pulled me against him. Something inside me—a force greater than my own will or understanding—strained against my ribs, expanding outward with such completeness, such power, that I ceased to breathe. The beating of my heart became everything, my whole being, sending through every limb, every finger, every inch of flesh a tide of awakening.

I closed my eyes, my lips parting in wickedly painful anticipation of his fervent kisses . . . and he bent his neck, the heat of his breath blazing my skin as he pressed his lips to the rim of my ear.

"One hour," he said huskily. His hold on my wrist lightened. "In the courtyard. Meet me there. I'll have the horses ready. The sun will be up by then. Rouse your companion and we'll be off to Vincennes."

Slowly, I opened my eyes, taking in his words, still waiting for more. More of his touch, his nearness. More of *him*.

But then he released me altogether, stepped back and started toward the door. It felt as though I had been suddenly nudged to the edge of a cliff and it began to crumble beneath me, leaving my toes dangling over the edge, my balance out of kilter, a great abyss gaping before me.

"One hour," he repeated . . . and left.

A cold rush of air filled my lungs, like the first draw of breath outside on a crisp winter morning. I stood alone, shuddering, gulping for breath. I could still feel the imprint where his fingers had encircled my wrist. I felt the warm moistness of his whispered words on my ear and neck. The pressure of his chest crushed against mine.

I felt myself . . . falling. And I embraced it in all its delirium and with it the uncertainty, secrecy and suffering that would, undeniably, accompany it.

Through my open door, I heard Patrice stir.

"Isabeau? Are you awake?" She slumped in the doorway. Her hair lay flattened on one side and on the other it stuck out sideways. She let out a huge yawn. "Dressed already, are you?"

"Change your clothes, Patrice." My own voice was distant, unfamiliar to me, as I sought to free myself from the memory of only minutes ago. "We're leaving for Vincennes within the hour to meet with Bishop Stapledon."

Groggily, Patrice complied. I sat on the edge of my bed, waiting for time to pass so I could see him again. But nearness alone would not be enough to quench the flame that had kindled inside me.

I had felt it the day I visited him in the Tower . . . no, further back than that—at seventeen, when Mortimer, just returned from doing the king's business in Ireland, came to report on his task to Edward. I had hung back, agonizingly aware of my large size. Mortimer had looked at me kindly and remarked on my beauty. From that day on I walked, and later waddled, with a certain swelling of pride and confidence, rather than embarrassment.

Even then, I had loved him for his words alone.
My dear and gentle Mortimer.

28

Isabella:

Palace de la Cité, Paris – June, 1325

THE AIR SMELLED OF rain. I inhaled deeply.

The yard of the Palace de la Cité was embraced snugly within a ring of whitewashed walls, which at that early hour shut out not only the intrusive clangor of Paris, but the warmth of the low morning sun as well. Patrice and I huddled together in the shadows at the yard's edge, waiting for Mortimer. The wind lifted in the barest of breezes, making the air distinctly cooler than the day before. Storm clouds, only barely visible over the top of the city's walls, gathered in the south, blotting out the blue of the sky there.

"A passing summer shower," I declared, hopeful. "And not even a full day's ride to Vincennes. It will renew us."

"We'll drown," Patrice grumbled. Her lower lip jutted out in rank displeasure.

My heart leapt when I saw Mortimer emerge from the stables leading two horses. Behind him were three other men with extra mounts—one I did not recognize and the others... Gerard d'Alspaye from the Tower and . . . could it be? Yes, it was: Arnaud de Mone.

Patrice wrung the hem of her cloak, twisting it murderously in her hands until the corner of her garment was a thick rope, as though she might loop it around Arnaud's neck and strangle him outright in the full light of day for all to witness.

But as they approached, instead of rushing forward and blazing her anger, Patrice retreated safely within herself. Her chin dipped and her shoulders rolled forward slightly.

"Stay here," I told her, putting my arm around her. "I'll be back in a few days. Not so long. Then we can go to Fontainebleau." When that brought no response, I squeezed her closer. "Châteauneuf then? You used to love it there when we were young. Remember how we would hide in the hedges as they called us to supper? They never could find us."

Patrice raised her face to stare coldly at Arnaud across the short distance. The men had halted in the open to steady the horses. Mortimer acknowledged me with a wave and then motioned to someone else. Soon, more men and horses appeared, until there was a small contingent of a dozen or so Englishmen.

"No, I'm going with you," she said.

At the sound of her voice, Arnaud looked in our direction. Patrice marched up to him and, with the barest hint of a smile, said, "It has been a long time."

"It has." He smiled back sheepishly and extended her the reins to a sleepy-looking bay palfrey. "I picked her, for you. She has the gentlest ride they told me. I remembered you once saying how much you disliked being jostled about."

She took the reins in her left hand, thanked him softly and with her other hand slapped him so hard across the cheek he stumbled sideways and slammed against the ribs of his own horse. The men behind him guffawed. Arnaud recovered his dignity, at least outwardly, and cut her a pained glare. A welt marred his fine features. As he opened his mouth to speak, Patrice reeled away, ducked around the front of the horse and pulled herself up into the saddle as nimbly as any young boy.

Mortimer sidled over to me, leading two horses. He wrestled a smirk. "They know each other well, do they?"

"They did."

He held the stirrup for me. The amusement had faded from his countenance, I noticed. "Ahhh. He has a wife, did you know?"

"What?" My heart sank for Patrice. I placed my toe in the stirrup as he helped me up. "This is recent, I take it?"

"If five years ago is recent, then yes."

"Oh. He never said anything. My damsels all swooned after him when he came to court. He rejected them all—except for Patrice. She will be deeply hurt to hear it . . . if she could be more so than she already is."

Mortimer handed me the reins and curled a finger to entice me closer. "Do not judge him too harshly, my queen. His wife—it was an arranged marriage—she bore him a daughter within their first year of wedded bliss. Well, truthfully, I do not know if they were ever happy, but it became complicated at that point. The child was small, feeble, not normal. Its eyes were oddly shaped and bulging. Its head too large for its body. In time, they could see its legs were bent strangely and that it would be a cripple. But even worse, the little girl died. Arnaud's own mother accused his wife of strangling the babe. There were marks on the child's neck, she said. His young wife went quite mad. Tried to hang herself from the rafters of the tithe barn. Arnaud found her in time, but the damage was done. Even though he had saved her life, when she awoke she had no idea who he was. The Poor Clares without Aldgate took her in. She digs the vegetables to earn her keep. It's all she can do, sadly. He goes to visit her every week, or he did, until coming here with me. He only spoke of it to me after we shared a cask of ale—and not again since."

Indeed, I thought differently of Arnaud then. But I was not so sure, even if she knew, that Patrice would forgive him.

I combed at my horse's golden mane with my fingernails while Mortimer's men loaded my baggage onto some pack horses to the rear. As I waited, I could not help but notice the slightly older, lean-faced man with dusky brown hair who had entered the courtyard at Mortimer's side.

Mortimer went and spoke to his men, and last to the dusky-haired man. "Who is he?" I asked as Mortimer returned to check the cinch on each of our saddles, before climbing onto his own horse.

"Sir John Maltravers. An old and true friend. He was with me at Bannockburn and in Ireland. He sided with your unfortunate cousin Thomas of Lancaster at Boroughbridge. Maltravers fled the battlefield with his life and made his way to Scotland, then to Sluys in Flanders and finally to France."

Maltravers' left hand was sharply angled in form and the last two fingers were shortened. It sent a chill through my spine to think of what it must be like to have parts of one's body hacked off and see your own blood spurting freely onto the ground.

Our assemblage complete, we left the Palace de la Cité, traveled across the bridge over the Seine and proceeded through the streets of Paris, which were already teeming with life and commerce.

"He was with me in Meath, too," Mortimer went on. "The Scots, led by Edward Bruce, had already been chased from the south of Ireland. During a minor battle—I don't even remember the time of day or the place myself, only that it was raining—I saved Maltraver's life, or so he swears. There was an Irishman bearing down on him with an axe. I killed the bastard. Maltravers insists he owes me his life in service. Between Gerard, Arnaud and him, and a few others in England, I've had no trouble getting messages wherever they needed to go."

I glanced behind us as we turned onto a main road beyond the city. Rain began to splatter on us in drops as big as spoonfuls. Patrice flipped the hood of her mantle over her head, but I left mine resting on my shoulders, lifted my chin and let the rain fall upon my face.

TWICE, WE STOPPED: ONCE for a midday meal of bread and cheese and another time to water the horses and watch a rare pair of egrets at river's edge.

ISABEAU

I refused to hurry on Bishop Stapledon's behalf. More than that I wanted the day to last. The rain clouds had been swept away by a warming breeze and the sun shone in full splendor over France. A journey that should have taken no more than a few hours instead lasted most of the day.

The road that led to Vincennes was a tunnel of speckled light miles long through a verdant, twining archway. On either side, the stout trunks of ancient oaks leaned inward like old men with crooked spines, joining their branches above the expanse of the road to provide a canopy for travelers against glaring sun or soaking rains. In the deepening shadows of twilight, squirrels leapt from limb to limb. As we reached the end of the road, the trees parted to reveal the grand palace of Vincennes ahead across a meadow shorn low by wandering, half-wild sheep. Around us, the forest embraced the palace grounds in a mantle of greenery. Birds hopped from bough to ground and back again, trilling their delight as they gobbled up insects and scavenged for more.

The dread I might have felt at having to meet with Bishop Stapledon had been lightened immeasurably by Mortimer's company.

His eyes still set on the sight before him, Mortimer smiled broadly. "I have not yet been to Vincennes. I hear it is a place where the senses are exposed to much delight, where beauty lies all around you and there is much sport to be had."

He then turned to look at me, but I quickly looked away before our eyes met.

The sun had finally dipped beyond the tops of the trees. I peered ahead through the creeping grayness and saw a mounted figure riding out from the palace gates toward us. The rider was too lithe on his mount for it to be the bishop. The clothes were that of a noble. The horse in royal trappings. The rider's head was bare and there was still enough light to give away his fair, silky hair and the youthful wedge of his jaw. I nudged my horse in the flanks to breech the distance.

"Mother!" Young Edward cried out. "Mother! Greetings! Did you think I would never come?"

A small party of six guards in royal English livery clipped along behind him on their horses, hooves flailing rocks. We were both on the ground, enveloped in a drifting veil of dust, and locked in an embrace before anyone else reached us.

I pressed my cheek to his and abruptly thrust him back for a look. "You have grown!"

"Almost as tall as you now," he said, his voice chiming with pride.

"Taller, I'd judge," Mortimer added.

Young Edward surveyed him with a skeptical eye. He had been too young when last he saw Mortimer to remember him. "English?"

"Sir Roger Mortimer." Mortimer slipped from his saddle to bow before my son. "At the service of the queen *and* my prince."

My son looked from me to Mortimer, then back again.

I embraced him once more and pressed my mouth close to his ear. "I shall explain later. Do not fear him." Then I stepped back, clasping both his hands. "Bishop Stapledon?"

"Here. And in a right terrible mood. He flew into a rant to see me here in France so soon. He's praying for your soul in the chapel this very moment. Mine, too, I wager." Young Edward grinned devilishly. "Prettier than I imagined here. You told me so many times and it *is* true, Mother. The cities, the castles, the walls around them—so big. Glorious! Such riches. I should like to be the King of France." His eyes were wide with wonder and the lilt of his voice matched his expression. Such a different young man than the one who had sat sullen-faced like a beaten prisoner beside his father that late night at the Tower. Then his mouth slipped quickly into a frown. "He . . . Father, he ordered me to bring you home soon"—he smiled again as suddenly— "but I'm in *no* hurry to go back. I've missed you so. I begged him to let me leave two weeks early, but he only let me come after I'd sworn him an oath—something about marriage, as if I had any notion of that."

I shared a fleeting glance with Mortimer.

"What did he make you promise, son?" I took him by the hand as we went forward. His guards parted to make way. Their horses snorted and tossed their tails, still invigorated by the brisk gallop.

He shrugged and twisted his mouth up, trying to recall something that, to him, seemed entirely unimportant. "I don't remember, exactly. Only that I could not marry without his permission. Phhhh . . . I will not marry until I am twenty, anyway. Twenty-five, maybe. Too much to do before then. I wish to fight battles first. That is how you become a great king."

"Are you hungry, Edward?" I hooked my arm through his as we began up the polished steps of the palace. The windowed walls stretched out almost endlessly to either side.

"Famished! I've been waiting to eat for hours. The bishop blurted out that you were coming. I think he regretted saying so. Ah, allow me to introduce Sir William Montagu to you." Young Edward motioned one of the knights forward from his retinue. The man was perhaps a decade his senior, but sly in his movements like a fox watching prey.

"My lady." Montagu bowed low and swept his hand to his waist.

"Sir William. I hope you'll look after my son. Keep him from trouble?"

He flashed a laconic smile at me. "Oh, indeed, my lady. It is my life's duty to safeguard my lord."

"You were sent by King Edward?" I asked, suspicious.

"My father had served as King's Marshal in Gascony, but he is not quite so welcome at court these days and so I have not been there much myself since I was very, very young. It was, however, not the king but my lord, Edward, who requested my service. We met briefly once when I was preparing for a tournament at Warwick. I was undefeated in foot combat that year. I taught him how to wield a sword properly. One day he shall better me."

I was surprised to hear such articulate detail from someone who, at first sight, looked the part of a bloodthirsty Norseman straight from a village raid.

"I am pleased, then," I said. "Edward, we will let the bishop wait until tomorrow. I'll not have him spoil our happy reunion."

IN THE LARGEST OF my rooms, the one that served as both a solar and a dining area, was a long table with chairs enough for a dozen friends. The table was so stout one could have led a horse across it. Each chair was padded on the seat and backed with black leather. Golden crowns and fleurs-de-lis colored the floor tiles and the walls of wainscoting were painted in the royal blue and white. On either side of the fireplace a pair of carved leopards thrust upward with their raking claws to hold the mantel aloft, whereon was a relief of France's greatest king: Saint Louis.

Patrice and I changed into fresh gowns in my bedchamber. She brushed my hair, plaited it and wound it in a single coil at the back of my neck, pinning it in place. Mortimer had declined my invitation to supper, not wanting to impose himself between my son and me so soon after our reunion. When we were told the food and guests were ready, I was met with a second surprise that day as we entered the adjoining room.

"Edmund!" I exclaimed, seeing my brother-in-law the Earl of Kent before me. I almost withdrew in shock, remembering the day he had warned me of Despenser's plans and I had fled. I never learned if his warning had been in earnest, or part of a larger plot to accuse me of a false crime.

His head stooped, Kent knelt on both knees before me and flattened his palms on the floor. "Sister . . . Isabella, I tried to save you, the children . . . but it was not enough. I could have spared you so much, if I had only known more of Despenser's plans. Please, you must believe me." A tremor rippled through his body. He gave a small, but distinct sob, then held his breath.

It was too much of an act and too abruptly done. "Why should I?"

He raised pink-rimmed eyes to me. "Because, I was deceived. Lord Cromwell came to me earlier that day. He told me he had overhead the king say that he was sending someone to take the children . . . and that your French ladies would be banished forthwith as well. Despenser sent him—I have no doubt. I was followed. I thought I would succumb to some murderer's cold knife as I ran. But they only wanted to make sure I would go to you. They knew I would. Despenser pointed the finger of blame on me when the campaign in France failed, but it was he who failed to send more troops when I asked for them and because of that I—"

"Yes, Edmund, I know. Because of that La Réole fell. You could not hold it." I did not mention that, although what he said was correct, he had himself failed in many other ways. Thus far, Kent had offered nothing but his own personal grievance against Despenser. "Still, what reason have I to believe you are not here on Edward's behalf? Declaring your innocence is not enough. I want to believe you, but I . . . I do not know if I . . . Please, it is best you go. If you have something from Edward to tell me, be done with it and go. Otherwise . . ."

I wanted to believe in his honesty, that I could count him a friend as well as a brother, but there was too much in the way of circumstances standing against him.

He dropped his head again and mumbled, "I am not a spy, Isabella . . . and I did not betray you. I swear it on my life, on my children's lives. But I have no proof to give, only my word. If you command me to, I shall go . . . although I will forever swear on the Holy Gospel that what I said is true."

I laid both my hands on the top of his head. "Edmund, I'm so sorry, but still—it is *not* enough."

Seemingly resigned to his banishment, Kent drew himself up and turned to depart. He had not gone two steps when Edward—who I had not known was in the room until then—grabbed him by the sleeve and dragged him back.

"Mother!" Young Edward protested. "Believe him! You must, I say. I was there—at the counsel meeting at Westminster. I heard him defend your honor when Father complained of you. Even when Despenser threatened him. He said he could not call himself honorable if he did not have a care about you, the mother of his nieces and nephews. Do you need any more proof than that?"

If I had faith in only one person, it was my son.

Perhaps it was as much the shroud of humility Kent wore as my own son's words that convinced me. "No . . . no, your word is enough. I believe him now." I took a step closer to Kent, who kept his eyes downcast, and took his hand." Forgive *me*, Edmund, for holding any blame on you all these months. It has been difficult, for me—being apart from my children."

"Then let me help you be with them again."

My first thought, as it always was until then, was to question why anyone would ever come to my aid or show me even the slightest gesture of kindness. I had been neglected, ridiculed and cowed into submission so many times by Edward, I had come to believe myself deserving of such treatment. But it would be so no more.

29

Isabella:

Vincennes — June, 1325

MORNING . . . AND MORTIMER AT *my door once more.*

Patrice let him in, but not without a sidelong glance.

I dismissed her because I did not like her reproachful look.

"But I wasn't going anywhere," she countered impudently, her brow crimping in the middle.

"You were on your way to help Marie and Juliana," I coaxed. "They are beginning work on a new tapestry this morning, remember?" Mortimer stood patiently behind her, his face impassive.

Her plump lips twisted into an unflattering scowl. She despised tasks like needlework and weaving, having no patience for them. "But I—"

"Tell them I'll be there before noon, will you? I'm quite eager to see how the colors Juliana has chosen will look."

She spun on her heel and stormed out the door, nearly slamming it behind her.

Alone now, I gestured for Mortimer to take a seat at the table. He declined, stating that he would be brief, because he did not wish to draw attention to our meeting.

"Perhaps, then, we should meet in secret, Sir Roger, if our being together openly is cause for rumor."

"I think that would . . ." he looked away, "that would be even less wise." He turned sideways to me, as if to emphasize his hurry.

"Why so?"

"You need to ask?" He flicked away a speck of mud on his leggings, and then shifted his eyes to the ceiling.

Yes, Patrice had told me of the rumors already circulating that Mortimer and I were lovers. Untrue, of course, but why did they make him so uneasy?

"His Grace, Bishop Stapledon," Mortimer went on, "will ask you to verify the documents as originals, and once you have approved he will give them over into your care. The treaty is an easy matter. Your son's presence here, not so. He will demand a date for the bestowal of the titles promised him and for the ceremony of homage. He will chastise you for not having returned to England already. Recite your wifely duties to you. Remind you that your funds are discontinued. Threaten you. In short, he will say more of what he said the day before yesterday, but only after he complains profusely of having to wait to see you."

"You have spoken to the bishop already?"

"No, I do not need to. The premise for his business here is well known."

"And how did you learn all this?"

"How is not important."

"Then when?"

"Before he came."

So then, Mortimer *did* employ spies. He had probably even done so while he was in the Tower. "I will tell him I need to confer with Charles first. That plans must be made, for Charles will want to make a ceremony of it."

He nodded. Still, he avoided looking at me. His words were almost

248

terse. "Yes, delay—for as long as you can. Edward will learn everything, eventually."

I moved around to stand before him. "Have I done something wrong?"

"Why would you think that, my lady?" Finally, he afforded me a glance. He had not moved since entering and speaking his first word.

"Because you were not so curt yesterday. And now you go beyond informing me and make yourself my advisor. You must feel I have need of guidance. Tell me—what have I done?"

Before he answered, I knew.

There was nothing, it seemed, that Mortimer was not aware of. No secret unsealed. No stone unturned. And if he knew of last night already—of my talk with my son and Kent—then perhaps he knew my heart, too . . . which was why he did not wish to stay. He could not trust himself either anymore. Lowly, I said, "I did not tell them everything."

Mortimer rolled his head back as he let out a sigh. "Ahhh . . . I beg you, please, please, be careful to whom you speak and of what. One word . . . one small, seemingly insignificant word could undo *everything*." He rolled his fingers into fists, clenching them as hard as if he were crushing rocks.

I did not care to be chastened by him. "The Earl of Kent can be trusted."

He opened his fists and looked down at his hands, pondering his response. "At times, perhaps."

"I think I know him better than you." Although in truth, I knew him to be impulsive and irresponsible. Still, I needed allies. "I remind you that Edward has too often given lands and privileges to Despenser that should have belonged to Kent. He has as much desire for revenge as anyone."

"Of course." He lowered his head in a slight bow, as if to excuse himself from my presence. "Can we speak later? A ride, maybe? Noon?"

I agreed and he was about to leave when he hesitated at the door. "Something else?" I asked.

He shook his head. "It can wait."

WITHIN THE HOUR I was holding audience with Bishop Stapledon in a meeting room off the great hall. He did exactly as Mortimer had fore-told—every point, every protest, every demand, every censure. Knowing precisely what would gurgle from his misshapen mouth, I was shaken by none of it.

Stapledon caressed the jewel in the center of the crucifix dangling from his creased neck. "The king commands you to return home—with me."

"Home? You mean to England? But I *am* home, Bishop Stapledon. Why should I leave France? Give me good reason." I needled him, but I took pleasure in his frustration, much as he took pleasure in conde-scending to me.

"To remove you from evil influences, my lady. France is teeming with them. Paris is naught but a pit of vipers."

"You mistake harmless earthworms for snakes, your grace. I shall not leave here with you, nor will I with anyone anytime soon."

He bit his lower lip before responding. "When then? My lord king looks forward to the pleasure of your company again. He says to remind you that your other children are wondering when they will see you again."

A well-aimed arrow to my heart. Doubtless he had kept that in his armory of bribes until I showed absolute reluctance to quit France. I could not, however, let on to Stapledon that my children were the weakness to my resolve. I parried. "Tell my husband that I will consider returning on two conditions: One, that Lord Hugh Despenser is banished from court forever and the king is to sever all correspondences and ties to him, and two, that all my lands and allowances be returned immediately and never again taken from me."

"He will not agree to such strict conditions, my lady. Mostly, he will not allow you to set the conditions of your return."

"I care not if he 'allows' it. Tell him. But be precise. I have given in to much—*too* much. I am a wife who has tired of mistreatment, not a mindless, misbehaving child to be scolded into better table manners. I will not compromise on those two things." Then I folded my hands on my lap and looked away from him, toward the single window, to indicate I had no more to say on the matter.

As I waited for him to go, he stopped, inspected the impressive set of antlers hanging on the wall above the hearth, the remnant of some long ago hunt, and said with his back still turned, "The king knows of Mortimer's arrival in Paris. I caution you, my lady, to keep from him. He is a traitor and a villain."

I said nothing to him. Whether I was with Mortimer or not, Edward would assume we were lovers.

Let him.

Let him seethe with envy. Let him, in his hypocrisy, turn to his beloved Hugh and then call me the 'unfaithful' one.

God will be my judge, not him.

"My lady?" A young page poked his head timidly inside the room. A hand appeared, then a leg. He squeezed between the door and its frame. "I am to tell you your horse is ready, to the rear of the palace . . ." He scratched at his ragged mop of brown hair with dirty fingernails, thinking hard. "Beyond the garden, near the pond. No, no . . . near the palace, beyond the pool? Or was it beyond the—"

"Thank you, I will find it," I said, sparing him further confusion.

AT THE GARDEN'S EDGE, I stood by the reflecting pool, far from the palace. Trickles of perspiration ran down my breastbone. I lifted my face and let the sun pour its light upon me. It must be well past noon, I thought, and Patrice would be angry with me for not keeping my word to join her. I felt little remorse for my absence, however. Patrice's moods were becoming quite insufferable and I found myself growing increasingly intolerant of them.

A frog croaked nearby and plopped into the water. I looked toward the sound, beyond a cluster of purple and yellow irises, to see a pair of shiny, bulging eyes peeping at me above the silver-blue surface. Drifting clouds reflected in the water, rippled by fishtails. Damselflies danced above. Beyond the pool lay the forest of Vincennes: the elms, the beeches, the woodland wildflowers.

And there, on the path into the woods, stood Mortimer, waiting.

Stooping, I plucked a violet from the grass and strolled unhurriedly around the edge of the pool, until at last I neared him. At his feet was a basket brimming with fruit: mulberries and strawberries, peaches and even a pomegranate. He inclined his head toward the trail leading into the woods. Beside him, two horses were tethered to the lower branches of a small tree and were stripping its tender leaves away.

"The bishop, I noticed," he said, "is keenly aware of your every move. He is watching us from a window this very moment."

I turned and peered past him at the palace, squinting in the midday brightness. I thought I saw a figure standing at one of the open windows, but it could have been a servant going about his duties or someone admiring the garden from above. Since Stapledon's warning earlier about his knowledge of Mortimer's presence, it was fair enough to believe what Mortimer said. No doubt it was precisely why Edward had sent him—to spy on me. I gave Mortimer my hand and joined him on the trail.

We were soon on our horses, his basket of fruit balanced on his horse's withers. The cool shade of the trees revived us as we delved deep into the woods, taking side trails so we could not be easily seen or found, until finally the trail thinned so much that we came down from our saddles. We tied our horses to a dead bush and sat down beside a gurgling brook only half a stride across.

He collected mulberries in his palm and gave them to me. "I was . . . perhaps, too harsh this morning."

"When you scolded me, you mean?" I teased.

"I only meant"—he turned sideways on his elbow, the pomegranate in one hand, his legs stretched out so that the toes of his boots dangled over the brook—"to caution you to trust sparingly. I spoke to Kent this morning. He bears a grudge against Despenser for having robbed him of various privileges. He swears Norfolk is of the same vein. But Kent, he is the sort . . . shall we say, there are sharper-minded men than him? As for important duties—be parsimonious in granting him those. He will make a mess of things without even trying. My lady, you gambled by bringing him into the fold. For now, his heart is loyal to you. There are those, however, who would think nothing of sacrificing you as an example . . . or for their own ambitions."

I plucked up a sprig of mint, pinched at a leaf and held it to my nose. "I know that—better than you think I do. But who *am* I to trust? Am I to review with you every person, every move, every thought before acting?"

"What I am telling you is to be careful. You trust with your heart and not your head. Hearts can be deceived."

"It was my heart that told me to trust you. Was it wrong then?"

He hung his head, perhaps sensing the futility of this argument. "I've spent too many days, weeks . . . nay, years agonizing over this to let it be too easily undone."

"Sir Roger—"

He held up a single finger to hush me. "We're alone. 'Roger' will do."

"Agonizing over what, Roger? Revenge?" His name felt thickly strange upon my tongue, but in my mind I practiced saying it over and over until it became an incantation.

He thumped the pomegranate on the ground between us. "You think I am doing this only for revenge?" The look he gave me then was grave and foreboding. "I risk your life as well as mine by being here."

By being here? I didn't know whether he meant by being in France or by being here right now, with me. I only knew that I felt suddenly, overwhelmingly panicked. Why was it that when I was with him, one moment I was never more myself and the next I could not have leapt from my own skin fast enough? Roiling in confusion, I shrugged. "What other reason could there be?"

The pomegranate tumbled away with a push of his fingers. "*This,*" he whispered, raising himself up to kneel before me. He slid the palm of his hand across my cheek, down my neck and around until his fingers were entwined in my hair, pulling my face to his.

"Isabella," he whispered. His breath washed over me in a flood of awakening.

I tilted my chin upward. His lips sought mine and found their answer readily as I returned his kiss.

His kiss.

I sank back onto the ground, pulling him with me, bits of leaves entangling in my hair, the sweet scent of crushed grass and wild mint surrounding me . . . and I did not stop him, but encouraged him, invited him, to do as he wished . . . as I wanted . . . as I had ached for.

As I had longed for all my life.

EVERY DAY I WENT and found him, begged his advice, echoed it . . . not because I needed it immediately, but because I needed an excuse to be *with* him. He came to me as much as I sought him. Sometimes, I had merely to think his name and he was there. At my request, Mortimer was given the room next to mine. Between his bedchamber and my wardrobe room was a secret panel, concealed on my side by rows of gowns and on his by a wide tapestry.

There were times when all was dark and quiet that I would go to him. And he would take my hands, pull me to him, cover me in kisses—my lips, my neck, my breasts—peeling away my clothes until they lay in a tangle at my feet. Then he would carry me to his bed and make love to me, slowly, gently, fiercely. Afterwards, we held each other and spoke in drawn-out whispers. Our fingers wandered over one another's bodies. We savored every moment of our togetherness, knowing that daylight would come and usher us back to our separate roles: the cast-off queen and her... we had not quite established to the rest of the world what he was to me yet. A counselor, perhaps? My commander? In private, at least, Roger Mortimer was my lover.

During the day, there were also stolen moments, rarer ones, but all the more feverish in their brevity—usually in my wardrobe. It is not a simple thing for a queen to accommodate her lover at will. Most often, it had to be arranged in advance, coordinated. That was where Patrice and Arnaud came to be of help. Marie was far too virtuous to entrust with the details of our affair. I could have trusted Juliana, but she had departed for Corbeil for the birth of her third child. It was unlikely she would return to attend me afterwards.

Although I had confided to Patrice the unhappy story of Arnaud's wife and child, she still refused his attempts at anything more than a casual friendship, so it was yet bitter between them. Otherwise, there was nothing the two of them would not do on my or Mortimer's behalf. Clever spies that they were, they guarded our doors and our secrets, concocted alibis for us, and kept us acutely abreast of Stapledon's whereabouts.

There was one more way in which Patrice helped. I was frightfully aware that what Roger and I were doing could result in a pregnancy and that was a risk neither of us could afford. So it was that I sought Patrice's advice on the matter.

"You wish, then, to prevent this altogether?" She drew a stitch slowly through a piece of embroidery that she had picked up out of boredom, for Patrice usually loathed such tedious domesticity, preferring to gossip instead. "Or to . . . take care of '*it*', should the need arise?" She tilted her head at the word '*it*', which only accentuated her highly arched brow more.

"I . . . I don't know. It seems as though, after my first child at least, I conceived almost every time I was with Edward." I sat down on my stool, running my fingers over the teeth of a jeweled and silver hair comb. I had considered the giving of my body to Edward to be a sacrifice of sorts—I loathed his touch every odious time, fought nausea and tears as he ground his hips into me and then ended with a grunt and a twitch. My only consolation was in the brevity of his lovemaking, if one could even call it that. I put my duty as a queen above my repulsion and learned to absent myself in mind. Yet now, with Mortimer, I was never more enthralled in each moment, eager for the next.

A child could come of it and . . . already I could be . . .

Patrice jammed the needle into her thumb, squealed and gave me a serious look. "Then I will tell you how to keep it from happening. But you must do it every time afterwards, within hours, or else you will grow a baby inside of you and then . . . that is more dangerous to take care of. Do you understand?"

"Yes."

"I need rue from the herb garden. Vinegar from the kitchen."

I sent a servant to fetch me both and a few other ingredients Patrice requested. Within the hour she made me a preparation out of the rue mixed with wine. This I was to drink every day. The vinegar was stirred with finely ground willow bark into a watery paste. This I was to wash my private parts with after being with Mortimer. The elixir of rue, as Patrice warned me, did make me bleed more heavily during my cycle, which sometimes left me light enough in the head to keep me in bed. Despite that, I was religiously observant of these practices. The Church may have frowned upon them, but so it did adultery, too. And I meant to give no proof of that to the world.

Bishop Stapledon, I knew, collected information and fed it to Edward at every instance, augmenting the rumors that were already rampant: that I had no intention of returning to England on congenial terms, that my son's filial devotion to me had displaced his fealty to his own father, that a scheme was afoot to either overthrow him or murder his favorite, and that I had taken a lover—a traitor to Edward, no less.

In every rumor, they say there is a grain of truth. Sometimes, 'they' are not altogether wrong.

30

Isabella:

Vincennes — October, 1325

AS THE WEEKS WORE on, like a pestering horsefly Bishop Stapledon appeared more and more frequently, demanding to speak with me on insignificant matters. I began to delay and then avoid him, perturbed at having my privacy so frequently invaded. When I did meet with him, I was brusque, wickedly pointed and liberal with my arguments. He chafed at being defied by a woman, inserted his strict interpretations of scripture repeatedly and fulminated, comparing me to Eve and Mortimer to the serpent in the Garden of Eden. But if I felt any trace of sin, I denied it completely.

In late September, Young Edward was formally invested with the titles of Duke of Aquitaine and Count of Ponthieu and Montreuil. A day later he placed his hands between Charles' and swore homage. He conducted himself with the aplomb of one twice his age, but it did not go without notice that instead of bowing his head in obeisance throughout the ceremony, he kept his chin up and his eyes directly on Charles', as if already he considered himself his uncle's equal—or perhaps even his superior. When Charles withdrew his troops from Gascony in terms with the treaty, again Bishop Stapledon demanded I return to England, since there was nothing more to be done in France. Once more Charles openly denied him.

Young Edward also refused to go back to England. It was then that events began to precipitate more rapidly.

MORNING HAD NOT YET arrived. I lay in Mortimer's bed, his arm lightly over my waist, his chest warm and hard against my back, his breath stirring the hair at the nape of my neck. For hours sometimes, I would feel the steady rhythm of his heartbeat as he held me, listen to the intake of his breath or memorize the lines in his hardened face, the shape of each muscle, the length of every finger—for the only thing I had come to fear was the prospect of being without him. I moved gently from beneath his arm and looked over the edge of the bed for my clothes.

"Back to sleep," he murmured, reaching out and pulling me to him. "All's quiet now. I'll not let you go, Isabeau." He had taken to calling me by my childhood name. Coming from his lips, it had an entirely different sound. Sweeter, more longing.

"I should go back, Roger." I felt compelled to return to my own room. We treaded dangerously, flouting discretion by the frequency of our trysts—all of which only heightened their intensity and made the promise of being together again even more powerful and undeniable.

"But I'm not done with you," he whispered.

He kissed my neck, beneath my chin, and began his way downward. Before he reached my collarbone, I had forgotten about going. I was so easily persuaded.

His knee wedged pleadingly between my legs. I put my hands around his neck and pulled him over me.

"Say that you will love me like this forever," I said, "no matter what happens."

He smiled as if in a dream. "Isabeau, there is only now—only you and me." Then, he chased away the uncertainty of the future as if it were but a pebble flung from his hand.

I was lost within our lovemaking when a pair of fists banged upon his door and toppled us from our heaven.

Mortimer ripped himself abruptly from me and rolled from beneath the sheets, so that a blast of cold air shocked me into both fright and awareness. He leapt into a pair of breeches, fumbling with a knot in the cord as he went to the door. The single candle on his nightstand, burnt down to a stub, wavered and struggled.

"Who is it?" Mortimer said gruffly. A low voice answered him, but the words were unintelligible to me.

I began to get up to put my clothes back on and hurry through the secret door back to my wardrobe, but he gestured for me to stay. I burrowed beneath the blanket and pulled it up over me, certain the door would crash down and soldiers rush in to arrest us. But I heard only the click of a latch and the creak of hinges as Mortimer let someone in and locked the door again. I peeked from beneath the blanket. It was Arnaud.

"The bishop," he said, catching his breath. "He left. Said he was going back to England."

"Did he say why?" Mortimer asked.

"He told Maltravers his life was in danger—that he had received a letter warning him he would be murdered if he did not quit the country at once."

"And who sent him this 'letter'?"

Arnaud drew a piece of crumpled parchment from inside his sleeve and handed it to Mortimer, who gave it a cursory look. "It was not signed, my lord."

A threat upon the bishop's life? Certainly this was not Charles' doing?

"I trust you let him go?" Mortimer suggested.

"Should we have stopped him . . . or followed him? Should we now?"

"No, no. It is a relief to be rid of him." He thanked Arnaud for his swiftness in reporting the matter. As soon as Arnaud had left, Mortimer came and sat down on the bed.

When I finally looked, he was holding the letter over the candle. The flame licked at its edge and then curled upward, turning the yellow parchment to floating wisps of burnt black.

I raised myself up, clutching the covers to my bosom. "He will accuse you."

"I shall deny it absolutely. All that matters now . . . is that he's gone."

"Back to England—where he shall tell Edward of us."

"Hmmm, he shall, I suppose. But I am sure Edward already knows. What's important is that Stapledon left without you. And you're still here with me."

31

Isabella:

Vincennes – July, 1326

MANY LETTERS WERE CARRIED abroad as a long winter passed into a fleeting spring. Then summer arrived prematurely on an arid, unrelenting wind, and replies began to pour in. Several more times Edward demanded my return. I called for Despenser to be banished forever from England. Edward again refused. Meanwhile, I also engaged in lengthy correspondences with Count William of Hainault regarding both the hand of one of his daughters for Young Edward and to implore his help. Those letters were met with enthusiasm and openness. But there were other letters—letters that were to threaten our plans. From Edward to Pope John. And from the Pope to Charles. Letters regarding my relationship with Mortimer.

Even worse, I did not realize to what lengths Bishop Stapledon would pursue revenge until my cousin Robert of Artois arrived in my solar at Vincennes unexpectedly. In the long golden light of a summer evening, Robert's face appeared ashen with concern. He turned his feathered cap in his hands, hunting for the proper words. I could not ever recall seeing him without a glint of merriment in his eyes or a grin teasing at the corners of his lips.

"Trouble from England," he mumbled, his mouth suddenly plunging in a sullen frown, "and elsewhere."

"Should that surprise us?" I tried to make light of it, but the slump of Robert's shoulders said that the news would be a heavy blow. "Does Edward order me back again? Or does he threaten to steal his heir back from beneath Charles' nose?"

"Lord Despenser told Pope John the only reason you have stayed in France until now is because Roger Mortimer has threatened your life, should you leave."

"That's a lie," I said, incredulous. "I choose to stay and I have been plain about why I am here and not in England. Because of Despenser. Oh, it does not surprise me one whit to hear him deflect the blame. Well then, I shall offer no retort. He may as well have accused me of witchery for putting a pinch of herbs on my pillow."

Robert cleared his throat. "The Pope has demanded that King Charles turn Sir Roger, and you, out."

On the stool next to me by the window, Marie laid down her needle-work. Patrice, who had been straightening the clothes in the wardrobe, dashed into the room, aghast.

"What say does the Pope have in where I am or what I do?"

"Complete say where it concerns morality." Robert ran a finger along the spine of the pheasant feather on his cap. "King Edward has written to the Pope repeatedly. It would seem, fair cousin, that your relationship with Sir Roger is much talked about, both on the continent and in England. King Edward claims"—he lowered his eyes—"that Charles is harboring adulterers. The Pope, by indication of his decree, gives credence to the accusation." Robert tugged a letter from beneath his over-tunic and held it out, but did not move toward me.

I crossed the room on weak knees, took the letter and read it.

ISABEAU

Our Dearest Sister,

Your work here has been of immeasurable value. We have reached an agreeable peace with England. You services are, however, concluded and I have no cause to continue to support you. It has come to bear that I can no longer grant you refuge, either. Pope John has decreed that your behavior, as a married woman, is intolerable and sinful. To disregard him on this delicate matter would be to accept excommunication. My faith is foremost. I cannot afford estrangement from the Church or the relinquishment of my soul. With even greater regret, I have forbidden any of my subjects to give you aid, on pain of banishment. I pray one day we will both be resolved of these unfortunate issues. Therefore, I ask you to go, but in peace and with my blessing.

God grant you a good and long life,
Charles, by the grace of God, King of France
Fontainebleau

I held the letter, my heart slowly going cold. My own brother, who had so vehemently defended me, given me succor, supported me in my grievances against my husband—he, too, was abandoning me?

I staggered toward the closest chair and crumpled into it, my body as limp as my will to go on. I wanted to call Mortimer to me that moment, wanted to throw myself into the comfort of his arms. He could put everything right. But I could not, not now—not with Robert here before me and this condemnation, this damning sentence of adultery and treason, swinging above my head as God's absolute and eternal judgment.

Robert came to me, kissed me on the forehead and brought his mouth close to my ear. "Count William of Hainault is expecting you and Sir Roger in Valenciennes. You are to leave this very night. Everything has been prepared for you." As he drew back, his hand lingered on my shoulder.

Charles? I mouthed.

He nodded in answer.

SHORTLY AFTER MIDNIGHT, ROBERT returned to my apartments and led me and my damsels away. Arnaud de Mone also escorted us, telling us that my son and Mortimer would meet us when we were safely outside the grounds. It would soon be discovered whose company we kept, but for now we would give the appearance of departing separately. The few sleepy-eyed servants and men-at-arms that we passed on our way to the outer wall kept their distance, as though we were lepers to be avoided.

At a low door in the outer wall, Robert whispered to the watchman and we were all ushered through, then along a footpath across a sheep meadow. Before we reached the hedgerow which marked its perimeter, our shoes were slick with manure. In single file, we scrambled through a hole in the bushes. Thorny branches tugged at our hair and caught on our clothes. Once through, we stood at the edge of a stream. One by one, Robert and Arnaud helped us down the steep bank. Lifting our skirts to our knees, Patrice and I waded through the cold water. The bank on the far side was less steep, but thick with stinking mud. Bedraggled, we slogged along with our shoes squelching. Soon, we found ourselves in an orchard where green pears clung tightly to their branches.

Behind me, Marie stumbled over a fallen limb and whimpered. I stepped aside and waited for her to come up beside me.

"I do not think I want to leave France again, my lady," she said woefully. She slowed her steps, frowning.

I took her trembling hand in mine. "Then I will release you, but not yet. Come to Valenciennes. When we leave for England, you needn't come with us."

She gasped. "Oh, I would never dream of leaving you, but . . . but England is such a dreadful, horrible place and the winters so gray and cold and so—"

"How much further?" Patrice demanded of Robert, as she veered to the side of our ragged line.

Robert jabbed his finger at her in warning. Then he held his hands wide to halt us. Thankful for the reprieve, I sank down. My shins ached from the long walk and the soles of my feet were tender from stepping on too many stones and sharp sticks. Robert brought a finger to his lips. Peering into the half darkness, I held my breath and heard, distinctly, footsteps on the path ahead. The night sky was veiled by wispy clouds, letting only patches of starlight shine through, and the moon was not out.

A doe and her fawn appeared on the path before us. The moment Robert rose to his feet and gestured for us to follow, the deer and her offspring bounded off into the tangle of pear trees.

A mile later, we came to a small farm in a clearing. There, we were joined by Young Edward, Mortimer and nearly a dozen of his men, among them Sir John Maltravers and Gerard d'Alspaye. We dressed ourselves in more humble clothes and took on the guise of a merchant's household, journeying north on business. Patrice fussed over trading her beautiful embroidered gown and ivory hair adornments for a kirtle of itchy fustian and a wimple that covered her swirling ringlets of raven hair.

We were provided with pack horses carrying bundles of linen. Within the bundles of cloth, however, were tucked bags of silver. We were also given a cart pulled by two red oxen that was stacked with barrels of wine from Gascony, salt from Bourgneuf and more silver buried beneath. Our leave-taking had been an event in planning long before Charles had penned compliance to the Pope.

I glanced at my son's face in the sheen of moonlight as we gathered between the whispering woods and the dark road leading away northward from Vincennes. He held his chin aloft, drawing the night air fully into his lungs.

"You understand," I began, keeping my voice low, "why we are going to Valenciennes?"

Young Edward shrugged. "I understand that the Count of Hainault, who is a rich man with many soldiers at his bidding, has four daughters. You want me to marry one of them?"

I nodded with a dose of trepidation. I had never truly asked Young Edward if that was acceptable, but had merely explained why he should accept a wife in exchange for ships and soldiers.

"What if I will not?" he asked.

"Then we . . . I could not go back to England."

"But I could?"

The teasing tone in his voice afforded me little reassurance. "If you wished."

"You would not stop me?"

"No." Although I would have expended every last shred of my energy trying to convince him not to go. "But you've stayed this long, haven't you? Why? To please me? You could have left with Bishop Stapledon at any time and what could I have done to stop you?"

"Please, I wouldn't have. The Bishop of Exeter bores me to death. Always lecturing. I'll be damned to hell when God says I am, not him. I never liked Lord Despenser. No one really does—except Father. And what's bad for the king is bad for England." He drew his shoulders up, sitting as tall as he could. "But you'll allow me to speak with the count's daughters and make up my own mind, yes? My wife will be passing fair to look upon and kind . . . and clever, like you. And if I like none of them, then I shall choose none. We will go on to some other court, try again."

"That would be difficult."

"It would, yes." He shot me a quick look. "But if I'm to have a wife, she must make a good wife for me and I must like her . . . and she me."

If there was any blessing in what I had suffered through with Edward all those years, it was my children, most of all Young Edward.

Before the silence that began to settle between us gaped uncomfortably, Mortimer rode around the corner of the byre.

"My lord," Mortimer addressed, dipping slightly from the waist in his saddle, "will you lead the way?" He raised his hand to indicate a road that plunged deep into the forest. Young Edward hesitated a moment, then rested the heel of his hand on the pommel of his untried sword and gave his mount a nudge in the flanks.

ISABEAU

A rising wind whipped the tree branches above us into a sudden clatter. Small trees swayed and bent. I brought the hood of my cloak up over my head. Our procession drew closer together, the nose of each horse touching the tail of the one before it, as we bumped along through the darkness.

A violent gust ripped my hood from my head. The first of the rain came not in pattering drops, but slamming downward in heavy sheets as if we had plunged beneath a great waterfall.

PART III:

I bear the name of King;
I wear the crown, but am controlled by them,
By Mortimer and my unconstant Queen,
Who spots my nuptial bed with infamy.

Edward II,
from Christopher Marlowe's *Edward II*

32

Roger Mortimer:

Saint-Denis — August, 1326

A N AMUSING SUPPLICATION. YOUNG Lord Edward, in no attempt to hide the letter, handed it to his mother almost immediately. She, in turn, shared it with me:

Our Fair Son,

Daily I pray for your safe return to England's shores, for the longer you remain in France, the greater, I fear, is the menace to your welfare. Your mother has fallen under ill counsel in Sir Roger Mortimer. For many years I gave him patronage and entrusted him with high stations and important duties, only to have him join in league with my false cousin, Thomas of Lancaster. Mortimer's nature is one of brazen arrogance. He fails not only in gratitude, but flaunts his undeserved freedom in mockery of me. I can but imagine what fantastic lies he has told to delude the queen, your mother. Despite my pleas of concern, she rebukes me. Mortimer, as you know, is my sworn enemy. She cannot see her very life is in danger.

I have knowledge of marriage negotiations, entered into on your behalf, of which I have offered no consent. Do not forsake the oaths you swore to me at Dover to withhold from all such contracts. They were requested and sworn for good cause. Honor your trust in me. Be not led astray.

For you, out of love, I beg you to listen to me, your father and king. Cleave yourself from those whose sole purpose is to use you, an innocent, as their instrument of evil. They bear neither love for you nor care for your future. Be not disobedient. Come home. Shame me no more by these vile associations. Relieve me of the grief that your continued absence has inflicted.

Our Lord protect you,
Edwardus Rex,
Lichfield

Four years had gone by since I knelt before Edward at Shrewsbury. Four years in which to think. Four years in which to design my revenge. Five hundred days and more rotting in the Tower have a way of filling a man's head with malice. It also teaches a man patience.

We went first to the Abbey of Saint-Denis. There, Isabella lit candles, knelt before the tombs of her father and two oldest brothers, and uttered copious prayers for their long-dead souls. Her son, Young Edward she often called him, mimicked his mother's every reverent move. It was a ploy spurred by Charles' insidious genius that had brought the boy to France—one that preyed cleverly on Edward's dependable stupidity. Not only did Young Edward despise Despenser enough to wish him gone as much as I or his mother did, but in him there was just enough of ambition to entice him to our plan.

The next morning, I joined Isabella in the cloister. I took her hands in mine and placed a cordial kiss upon her knuckles. Then she hooked her arm through mine and we turned to walk toward the little orchard of pear trees beyond the abbey walls. We paused to let a line of monks pass, their shoulders stooped forward and hands folded in perpetual prayer.

When we stepped past the first row of trees, their branches hanging low, I plucked a half-green pear and turned it over in my palm, inspecting it for worm holes. We walked along side by side for awhile, until our steps slowed in unison. Before she could look at me, I moved to stand behind her, so that I could memorize the curve of her lower back, the indentation of her waist where only last night I had slid my arms around her and pulled her to me.

"We will be apart, Isabeau, for weeks perhaps. You must go to Ponthieu. As for me—as soon as Gerard and Arnaud have readied the horses we will be on our way. To Amiens first, then Courtrai, then on to Zeeland." To Zeeland, that soggy, reed-clogged spread of land along the coast, where I would commission the finest vessels from Sluys all the way to Dordrecht. Ships to carry men for the army that I would lead. The army that would overthrow Edward and Despenser. "Once you have collected your revenues from Ponthieu you can join me at Valenciennes. There the prince can pick his bride. For now, though, if we are to return to England in sufficient force, I need more men, and the means to pay them. Promises of plunder alone will get us little more than vagrants and criminals. I need trained men, fine horses, ample weapons and supplies. I cannot have less, Isabeau. I have waited too many years already."

"How long do you think *I* have waited?" She stepped away and leaned into a crook of the tree, her gaze intense. "I was suffering long before you fell from favor, Roger."

"Yet you have survived and risen. I swore to you I would not fail at this. And I will not. Do you believe in me?"

A breeze lifted over the pastures surrounding Saint-Denis and teased long wisps of her hair from its pins. "I believe that you will do everything you can to see it through and beyond. But I also believe there are things not in our control, things we cannot foresee. I only wish it were a year from now, Roger. We would be back in England and all this would be done with."

"It *will* be over with . . . one day. You realize, don't you, that we will have to do more than just remove Hugh Despenser? Are you prepared to do what needs to be done?"

Looking down thoughtfully, she blinked. "He will be tried by parliament for treason, among other things, and found guilty. There is only one outcome for that. His blood, then, will not be on our hands."

"And your husband, the king? What do you think will become of him?"

That question was harder for her. "I do not know."

"If he is permitted to remain on the throne, then what happened with Piers de Gaveston, with Despenser, would happen all over again. Edward has a weakness. A weakness that cannot be cured. He depends on others who then take advantage of him. He should not be allowed to rule freely again. *That* is something you do know, isn't it?"

A crevice furrowed the narrow space between her brows. "Yes, you're right. England would be better off with my son as king."

And with us as his regents. Finally, she had put all the pieces together.

"Ah, there," I said. "Gerard is coming to fetch me."

When Gerard d'Alspaye noticed the queen, her form molded to the tree, he stopped short and beckoned. I raised a hand in acknowledgment. "A moment, Gerard. Final orders from my queen first. Bring the horses this way."

He bobbed his head in reply and returned to the abbey.

For several moments, we could not look at each other, Isabella and I. We simply stood there, close enough to embrace, saying nothing.

At last I spoke, my low words intermingling with the rustling of leaves on the warm summer wind. "I must go."

She bit at her lip to keep it from trembling.

"Think of it as only a day that we must be apart," I said to her. "And when that day is done, one more day. And one more day. Until we are together again."

Sir John Maltravers, with his wounded hand curled into his chest like a battered claw, appeared first through the abbey gate on his horse, leading my train of armed men.

I walked away, each step becoming heavier than the one before. I felt the pull of her stare, pleading for me to rush to her and take her into my arms. It was damnably hard, but I forced myself not to look back.

The sooner everything was arranged for the invasion, the sooner Isabella and I would be together again.

33

Roger Mortimer:

Hainault — August, 1326

TWICE BEFORE, I HAD visited Count William of Hainault and his brother, Sir John, in Mons. Once soon after fleeing England. A congenial visit, and short, during which I made no requests. A second time, after Isabella had first arrived in Paris, to discuss business.

Under a strong afternoon sun, Count William, Sir John and I took a leisurely ride through the Hainault countryside. I suspect the count wanted me to see his expansive dairy herd so he could explain to me the superiority of his cows to English ones—a suspicion which was born out. I listened to his bombast with dulled senses, occasionally inserting a polite question to pretend an interest in milk production and growth rates.

Sir John sat upon his horse straight and strong, as if born to the saddle. His brother, who was much older, resembled an egg trying to balance on its bottom. Swaying with every stride of his mount, the count gripped its ribs with his knees and held the reins murderously tight.

Finally, exhausted by his constant efforts, Count William halted his horse abruptly. He rested one hand above the protrusion of his belly, stifling a belch, and shaded his eyes against the August sun with the other. "Queen Isabella has attempted reconciliation with her husband, the king, has she not?"

"On many accounts, my lord. In person, by letter, through her brother, King Charles . . . even by appeal to the Pope to try to reach some compromise."

He dropped his hand from his brow and turned his shrewd, piggish eyes on me. "By 'compromise' you mean the banishment of this Lord Despenser?" The cows, with their bony hips and sagging udders, swished the flies away with their tails and chewed on great wads of cud. My horse dropped its head and nosed the hindquarters of a pregnant cow. I tugged at the reins, urging him away before he took a hoof to the foreleg.

I nodded. "His Grace, Pope John, upheld Queen Isabella's request. King Edward flatly refused to honor it."

"Naturally." William shared a knowing smile with his brother. "Yes, we have heard of Edward's unusual fondness for this Despenser, even here. Stories of the English court are ever a source of amusement and shock. We are simple folk, Sir Roger. We fish. We farm. We weave and dye. We place our lives at the mercy of the sea in the name of trade, so others might have the needed goods that cannot be purchased in their homelands. Between our prayers and our duties, we haven't the luxury of enjoying life's pleasures. One is left to wonder how much more prosperous the English could be if they squandered less of their time in frivolity and spent more of it praising God's grace and blessing His bounties."

Again, I nodded. In truth, I detected a sermon and I despised getting them from men who paid for my sword while they idled in opulence, protected by high walls. But the count had something of value to me—an army—and so I tolerated him. English exiles alone would not be enough. I needed the Hainaulters with their honed blades and well-trained horses. I needed their might. I needed his money. He needed a source of commerce to ensure his lasting wealth. And . . . he wanted a legacy. A marriage pact. A daughter of his joined to England's heir.

"There are goods to be had in England, my lord," I said, "from which you might earn a greater profit. Then, you could build more ships, more barns, more churches: to trade, increase your herds, give thanks to God, whatever you so please."

Like any man, Count William served himself.

I ENDURED HIS COMPANY for two more days. He talked too much, of nothing in particular, and when it came to money, he could not be shut up at all. He had amassed great quantities of it by driving hard bargains. His daughters, of whom he spoke with as much affection as he did his dairy herd, he had long ago figured were among his greatest assets. With twelve children of my own, I could well understand. Better to think of their rearing as an investment than a burden. My relief finally came when the count left for Valenciennes.

The next day, Sir John and I rode out from Mons to greet Queen Isabella and Lord Edward. Although far from eloquent in speech or manner, I found Sir John to be less one-sided in his conversation. Like me, he realized the strength of his sword over that of his purse.

His deeply set eyes took on a faraway look. "I hear Queen Isabella is beautiful."

"Some say she is." Only I knew how much so.

Beyond an expanse of farmland lay a village that was no more than a blacksmith's shop, a few houses, and a mill on the nearside of a bridge at stream's edge. From between the houses, a party of riders approached at a gentle walk. Before they reached the bridge, I knew who it was. I gave my mount a sharp prick of my spurs and took off at a canter, Sir John quickly beside me.

Before Isabella and Young Edward were within a stone's throw of us, Sir John had dismounted, rushed forward and dropped down on one knee in the middle of the road, his head bowed. Although Isabella's eyes were on me, she brought her gray palfrey to a halt before Sir John. Young Edward came abreast of her.

"Sir Roger." Isabella's face broke into a broad smile.

"My queen." I leapt to the ground and returned the smile. Then I bowed to her son. "My lord." I was about to go forward to help her down from her horse when she dropped her gaze to Sir John and stayed me with her palm.

"Who might you be, sir knight?"

Still, he kept his head down. "John of Hainault, good lady, and I swear I shall defend you all my life."

"Then stand, Sir John."

In one motion, he was on his feet and lifting her by the waist as if she weighed no more than a bird.

"Your kindness is too much," she said. "I thank you, a thousand times over, although my gratitude hardly seems sufficient."

"It is, my lady. It is. I need no more."

"Sir John," the prince said, clenching the reins of his horse impatiently, "you came to escort us to Mons?"

"Yes, my lord." Sir John gave a cursory bow. "If you will follow me."

WHEN ISABELLA CAME TO me that first night in Mons, we wasted no time with words. Eager to press my flesh to hers, I tore the layers of clothes from her body roughly. We tumbled onto the bed as my own garments flew through the air, her hips arched high, her legs wrapping invitingly around mine as I knelt before her. I explored her, caressed her, kissed her as she writhed on crumpled sheets. Her moans of pleasure became a plea for ecstasy. Open-mouthed, her hands slid down my back and clamped hard around my buttocks as she pulled me greedily to her. I lowered myself over the length of her body, seeking entry, finding it with one strong thrust. She shuddered, her fingernails imprinting into my skin. I drew back, feeling the crash of blood with my heartbeat. Then I drove again, and again, she moving with me, her hips rocking in rhythm with mine, until the pace of our coupling reached an uncontrollable frenzy. Each wave hurled us higher, further. Until at last we were both drowning in each other, gasping for air, as if crashing toward the depths of a bottom-less waterfall. One, falling together. Her breath came quick and shallow, but still she held me to her. As she lay beneath me, I was not thinking of war or revenge—only her and how it was to be with her.

I reached over the edge of the bed to retrieve the wad of sheets that had fallen to the floor and pulled it up over us in false modesty. "Have you spoken further to your son about the count's daughters?"

Isabella rolled to me and nuzzled against my shoulder. "I have."

"And?"

"He says, quite adamantly, that he will not marry until he is twenty-five." She giggled like a girl of ten. "He does not know what he is missing."

"Did you tell him that is too old? I've known men that were grandfathers before thirty."

Her fingers wound into the knot of hair at my neck. "You are almost forty and you are not." She kissed me playfully on the underside of my chin.

"The count wants to join his house with that of Plantagenet and Capet. Besides, your son is old enough to discover the pleasures of having a wife in his bed every night." It seemed a very logical device to me. At the same age Young Edward was, I had been betrothed. At fourteen, I was married. On our wedding night, I bedded Joan. In less than a year our first son was born.

Isabella slipped her hand from me and rolled away. "When we return to England, will you go back to Ludlow?"

Ludlow. Where my wife would be waiting. I had tried not to think of that. I had other plans. There was too much else to do. I caressed her shoulder, as if I could sweep away her worries with a touch. "Isabeau . . . I want nothing between us to change. I will write to her that my duties are too many. She will live comfortably. It will be understood."

She lay still, without response, as though she were waiting to hear more.

"Isabeau . . . Isabeau," I whispered, stroking her hair, "I love you."

I had never spoken the words before, not even to Joan.

She turned her face toward mine, seeking a kiss. "And I"—her legs slid around mine as she pulled me onto her—"love you, my gentle Mortimer."

But where she discovered contentment and joy, I felt a great burden settled on me. To say that you love someone is far different than to live as though you do.

AT VALENCIENNES, COUNT WILLIAM and his wife, Jeanne, welcomed us formally in their great, glittering hall. Count William presented Isabella with a bronze unicorn aquamanile. To her son he gave a silver-gilt plate from Byzantium, depicting David's triumph over Goliath. Young Edward gave the count's daughters identical ivory-backed mirrors and their mother embroidered silks from Persia, courtesy of King Charles.

Three fidgeting girls ranging in age from fourteen to nine—the fourth being noticeably absent, although no one had yet mentioned it—stood lined up like a collection of dolls near a row of windows to the east. The morning sunlight struck harshly upon their blanched complexions.

Young Edward, seated by then between his mother and the count, appeared wholly unimpressed.

Eighteen months had passed since I had visited the count's court and looked his daughters over. Then, I had thought them promising enough, but in truth, I admit, they were more pleasant and healthy than pretty—the three present, at least. Margaret, the oldest, had grown more broad than tall in that time. She resembled Sir John more than her father, with stout arms and broad shoulders and a silver-yellow rope of hair that hung all the way down her back and to her knees. She was robust and sturdy, like a well-bred ox. Good perhaps for bearing children, but not altogether enticing to a young man entertaining his choice of brides. The youngest two, named Joan and Isabelle, huddled close to one another, too frightened to speak, and neither of them old enough to have burst forth with the first firm, budding curves of womanhood. Both still had the plump bellies of overfed babes, not unlike their father. In different clothes and with cropped hair, they could have passed for boys, so plain and unmaidenly were their faces.

The countess uttered profuse apologies for Philippa's tardiness. While we waited for them to find the girl, the queen and countess exchanged compliments on the gifts. Too soon, the awkwardness was replaced by stone-dead silence. It was not going well—rather badly, in fact.

"Margaret," I broached, beginning with the oldest, as I turned to Count William, "does she hunt or hawk?"

Margaret took a step in retreat.

The count looked at his wife blankly, awaiting her help to answer the simple question. Clearly, he left the raising of his daughters to his wife. Countess Jeanne rescued her husband from his ignorance. "She rides when she must . . . and she has a lapdog that she will not part from, but she is . . . she is of a fragile nature and prefers gentler pursuits."

I wondered what 'fragile' entailed. She looked more like a plow horse to me than a butterfly whose wings could be crushed between the fingertips. "Yes? Such as . . ."

The countess replied with the common domesticities: needlework, the reading of the Gospel, letter-writing. And so the forced conversation went, which was even worse than it had begun.

Young Edward stretched his lanky legs and yawned, his eyelids sinking as he gazed out the window. In those clumsy minutes, I could see Isabella beginning to fret. Our chances of convincing her son to select a mate were sinking rapidly . . . as was our hope of overthrowing Edward and getting rid of Despenser.

I glanced at the prince, only to see him leaning back in his chair, asleep. It was only the stringing together of sharp words and the firm stomping of her foot as Philippa finally, and reluctantly, entered the room that awoke him. She came to a halt beside her youngest sister Isabelle, standing not much taller even though she was four years older, and threw her hands upon her hips. Although not any prettier than the other three, she had a confidence to her demeanor that they lacked.

Wearing a look of irritation, Edward leaned forward and peered at her. He rose from his chair and flew to her in great swooping strides.

"You are late," he told her.

She stuck her dimpled chin out. "I had better . . . I mean more pressing things to do."

"Better than being presented to the future King of England? Do tell. I should like to hear." He walked a full circle around her, appraising her from various angles. Her face was oval, her frame tending toward broad rather than slender, and her curves of a matching roundness. Not plump, but robust. Unlike her sisters, whose hair was bound in either a caul or covered by a wimple, Philippa wore hers loose, a mass of glistening golden brown that hung to her waist, bits of straw entangled in it.

"My favorite mare delivered a foal not an hour ago," she boasted. "A black colt with a blaze. He is already standing. I was not about to leave him."

"You ride?" he asked, stopping in front of her squarely.

Philippa smiled and drew her shoulders back, brown eyes twinkling with pride. "I do. Every day."

The countess dug her fingernails into her legs and glared at her daughter.

Finally noticing the scowl affixed on her mother's face, Philippa quickly retracted her words, her tone notably less pert and more congenial. "At east, I would like to . . . my lord."

Pleased, he nodded. "Good, then we will ride tomorrow, Lady Philippa." He bowed his head to the count and countess. "If I may beg your leave. I should like to take my rest now." He glanced at his mother. "Our journey was a hurried one."

Before going, he took Philippa's hand, but rather than kiss it, he drew her a step closer. "It would please me if you would sit beside me at supper. We could discuss your new colt."

Without giving her time to answer, he turned and left. Margaret crossed her arms and, pouting, turned her face away from her sister. The two youngest, holding hands, looked down at the ground and shifted on their feet. Their parents glowed with satisfaction.

Isabella and I did not need to share a look to know that with that one fleeting stroke of fate everything had fallen into place.

FOR FIVE DAYS STRAIGHT, Edward and Philippa rode together, much to her mother's displeasure, but on the sixth day a heavy rain prevented them. So instead, Young Edward taught her how to play the game of English tables. Before the afternoon was done, aided by both luck and wit, she was beating him soundly. He took it in good humor and, being obstinate, challenged her to another game and another after that. Their fun ended when the priggish countess voiced her disapproval because the game used dice—the devil's playthings, she declared.

An intelligent girl, Philippa would make a good queen for any king, although I questioned whether she was strong enough to survive child-bearing. Margaret would have been a better brood mare, but he would have grown quickly bored of her, dull as she was.

Soon, Young Edward made it quite plain to his mother that he had made his choice: Philippa it would be.

An agreement was quickly struck with Count William. Philippa's dowry—the men, money and sailing vessels that were already being gathered—would be delivered within the month. In return, the wedding would take place in two years. Philippa was too young yet for bearing children. But time would go by quickly. The sooner Young Edward got a son on her, the stronger his rightful claims to the thrones of England and France would be.

Near a hundred ships were filled at Dordrecht with the provisions of war: Flemish horses trained for battle, a thousand staunch fighting men, food enough to last us the journey and longer in case we met resistance, and the weaponry to hew our way through if we did.

On a cool morning in late September, we pulled up our anchors and slipped out into the flat, blue-gray sea, which mirrored a drab sky . . . a sky which soon began to choke with more and darker clouds—low, heavy ones, warning of storms. Our sails caught the mounting wind, hurling us over the rising waves at dangerous speeds. For a while, Young Edward clung to the rail at the prow, the wind tearing at his hair as he squinted to see, glancing from time to time without apprehension at the storm chasing us. Before the rains came, though, Isabella fled to her cabin, quaking in fear, as if to escape some demon of sea and wind that haunted her.

For two days, we wandered over the water without mastery of our destination. The hull filled with the sour stench of vomit. Isabella slept not at all, but prayed. Prayed to God to find shore. To be delivered, if not to England, then safely, somewhere.

I dreamed of finding King Edward quivering before me, begging for his life. When I did, I would shut him up in a very small, very cold room and mull on it . . . for years.

34

Roger Mortimer:
Suffolk – September, 1326

T HE GALE HEAVED OUR ships over the surging waves and dropped them like brittle sticks beneath a pounding waterfall. We sailed on a ship called *The William*—named, in vanity, by our benefactor, the count. Although it was a stalwart vessel, no expense had been wasted on the unnecessary. In its sterncastle was a cabin, austerely furnished for the queen's voyage with a bed made of planks, a small table affixed to the wall and a stool. The cabin was meant for no more than two people. Sitting far back on the straw mattress, which was beginning to stink of mold, Isabella clung fiercely to her damsel Patrice. With every roll and tip of the cog's unsteady hull she held her breath, shut her eyes and prayed. I nearly asked her to beg a favor of God on my behalf. Death was a possibility that day and it had been some years since I had confessed. But I resisted. I had sworn not to fail on this quest, storms or no. This terror was a passing inconvenience. We would make land. We would march. We would win England back from Hugh Despenser and exact payment from him.

Not until the following morning did the storms relent. We had lost not only our bearings, but also three of our ships. Two carried food supplies and a small number of mercenaries; the other was a taride, in which canvas slings had been set side by side in the below-deck compartment of the deep hull to help keep the horses safe from injury. Thirty-five of our horses, some of them trained Flemish warhorses, had been lost. We would have been at less of a disadvantage had we tossed our gold into the sea. Gray dawn revealed the broken mast of yet another cog as a stunted, jagged knife of black to the east. It was taking on water and so we loaded all its men and what supplies we had room for onto two of the other ships.

Then, far to our west, through a rolling, low fog . . . a hump of land stretched across the horizon. As the sky lightened and the mist lifted, the shoreline came into better view. I stood on the platform of the aftcastle and studied it. Shingle littered the strand in sharp, scattered clumps where the waves broke at high tide. The tide was low now and so we let down anchor far out. With small rowing boats, we began to unload men and supplies. The storms had brought with them the first frosty bite of autumn and every man shivered as he worked.

Waist-deep and impervious to the icy cold of the sea, John of Hainault reached for Isabella with his huge hands. Waves crashed against his thighs, but like a deeply rooted tree he stood firm. Isabella leaned out from the little rowing boat we were in with the prince and lowered herself slowly, shaking, into his bulky arms. As he carried her to shore, the hem of her skirts trailed in the water. Then he set her down on English soil— or what we, for now, assumed was. Still accustomed to the sway of the sea, she wobbled. A priest, Father Norbert, caught her by the elbow to steady her. I had not exchanged more than a few words with him, but already I disliked him more than most holy men for the way he constantly shepherded Isabella aside and preached to her of virtue and godliness. Having been in Cologne the past year carrying out business with Emperor Louis on behalf of Bishop Stratford of Winchester, he had joined us at Dordrecht seeking passage back to England. Together he and the queen sank to their knees and gave copious thanks to God.

I leapt into the water. The tide shoved hard at the back of my calves. Coarse sand seeped into my boots. Its grit rubbed against my shins and ankles before settling around my toes. Garlands of seaweed tangled about my feet as I trudged through the shallows and stumbled onto shore.

Meanwhile, Lord Edward bounded through the waves, splashing, until he stood ankle-high in foaming seawater. He gazed up and down the curving shoreline. Overhead and around him, a cloud of gulls tumbled and jeered. He stooped momentarily in surprise, laughed and opened his arms broadly. Then, he swept one leg through the water and kicked, sending sprays into the air.

He could have come home long ago, had he wanted to. However, he had stayed in France. I suspected it was not out of love alone for his mother, but from pure ambition for his uncle's throne. Perhaps his father's, as well.

Near me, a plover studied the pebbles around it. It gobbled down a wayward insect, trapped in a pool of tidal mud in the shape of a footprint. Isabella, who had finally taken respite from her prayers, approached the bird slowly. Disturbed by her closeness, it took flight and flapped along the low, sandy cliffs until it found a length of beach where more tiny pools of tidewater lay trapped in an outcropping of rubble.

"Where are we?" Isabella wondered aloud, crouching over the lone footprint. There were no more tracks. Some time had passed, hours or perhaps a day even, since its maker had trodden there. Instinctively, she looked to me. But I had made it a habit to keep my distance and speak rarely to her in public, instead allowing Sir John to plod in her shadow like a pup begging for attention. He had been but a few steps behind her.

Sir John blinked and scratched at his unshaven neck. In his clumsy, thick accent, he said, "I do not know, my lady. I have never been to England."

Had I met John of Hainault under other circumstances and not known of his birth, I would have called him an oaf and hired him at a pittance to pull the oars of my boat. He had arms as thick as my neck, a flattened nose and a broad forehead with a ridged, bushy brow, all of which gave him the look of a rustic simpleton. Yet had he cause to, he could have cleaved me in two at the spine with one flick of his axe.

With most of the soldiers and arms ashore, our provisions were now being unloaded: barrels of salted fish, sacks of beans, and casks of cider. A soldier passed by with a flitch of bacon flung over his shoulder. Hunger gnawed at my belly. More than food, though, I thirsted for a long pull of ale. Something to dull the stabbing ache in my head and I needed to wash the taste of salt from my tongue. I called for a drink.

"No man eats," I told the soldier, "until everything is in order and accounted for." It would give them incentive to finish their duties, I reasoned.

Nearby, Isabella slumped down on a piece of driftwood next to a leaning clump of sea-holly. She tugged the hood of her mantle up over her head. The waves and wind roared in my ears so that I could barely hear the frail whisper of her voice.

"It's cold, everything stinks of seawater, and I am weary to the bone." Isabella cupped her hands to her mouth and blew warm air into them. At that moment, she looked like some haggard old fisherwoman, wizened by harsh winds, not like a queen in the prime of her beauty. Deep creases had formed around her eyes. Her shoulders were rolled forward so that her back was hunched, as if she had carried the equal of her own weight for years on end. The brightness that was Isabeau—the vitality and ardor that I had come to experience so intimately—was gone.

I had Arnaud bring her a blanket to ward off the autumn chill. But when he offered it, she waved it away.

"I need a fire, not a damp rag," she complained through blue lips. "I am cold. Cold and wet."

The count's brother, who had taken it upon himself to be not only her champion, but her caretaker as well, overheard her. Soon there was a fire and a little shelter made of reeds and sticks to shield her from the wind. She called for ink and parchment. Patrice found her a wooden box to serve as her table. Isabella's hands trembled as she wrote.

A useless task, I thought. What good would pretty words do when we had an army to move?

She paused, wiggled her fingers and pulled them inside her cloak. I longed to hold her against me to warm her, but that was not my place, as her advisor. Instead, I gulped down the last of my drink, turned away and went in search of Maltravers.

I found him bringing the remaining horses ashore. Plowing through knee-deep water, he pulled hard at the reins of a chestnut mare, blurting out a curse every time she resisted.

"Your horse?" I called to him.

He squinted at me with one eye. "Mine? Thank the saints, no. She's a stubborn mule. Mine broke its blessed leg. Kicked at a hurdle in a fit of terror. I'll need another." With a grunt he yanked again. Her neck arched as she dug her forelegs into the muck.

I waded out to his side, caught the reins close to the bit and stroked her muzzle. In moments, she had settled and began to walk willingly with me. On shore, I gave her a firm pat and chastened her. "Whose is she?" I asked.

Maltravers spat into the sand at his feet. "The queen's, I was told."

"Ah, I remember now. Given to her by Countess Jeanne. But she still preferred her old mare—the gray. The other horses . . . What of the taride carrying the Flemish ones? Did it go down?"

"Blown away by the storm, someone said. With good luck it will be found, but I wouldn't count on it soon. It could be anywhere." He wrung out the tail of his shirt. "The hay was ruined, all of it. We've some oats and fresh water, but they won't last more than a day."

"We don't need more than that. This is England, man, at least I think, and it's far from being winter." I looked along the shoreline for a meadow or some indication of fresh water. "The shore, there to the north, where it bends westward . . . Do you see the reeds of an estuary? If the water is less brackish there . . . A river." But which one? Our intention had been the beach of Thanet, north of Dover, where Edmund of Kent, who had left Valenciennes two weeks earlier, awaited. But I doubted the river was the Great Stour. We had been pushed too far north for that. The Deben, perhaps? "Leave the horses and provisions to others for now, Maltravers. Take some men with you. Follow the river. Find out where we are," I told him, hoping it was not so close to London that we would be set upon like salmon leaping out of the water and landing on shore. "And learn the whereabouts of the king."

The whimpering Edward would stay where it was safest—yet never far from his dearly beloved Despenser.

THE SCENT OF WOOD smoke filled the afternoon air. Cooking fires, most surrounded by dozens of hungry soldiers, were closely tended. The ships had been quickly emptied and were preparing to sail out on my orders. The likelihood was great that someone had already spotted the fleet. Soon enough, word of our arrival would spread like fire in a dry hayloft. With the ships gone, not only would there be less cause to cry foul, but our band of mercenaries would be unable to abandon us if our situation went too suddenly bad. Although I trusted John of Hainault because of his incurable devotion to Isabella, it would be all too easy for his men to skulk away and return to the continent if they had the means. I had prevented that from happening. They would serve the queen and her son until they were released from their duties—for however long they were needed.

The heavy clouds of that morning scattered northward. Patches of bright blue invaded the sky between. I sent a couple of men to find pasture for the horses, figuring that was an easy enough task for them. But when they returned, which was long before Maltravers, it was not with fodder or grain.

Two soldiers warbled a tavern song from the bench of a tottering cart drawn by a swaybacked nag. They laughed raucously, whipped the old horse with a willow switch and shouted to their fellow soldiers, "Ale! Ale!" A hail that brought thirsty, tired men in throngs, who shoved and grappled at the dozen casks.

The cart's bed was emptied by the time I reached it. Parched men-at-arms guzzled down ale in torrents. Some men shared in the spoils, but others thought nothing of slamming a fist into someone's gut to take what they wanted. A cask fell from the grasp of a Flemish soldier and broke into splinters on the ground. Liquid gold and bubbling foam soaked into the earth. A nearby Englishman kneed the Fleming in the groin for his wastefulness. Then, he pulled a knife and twirled it in his grip.

From behind, I whipped my sword free of its scabbard—a sound which made heads turn and bodies fall back in reflex. I brought it to where his neck met his spine. "Do it. You'll serve as a fine example of what happens to those who quarrel."

The knife fell from his fingers.

I stepped past him and turned around, my blade held straight before me. Slowly, they put down the casks and cleared way. "Not one day in England and already you cannot tolerate each other. Why did you come? You are worth nothing to me like this. Nothing! If you cannot discipline yourselves, I will gladly do it. And I will think nothing of getting rid of any one of you who dares poison this army with disobedience. You . . . and you, over here!" I pointed to the two men who had stolen the cart. "Here! Now!"

Then I turned to a young squire beside me. "Summon Lord Edward."

The fatter culprit stumbled to me and let out a belch stinking of vomit. I held my breath until it wafted away. The other man, short and thin with a long, skeletal face, swayed left and right, then crumpled to his knees. Someone kicked him from behind. He crawled to me. I stepped on his outstretched fingers and he let out a kittenish wail.

"What were you sent to do?" I said.

"Find food . . . for the . . . the horses."

"Did you?"

"Ahhh, no, my lord."

"And did you pay for this? Any of it?"

He did not answer. I ground a heel into the bones of his hand. He wailed again.

The bigger one answered for him. "We hadn't any money. So we took it. Was that wrong, lord?" He dragged a forearm across his beard to wipe away the last drops of ale.

I went toward him, to the relief of the man whose hands I had crushed. "Wrong . . . and stupid." I rammed the butt of my hilt into the soft flab of his belly. "We have ale of our own. And we do not—do *not* steal from the very people we wish to welcome us."

I beckoned to Sir John as he pushed his way through.

He looked at the cart and its depleted contents. "Thieves?"

"What do you do with thieves, Sir John?"

He thought about it. "Cut off a hand."

"No!" Lord Edward broke through the crowd. "No. I think that . . . that would be too harsh a punishment. Sir Roger, what do *you* do to men who steal?"

"Depends on who they steal from and what, my lord prince. But in Ireland, we would strip them naked, then tar and feather them. Devil to scrub off. Left them stinking for weeks, too. Not even the camp whores would come near them."

"Do it, then." Pleased with himself for having a measure of authority, he turned on his heel and left.

But as I watched him go, Isabella was making her way through the commotion. Men parted at the appearance of her spectral form. Her skin was pallid, her eyes dark and sunken. Her hood had fallen back and her pale hair flew wild behind her.

"Your name?" she asked the bigger one as he swayed on his feet.

"Gurney, my lady. Sir Thomas Gurney."

"And him?"

"William Ockle. We are both of us close acquaintances of Thomas Berkeley."

My daughter, Margaret, had married Thomas Berkeley when she was fifteen. Two years later his father died, making him Lord Berkeley. But by then I had my falling out with King Edward. Margaret was shut up in a priory somewhere and the young Berkeley imprisoned. "My lady," I interrupted, "I doubt my daughter's husband would keep company with pilfering sots."

Isabella let out a long, worrisome sigh and closed her eyes a moment. "Before you take your amusement in them, send them back to whomever it is they stole from. Let them utter apologies and beg forgiveness. Then, pay the victim for all this from my own coffers. I will not have the people of England running in fear from those who have come to liberate them." She closed her eyes halfway again. Her voice was thin, ethereal. "A word with you, Sir Roger."

I gave her my arm and felt her lean heavily into me as we walked slowly toward the shore.

She unhooked her arm and went to the water's edge where the sea lapped at her shoes. Upon the horizon, the sails of the count's ships were already disappearing. She was so absorbed in her thoughts that she did not remark on why the fleet was leaving, nor did she flinch as a cawing swirl of blackbirds encircled her.

I looked around. No one had followed us. Not even, for once, Sir John. He had stayed behind to see that the queen's wishes were carried out explicitly.

I went closer to her. "Did I do something to displease you just now?"

"That? No, no. It's only that . . . that . . ." Worry wove itself through the frail threads of her voice. "When I first came to England, to London, its people came out in throngs to cheer me. They threw flower petals before me. I was young then. I thought it wonderful. They did not even know me then, but they loved me. I was their hope. For an heir. For peace. Since then, though . . . how terribly wrong everything has gone." She wrapped herself in her own arms as the wind tore at her hair. "Now, I have returned. With a foreign army. And I fear they will hail me not with flowers, but with arrows."

"You assume the worst, Isabella. You defied Lord Despenser. Something no one else has dared to do. England will welcome you gladly. And it is your son—their newest hope—who shall ride at the head of our army. One day, soon perhaps, he will become their king."

"Soon? Perhaps we should not assume too much, my lord." Her chin drifted to her shoulder and she turned to look at me with narrowed eyes. "I have letters to be dispatched to the people of London and its mayor. I shall write another soon to my cousin, Henry of Leicester, but for now . . . for now we must sow the seeds for our favor in London. If Edward is there and London turns against him . . . But we cannot go there until we know that we will be welcomed heartily. Do you not think that wise, Sir Roger?"

She was thinking as a queen thinks now, not like the embittered consort of a neglectful king. If London could again love her—

A cry reached us from atop the edge of the low cliffs. I recognized Maltravers' crooked arm as he waved to us. With him were twenty men on horse—many more than he had taken along to discover our whereabouts.

"Is that . . ." she stood frozen, not trusting her own eyes, "who I think?"

"Sir John Maltravers has returned to tell us where we have landed, I assume." I strained my eyes against the glare of the setting sun behind them. Next to him, a banner fluttered and snapped in the wind. Across its crimson field stretched the golden lion of the Plantagenets. "And with him—Thomas of Norfolk."

So Kent had spoken true. Even the king's own brothers had abandoned him.

35

Roger Mortimer:

Walton, Suffolk — September, 1326

ISABELLA RAN TOWARD THE low ragged cliffs where Maltravers and Norfolk were. The sodden hem of her skirts dragged upon the ground. Her foot raveled in the hem. She stumbled, nearly righted herself and then tumbled forward. Fast on her heels, I caught her around the waist and snatched her to me, pitching my weight sideways. My shoulder and arm hit the sand with a muffled thud, absorbing the shock of our fall. We rolled twice before coming to a stop. She had landed on top of me, her small back hard against my chest.

Rather than her gratitude, I received the sharp point of her elbow grinding into my ribs, then a jab.

"Let me go," she grumbled. Struggling against my hold, she raised her voice sharply. "What are you doing? I said let me—"

I clamped a hand over her mouth. For a moment I thought she might sink her teeth into my palm, but she expelled a breath and I felt her stiffen in my arms. With an abrupt heave, I rolled to my side and dumped her unceremoniously onto a bed of shingle. She snapped upright and thrashed the sand from her face with the fury of a cornered cat.

I stood and offered my hand. "Saving you from a fall, I thought, and from your own impatience. If that *is* Norfolk, then I suggest you not throw yourself at him, or anyone, until we know a few things more. Where the king and Despenser are, for one. And if they have sent an army against us, for another."

She spat at my outstretched hand and helped herself to her feet. "I would have looked less ridiculous if you had let me fall." Still whisking away the last grains from her lips, she walked, this time with forced restraint toward Maltravers and Norfolk, who by then had discovered Young Edward and ridden toward him. The two men dropped from their saddles and paid their respects to him. No alarm was raised with Norfolk's sudden arrival and William Montagu was, as ever, fully armed and not more than two steps behind Edward.

We picked our way hurriedly along the crumbling cliffs, until we reached a place where their crest eroded into a dune that curved southward along the shore. Beyond the dune, to the west, were grazing marshes dotted brown by the faded sprays of sea lavender, but the recent storms had left the ground a soggy, stinking mess where no herdsman would have dared release his cows. Norfolk must have come from the south then, along the shore, not by the river estuary.

"Why don't you trust anyone?" Isabella said as I came abreast of her.

"There are many I trust, my lady."

She kept her chin forward, her strides strong and purposeful, despite the fatigue that still showed in the dark moons beneath her eyes. "But many that you don't?"

I lowered my voice as we approached the gathering crowd. I had placed my trust too lightly before and nearly paid with my life. I only sought to spare her the same. "It would serve you well to be as cautious, my lady."

I heard only a slight, but obdurate 'humph' from her mouth. She pounded yet more sand from her clothing and drew her shoulders back proudly.

"Lord Thomas, my dear brother," she called.

As soon as he saw the queen, the Earl of Norfolk swept forward in a long, low bow to Isabella. He was a year older than Edmund of Kent, somewhere in his mid twenties, with boyish, sandy locks that fell across his eyes with every tip or turn of his head.

"Welcome to Suffolk, my lady." He straightened abruptly and a tepid, yet charming smile broke across the perfectly molded features of his face. The smile disappeared as his attention wandered to his shoulder. He flicked a speck of dirt from it. "My dear nephew . . . and sister . . . how good to see you. Unexpected and yet overdue. You look . . . well." He had hesitated as he perused Isabella's wind-tattered hair and soiled clothing. "Edmund was expecting you in Kent, but no bother. It is as well you are here. We are a short ride from Walton, although my lovely Alice will be quite cross with me at the lack of notice. No worry. Her anger will vanish in the merriment. You'll come then?" He enticed her to his invitation with a tilt of his head. "There by nightfall if we leave now. A roaring hearth. A warm, dry bed for you, my lady. And the best wine."

If we had landed near Norfolk's manor at Walton in Suffolk and that was to our south, then the river nearby would be the Orwell. Three days' march from London.

"Your generosity overwhelms us, Lord Thomas," she said, her words slow and thoughtful as she cast a swift glance over her shoulder at me, "and we are indeed fortunate, blessed I say, to have come upon you. I shall give thanks to Our Lord that we have found ourselves in good company after such a perilous voyage. But, if I may beg it of you . . . we must have news first, before we decide any course."

"News, ah yes. Of your husband?" Norfolk gave me a sidelong glance and I thought I detected an impish wink. "I daresay you've not missed him at all."

Deftly, she deflected the barb. "Thomas, tell us, will the people of England welcome their prince home?"

He returned his gaze to her. "Why ever would they not, dear sister?"

"Because of them," Young Edward broke in flatly. He tossed his head back, indicating the mass of soldiers looking on behind him, most not of English birth. By then, the Hainaulters were aware there were no ships to carry them back to the continent, should the tide of judgment turn against us.

Norfolk tugged at his chin, one finely curved eyebrow dipping down. "Hmm, an interesting lot. Not a mere escort, then, are they?" He let out a ripple of laughter and clutched his stomach. "Oh, I have news . . . yes, fantastic news indeed, fair sister. Edward has been expecting you for some time."

I scanned across the marsh, broken across its green expanse by only a weedy stream, and down the coastline for indications of a royal army encircling us. But I saw no horses hidden amongst the far away hazel copses to the northwest or soldiers hunched down in the reeds. Aside from a few cow paths through the tall grass and our bedraggled army of less than a thousand men crowded now between the south-lying dunes and the marsh, there was little sign of life at all.

"My brother, mighty king that he is, ordered some two thousand odd men to Kent and as many here. But how many do you see? Any at all? Did any ships pursue you? Any? Not one, I venture. And do you know why? Because, plainly put, no one will heed a thing he says. Sad, truly it is. But is it any wonder when Hugh Despenser robs them all with my brother's blessing? So, you ask, sister, if England will welcome their prince?" He strode over to Young Edward and threw his arms around his nephew, clutched him to his chest and planted a kiss upon his head before releasing the bewildered and slightly offended young man. "They will shove each other aside to have a look at you and proclaim their love. They will flood the streets with wine, feed your men with their last cow and offer their virgin daughters in thanks. By God's ears, they will more than welcome their prince. They will do all but build shrines in his honor, so as not to blaspheme. To Walton, then? We're wasting daylight, bantering about. Come, come."

He extended his hand to Isabella. She took it, but with reserve.

"You'll tell us more along the way?" she probed.

A mischievous grin plied at his mouth. "Much, much more, my dear, sweet sister." He laid a kiss upon her knuckles, then one on each cheek, brushing her lips as he pulled back.

As soon as our column of disciplined mercenaries and once-exiled Englishmen was in formation, we began our march along the shoreline with Norfolk as our guide. In time, the flat marshes yielded to dryer, rolling ground spotted with clumps of heather and gorse. King Edward, we learned, was shut up in London with Despenser. The city was wickedly restless. Rumors of our coming had been sweeping across the land all summer long. Our delay in gathering funds had proven to our benefit, as any sympathies there might have been on the king's behalf had trickled away with the mounting resentment toward Despenser.

Not all the news was good, however. London's masses were fickle, as swift to embrace as they were to exchange blows. It was not yet safe for us to go there. But within the Tower was Isabella's young son John . . . and likely living in less comfort were two of my own: my oldest, Edmund, and my namesake, my Uncle Roger. Isolated within the squalor and darkness. Deprived of their freedom. Just as I had been.

WE—OR ISABELLA AND her son, rather, as I took housing at a nearby abbey—stayed only the night in Walton, much to the displeasure of Norfolk's wife Alice, for whom Isabella had much fondness. If, as Norfolk claimed, Edward's summonses were going ignored and London was not decided in its loyalty, then we had to go where sympathies would assuredly be in our favor—to the Welsh Marches. Isabella's letters to London and to her uncle, Henry, Earl of Leicester, were dispatched with great haste.

As we went deeper into England, Isabella donned her widow's weeds—a high-necked gown of plain, black serge and the modest veil to match. We followed the River Orwell to Bury St. Edmunds, where Isabella again prayed. What was offered to us in the way of food, she ordered, was to be promptly paid for. In those simple gestures performed over a few scant days, Queen Isabella began to win the battle that King Edward, in nineteen years, could not.

None but a few dozen men rallied to the king's banner, most of them pardoned murderers. Barely enough to guard his person even in the most impenetrable of fortresses. Norfolk stayed behind in Walton to further our cause, but he sent with us sixty men and along the way more and more joined with us.

As we rode on to Baldock and then Dunstable, the people of England, who had at first scattered in confusion and reluctance, now began to greet us openly. Young Edward sat tall in his shining armor. While still a boy, he had changed during his stay in France, not so much in looks, although he had grown taller, but in his manner. He now strode with the confidence of a young man who had discovered his place and purpose in life. He spoke more boldly and commanded with stern glances, where once he had observed everything with quiet obedience.

The belief that he was born to be a king had taken hold of him. Even though that was the very thing I had hoped for—a thirst to lead, a glimmer of vainglory—it carried with it the hazard of untold troubles, as well.

Pride, if left untamed, could bring a man to his death. A king, even.

36

Roger Mortimer:

Oxford — October, 1326

B Y THE TIME WE reached Oxford, hundreds lined the roads. The gates to the city stood gaping. Young Edward led the way like the Messiah delivering the promise of paradise.

Our progress slowed to a crawl. We lurched and halted. Heralds shouted to clear the way, but the mob only pressed closer, clogging the streets and alleys. Faces smeared with grime and soot appeared in windows and doorways. Hands writhed from a twisting mass of bodies all around us, grabbing. Finally, at my orders, our pikemen lowered their weapons to clear a path. With his mother beside him, Lord Edward rode just behind the glinting sweep of blades, his shoulders drawn up tall and a smile on his face. Every now and then he nodded or raised his hand in greeting. They cheered him as he passed. They called out for their beloved Isabella.

We had meant to make our way to the church—for, of course, Isabella would stop there to heap God with yet more thanks, as if He had forgotten those she had showered Him with that very morning—but by the time the church came into sight we found ourselves at a complete halt again. Cries rippled through the crowd. Around a corner I saw the curling, ornate tops of crosiers bobbing above the throng. The horde fell back as if on cue. Adam of Orleton, the Bishop of Hereford, led a small army of bishops and clergymen toward us.

He bowed to the prince and they exchanged a few words of formal greeting. Arnaud helped Isabella down from her mount and she hurried forward, a haze of dust swirling around her.

Orleton's long arms encircled her with fatherly tenderness. "Child," he breathed into her ear, "I have prayed for your safety every night and every morning since you left for France." Then he kissed her once on each temple and held her at arm's length. "I understand you had a rough voyage." He scrunched his feathery, graying brows together in concentration, and then arched his left one high. "You look surprisingly well."

"Oh, you are much too kind, your grace," she replied. "I have suffered so much anguish this past year. If I look well at all, it is only because my spirits are lifted to see you at last."

Barely two weeks past, this very woman had feared whether England would open its arms to her or pelt her with stones until every bone in her body was shattered. Since then, the blush had returned to her cheeks, her eyes glinted with mirth and a beatific smile graced her lips at times like this. She thrived on the adoration of the masses. All the while, she had maintained her outward piety—to my increasing frustration. I much preferred her private, shameless side. Not since before we left from Dordrecht had we been alone together for a single night . . . not even for a transient moment in which to steal a tantalizing kiss.

"My lady," Orleton said, "this is Frances Willington, Master of the Guildhall here in Oxford. He brings you a gift."

Before her stepped a short little man who looked down at the ground timidly. He glanced up, then back down and thrust out a silver chalice to her. "For you, my lady queen. An offering of peace and welcome from the citizens of Oxford."

She took it from Willington and looked inside. From it, she took only a sip of the blood-red wine, thanked him sweetly and then passed it along to her son. Young Edward savored a swig on his tongue. Then, he tipped the chalice back and guzzled down the remainder. When the last drop was drained he thrust the chalice above his head and the townspeople erupted in a roar of cheers.

"Sir Roger," Orleton said, approaching me so I could hear him above the din, "it has been long since we spoke in person. Years, has it not? It was never easy getting letters to you. You never stayed in one place. But what a great blessing to know you have arrived safely at last."

"I am indebted to you, good bishop, for letting me get away with my head still on my shoulders."

"You have it for now, my lord, but I warn you the king has placed a high price on it." He motioned for us to follow him and his clinging flock of clerics to the church. The crowd slipped back, but Isabella and Young Edward suffered the occasional dirty hand pawing at their clothing and hair.

"Has he? How much am I worth?" I said.

"A thousand pounds sterling."

"Is that all?"

"I am sorry, but yes. He attributes this insurgency to you alone, blaming no other. He wants you dead for it. The queen, the prince, even Kent, he has decreed, are to be left unharmed. By now he knows of Norfolk giving you succor, as well." Orleton hoisted his crosier to clear the church steps of onlookers. As we ascended, I cast a glance behind us. A mother had thrust her infant to arm's length at Isabella. She took the babe from its mother, held it aloft, then brought it gently down and kissed its fat cheek. Further back in the crowd, Young Edward strutted past a line of swooning maidens to stand at his mother's side.

We entered the church and Orleton and I stepped aside to let our following of clerics—two other bishops and a large cluster of abbots—pass as we waited for Isabella and the prince.

"I hear his general summons went unheeded," I said.

"It did. He called upon thousands to array, but as soon as the barons heard Norfolk and Kent were ignoring him, they all spewed out excuses as if they were avoiding an invitation to supper. Desperate, he offered freedom to any criminals who would fight for him. That got him some response, but London turned a deaf ear. Even the bishops there are stalled in argument as to whether to stand behind the king or oppose him. Edward has since fled the city."

I imparted a smile to Bishop Orleton. "So, we have flushed the fox from his den?"

"You have."

We paused at the broad archway beyond which lay the nave of the church. Isabella began up the steps, her son next to her. A growing throng of knights and nobles trailed them closely.

"I believe the queen expects a Mass," Orleton stated, "although it will not be long. I admit I am ill prepared today. Will you join us?"

"I should . . ." I fumbled for a plausible diversion. "I should see to the quartering of the soldiers. Pardon me, your grace. I should go."

He nodded in understanding and led the queen and her son to the front of the nave. I retreated into a vestibule as the barons trickled by. They all appeared eager to take Mass with the queen and prince to gain their favor. I searched for Maltravers in the passersby, but could not find him.

"My lord?"

I turned at the hoarse whisper to see Simon de Beresford in the shadows behind a column. The light from the open door fell upon only half his face. I waited until the last of the conveniently reverent drifted by before going to him.

"I have news," he said.

"Go on."

He stuck out his hand. "You are in the queen's pay now, not a penniless prisoner. I expect something for my troubles."

"You'll get more than the occasional coin if the news is worth enough."

From inside the nave, Orleton's words resounded:

"Almighty God, to whom all mankind surrenders its will, we beseech thee, in your everlasting glory and power, to be our guide in this time of darkness. Grant us the wisdom and the goodness to overcome evil, and to—"

Simon pulled back into complete shadow as a monk poked his head through the door to the nave, then pulled it shut, muffling the bishop's sermon.

"A knighthood?" he asked.

"It can be arranged."

"How soon?"

"That is not up to me. Besides, you'll earn it when I say you have. Now, what news?"

"Of the king."

"How big is his army?"

Simon's teeth glimmered in the darkness. "Army? I would not call it that. He has with him but a skeleton guard and a smattering of archers. No more than twenty altogether."

Twenty retainers who must have all been cruelly aware how futile their duty was. "Who else is with him?"

"Of importance? It is known he left London with his corrupt treasurer, Robert de Baldock . . . and Lord Hugh Despenser, naturally. As for where they are all now . . ."

I slipped my hand into the purse at my belt and drew out two gold nobles bearing the likeness of King Edward. They would be worthless soon enough, but the gesture would placate my spy for now. I pressed them into his palm. "Where were they lately?"

"In Wallingford not three days ago. They took the road to Cirencester."

West. Most likely to Gloucester. From there, they could take refuge in Wales, or Ireland even. If they fled England altogether, Edward's son could be crowned in his place.

"Find them. And if you can lead me to them—there will be a

306

knighthood for you. I'll see to it."

A desolate hour it was for King Edward. And an even worse one for Despenser.

Bishop Orleton's voice pried through the crack between the great oak doors:

"—snake has entered Eden and the seed of Satan infected our king. This 'affliction', Lord Hugh Despenser, has caused our king to do much wrong: in the governing of his kingdom and its people, in his private deeds, and in the estrangement of our dear and beloved queen, who has been only ever faithful to him and tolerant of his faults far beyond duty. We are blessed that Queen Isabella returns to us now, with our noble prince, Edward, at her side. Together, they will free us of this scourge, this plague of immorality and avarice, and return our beleaguered England to the right and true law of God. Our Heavenly Father, the Holy Spirit and Christ Jesus be with you all."

"Amen," I rejoined.

THAT NIGHT IN THE high-raftered guildhall of Oxford, there was a feast to celebrate the return of Queen Isabella and Lord Edward. Roasted pig, mince pies and puddings were served. Fresh straw had been strewn over the floor, making it smell like a well-kept stable, although the scent was barely strong enough to overpower the stink of too many knights crammed into too narrow a hall. At the head table, I sat next to Isabella. To her right was Lord Edward and to my left Bishop Burghersh of Lincoln, who quickly gorged himself on an excess of fresh herring and went to bed early with stomach pains.

I was heady with my rising wave of good fortune and a generous helping of mulberry wine. I raised my goblet—my fifth of the evening—and shouted, "Two thousand pounds sterling for the head of Hugh Despenser!"

"Allow me the honor!" boomed a gravelly voice from the back of the hall. "But do you want his ugly head with or without his body attached?"

Laughter rolled through the hall and broke apart. The lute played on, while the little man with the nakers at his belt thumped a frenzied rhythm. Dancing girls flailed their scarves to catch men about the waists teasingly. One young man snagged his temptress, reeled her in and pinned her down on a table. She raked him across the face with her fingernails, prematurely ending his debauchery.

I slid my chair back. On swaying legs, I climbed up onto my seat to see who had arrived to claim the prize for Despenser's head. Isabella tapped lightly on my calf, but I ignored her, searching through the throng of overstuffed, lascivious merrymakers.

"Come forward," I commanded. My head was so light that faraway faces blurred together. I was answered by only a hush that very soon returned to a buzz of conversation. Cups clinked together. Dogs growled over fallen scraps.

Isabella pinched the cloth of my leggings. "Please, Sir Roger."

I complied, sinking down into my chair with a long belch. I plucked up my goblet and raised it to her. "To England's most beauteous of queens: Isabeau the Fair."

John of Hainault, seated down the table from her, lifted his goblet high. "To Queen Isabella!"

She rolled her eyes. "You should sleep well tonight, my lord."

The prince, who minutes before had been seated next to her, had abandoned his chair and was enthralled with the antics of two small, trained dogs over by a side table. I leaned in close to the queen and whispered, sweet and unctuous, "Better than well, with you lying next to me. Do you not dream of it yourself?"

Her lashes fluttered. She stirred the food on her plate with the tip of her knife. Slowly, she turned her eyes on me. Green as the Welsh hills, they were. Her skin as creamy as milk fresh from the cow's udder. I wanted to know every inch of her and I would use every minute of the night to do it, sleep be damned.

She laid her hand lightly on my forearm "Patience, I beg. There are more important things."

"More important?" Under the table, I trailed my fingertips from the middle of her thigh to the point of her hip.

"Your lodgings tonight are to be at Oseney Abbey, outside the town's walls." With an apologetic smile, she nudged my hand away, and then inclined her head in thought. "Two thousand pounds? Is that enough, you think?"

What? I struggled to sweep the cobwebs from my head. *Ah yes, Despenser's head* . . .

The clink of metal rang sharply in my ears. I looked up to see a square-shouldered man with thinning coppery red hair standing before us, both hammer-like fists propped upon his broad hips. His mail was dulled by road dust and the leather of his boots was cracked from wear. Over his mail he wore plates of armor. His spurs were of gold.

This time, it was Isabella who stood. "Uncle Henry?"

Henry of Leicester, or Lancaster as he fancied himself, flung his arms wide. Isabella rushed around the table to him. He grunted, even though her embrace was brief. My head rushed with blood. I held no quarrel with Leicester, but I had far from forgotten that his brother had failed me.

"My lord," he addressed the prince briefly and returned his attention to Isabella. "My lady and dear niece. When you wrote to me, you told me you had also written to the people of London. You said as London goes, so goes England?"

"I did."

"Pray it does not, my lady. In heart, perhaps. But not in the same manner. When your letter was read there, it caused a great deal of . . . unrest. The citizens rose up in your name. Rioted. Hunted down those loyal to the king and Lord Despenser. Mayor Chigwell swore allegiance to you and was spared. Others were not so fortunate. They took the Tower from Lady Eleanor de Clare. She gave your son, Lord John, up without a fight. Thought they'd treat her more kindly for it."

At the mention of her son's name, Isabella clutched her stomach.

Young Edward rushed forward to stand before Leicester. "My brother—is he all right?"

"Yes, yes, for now he is. Warden of London, they made him. But I'd advise you to waste not a moment in sending someone to look after him."

Isabella pressed her hands together in a quick, silent prayer. Then she returned to her seat and cast an authoritative look at John of Hainault. "Sir John?"

"Yes, my lady," he said. "I will leave in the morning, at first light."

Before they could lay out the details of Sir John's mission, Leicester interrupted. "Your pardon, my lady, but I came for other reasons, as well." He hoisted his belt. "I was denied an earldom out of enmity and spite. My grudge against Lord Despenser, however, is over more than land. My brother is dead because of him. "

"If your brother had joined with me when he promised," I said, my tongue tinged with bitterness, "he might not be dead at all."

"Or, you *both* might be dead," Leicester countered.

Before old grievances could be resurrected, Isabella intervened. "Please, my lords, we do no good to guess what might have been. Let us go forward, together. In a common cause. Lord Leicester, if you will remain with us, the council will discuss the earldom of Lancaster. I see no reason to keep it from you."

I wondered what 'council' she referred to, there were many lords of late who had thronged to her side, but then a more immediate concern gripped me. I scooted my chair back, rose and spread my hands on the table. "Lord Leicester, since you know of London, if those in the Tower were liberated, when can I expect to see my son, Edmund, and my uncle, Roger of Chirk?"

"There were many held in the Tower, Sir Roger. If they were there, I imagine they have indeed already been set free. Perhaps you will learn more soon, but I don't know any more than that."

A fog of sorrow crept over me. I had advised Isabella to avoid entering London because it was too dangerous there, even though I knew her son, mine and my uncle were in the Tower. I lowered myself slowly into my chair. After so long, I was not yet sure I wanted to see my uncle. The stubborn old bastard would argue I had not redeemed myself. And I hadn't. Despenser and the king were not yet in my hands.

The earl's voice rattled me from my roiling thoughts. "Might you care to know," Leicester said boisterously, "what has become of Bishop Stapledon?"

It was not a question, but an announcement.

"Lord Wake," Leicester beckoned with a commanding gesture. Lord Thomas Wake shoved his way forward from the back of the hall and brushed past the prince. Wake, who was the brother of Kent's wife, Margaret, had been in Paris for much of the past two years, but when Isabella and I were forced to leave there, he, too, had left. Until now, I had not given much thought to his whereabouts, but obviously he had taken refuge with Leicester. Against his chest, he held a basket. The sweet, pungent stink of rotting flesh mingling with blood seeped through its cracks and permeated the air.

Young Edward drew his forearm over his mouth and nose, retreating as he did so.

As Leicester threw back his head in laughter, Wake flipped aside the basket's lid and pulled from it—the head of Bishop Walter de Stapledon of Exeter.

Not by my hand . . . but I exulted in it.

37

Isabella:

Oxford — October, 1326

T HE BASKET DROPPED TO the floor at Lord Wake's feet. With his fingers entwined in Bishop Stapledon's blood-matted fringe of hair, he lifted it high. One of the misshapen ears, attached by only a loose strip of skin, flapped with every twist of his arm. A squirming clump of maggots fell from its nostrils. With sinister glee, Henry, Earl of Leicester, squashed them beneath his foot.

A woman's scream tore through the stunned hush. Then broken shouts rose to a rumble of cheers, swallowing up her cry.

A burning river of bile rose in my throat. I swallowed it back. Horrified by my own fascination, I studied the distorted features. The bulging, crimson eyes were rolled back into the head. The skin, mottled by green and purple bruises, stretched taut across the cheekbones, except where gashes exposed the bone beneath. Flies swarmed around it in a humming cloud as Wake thrust it in my direction. I averted my eyes. My gaze came to rest on Mortimer.

He stared at the grotesque trophy intently. An eerie grin pulled at the corners of his mouth. Although shocked, I hardly mourned the bishop's death and would not have expected Mortimer to, either. Still, I could not allow Mortimer or anyone to take delight in such gruesome acts. Revenge was a sickness that corrupted the soul. I had seen it in Edward.

My face still turned away from the sight, I raised a hand to quell the crowd. "Take it away, Lord Wake," I uttered.

I heard the scuff of the basket over the floor as he scooped it up and the thump of Stapledon's head as he dropped it inside, then his footsteps dragging away to the end of the hall.

"My Lord Leicester," I began, "this was an act of rage, a murder which I cannot condone. May the Lord God forgive those whose hands are stained by this wicked deed. They did not know, in their hysteria, that the Devil led them to commit it." My voice, I realized, quavered. I had known this uprising would not be a bloodless one. I only prayed it would all end swiftly and my son, John, would remain safe.

"And yet, my queen," Mortimer said, his words low but clear, "is there not some measure of justice in the act? We were all spared the tedium of a trial, which would have ended the same. I say the Londoners are to be commended for their expediency."

His declaration was met by nods of approval. I resisted the urge to correct him for contradicting me so abruptly, and in public. For too many years I had held my tongue with Edward. Never again would I allow any man, including Mortimer, to silence me. "Whether it is right, Sir Roger, to take an eye for an eye is not in question. Justice should not be dispensed in so reckless a fashion."

"Reckless?" Mortimer echoed with sarcasm. "What would you advise then?"

Perhaps it was the drink that made him irritable, or that I had rebuffed his overtures only minutes before, but there was a distinct surliness to his words I found intolerable. I tried to remain calm, to be the steady ship in this rising storm, but the rising pitch of my voice told otherwise. "Even the guilty deserve to hear an account of their crimes. And the punishment should be a fitting one, not one meted out by butchers' knives and bricks."

"The punishment for treason is death."

"You, Sir Roger, were declared a traitor and yet . . . you were allowed to live."

Mortimer gripped the table edge and slowly raised smoldering eyes at me. His lips twitched in a snarl like a dog that has been beaten by its master, yet dared not bite. "I never betrayed England. *Never.* I spoke out against Lord Despenser—that was my crime."

Regret flared inside me, warming my ears. I had spoken without thinking. Yes, Mortimer lived because I had begged for his life and I had cruelly seized this moment to remind him of that. Still, it was an unfair blow. I would make amends later, but a guildhall full of drunken men thirsting for retribution was not the place to sort out private grievances.

"So it was for many, my lord," Bishop Orleton said, rescuing me from further blunder. "There are innumerable wrongs that remain to be righted, but we cannot leave justice in the hands of a feverish mob. Do you not agree?"

Mortimer flicked a crumb from the table. "Of course," he spat between tight lips.

Before anything more could come of my cruel stupidity, I changed tack. "Lord Leicester, where are my daughters?"

"Now? I wish I could tell you," he replied. "They were at Pleshy through May. Marlborough until a month ago. But they were taken from the Lady Monthermer then. Some say the Earl of Winchester, the Elder Hugh Despenser, has hidden them away somewhere."

My heart plummeted. It was ill news for them to be in the hands of a Despenser. More than anything, I wanted to see them again, to feel their arms around my neck, hear their small voices calling for me.

"My dear lady, my good lords," Leicester implored, raising his broad hands up high and turning about, "who, then, will bring you the younger Despenser's head?"

The crowd shouted its approval for Leicester. Tankards were thrust high, spilling ale. Spoons clanged on pewter trenchers.

"Find Despenser!" he cried. He drew his sword and jabbed it toward the rafters. "Hunt down the thief who has stolen our riches, murdered loyal men and depraved our king. Force him to his knees." With a jerk, he hacked his blade downward. It bit into the floor planks with a splintering crack. "Free England of its tyrant!"

My daughters were forgotten. Like hounds on the trail of wounded quarry, they clamored for another beheading. Beside me, Mortimer was silent, clenching the handle of his table knife. As the roar of the crowd died away, Leicester sheathed his sword and smugly took the seat next to Mortimer, that which had been abandoned earlier by Bishop Burghersh. Mortimer, at once, slid his chair back, bowed to me without meeting my eyes and left the hall.

Even as I watched his back disappear through the mill of bodies clogging the doorway, I thought of my girls and how long it had been since I held them.

THAT NIGHT, I WRITHED in my bed, alone and tormented. I had planned for this, prayed for it. To return to England. To command its people in my son's name. But justly.

There were those, however, who would not be satisfied until the blood of their enemies flowed freely. I counted myself among them, because there were things I had not forgotten. Things I could not forgive.

At midmorning, I sat at council with the prince, the bishops of Lincoln, Ely, Durham and Hereford and a dozen barons, half of them Leicester's proponents, while he procured their blessing to grant him the earldom of Lancaster at the next meeting of parliament. Leicester also declared we would march to Gloucester, where we would surely learn of Despenser's whereabouts. All agreed—those who spoke, at least.

Mortimer was absent from the meeting. The message he sent was that he could not come, because provisions had to be gathered to feed the growing army before setting out again. With the Earl of Leicester's arrival, our numbers were nearly doubled. Nothing would stand in our way. I should have been glad for that, glad that England had embraced us so heartily, but I had seen the first clouds of another storm brewing.

The more I looked upon Leicester, who was my half-uncle through my mother's mother, the more I saw the image of his dead brother Thomas of Lancaster in him. And it frightened me. Frightened me because it was the past hurtling forward into the future. Once, nearly a lifetime ago, I had calmed the rough waters between Lancaster and Edward. In the end, it was all for naught.

It could not come to the same between Leicester and Mortimer.

38

Isabella:

Vale of the White Horse — October, 1326

A COOL MIST HUNG in the morning air as we crossed the bridge over the Thames and headed west toward Gloucester. Like a snake through wet grass, the column advanced silently. By afternoon the mist had become a steady rain, soaking us all to the bone and forcing our heads down.

Mortimer peeled back from the front of the line and came abreast of me on his mount. "You needn't ride in the rain like this, my lady. Why not make use of your carriage?"

I kept my gaze forward. To the front, Young Edward's standard flopped heavily at the top of its pole. Scattered throughout the length of our column were dozens of other standards: sodden rags dangling limp at the ends of sticks, their colors and emblems indistinguishable.

"The people must be able to see me, as well as their prince," I said.

"There will be no one about on a day like this to see you, anyway. You'll take ill."

I lifted my hood from my head. Raindrops pelted my face and stung at my eyes. "I thank you, my lord, for your concern, but lately you seem to have appointed yourself my conscience, as well as my voice."

He looked at me, momentarily perplexed, and then scoffed. "That? That was two days ago. It was an offhanded comment. I merely said what others there were thinking. If you were not as happy as I was to see Bishop Stapledon dead, you were at least relieved."

The rain drummed on the soggy ground, on tree limbs, on shields and bodies, rising in a roar so loud no one more than a few feet away could have heard our conversation.

"You contradicted me," I said.

"I disagreed with you. If I am to counsel you, then—"

"If you are to be *among* my counselors, you must heed my wishes. When I need advice, I will ask it of you."

He propped a hand on his hip above his sword and worked his jaw back and forth. Drops of water gathered in the stubble on his chin and streamed down his neck. "And is my advice of value to you?"

"Very much so. More than anyone's."

At that, the firm set of his mouth slackened. He dropped his eyes. "So if I disagree with you, if I have something that needs to be said, how am I to let you know?"

"When we are together, the two of us alone, you can say anything. *Anything.* Only, in public, I must be the one who says what is to be done, whether in truth it is you who decides it or me. We cannot, in front of anyone, even *appear* to disagree." Water ran hard into my eyes and mouth and seeped into the fibers of my clothes. I shivered, but not from the cold and damp. "I will not have anyone turn against you, as they turned against Gaveston and Despenser. You mean too much to England and to my son's future. *I* need you too much. So let it be me who speaks. Let it be me they question or confront. Not you."

I reached out my hand. He looked long at it before he finally leaned out, took it and kissed it. He squeezed my fingers before letting them go. "Tonight, we will discuss our plans?"

"I cannot promise tonight, but most certainly soon. At length."

"Alone?" he added, a playful smile on his lips.

I forced a serious look as I teased him. "I thought I might invite Bishop Orleton and Bishop Stratford. Would you mind?" But I could not stop myself from returning his provocative smile.

I lifted my face to the sky, expecting raindrops to patter on my forehead, but only a light drizzle brushed my cheeks. The downpour had passed. An easterly wind pushed along the low, broken clouds. In time they yielded to patches of deceptive sunlight, for it was hardly warm. Beyond Abingdon, we halted to take rest in a broad valley. Mortimer rode to the back of the column where it was reported that two wagons carrying supplies had become stuck in the mud. I noticed he often fussed over such details to busy himself, for thus far our 'invasion' had amounted to little more than a royal progression through the countryside.

Patrice brought me a dry cloak and food. While we sat on a stone fence, nibbling at soggy bread and cheese so moist it turned to mush in our mouths, I gazed absentmindedly at the view around us. Our army filled the valley, looking like the Exodus of Moses' people from Egypt. Men sank to the wet ground to rest their weary legs and dry weapons on the scraps of cloth they kept tucked away. Squires and grooms tended to horses. Priests floated through the mass of bodies, sprinkling blessings on indifferent soldiers who were more intent on filling their bellies than purging their souls.

Some distance from the road on which we had come ran a long, low ridge, its thick mat of grass yellowed by autumn's first hard frost a few days past. In the middle of the hill stretched a figure with sprawling limbs and a long body, carved from the turf to reveal the white chalk underneath. Had we not stopped I would never have noticed it, for we were passing in the opposite direction to which it faced. I puzzled over it for some time before Mortimer returned to relieve me of my curiosity.

"A horse," he said. "Marked in the earth by those who lived here long ago. Before the Romans came."

I handed Patrice the remains of my meal and told her to give it to some of the men. Mortimer joined me on the fence, gnawing on a hunk of salted pork and washing it down generously with ale.

"Why go to the trouble?" I stood and took a few steps forward, although my perspective changed not at all, since the horse carving was half a mile away. "I can't see it serves any purpose."

"Why do we build churches if God is all around us?" He swallowed the last of his meat and drained his flask, wiping his mouth clean with the tail of his cloak. "They worshipped a horse goddess. It was a tribute to her: Epona. Women prayed to her to make them fertile."

I almost asked him if Joan had prayed to the horse goddess for her twelve children, but before jealousy took full hold of me, something caught my eye. I took several steps forward. To the north of the horse carving, riders crested the hill at a full gallop. I pointed to them. Mortimer squinted, peering into the distance.

"More men coming to join us?" I asked.

He shook his head. "No. We've stopped. They would not be in such a hurry for that. Messengers." Only a handful, but they rode with determined swiftness. "They've come from the London road."

A knot of dread drew tight around my chest. Immediately, he called to Arnaud, who still had his horse nearby, and told him to bring the riders to us. Arnaud had barely taken off at a canter when a scowl marred Mortimer's face. Leicester was approaching—and with a dozen knights tripping along behind him.

"Ah there, dear niece," Leicester hailed merrily. Then with a tip of his head to Mortimer, "My lord." He lifted his face to the sky. "We'll travel more swiftly now that the weather has broken. I took the liberty of sending men to gather news of the king. He came this way not a week ago. We're on the right path. I wager we'll find him before we get to Gloucester."

"We'll find him when he's run out of places to hide," Mortimer said mawkishly.

Leicester glared venomously at Mortimer, but just as Leicester took a step forward, shouts rang out from below. Mortimer bolted off, sprinting downhill, toward the sound of hooves sloshing through puddles. Halfway down the slope, he met the newcomers. One, a younger image of Mortimer, swung himself down from his saddle. In an instant, Mortimer embraced him.

"Edmund," I heard him say.

As if abruptly aware others were watching, Mortimer let go and took a step back. Another young man stood shyly behind the first. Mortimer cocked his head at him. "Roger . . . is it . . . is it you?"

Edmund and the younger Roger Mortimer. His sons.

He embraced young Roger only briefly, before he thrust him, too, away. With a jerk of his hand, he motioned them to follow and led them to where I stood with Leicester and the others.

Edmund Mortimer patiently endured his father's stilted introduction before he began spewing out his news. "Sir Henry de Beaumont is on his way. He was but a day behind when you left Oxford. He has a hundred and fifty with him."

"No more?" Leicester questioned. "I expected better of him than that."

"It is a hundred and fifty less for the king," Mortimer said. "What news do you have from London, Edmund? Any of John of Eltham, the queen's son?"

"Safe in the Tower, for now. Although no one dares to venture out into the city, as yet. It is still dangerous."

I feared for my son. For now, however, there was nothing I could do to help him. Nothing any of us could do but wait and hope. "My daughters—do you know where they are?"

"At Bristol, my lady. I have that on good word."

Relieved to finally know where they were, I crossed myself and said a swift prayer for their safety. "Whose word?"

"Lady Eleanor de Clare, it seems, was very willing to give out information to save herself. According to her, the Earl of Winchester was told by his son, Lord Despenser, to go to Bristol and hold it at all costs. Winchester left London only two days after the king did."

My heart plunged into my stomach like a boulder shoved from a cliff. They were indeed in the hands of Despenser. He had used my children against me before; it should not have been any shock that he would do so again. Somehow, I had known it would not be easy to get my children back. Not even with an army at my bidding and the greatest lords in the land beside me. My hands shook as I pulled my cloak around me, trembling. Leicester and most of the others would still want to pursue Edward.

"My uncle?" Mortimer asked.

Edmund's chin dropped. "They say he was taken away."

"From the Tower?" Mortimer stared hard at him, confusion evident in the furrowing of his brow. "By whom? To where?"

"Winchester. To Bristol, as well. But he was not well."

I touched Mortimer on the arm. "Why would he take your uncle with him?"

He spun away, raking his fingers through his hair. Suddenly, he gave a dry laugh of realization. "To bargain with. Bristol is a feint. A double one. Your children to use against you. My uncle against me. Cruel *and* clever."

Henry of Leicester swaggered forward, his thumbs hooked in his sword belt. "It has already been decided. We're going to Gloucester. To find the king and Lord Despenser."

Mortimer rounded on the earl. "They will be found! After all, who do you think is going to hide them? The Welsh? More likely than not, they'll stay out of this entirely. It would be their death warrant to come to the aid of a powerless king, running for his life. No, if the queen wishes it, we go to Bristol first. Get our hands on the Earl of Winchester, free my uncle and return the queen's daughters to her."

Like a sparring cock, Leicester puffed out his chest. "Bristol is protected by the Avon and the Frome. It has the thickest walls of any castle in England. You won't be able to take it. No one ever has."

"Then we'll lay siege."

A stale, broken laugh shook Leicester's belly. "A siege could go on for months."

Mortimer thrust his jaw out, confident. "So it could, if one were ignorant of Bristol's weaknesses."

"I told you, it has none," Leicester argued. "And while you loiter outside Bristol for weeks on end, the king and Lord Despenser could escape to anywhere—to Ireland, to the continent, to—"

"Can't you understand?" he screamed at Leicester. "If the king abandons his kingdom without appointing someone to govern in his place and placing the Great Seal in their care, we have *every* right to put his son in his place. We could take England back without levying a single blow. So let them abandon England. Bloody let them." He glanced at me, then lowered his voice. "And by God, Bristol will *not* resist me."

I laced my fingers together, brought them to my lips and shut my eyes tight. Before I could beseech God to return both my daughters and my son to me, I heard Young Edward's voice. I looked to see him bounding up the incline toward us. Sir William Montagu and ten more bright and bold knights followed him.

"Perhaps," Mortimer said to Leicester with marked sarcasm, "if you are so intent on hunting them down, you should tell the prince we are going on to Gloucester instead? That we haven't time to save his sisters."

"Sisters?" Young Edward strode into the midst of the group, glanced at Leicester, who was still fuming, and then inquisitively at me. "Hunt whom down, Mother? And what news of my sisters? Have they been found?"

My hands dropped down to cover my heart.

"My lord prince," Mortimer said with a flick of his hand, "these are my sons, Edmund and Roger."

Young Edward listened intently as Edmund Mortimer repeated his news.

Then, with a coy smile, Mortimer turned to me. "My lady? Bristol— or Gloucester?"

In my heart, I knew the answer. But it was precisely what Despenser expected of me. I shook my head and looked down. I could not think to speak, could not raise my voice in authority when I most needed to.

"P-perhaps . . ." I stuttered, "perhaps Winchester could be persuaded to give himself up? His hostages—" At the word, I halted, a black cloud of fright enveloping me.

"Lord Leicester," Young Edward said, his confidence rising with each word, "will you give the word to march?"

"To where, my lord prince?" Leicester's lips twitched as he fought a snarl.

The prince blinked at him. "Bristol, of course. Where else would we be going?" With a wag of his fingers, he gathered his band of young knights about him and departed.

Leicester had lost the argument. In the future, I doubted he would always yield so easily.

So it was that we turned for Bristol, great in numbers, but divided in purpose. With each mile, my uncertainty faded. Not one more day would I suffer, if there was even the slightest chance of getting them back.

39

Roger Mortimer:

Bristol – October, 1326

T HE RAINS ABATED, AND so I drove the pace, aware that rest beckoned at the end of a long road. Food to feed our soldiers and wood for fire to warm them were easily come by, for no one seemed to care that King Edward had proclaimed many of us, myself foremost, as outlaws. The irony of it all amused me. Only a few years ago, I had ridden at the head of a straggling army, begging for scraps in a land already stripped bare, while men weary of empty bellies slipped away into the night. Now we had but to approach a town and the gates stood gaping before us. Whenever I demanded provisions in the queen's name, they were given without question, often eagerly; but while I reveled in the ease with which success had so far come to us, I had also grown quickly bored of it. There was no thrill without a chase; no conquest without a contest.

The queen sent an envoy to Bristol to demand entrance, while she and her son remained safely behind with the army. The envoy also carried word that our numbers would shortly be augmented by those of the Earls of Kent and Norfolk. If Bristol resisted, it would soon be overrun.

Not far outside the city, I waited for a reply with a delegation, which included Leicester and the bishops of Hereford and Stratford. Bristol's white keep thrust starkly against a menacing sky. The castle walls looped within a tongue of land between the River Avon to the south and the River Frome to the north and west. It had been years since I was inside those walls, but if my memory held true, the castle was not as impenetrable as Leicester swore it to be.

Our answer came quickly.

The messenger, a youth less than half my age with a knot of black curls bunched into a forelock, dropped from his saddle to bow before us. "My lords," he said almost cheerfully, "a good morning to you."

One hand resting on his sword hilt, Leicester spat at the messenger's boots. "It will be, if you bring us good news. What does Bristol say?"

"We extend a hale welcome to our fair Queen Isabella and the noble Lord Edward. The town's gates stand open, my lords."

With his fingernails, Leicester scraped at his scraggy chin and grunted. "What of the castle? What says the Earl of Winchester?"

A cold wind raced across the open field to our west, tearing at our hair and clothes. In the distance, a column of black clouds advanced toward Bristol.

"The earl wishes to negotiate."

At that Leicester slapped at his thigh, laughing. "Negotiate what? He's surrounded."

He bluffed. Bristol was not surrounded. Not yet. Any fool looking out from the castle keep could see that. We would have to wait for the others to arrive before we could sufficiently position ourselves around the town without spreading too thin.

The messenger's jaunty smile dissolved. He forced his back straighter and met Leicester's patronizing gaze. "He requests pardons for himself and his son, Hugh the Younger, Earl of Gloucester."

Leicester sobered abruptly. We exchanged a glance.

"Why," I asked, "does the elder Despenser speak on behalf of the younger one?"

The messenger cast his eyes downward, as if it were the one question he had hoped not to hear. "He did not say, my lords, but"—he looked up again, tentative— "I can tell you the younger Lord Despenser arrived here with his father."

Blood surged through my veins. The wolf was near. The hunt had begun in earnest.

I sprang down from my saddle and in one bounding stride reached the messenger. He recoiled, but not fast enough. I grabbed the front of his jerkin, yanked him to me and closed one gauntleted hand around his slim throat.

"Perhaps, you could be persuaded to tell us"—I tightened my hold on his neck—"whether Hugh the Younger is still within?"

His face flamed red, then took on a bright, purplish hue. Slowly, I uncurled my fingers until he drew in a ragged breath.

He gulped and sputtered, struggling for air. "I do n-n-not know."

Again, I squeezed. Great drops of rain splattered against my face.

"I swear," he croaked, his knees beginning to buckle.

"And the king," I asked, "did he come to Bristol with them?"

He tried to shake his head, but my grip prevented it. I let go and shoved him down into the muck.

He collapsed to his knees and threw his hands out before him, kneeling like a dog. Coughs rattled his body until he retched, his spine arching with each convulsion. When he had finally regained his breath, head still bowed to me, he answered hoarsely, "My lord . . . I swear on my life, I know nothing of the king. He was not with the Despensers when they came here."

If this stripling spoke the truth, the king and Despenser had separated. But why?

I stuck out my hand to him. He gazed long at it before he took it. Then he got to his feet, wobbling.

"The Earl of Winchester's request is denied," I said.

Once, I had asked the same grace of Edward for my uncle and

myself. If Despenser was still within . . . if he actually was, he would receive no mercy from me.

Leicester dropped from his mount and came at me, flailing his arms. "Denied? You can't mean to lay siege? Bristol could stand a year against us."

I motioned the earl aside so our voices would not carry. Rain and wind whipped hard, forcing us to turn our faces away from its assault. "Do you want this over with . . . or do you want both Despensers dead?"

He threw his head back, sucking air between his teeth. It was too sweet a temptation for a man as vengeful as Leicester. "Dead."

More ox than fox, Leicester had to be led by the nose to see anything less than obvious. So I led him.

"Then listen. Ten years ago Bristol defied the king over a matter of taxation. The Earl of Pembroke and I were ordered to bring the town to submission. There was a more effective weapon for that than starving them out: terror. With only two trebuchets and a mangonel we hammered the town with stones. Less than twenty days later Bristol fell. This time, with the town already throwing open its gates, we will not have to loiter here as long."

By then, I had his full attention. I continued. "Since Bristol was given into their lordship, the Despensers have permitted the building of houses that abut the castle walls. All we need to do is lull them into complacency. Let them think we have the patience and means for a siege—they have no contact with the outside now. We can scale the walls from the roofs of those houses. With enough men, the garrison will be easily overcome. All of Bristol will be ours, Winchester *and* Lord Despenser our prisoners . . . and the queen's daughters back in her care.

"Put them on trial then—I give you free rein there, Henry. We know what the end will be. But negotiate with Winchester . . . and you will have lost your chance at that which you most want." I could have gone on, but Leicester was not so stupid he could not get my point.

In a freezing rain, the messenger raced back to the castle, no doubt eager to be out of my reach. I could have promised pardons and then reneged on them, as Edward had done to me at Shrewsbury, but even when dealing with my enemies I would maintain my honor and not offer lies to gain the advantage.

There would, however, be no compromise. No clemency.

I DISPATCHED PATROLS AROUND the perimeter of the city to watch for anyone trying to enter or leave the castle undetected. My spies went to work harvesting information from the townsfolk, journeying craftsmen, and nearby farmers. At every road, our soldiers blocked the way, ruthlessly interrogating travelers. Very soon, they brought to me a Flemish cloth merchant, who had come directly from Gloucester, where, he said, King Edward had issued another summons to gather an army to him. Those who heard the king's order had laughed and ignored it, going about their business as before. The Fleming had heard Despenser was with the king, but he could not say it as a certainty. Since one man could not be in two places, Despenser had either been with the king at Gloucester all along, meaning the envoy had lied, or he was still inside Bristol Castle, fool enough to think the king would raise an army and rally to his defense. Electing to come to Bristol had been a calculated risk. I only hoped that it was one that would not cost me—and England—more than could be gained from it.

I did not worry Isabella with the news that Hugh Despenser the Younger might be inside Bristol Castle, for in truth I did not know that he was. Yet with each passing day, I could tell by her silence that she had begun to doubt not only me, but her own judgment, as well.

For six days we idled outside the town walls. Kent and Norfolk, who finally arrived on the third day, were stationed to the south and east, Beaumont and Wake to the west. The larger part of our army, Leicester's forces and the remaining Hainaulters, were encamped on the far side of the River Frome, north of the Abbey of St. Augustine's where Isabella had taken up residence.

Whenever the rain let up, our archers lobbed their missiles from rooftops at sentries on the castle walls, while the garrison archers returned the volleys. Within their homes, the townspeople huddled as stray arrows thwacked against their roofs. If not for the frequent rain, undoubtedly the garrison would have returned flaming arrows and burned Bristol to the ground in its own defense.

Meanwhile, east of the castle and within plain view, we hauled timber, sawed it and fit it together as we built our siege engines. But the carpenter's work was woefully slowed by the heavy rains that soaked the earth and turned the fields into marshes, a situation that rankled the engineer I had brought all the way from Koblenz for just such a purpose. He threatened to quit England when I forbid the machine from being moved into range the moment it was finished, until he found the point of my sword pressed to his throat. His mind changed quickly.

For six days straight, Winchester offered to give himself up, although he made no further mention of his son. And every time I sent back the same answer—that his life and his son's were forfeit.

On the seventh day, I returned no answer. He would have it soon enough.

40

Roger Mortimer:
Bristol – October, 1326

I SABELLA STOOD ON A grassy knoll to the east of the city, the hood of her mantle pushed back onto her shoulders and her feet braced to withstand the buffeting wind. She surveyed the vast army that engulfed the town and the high walls behind which her daughters were. Beside her was Bishop Orleton, his gold embroidered amice pulled up over his head to cover his ears and ward off the cold.

"My lady," I hailed as I tramped over the slick, wind-bent grass of the small hill. "Your grace."

A polite smile curved Orleton's fine lips as he nodded in greeting. "Will we see you at Mass tomorrow, Sir Roger?"

"Is tomorrow Sunday?" I figured if I needed to speak with God, He would know where to find me, whether I was at church or not.

"No, but it's All Hallow's. We will honor all the saints and martyrs who—"

"Your pardon, good bishop, but I regret I must tend to my querulous flock of misfits, even on holy days, lest they add murder to their litany of sins."

"You have been engrossed in other details as well, I see." He turned his gaze to the open area at the western foot of the hill.

There, rising from the marshy meadow like a dragon out of the earth's messy bowels was the monstrosity which had consumed me lately: the trebuchet. I had finally ordered the great machine to be moved into position. The threat of it would distract from other goings-on within the town walls.

Isabella quailed visibly. "What are they loading in the trebuchet, Sir Roger?"

"A horse's head, my lady. It was an old cart horse with a bad leg," I added, trying to convince her that a lame beast was more useful dead than alive. It had taken a small host of footsoldiers to haul on ropes as the counterweight of the trebuchet was brought into place. Large shields covered in wet hides had protected the workers from the garrison's arrows. "Its injury became infected. It was a kindness to put it out of its misery."

She turned sorrowful eyes on me. "And you will . . . throw it over the castle walls?"

"Where it will rot and raise a holy stink." The horse had been put down two days ago and already its corpse was emitting a stench strong enough to bring the buzzards circling. I omitted mention of the other grotesque warnings that would follow, should other plans fail. Shortly after our arrival, Sir John Maltravers had captured a small reconnaissance party of Winchester's. If the captives did not provide more useful information than what had so far been extracted from them, their severed heads would be the next thing lobbed over the walls.

Pulling her fur-lined mantle tight to her breast for warmth, Isabella looked at Bristol's stout walls. "Why do we not offer the earl terms? Let it all be over with."

"The ladies Joanna and Eleanor will not be harmed," I assured her, although I avoided arguing with her about Winchester. I meant to see the man's head on a stake for all he and his son had cost me. "Trust me in this. You'll have them sooner than you believe."

"My faith in you, Sir Roger, is not in question." Her voice was airy and strained. "My daughters are still in danger. That is all I know or can think of. It robs me of sleep and wrings the blood from my heart."

A gust of wind, carrying the faint tang of salt air, ripped across the open ground. Golden strands of hair lashed at Isabella's face. She ran her tongue over chapped lips, as if to speak, then turned away and took the arm of Bishop Orleton. They descended the hill, where horses awaited to take them back to the abbey.

I did not tell her that before noon tomorrow, Bristol would be ours. If I had, she would not have believed me anyway.

Overhead, gulls shrieked and dove against a clearing afternoon sky where high clouds raced eastward like tufts of lamb's wool tumbling in the wind. In the meadow below, the crank of the trebuchet's winch screeched as the men gave it one more turn. The beam groaned in answer against the strain. Father Norbert waved his hands in a blessing of the machine— although I was sure he had been dragged there and forced to do it. Then, the engineer released the pin. As the counterweight slammed downward, the sling flew through its chute, and then arced out and up. Father Norbert dropped to his knees and raised his hands to heaven, crying out for God's wisdom to rain down and make the Earl of Winchester relent of his evil ways.

A pleasing sentiment . . . but inside the castle was probably another priest, asking for God's protection.

CLODS OF MUD PACKED the soles of my boots as I trudged to the Earl of Kent's pavilion. He expected a report on the trebuchet and so I went, hoping it would be short. As I stopped before the earl's quarters, Gerard d'Alspaye hailed me and approached, his feet flinging streaks of mud against nearby tents with each stride.

"Leicester's men will be ready, come morning," he reported.

I drew my sword, scraped the mud from my soles and slipped it back into its scabbard. "Good. Make certain, though, that they are all in place well before nightfall."

Gerard went and I nodded to the young man standing guard before Kent's pavilion. He announced me and drew aside the flap.

"Come in, Sir Roger." Edmund, Earl of Kent, pushed a map across the table at me with the point of his knife.

It was dark inside the pavilion, despite being midday. Rain had fallen weeklong and although a drop had yet to fall that day, heavy clouds still cloaked the sun. A rising wind hammered at the walls, threatening to topple the pavilion. Already two had fallen that afternoon, one of those being Leicester's, which had sent him into a terrible dudgeon.

"Did it work?" he asked.

"Well enough," I said. "But the mud is shin-deep in places. Moving the trebuchet into better positioning to hurl stones at the walls or towers will be near to impossible. We'll have to be content with sending them putrid offerings of peace. Just as well, though. The queen does not want her daughters put in danger." The whole industry, however, was no more than a ploy, meant to convince Winchester that he should accept his fate. Kent was better left in the dark until the assault began. If he learned of it beforehand, he might ruin it simply by trying to take part in it.

Kent twirled his knife between his thumb and forefinger. "He brought this upon himself."

"Winchester?" I bent over the map to study it—a map of Wales and the Marches, with a tattered hole where Gloucester should have been.

"Edward." He scratched furiously at the table with his blade, making a deep gouge in the wood. "I tried to tell him it would come to this. Everyone did."

"Ah, and I thought you'd asked me here to discuss the accuracy and range of our beloved war machine." A sneer flitted across his mouth, telling me he did not share in my sarcasm. I smoothed the torn edges of the map with my fingertips, trying to push them back together. To appease him, I sobered. "The king, your brother, does not accept blame readily. When you gave him advice he didn't want to hear, he took it as an attack on his person. So instead, he chose to believe the one who flattered him when he doubted himself, consoled him when he felt offense."

"And why did you not do that, Sir Roger?" Kent arched a pale brow and tilted his head to one side. "You were high in his favor once. You could have been the one sitting at Edward's right hand, had you said what he wanted to hear. Yet you defied him."

"For the same reasons you did, my lord. Because I could not curry favor with a man who had been led so far off the path of what was right and just." Besides, Despenser held a power over Edward that no one else ever would. "But it is as you said—you tried, I tried, others did. To no good end."

Kent, however, was only half listening.

"My lord," I said, "why did you ask me here?"

He slammed the knife into the table, embedding its point. "My brother's rule has been nothing but disaster," he blurted out. "Someone else, someone more fit to wear a king's crown, should sit in his place."

For a moment, I wondered if he meant himself. Like me, Edward's brothers had been cheated out of much in favor of Despenser. They would want their due, and the opportunity was at hand. But there were three in line ahead of Kent: the princes, Edward and John, and his full brother, the Earl of Norfolk. Kent was hardly arrogant enough to reach that far.

I plied carefully. "You speak of removing Edward from the throne. Is that wise? There may be some yet who would consider it treason." While England had rushed to our aid, eager to cast away Hugh Despenser, the question still remained of what to do with Edward. In one aspect, Kent was completely right: Edward was incapable of governing his kingdom properly.

With a loud sniff, he looked down sulkily and shrugged. "I didn't want to turn against him, you know. How does a man betray his own brother?"

So Kent doubted himself. That made him unreliable. Still, it per-turbed me to come here for no more reason than to absorb his guilt. A tavern whore would have more compassion for him than I did. Bristol Castle was about to fall and with it the Despensers. I preferred not to waste any more time in this manner, yet I needed to know where he stood. "Are you willing to carry through, my lord, once they are found?"

"I see no other way to end it. The earldoms of Gloucester and Winchester—they should have been given to Thomas and me, not to those ingratiating weasels." He threw himself onto a pile of furs, locked his hands behind his head, and gazed up at the ceiling pensively. Outside, boots slurped through the mud. Two soldiers complained of the snoring of a third as they passed by, bantering ideas about as to how to silence him. As the voices faded into the lazy hum of camp noise, Kent flipped over, propped himself up on his elbow and jabbed a finger at me. "A word of warning, Sir Roger: do not aim too high."

"I aim at nothing," I replied tersely. "I only mean to correct the wrongs that have been done."

"Do you?" His fine lips tilted into a curious smirk. "Oh, I think you're like any other man who has stepped into the circle of power. Temptation calls your name. It whispers promises of immortality in your ear. Speaks to you of glory and greatness. What man wouldn't harken to that?"

I did not answer. If Kent wanted to accuse me of ambition, it was only because he lacked the ability to take action himself. And if not me, then who? Yes, I had failed before, but this time I would succeed. A blast of damp air tossed the map onto the ground and I bent to pick it up.

"My lords." An apologetic guard peered through barely parted tent flaps. "Sir Roger, a messenger to see you."

Before Kent or I could reply, Simon de Beresford slipped past the guard and entered, the rank smell of wet horse and rotting leather wafting after him. Mud was splattered over his legs and chest.

"You bring word of the king?" I asked.

Ignoring me, Simon edged closer to the side of the table where an untouched loaf of bread and a flagon of wine sat. He wore the gaunt, weary look of one who had been on the road too long and needed the relief of strong drink.

I scooped up the loaf of bread and tossed it to him, but left the wine where it was.

Simon caught the bread in his grimy hands and tore it in two. "Stale," he proclaimed, yanking a forearm across his snotty nose. Then he tore off a piece with his teeth and gnawed on it. "Something to wash it down with?"

Indignant, Kent tucked his chin in. "Who is this . . . this dung-fly?"

"Simon de Beresford." With exquisite slowness, I poured a cup of wine and gave it to Simon. "A spy. Mine."

At that, Kent scrambled to his feet, his eyes wide with curiosity. "Well, then, what have you to say, Simon de Beresford? By your looks, I say you've come a long way without rest. Important news?"

"Important news deserves good pay," he returned sharply, "especially when it involves England's future." He guzzled his drink, then pushed the cup along the edge of the table, wanting more.

"You'll get your reward," I reminded him, ignoring his gesture, "later, as we discussed."

"And a hefty one it will be, I don't doubt. Although I have, at times, wondered if you haven't offered me things which are not yours to give away. Still, a man has to eat, to drink . . . to partake of small comforts along the way. I cannot accept other duties when my every waking hour is spent on uncovering the king and his pet snake."

Nearly tripping over his pile of furs, Kent turned and went to a small chest on the far side of the pavilion. He flipped the lid open, snatched up a trinket and hurled it in Simon's direction.

A band of gold flashed in the dimness. Simon flung a hand out and caught the ring. Palm open, he nudged at it with a finger. "Coin is better, but this will serve . . . for now."

"Your news?" Kent probed in an irritated tone.

Simon slipped the ring into a pouch at his belt beside the long knife he wore. "King Edward and Hugh Despenser set sail from Chepstow two days ago."

I took a step back, absorbing his words. Gone? To where? Bloody hell . . . bloody damnable hell. Those who would not be overjoyed to hear it, those who wanted bodily revenge on Despenser, would blame me for letting them go.

"They've left England, both of them?" I questioned. For a week I had held hope that Despenser was inside the castle. With him in our hands, Edward would do whatever we begged of him, including giving up his throne. But if Despenser had slipped away under our noses, or left before we even arrived, it was a grand opportunity missed and Leicester would use that failure against me. "You're certain of this?"

"Leicester said he was here," Kent muttered.

"He *was* here," I retorted, tired of Kent's childish sulking. If allowed to, Kent would kick at the dirt and whine about this for days before a sound thought for action entered his head—days that could not be wasted.

Kent stomped his foot. "All this, this . . . waiting and wasting time. Turning away from Gloucester, where we might have had them. To come here. For nothing."

"It wasn't for nothing. Your nieces are inside." And my uncle. But I said nothing of him. This siege could not be regarded as my personal blood feud, whether it was or not. My every move would be scrutinized by not only Kent, but others grappling for position in the rising momentum of this upheaval.

"We could have had him," Kent whined.

"Unlikely," Simon calmly interrupted, "unless you would have sent a small party ahead after him. You missed him by less than a day." He took the flagon of wine, brought it to his mouth and downed its contents in one long swallow. "Despenser came to Bristol to retrieve his money. Sacks of gold, most of it hidden here. Some in Gloucester, too. But when he learned you were coming, he left in the middle of the night. Couldn't take it all with him."

Even desperate and running for his life, Despenser could not abandon his hoard. It was the only means they had left. Wherever they were going, even if no one would voluntarily give them succor, not many would turn down money.

Then, it struck me with the force of a well-aimed lance blow to the chest.

England was without a king.

41

Roger Mortimer:
Bristol – October, 1326

TOO LATE, I REALIZED my mistake in allowing Simon to deliver his news in the presence of Kent. I had but one means to circumvent the damage that could be done and turn it into opportunity. One way to preserve what I had so far gained.

I went to St. Augustine's in search of Isabella, but was curtly reminded by an agitated monk that it was All Hallow's Eve. The queen and Lord Edward were within the Lady Chapel, praying in honor of all the martyrs since before the time of Christ. For nearly an hour I waited, expecting her to emerge from her devotions. Impatient, I paced the length of the cloister court. From somewhere, the faint scent of wood smoke drifted on a dying breeze. I looked up to see a sky that was black for lack of star or moon. Drifting clouds were edged in silver. They must have already lit the bonfire in the market square to ward off the wandering souls who had not yet found their way to heaven or hell. A passing beggar, who was leaning on a crutch fashioned from a weathered branch, his teeth half gone and a putrid wound on his neck seeping puss, offered to share his blood pudding with me. I refused, telling him if I wanted to gorge myself on pig's offal I would gut him. He limped away in a hurry.

Finally, Patrice came to fetch me, saying the queen had already taken to her quarters for the night, but would see me briefly. She led me to the queen's room within the abbey, where Arnaud stood guard at the door. His presence took me by surprise, although a welcome one it was. If Isabella had intended to grant me nothing more than a few minutes, she would not have posted her most trusted squire outside her door. The moment I was through the threshold, Patrice closed it behind me.

Though spacious, the room was austere, furnished with only a four-postered bed, a square table, two chairs, and an unadorned hearth. On the wall to the right of the bed hung a wooden cross, carved with a crude figure of the Christ, who dangled with arms outspread and his face turned upward in agony. Beneath, four tallow candles flickered meagerly.

A sigh wafted across the room.

I looked toward the single window, its shutters open to the cool night air. There, hugging her knees to her chest, Isabella sat on the narrow window ledge. The pointed, satin toes of her slippers peeked from beneath the hem of her nightshift to show bare ankles. Her favorite red mantle, plush with fur, had slipped from her shoulders, as though she had grown mindless to the chill in the room. Her breath fogged the air.

I tended to the neglected hearth, until the fire within it sent up flames that licked the mantle. The sparks jumped from the kindling and the heat rose so rapidly that I stepped back to avoid being scorched.

Still, Isabella had not moved. "I knew I would not be able to sleep," she said. "All day I prayed to God to deliver my girls and John safely to me."

I poured two goblets of wine and handed her one.

Finally, she looked at me. "You must have felt as I do, at times."

"And how is that?" I drank my cup halfway down.

"Guilty . . ." She looked long into her goblet before taking a sip. "Guilty that I could not always keep my children with me. Or protect

341

them."

"Why should anyone, father or mother, feel responsible for another's cruelty?" My own children had been shut up all over England. I hardly thought it my fault. I leaned against the wall next to her, close enough to reach out and touch her, but not so close I could not admire her beauty. A single golden strand of her hair dangled over her shoulder. The neckline of her nightshift dipped down to her breastbone. With every breath she took, my eyes were drawn to the gentle rise and fall of her bosom, as small and firm as a young girl's.

In one long gulp, she drained her goblet dry, as if she had not wetted her throat for days. Then she pulled the shutters closed, finally drawing her mantle up around her neck. "I left them."

"Despenser took them *from* you. You left because you had no other choice. You will see them, Isabeau," I told her as I poured her another glass, "very soon. I promise you. And word from London is that things are settling well. John of Hainault will look after your son there. Few are more trustworthy than him." Moving nearer to her, I set my own goblet down and lifted her cold hand to my hungry lips. "You will have the girls back soon, my love. Tomorrow. A few days. A week, at most. Winchester cannot last."

A shiver ran through her body and I leaned back to look into her face. "There is something I must tell you. Something I learned today."

"What?" she whispered, as if someone might overhear us.

"When we arrived here at Bristol, Leicester and I were told that Lord Despenser was inside the castle."

At that, her hand crept up to cover her mouth. I could sense the fear flowing in her veins and so I went on quickly. She had suffered enough worry already. "But he isn't. Not anymore. He had already gone from here and was on his way to join the king." Her shoulders slackened with relief. "Only hours ago, I learned that Edward and Despenser boarded a ship in Chepstow and set sail. They are no longer in England, Isabeau. Do you know what that means? It means that your son, Young Edward, can take his place, with you as his regent. You need not fear them anymore."

I kissed her fingertips, her wrist, her forearm. Her mouth quavered. I peeled back her shift at the shoulder and inched closer, my arm sliding around her, pulling her to me. With wine-wet lips, I kissed her neck. Her head lolled to the side. A shiver of longing, a response I had come to know well, ran through her. Every muscle in me wanted to feel her beneath me, to move inside her until we were both drenched in burning sweat. But more than just making her willing to bed with me, I wanted her to love me in a way that flouted what others might think or say. As I did her.

Dear God, I *loved* her. Not just that I had stolen her from Edward and had her a hundred times over . . . but, I loved *her*. The woman, not the queen.

Yet for as much as I loved her, I bloody hated the torment she inflicted on me. The way she made my guts twist inside out and my head go light even at the sight of her. Like now. Perhaps that was why I fought so hard to keep some measure of control over her, because I had so little when it came to being alone with her.

I whispered, "Tell me what you want, Isabeau."

One of her hands drifted across her body and up to her shoulder. She tugged her nightshift free, letting it fall in a drift of white at her feet. As she stepped over her clothes and past me, she brushed me with a hot hand. I heard the sigh of the covers as she peeled them back from the bed. The creak of the frame as she lay down. Her voice, soft as a swan's feather in my ears: "You, Roger."

Over my shoulder, I gazed at her. Arms sprawled above her head. One knee drawn slightly to the side. Her open mouth, her hand held out to me . . .

I went to her, leaned over her and touched my lips to hers. A low moan rose from her throat to hum against my tongue. I cupped the back of her head, tasting her, inhaling her. The heat of her flesh seared into my fingertips. I drew back slightly, gazed down into her glistening face and kissed her eyelids. Then, I plucked up the corner of the bed sheets, drawing them over her.

As much as I wanted her, there was something far more important that I had to do.

For a few moments, she blinked in confusion. Slowly, as if in a daze, she clutched the covers close to her bare body and sat up. Before she could part her lips in question, I told her, "I cannot be with you now, Isabeau, my love. Not tonight." I withdrew toward the door, my eyes never leaving her. "Tomorrow, before first light, Leicester's men will scale the castle walls. I must be there. Because I'm going to give you your daughters back, Isabeau."

And I'm going to find my uncle, so I can take him home to Chirk.

Isabella closed her eyes and sank back against her pillows. "Go."

And I left a queen alone in her bed. So I could do as I had sworn to.

42

Roger Mortimer:
Bristol – October, 1326

FAR AWAY, A DOG howled. Restless, I lay awake, listening to the sounds of an army in the night. The low, hushed voices of sentries as they passed one another. A horse nickering. Scattered coughs. The delusive titter of a camp whore. The crackling of a fire.

A cold, gusting wind rapped at the side walls of my tent. I clenched the handle of my knife tight beneath my blanket and held my breath, peering through the darkness at the tent flap even as my eyelids sank with weariness.

I should have sworn Kent to keep the news to himself. Better yet, I should have gone elsewhere with Simon before I allowed him to speak. If Leicester learned of this before morning . . . he would not launch the assault. Instead, he would come at me in a rage, blaming me. We would not take Bristol's castle.

And we would never find the king. Never bring Despenser to trial. Never . . .

MALTRAVERS ROUSED ME WELL past sunrise. I scolded him for not waking me sooner. With the help of a flustered body squire, I prepared hastily. Gerard, who was with him, had seen to it that my mail had been finely polished with sand and vinegar until it shone in the day's first light. I stepped from my tent, sword at my side and my shield strapped to my arm. We went on foot with haste to St. Ewen's Church, a stone's throw from the walls of the outer ward of Bristol Castle, where Leicester greeted me in high spirits.

"They've taken St. Nicholas' Gate at the bridge," he crowed, thumping me on the arm with a gauntleted hand. "No escape now. We have them, by God."

So, he had not yet learned Simon's news. My reprieve, I knew, would not last. Once the keep was searched and Despenser was nowhere to be found, the truth would come out.

I flipped the visor of my helmet up. "I'd have thought you'd be in the thick of the fighting, Henry."

He bristled. "When I sent for you, Sir Roger, I expected you straight-away."

Shielding my eyes from the morning sun with my hand, I looked toward the square, white keep, towering above the walls. Hurriedly, I scrounged for a plausible excuse—one I knew he would condone. "The town is filled with whores, Henry. Can't a man take a little pleasure when it's given to him?"

"Given . . . or bought?" He cuffed me on the shoulder blade. "If we go to Hereford, I'll introduce you to a girl there named Gwenllian who, for nary a penny, will do things I wager your wife has no knowledge of."

He was lecherous, just like his brother Thomas had been. If I let him, he would talk of such things until after the assault was long done. "I trust you told them to find Lady Eleanor and Lady Joanna? If any harm should come to—"

"Do you take me for a fool?"

"Not at all. I only wanted to make certain your men understood their welfare is of the utmost importance. Winchester is desperate by now. We can't trust him not to—" I broke off. Shouts burst from within the outer ward. Insults and jeers. Whoops. The noise of triumph.

I rushed through a clutch of archers arrayed in front of St. Ewen's. Their quivers were still full. They had not yet spent a single arrow in the attack.

With Maltravers and Gerard at my heels, I went across the narrow drawbridge spanning the moat. At the gate, more than a dozen pikemen stood on guard. They had stopped a knight and his squire who were escorting a prisoner from the castle.

A paunch-bellied guard lowered his weapon, aiming its pointed end at the knight's chest.

"Who's the prisoner?" the guard said.

The knight puffed his chest out and lifted his chin like a sparring cock. "The constable," he said with a shrug, indicating the gray-haired man, so slight in build and sunken in the face he resembled a skeleton.

"And who are you?" the guard interrogated.

He lifted his helmet from his head. "Lord Thomas Wake. Now let me by."

I shoved my way to them and said, "You did not hear? All prisoners are to remain inside the castle."

"But my lord," Wake protested, "the Earl of Leicester, wanted them to be brought to the camp."

I cast a look over my shoulder. Leicester had not followed us. Probably, he was waiting until he could be assured it was safe to enter the fortress. "They are to remain inside. No one is to take prisoners for ransom. Queen's orders," I added, although she had said no such thing, leaving all to me. One of these lump-headed dolts might let an important prisoner slip past them and I would not run that risk. "Have we captured the keep?"

"An hour ago," Wake replied with a sneer.

"Good, then you'll take the constable here back to the great hall. And you'll shove him into a clump with all the other prisoners and do nothing further with them until you hear from me. Understood?" Without waiting for an answer, I searched the faces of the other pikemen until I found one with an honest look to him, a boy of eighteen or so who met my eyes without defiance. "You, go to all the other gates and tell them the same thing. Quickly, boy."

Spurred by the commanding urgency of my voice, he hurried beneath the archway of the gate and went right, off toward St. Nicholas' gate. We followed him beneath the portcullis and found ourselves in the outer ward. Despite the mess that met our eyes, there appeared to be some kind of organization. The remaining garrison—those who had attempted to defend the castle, and judging by the scattered bodies, broken and bleeding, many had tried valiantly only to fail—were being dragged from the inner ward and forced to their knees just outside the keep. Behind me, Lord Wake could not stop his grumbling as his men yanked the simpering constable toward the keep. I had robbed him of a sizeable ransom. He would harbor a grudge toward me.

Though still shrouded in morning shadow, above the inner curtain the limewashed walls of Bristol's keep gleamed as white as a gull's breast feathers. Somewhere, in this sprawling expanse of stones jutting skyward, were the Earl of Winchester, the queen's daughters, and my ill and aged uncle. Once found, the earl would be brought before a tribunal, the gruesome outcome already decided.

Father Norbert, the queen's shrew-eyed confessor, stumbled through the maze of prisoners. He wrung the wooden crucifix that dangled from a piece of rope around his goose-like neck. Finally, he dropped to his knees and laid a hand on the forehead of a wounded man. The leather brace on the fallen man's wrist told that he was an archer, but his clutch of arrows was either spent or had been stolen. The angle at which one of his legs lay twisted indicated he had fallen from the wall. He was still alive, barely.

"Do you make a habit," Father Norbert complained as he caught sight of me, "of waging war on holy days?"

"You're wasting your time," I told the priest, before he could utter the first word of a *pater noster*. "Save your prayers for the living. Better yet, someone other than our enemies."

Father Norbert drew the sign of the cross in the air and uttered a few words of Latin, of which he probably did not even know the meaning. "All are God's children, Sir Roger. And he is a fellow Englishman. Men do not always choose on which side they will fight. Most are simply following their master's orders, as you and I do."

The archer's eyes rolled far up into his head. His body jerked as he gulped his dying breath, and then went slack. Father Norbert reached to pull the man's eyelids shut. Before he could, I grabbed the back of his black frock, twisted it to gain my grip and yanked him to his feet. "I follow no one's orders. But here's one for you, Father: go to the dungeons; if you find my uncle, Lord Roger of Chirk, come back and tell me where he is. And if you need to say a prayer, pray you find him alive. I didn't come all this way to bury him."

I told Maltravers and Gerard to go with him, to make certain he did not stop to dribble prayers over more corpses. As I shoved the quivering priest toward the gate to the inner ward, I caught sight of my son Edmund, lowering himself wearily down the bottom rungs of a ladder that leaned against the wall. Blood ran in streaks from a gash on his left cheek, dripping onto his surcoat, although he paid no heed to it.

"I thought I told you once," I said as he neared, "never to lower your shield until your opponent has exhausted himself first."

Edmund wiped at his cheek, smearing bright blood from ear to jawline. "It was strapped to my back." With a grin, he added, "I was one of the first up the ladders and over the wall."

"A foolish thing to do. A wonder, it is, that you're not dead." I had not spent two years in the Tower and as many in exile only to have my firstborn son throw himself on the first blade raised at him. The boy needed to learn caution. "Next time let the men-at-arms take the first assault."

At my admonishment, he hung his head, then sucked in a breath and raised his chin. "I killed three men on the wall."

"Who could've killed you," I reminded him. "I suppose, though, it's proof of your skill they didn't." As he soaked in the mild compliment, I realized I had not seen my other son in more than a day. "Your brother, Roger—where is he?" I asked.

"Scouring the keep with Sir Henry de Beaumont." Edmund stepped close and lowered his voice, as if guarding a great secret. "It seems Lord Despenser was hoarding half of England's treasury here. There are rooms stuffed with gold and jewels in there. Piles of it. Beaumont was doing all he could to keep the Hainaulters from pilfering any of it."

"No more the Hainaulters than our own. I just stopped Lord Wake from trying to abscond with the constable, no doubt hoping to barter his freedom with the man's kin for a fair sum." I surveyed the ward. "The queen's daughters? Have they been found?"

"In the chapel of St. Martin's, over there." He raised a reddened hand toward the little chapel tucked in the northwest corner of the ward.

Relief swept through me. "Unharmed?"

"Afraid, but without a scratch."

"Good. Send for the queen."

I wended my way through the chaos of bodies, climbed the dozen steps and entered the church through the half-open doors. At first, it appeared empty. Light filtered through a stained glass, rosette window high on the wall behind the altar, flooding the serene expanse of the nave in a wash of rose-red and violet. Within, all was quiet, but from outside, the desperate pleas for mercy that ensued from the lips of the defeated penetrated the walls.

Beyond the fluted pillars, I explored its depths cautiously. A whimper, followed by a small, shushed voice, emanated from a vestibule to the left. I walked beneath an archway toward the sound, stopping before a door that hung askance on its iron hinges. Gouges marked where it had been hammered at by the butt end of weapons. An axe had cleaved at the planks, leaving long, jagged splinters. I unstrapped my shield and laid it aside, then grappled at the handle, finally removing my gauntlets to gain a firmer grip, and dragged the door's bottom over the rough flagstones.

I gazed into a small, private chapel, its vaulted roof moored by closely spaced, squat columns. At its end was a humble altar and upon it a plain wooden cross and three lit candles. I moved toward the altar, watching for shadows to spring from behind the columns.

Again, a whimper. But this time a muffled growl followed it. Slowly, I slid my sword from its scabbard at my hip. I cursed myself for not having taken men in with me. If I turned my back now, whoever was there would have a clear target. I debated whether to retreat or advance. There could not be many of them, as there were only a few columns to hide behind and perhaps an alcove to either side of the altar.

But the queen's daughters were here somewhere. And if they were in this room, if those sounds were one of them in distress . . .

"Show yourselves," I called. No one spoke out. No one appeared. But I heard short, ragged breaths and knew I was not alone.

"I said come out!"

Low voices, more than one. Footsteps scraping. The whisper of a blade being drawn.

"Who are you?" a rough voice demanded.

"Sir Roger Mortimer," I replied, hopeful my name would stoke an ember of fear. But my days of distinction on the field of battle had passed long ago. Of late, I had done little more than see to the gathering of provisions and the quashing of brawls between arrogant mercenaries and petulant Englishmen.

"You should have bloody said so sooner." The hulking shadow of Sir Thomas Gurney emerged from the darkness of the alcove. He shoved his short sword back into its scabbard and scratched at his roll of belly fat. A broken-toothed grin twisted his ugly face. "Lord Leicester told us to guard the lambs if we found them—to the death. I was hoping you were one of Winchester's men, so I could."

I rounded the bulky column from behind which he had appeared. There, two quivering girls, still in their nightclothes, clung together behind the spindly legs of William Ockle. Of the two men, they had apparently perceived him to be the lesser evil and thus claimed refuge with him.

Ockle, however, cringed at their touch. The older girl peeked around his waist, her mouth agape and her eyes, the same green as her mother's, wide with terror. A trembling child was not the sort of fear I had wanted to inspire by my reputation. Then I remembered I still had my sword drawn and my helmet on.

"Lady Eleanor, I'm sorry," I offered, returning my weapon to its resting place. Then I removed my helmet, laid it at my feet and held my empty arms wide, palms open, to show I meant no harm. "I did not mean to frighten you. I am Sir Roger, in the service of your mother, Queen Isabella. I will take you to her."

Then the other girl poked her head around Ockle's other thigh. She sucked at her fingers, her cheeks still plump as an infant's. Around her shoulders was a ragged square of lambskin. It must be Joanna. And not much older than my own daughter, Beatrice, whom I had never laid eyes on.

My hand held out, I eased toward them. Eleanor pulled her sister back, but Joanna struggled against her grasp, tore free and flung herself forward. The lambskin fell to the floor. Just as I reached down to pick it up, Joanna grasped my wrist between her chubby hands and, without warning, sunk her teeth into the meat of my thumb. I let out a curse and jerked my hand away as she scuttled backward to rejoin her sister.

Ockle fought a smirk. Behind me, Gurney guffawed uncontrollably. Between snorts, he said, "I had a mind to tie that one up in a sack and toss her in the river. Feisty little brat, isn't she?"

I rounded on him. "She is the queen's daughter!" I lowered my voice, mindful of the girls. "Say any such thing again and it's you who'll be drowning in the river."

"She's spirited, is all I meant," he grumbled. "Wasn't an easy thing keeping her quiet. She nearly gave us away more than once."

"Best guard your own tongue, Gurney."

Eleanor stomped her foot. "Take us to our mother. Now!"

She raised her chin and glared at me. In the wan light, her hair shone like spun honey. She had her mother's fair looks and her father's fiery temper. I would have known whose whelp she was without being told.

A purple crescent of teeth marks had appeared at the base of my thumb and I rubbed at it, although that only made it throb worse. I forced a tepid smile, trying to win them. "Lady Eleanor, I said I'd take you to her. She won't find you hidden in here, will she?"

"I don't trust you," Eleanor snapped.

"Let's leave it go, shall we? We start over. Follow me, out into the nave, and we'll wait for your mother there. Agreed? I've already sent for her."

Impatient, Ockle wrung Eleanor by the arm and swung her forward. Joanna he dared not touch, instead simply trusting she would follow her sister. Gurney marshaled them with a leer. This time, my aching fist clutched at my side, I hung back. As they whirled past me, Joanna latched onto her sister's hand and dug her heels in. Eleanor stumbled. Soon, Ockle was dragging them both. Gurney flung curses unfit for the ears of babes. A snarl twisted Ockle's lips. For a moment, I thought the two men might turn on each other.

Risking harm to myself again, I wrenched Joanna from her sister and snatched her up. She turned surprised eyes on me, but before she could take another chomp, I teased her to my advantage. "You don't want to anger them, Lady Joanna. They've been known to throw little girls, like you, into boiling pots, pepper them and eat them for supper."

Her hand flew up to cover her mouth. A tiny whimper escaped her throat and she latched her arms around my neck.

Free of the added dead weight, Ockle clenched his fingers around Eleanor's thin arm and hauled her out the door and into the church nave.

I was shushing little Joanna, when Ockle suddenly let go of Eleanor. She bolted past the tall columns at the back of the church, where daylight streamed in from the open door and freedom promised.

I nearly shouted at Ockle to go after her. Then I saw a long shadow flying down the center of the nave, gaining speed, skirts flaring out.

Arms outspread, Isabella plunged to her knees and Eleanor tumbled into her mother's waiting embrace.

43

Isabella:

Bristol — October, 1326

"MOTHER! MOTHER!" ELEANOR CRIED.

My heart pounded with joy as my daughter squirmed in my hold. Two years ago she had been torn from my arms by Hugh Despenser. Two years in which she had grown. Two years lost. But my Ella, she had not forgotten me.

"Have you been well, Ella?" I asked, not knowing how else to begin.

"Eleanor, please," she softly corrected, still holding me tight. "No one calls me 'Ella' anymore." At last, she leaned back to study my face. Her nightclothes were crumpled and her hair mussed, wisps of it springing wildly from her plait. She looked as though she had been roused from her bed in the middle of the night. Gently, she wiped at my tears with the sleeve of her gown. A furrow of concern formed between her brows as she took me in. "I've been very well, Mother, and I'm so happy to see you. Aren't you happy, too?"

I attempted a smile, but it melted under the flood of my tears. "Oh, yes. Never more so."

Everything . . . everything I had done was for this moment. I crushed her slender body to mine again. Steady footsteps echoed against the high, vaulted ceiling of St. Martin's Chapel. Mortimer strode toward us, holding little Joanna.

"My sweet Joanna." I beckoned for her. "Will you come to your mother?"

But Joanna was only three the last time she had seen me. My face and voice were no longer familiar to her. She shook her head wildly and buried her face against Mortimer's shoulder. With a wry grimace, he tried to pry her loose, but she twisted her fingers in the back of his surcoat, clinging for dear life.

"It's all right," he promised and carried her to me. Then he knelt down at an angle, so that her face was turned toward me, but her eyes were shut tight.

Eleanor reached out and stroked her hair. "It *is* her, Joanna. Truly, it is. Mother had to go away, to France, where she grew up. But she's come home now. She won't ever leave us again. Ever."

I cringed at those words. I *had* hurt them. More than anything, I needed their forgiveness. But it would be hard with Joanna. She was too young to understand.

Eleanor nudged Joanna to me. Fingers shoved in her mouth, she shuffled forward until she stood shyly before me, looking down at the floor. Great blotches of red encircled her eyes where she had rubbed at them and she clutched an undersized piece of lambskin to her chest for warmth. As I drew my youngest to me, I could see the confusion in her face and feel the reluctant stiffness in her body.

A shaft of daylight intruded as the door to the nave flew wide open behind us. Outside, screams still filled the air. Joanna threw her arms around my neck and squeezed, a ripple of fear running through her small body. I scooped her up and stood. A dozen armed men tromped toward us, their spurs chinking.

"My queen, Sir Roger—Bristol is ours!" Leicester proclaimed from the doorway, sweeping his helmet from his head. "I give you . . . our prize!"

The soldiers closed on us, Wake triumphantly leading the way. He threw a stout arm up to halt the men behind him, and then stepped aside. In their midst cowered an old man, frail-looking and wobbling from exhaustion and a battering. He wore a nobleman's garb: a dagged edged cape draped over his shoulders and across it a heavy golden chain, but his leggings were rent at both knees and one sleeve was half shredded and stained red-brown. Blood seeped from a fresh wound on his arm. Someone shoved him from behind and he stumbled forward, his knees and then hands striking the floor. When he raised his bleary eyes to meet mine, it took me a moment to recall who he was: Hugh Despenser the Elder, Earl of Winchester.

His hair had turned a shocking white, his cheeks were hollowed and the shadows beneath his eyes gray and sunken.

"Please, my lady," he implored, his thin voice crackling with strain, "in God's holy name, I beg, have mercy on me. I swear—I sought to return your daughters days ago, but my offers were refused. I would not have kept them from you, otherwise."

"You asked for clemency without conditions," Mortimer said. "Did you think—"

I silenced him with a swift glare. Bowing his head, Mortimer clasped his hands behind him and took a step backward. It was not easy for him, I knew, to hold his tongue, especially when one of the men responsible for depriving him of his possessions knelt powerless before him.

Leicester swaggered past the clump of soldiers until he was before Winchester. He stooped forward, hands on hips, and cocked his head sideways to look at the earl straight on. "If you wanted to give yourself up, Lord Winchester, why did we find you crouched beneath a table weeping your eyes out?"

Winchester sniveled. Blood dripped steadily from the gash in his arm and pooled in the cracks between the tiles, seeping outward in fine rivulets of shimmering red. "I feared for my life."

"I suppose now," Leicester said as he straightened, "you've decided you *do* value your life more than your possessions. Pity you didn't figure that out sooner." The toe of his boot met Winchester's cheekbone with a loud crack.

Winchester crashed to the floor, wailing. He threw an arm over his face and rolled up in a ball.

Bellowing, Leicester gripped the pommel of his sword and drew it partway. I thrust my daughters away and grabbed his forearm. "My lord, no! Stop this! Now! He deserves a fair trial."

"A trial?" Leicester's jaw quivered in rage. He glared down his nose at me. Reluctantly, he slipped his sword back into its scabbard. "Yes, a trial. But a swift one—and soon. No sense letting him chew on his fate and that of his son like slimed cud. Today?" His fiery eyebrows lifted in suggestion. Suddenly, a scowl dragged the corner of his mouth downward. "Then we can get on with finding the king."

I thought perhaps Mortimer flinched upon hearing Leicester's words, but figured I must have imagined it, that he was merely fighting fatigue.

Small arms twined around my waist and I looked down. Her eyes round with fright, Joanna pressed her cheek to my thigh. I took her hand, then reached out to Eleanor and drew her to my side. "I'll be at St. Augustine's with the girls," I said to Mortimer. "They shouldn't bear witness to this. Send someone to fetch their clothes. I assume they came with some belongings."

His eyes were dulled by some distant thought, his lips drawn tight against his teeth, but after a few moments he nodded. "And the prisoner, Lord Winchester?"

At the sound of his name, Winchester twitched. I took some pity on him, for he was an old man now. He had followed his son's ambitions, not forged his own. I sighed and closed my eyes momentarily. I did not want this weight on my shoulders: the life of another. Rather, I would leave it to others. "The earl will be tried by his peers. Gather a tribunal at the chapter house of St. Augustine's at midday . . . and bring Lord Winchester. Until then"—I gave Leicester a warning glance—"Lord

Wake, will keep him in his care, unharmed."

I tugged my daughters forward. The soldiers scattered before us, but Leicester scrambled angrily into our path. "How many on this tribunal—and who?"

"I don't know, Henry! Now, please, get out of my way."

"But they'll have to be found and assembled," he insisted.

I had wearied of his doggedness, but more than that, I wanted a moment's peace with my girls. "Do as you wish. Now let us by."

With my girls at my side, I pushed past him. As we emerged from the church, the sun's glare nearly blinded me. I paused at the top of the steps to let my eyes adjust. Earlier, I had been intent on finding my daughters and so my surroundings had been a blur, but the carnage that now met my eyes horrified me. The mangled bodies of garrison soldiers were strewn across the outer ward. At the base of the church steps, one of the slain lay sprawled in a pool of blood. His shattered jaw dangled by a flap of skin. A ragged trail of blood marked his final progress as he had struggled toward sanctuary, unsuccessful.

Joanna burrowed into the folds of my skirt, whimpering. Bravely, Eleanor raised her chin and pulled me forward. I swept Joanna up in my arms. The cadence of Eleanor's strides increased as we neared the bottom, going wide of the dead soldier. She yanked harder. Her hand slipped from mine and she sprinted across the ward, the long plait of her hair unraveling behind her. A clump of captive garrison archers cowered on their knees. She ran past them and through a swarm of soldiers hauling sacks of coin by the armload.

"Eleanor, stop!" I called, certain she would heed me.

My eyes lingered a moment on the impressive treasure mounding in the ward. The Despensers must have decided to store their hoard here in Bristol, the one place they thought could not be taken. The clink of coins rang out as more sacks were flung onto the pile. Near the wall, the prisoners were being stripped of their armor and clothing, down to their breeches, and their weapons were cast upon a heap for sorting.

Hooves thundered over the cobbles. A mounted knight galloped between where I stood and the treasure. Beyond, I saw a tangle of horses' legs as more mounted men gathered. Eleanor disappeared amongst them. My breath caught at the back of my throat. A horse reared, its dark gray fetlocks dancing as its hooves circled in the air, drawing my attention. Then, Eleanor leapt out of its way and plunged behind a cart.

I pushed Joanna down onto the last step. "Stay here," I told her, even as she gazed up at me with wide, frightened eyes.

Frantic to find Eleanor and herd her to safety, I started forward, but Father Norbert stumbled in front of me and caught me by the arms. Blood stained his hands. "My lady, where is Sir Roger?"

His fingernails dug through the cloth of my sleeves and into my flesh. I shook my head and tore myself from his clawing grip.

"Please, my lady," he shrieked after me, his voice rising to a desperate pitch, "please, I need to find him!"

"The church!" I hurtled myself through the confusion. The cart Eleanor had run past blocked my path. I could not see her. Could not remember which way she had gone. My panic rising, I stopped and searched around me, disoriented. My blood raced through my veins, my breath came in rapid gasps.

Finally, I saw the cause for Eleanor's urgency. Young Edward had cantered into the middle of the ward, Montagu beside him and a string of mounted nobles clipping along close behind. He raised a hand to halt them and slipped from his saddle.

Eleanor sprang into his open arms. As if she weighed no more than a bird, Young Edward lifted her off the ground and swung her around. She trilled with laughter, her head thrown back. When at last he set her down, she reached up on tiptoes, pulled his face down and planted a kiss on his cheek.

"Dear Lord in heaven!"

I spun around to see Ida waddling toward me, barking at soldiers to get out of her way. Joanna was propped on her hip, her lower lip trembling in terror as she gawped at the chaos and gore around her.

"Oh, my lady, my good lady," Ida blabbered. "You're here after all!

They said it was you outside the walls, but I didn't believe them. Not until now." She was laughing and crying all at once. "Must have been angels watching after this one," she said, as she handed Joanna to me. "That and the Holy Ghost and the Virgin Mary and all the saints. Two ogres came and stole the girls from me this morning. I didn't know who they were or what was going on. I tried to stop them. I tried. Then they locked me up in a room with some of the other women and someone finally recognized me and let me go. I've been searching for the dears ever since. Little Joanna here—someone abandoned the poor child on the church steps. Pitiful. She could've been snatched up and taken away and we'd have never seen a hair of her again. I couldn't let that happen. I couldn't. I—"

"Ida, hush, please." I put my arm around her and pulled her close. "You needn't worry anymore. They're safe."

'I'm going to give you your daughters back, Isabeau,' Mortimer had said.

And he had.

THEY WERE DELICATE HOURS in my room at St. Augustine's, those first few, filled with long periods in which I simply stared at my girls, wondering if I would awaken from a dream and find myself back in France, or worse . . . in the Tower under the incessant scrutiny of Hugh Despenser. But each time Joanna or Eleanor stirred from their nap and stretched, my heart would suddenly flutter and a surge of warmth would flood my entire body, reminding me it was real. But I regarded it as a very fragile reality. Over and over, I thanked God for giving them back to me—and my gentle Mortimer for seeing that God's will was carried out.

I had not heard from Mortimer since leaving him in the church. The silence began to weigh on me as I recalled Father's Norbert's frantic urgency, although Arnaud arrived at my door late in the morning with some of the girls' clothes from the castle, so I knew Mortimer had followed through on my request. Blushing as her hands brushed his, Patrice took the clothes from Arnaud. I noticed how his eyes lingered on her, tired though he must have been from a fight that had begun well before dawn.

As he turned to go, I asked, "Arnaud, do you . . . do you know where Sir Roger is?"

Leaning with a thump against the door frame, he shrugged. "I only know that when he left the church, he was headed toward the keep, my lady. Should I send someone to find him for you?" His left elbow was tucked protectively to his ribs, as if he had taken a blow to it.

I kept my voice low, not wanting Ida to overhear. "If you happen to see him, tell him, if he can spare a few moments . . . tell him I would like to speak with him before this afternoon—about Winchester's tribunal."

Ever so slightly, Ida tilted her head. Although I knew that she would never betray me outright, I did not need her chastisement should she ever figure out the truth about Mortimer and me. The fewer who knew of it the better, especially now when so much hung so delicately in the balance.

As he pushed away from the door to go, Arnaud tried to straighten his arm, but a grimace flashed over his mouth and he pulled it back in close his chest. He dipped his head to let me know he would attend to my request, and went, one shoulder hunched up toward his ear. Patrice leaned so far from her stool to look out the open door, I thought she would fall off. One of the girls' kirtles, which had been lying in her lap, slipped to the floor. Still staring after him longingly, she picked it up and laid it over the chest at the foot of the bed with the other clothes.

"Patrice, go to him," I told her. "All this time you've been condemning him for betraying you, but what happened with his wife shamed him and hurt him deeply. That is why he never spoke of it. He has been loyal to you ever since he met you. And you will not look at anyone else. Not even while we were in France. So stop pretending you don't love him anymore. Go. Tend to him. Be with him."

Without a word, Patrice gave me a quick embrace and hurried off. Through the closed door, I could hear her call his name, the flurry of her footsteps as she rushed to him and then the pause as she must have embraced him.

Some time later, the girls awoke, groggy and mumbling. From time to

361

time, Joanna stole glances at me, as if still uncertain. I wondered what terrible things they had heard about me, but quickly banished my worries. They were young. In time, they would come to know again how much I loved them. I slumped down in a thinly cushioned chair as Ida bustled about, harping for someone to bring a brazier to warm the room and food for the children.

"When do we go back to Lady Monthermer?" Joanna asked, referring to Lord Despenser's sister in whose care they had been placed when they were taken from me. Soon, a novice shuffled in with a coal brazier, set it in the middle of the floor and left. Its heat did not reach far compared to a blazing hearthfire and it produced a black smoke that tasted of ashes, but it would suffice. Ida dragged a stool close to it, muttering that it was much warmer in the castle, and worked at mending some of the girls' clothes.

As my girls sat cross-legged on the bed, Eleanor teased apart the tangles of her sister's hair with a fine-toothed ivory comb, working her way slowly and gently from the ends up. "Never. And I don't think we will have to see Lady Despenser again, either. Mother's back and when she can't be with us, Ida will. And very soon, we'll get to see our brother, John. Would you like that, Joanna?"

"Which part? The part about John or the part about the witch-lady?" Joanna giggled.

The one window in the room was made of slats of horn, permitting only a glow of daylight to enter, but between two of the lower slats was a notch where the horn had broken. I rose from my chair and pressed my eye to the tiny hole, but saw only the short shadows of noon in the monastery graveyard. A shiver of foreboding rippled from between my shoulder blades to the base of my spine, reverberating through my limbs. My flesh prickled with goose bumps. Pressing numb fingertips to my cheeks, I turned to search for my fur-lined mantle. The sun had returned after a week's absence, but the day was distinctly cold and I could not stop trembling no matter how close to the brazier I stood.

The bells of St. Augustine's Abbey tolled noon. Although early yet, already it had been a long day. Mortimer had not come. I wrapped my mantle about my shoulders and kissed both of my girls on the forehead, promising to sit with them at supper.

Before I joined Leicester's extemporary tribunal, I would go to the Lady Chapel, there to say a prayer to quiet my soul and thank God again for the blessings that had come to me today.

44

Roger Mortimer:
Bristol – October, 1326

HANDS CLENCHED, LEICESTER STOOD in the doorway of the chapel, watching the queen depart. The sunlight cast his reddish hair in flame. A rumbling growl started deep in his throat and rose, until his bellowing roar filled the nave. He slammed a fist into the metal-studded, oak door and whirled around. In furious, swooping strides, he returned. A diabolic smile spread his lips far into his ruddy cheeks, his vexation replaced by pernicious delight.

He bent forward, clamped his hands on his knees and glared at Winchester. "Where is that bastard son of yours?"

"Not here," Winchester said, defiant.

"Of course he's not in this church, you bloody old fool." Leicester straightened and crossed his arms over his broad chest, his chin cocked to one side. "Now, tell us where to find him."

"I don't"—the earl pushed himself up, so he was kneeling—"know."

"Meaning you don't know where he is this moment? Very well.

Guard your secret, if you want. Carry it to hell if you value his life more than your own. My men will find him."

Drops of deep crimson oozed from Winchester's swelling lip. His pained snarl revealed that he no more believed Leicester would spare his life in exchange for his son's than I did. He swallowed and began to gag on his own blood, finally spitting out a mouthful before he could speak. "I mean, you idiot, he's gone."

Leicester's face blazed scarlet. "Thieving bastard!" His sword hissed death as he slid it free with both hands and brought it up high. "Tell me where he's hiding!"

"In the name of God, I swear, I do not know where he is!"

I stepped forward. "He's not lying to you, Lord Henry."

His weapon still poised, Leicester challenged, "How would you know?"

I told myself I had nothing to fear. Isabella already knew of Edward and Despenser fleeing England. But at that moment, I was not so sure Leicester would not try to sever my head instead of Winchester's once he heard the full truth. I raised an empty palm to him, as if that tranquil gesture could somehow tame the raging beast before me. "First, Lord Henry, put your weapon away. When you do that, I will tell you. As the queen said, it is up to the tribunal to decide his fate, not you or me."

"Arrrgh!" With a heave of his shoulders, Leicester swiped the blade sideways. It divided the air, just above the crouching Winchester's head, so close it stirred the old man's hair. Leicester muttered a curse, then slammed the blade back into its scabbard and braced his feet wide. "Now, tell me."

My mouth went stone dry, yet I held his gaze. "Late yesterday when I was meeting with the Earl of Kent, I received a report that Lord Despenser fled from Bristol shortly before we arrived. He met the king in Chepstow a few days ago." I paused, detecting a twitch of Leicester's lips and his sword hand tensing. "They sailed from there. Despenser's gone. So is the king. His son can be declared Guardian of the Realm now and a council selected to help him rule in his minority."

"You knew . . . yesterday? Is that right? And you said nothing to anyone?"

"No, I told the queen as soon as I learned of it. The Earl of Kent heard the news when I did. I assumed he would tell you." I lied. I was merely trying to deflect blame. Leicester, despite being thick in the head, must have known that.

"And you went to find the queen, to inform her before anyone else could? Convenient."

"It was my duty to—"

"It was you hoping to save your skin before I shredded it from your bones!" He threw his hands wide, his fingers curled like a lion's claws poised for the kill. His bitterness toward Winchester was forgotten as he turned his full flaming ire on me. "I wanted to go to Gloucester to hunt them down and you would not have it. Because of you, they—"

"It was the queen's wish to come here. She has her daughters back now. It was not effort wasted."

He stomped at me and shoved me back with open palms. Steadying myself, I kept an eye on his hands, in case he tried to slip his knife from his belt and slice open my belly. "She would have had them anyway," he said, "had we gone to Gloucester. Winchester would not have resisted once his son and the king were captured. Your reasoning isn't worth a pile of goat shit."

His right hand flinched and I leapt back, grappling for the hilt of my sword. But before Leicester could loose a weapon on me, a high pitched voice cried out from the outer doorway of the chapel.

"Sir Roger!" Father Norbert ran toward us, flailing his spindly arms. The soldiers who had escorted Winchester parted to let the mad little holy man by. He skidded to a halt before me, gulping. "Your uncle! Praise be to God, I've found your uncle."

Never did I think I would be thankful to see the pious little weasel, but his interruption had spared me an inopportune fight with a man who, in his madness, could have crushed me in his bare hands. "Where?"

Father Norbert hooked his skinny hand in the air as a gesture for me to follow. "This way. Come, hurry, hurry."

I said no more to the Earl of Leicester, but sped from the church on the tail of Father Norbert, who was as fast as any hare being chased by hounds. He led me across the ward to a door of one of the corner towers, its lock shattered by the hacking of weapons, and tugged it open. The caustic stench of urine burned my nostrils. Inside was a narrow stairway leading not up, but down—to the dungeon. Father Norbert plunged into the bottomless darkness. Almost immediately, I lost sight of him, although I could hear his light footsteps fading away. I stuck out my hand and groped along the wall like a blind man, lowering each foot with care. Pausing to let my eyes become accustomed to the dimness, I realized I could not hear the priest any longer.

"Father?" I said.

"Here," he called up. "Still coming, my lord?"

"Coming." I drew my sword. The steps were worn smooth in the middle, the stones damp with moss. I was aware of nothing but my own breathing, my sword firm in my grip. My feet fell in a steady rhythm as I descended in a leftward spiral. A yellow glow reflected off the wall and the smells, new ones, grew stronger, more offensive: the smell of old blood and decaying flesh. Someone moaned low and long, but as I neared the bottom the moan rose in pitch until it was a wail of agony.

"Hurry, Sir Roger," Father Norbert urged. But I could not locate the direction of his voice or see where he had gone to.

Another cry rent the air, but fell almost instantly into inconsolable weeping. The sounds I heard were the plaintive cries of the dying, those whose pain is beyond assuagement. If this was where Uncle Roger was being kept, I hesitated to learn the condition I might find him in.

I came to the bottom of the stairs and, seeing Father Norbert hopping impatiently on the balls of his feet before he turned to continue down the dark corridor, I stepped out, but I had not looked down to see there was yet another step to go. My heel tipped the loose flagstone. My balance shifted. Too late, I pitched my weight to my right, trying to break my fall against the wall. I toppled backward. My sword clanged against the wall and flew from my grip. The base of my spine struck the edge of a stone and I felt its bite like an axe blow, blunted only by the links of my mail. For a moment, I closed my eyes as the pain hammered through me. Then I pushed myself slowly up and leaned a shoulder against the wall. As I stooped to retrieve my sword, a fresh tide of pain rushed through me, threatening to overtake me.

Father Norbert was far ahead, a flitting shadow in the death-gloom. Somewhere behind him, torchlight wavered. On either side of the narrow passageway, the dank walls were interrupted by iron bars. The faint tang of rust mingled with the burning smell of piss. I looked ahead, but Father Norbert had disappeared again.

Unsteadily, I started forward. The first cell I passed I did not look into. The smell of disease was strong enough to let me know a corpse lay in it. A bolt of pain ripped from my lower back and down my leg. I staggered to the left, unable to bear my full weight on the right side of my body, and then forced myself onward. A blackened hand flew out of the darkness and clawed at my surcoat. Startled, I jumped back to see a man, naked but for his soiled breeches. His beard was long and thin, patches of it missing where he must have pulled it out. Festering sores on his belly and skeletal legs oozed thick, yellow pus. He licked his grimy palm and reached out to me.

"Come near, my son," he said, an eerie smile revealing toothless gums, "so I can bless you with the Lord's holy water."

A madman. I went wide of him, the heat of the torch in its sconce on the opposite wall warming my neck.

"Salvation awaits!" he cried. "You are an instrument of the devil! Confess and be saved!"

Ahead, another torch glowed faintly where the corridor divided. As I went, I cast a glance in each cell. Two were open, only one of those bearing evidence of any recent habitation in the form of a few gnawed chicken bones. Others were empty, but in some were shackled prisoners too weak, or too afraid, to investigate as I passed them by. None contained my uncle.

"We are all sinners, my son!" the madman cried. "Repent of your carnal ways and God will receive you into Heaven, where you will find everlasting—"

A ghostly wail drowned out his voice. I came to where the passageway divided. To the right, another short corridor and another division. Left, a dead end. I began to go right, because that is where the sound of a soul on the precipice of death was coming from.

"Sir Roger," Bishop Orleton called to me from behind.

Surprised to hear his calming, familiar voice, I turned to see him standing outside an open door, one made of solid wood. On the wall next to him, a single torch flickered, dimmed and then sprang back to life.

"In here," he indicated, stooping beneath the low lintel as he entered the room. But something in his tone spoke of sorrow and my pain was forgotten as my heart sank like a stone through my bowels.

Reluctantly, I followed. When I entered the dank, cramped room, Father Norbert scurried back from a low, straw-littered bed made of discarded planks. A candle stub shed a meager light on the long, rigid form stretched out on the bed.

I was not prepared for the sight that met my eyes.

Lord Roger of Chirk lay unmoving. His thumbs were clasped so his hands were spread like dove wings on his chest. His skin was the pallor of chalk. His eyes gazed into some distant realm, beyond my knowing.

Head bowed to avoid scraping his head on the low ceiling, Bishop Orleton approached my uncle, then pulled his eyelids down. He made the sign of the cross above him.

"Leave us," I heard myself say, although I do not remember the words passing over my tongue, for grief choked my throat.

The door groaned behind me. I was on my knees beside his death bed, staring hard through eyes that stung, expecting that at any moment his nostrils would twitch, his lips part, his chest rise in the weakest of breaths so I might speak to him, tell him I had come for him, and know he could hear me. I imagined his thin lips curving into a smile, his age-spotted, wrinkled hands reaching for mine, but they did not.

I had arrived too late.

WHEN I LEFT THE putrid dungeon and stumbled into daylight, I was in a stupor. The joy of winning Bristol Castle was swallowed up by the anger seething within me for not launching the assault a day sooner.

I ordered Father Norbert to take my uncle to St. Augustine's. The chancel, I knew, was full of monks tending to wounded men and the place would stink of blood and human filth. So I told him to lay the body out at the altar in the Lady Chapel, which was tucked behind the rear of the wall of the chancel's high altar.

When I found my uncle's cold corpse in the smaller chapel, Bishop Orleton was there waiting for me again. Twelve candles flickered on the altar. Over my uncle lay an unadorned white shroud—too plain for a man of his station.

"Lord Roger died only minutes before you found him," the bishop said. "I had enough time to tell him you had taken the castle . . . and about the king sailing from Chepstow. He did not respond, but still, I told him everything anyway. Sometimes the dying can hear, even though they have not the strength to answer."

"And did he . . ." I was about to ask whether my uncle had cursed or praised me, but in truth I did not want to know. "Was he in any pain?"

"He was not suffering, no. Natural causes, I would assume. I've known few myself who lived as long as he did."

The hushed blessings of monks mingled with the low moans of the wounded lying in the chancel. Some of those men, I knew, would die. Many already had. They, at least, had died free men. "Thank you, your grace, for your kindness. I . . . I will instruct Maltravers and my sons to escort his body home to Chirk."

I heard the scuff of feet on tiles and saw Father Norbert pause just outside the chapel. Squinting, he craned his thin neck sideways. His eyes opened wide in recognition of us, and then he spun about on his heel and scampered away.

Orleton clasped his hands beneath his vestments and bent his head. He drew a long breath. "The tribunal will meet soon. Some have probably already gathered by now." When I gave no response, he asked, "Shall I tell them you will be there shortly?"

I avoided answering him. "Who was called?"

"Leicester called Norfolk and Kent, of course . . . Wake and Beaumont, the bishops Stratford, Burghersh, myself . . . and you. A few other barons whose names I suggested."

"I am certain you chose wisely, your grace."

"You will be there?" he asked again, insistent.

"If I can." I lowered the shroud from my uncle's face and forced myself to study his features: the mat of gray hair, the dark brow, and the downward lines framing his mouth. It was his body, his face, and yet . . . it was not him. Had he chastised me with his last breath and then died with a horrific gasp in my arms, I could have believed that this cold, rigid corpse was indeed him. Yet there was no doubt it was. He was as dead as my father's father, who had not even lived till the day of my birth. Still, why did I expect to hear my uncle's mumbled curses, feel his walking staff hammer at the floor or suffer the light cuff of his gnarled hand against my skull? Why did I think he would swing his stiff legs over the edge of the altar, sit hunch-shouldered, glowering with contempt, and spit at me?

Even more, why had I yearned so desperately for his forgiveness?

He was dead. It did not matter anymore.

"I'll leave you here, then," Bishop Orleton said serenely, "with your uncle."

Although I did not turn to see him go, I heard his footsteps exit the chapel and turn the corner. Alone now, I fixed my gaze on a single candle flame. Then I sank to my knees, weary and drained, for I was not so young anymore. Too late, I remembered the fall I had taken that morning.

As I let my weight drop beneath me, my knees folding to meet the floor, a knife of pain slashed through me. Jaw taut, I covered my face with my hands, but a small cry leaked out, high and thin as a woman's keening after battle.

"Sir Roger! What is—" Isabella's voice echoed from the vestibule. She rushed to me and laid a soft hand on my shoulder. I tensed at her touch, resisting the impulse to shove her away.

She knelt and draped a caring arm around me. The fur of her mantle brushed the nape of my neck. "Your uncle? Oh, no . . . no. I'm so sorry, Roger. So very sorry."

My fists dropped to slam against my legs. She thought I mourned him, deeply, but rather than a salve to a wounded heart, her words instead stirred the embers of my black mood. "I failed him," I said, disdainful of myself. "He gave up waiting."

Her flaxen brows bunched together above narrowed eyes. "Gave up? I don't understand."

"Why should you?" I snapped, and shrugged her arm away. My breath hissed through my teeth as I drew myself up, my muscles flaming. She reached for my wrist, but I sidestepped her and turned away because I did not want her to see the grimace distorting my face. In the corner of my eye, I caught sight of Patrice, one hand clinging to a pillar that flanked the entryway of the Lady Chapel. "What?" I screamed at her. "Do you always spy? Be gone!"

She backed hurriedly away, shaking her head feebly in apology. "I came to find the queen—and you. Lord Leicester requests your presence at the tribunal."

Isabella answered before I could. "We'll be there soon. Tell them to wait, please."

The moment Patrice disappeared from view, Isabella rounded on me. "You will hold your tongue! I will not have you speak thus to me *or* Patrice. I love her as a sister, just as . . ." Her head tilted and her mouth turned downward. The sharpness was gone from her voice. "Just as you loved your uncle."

Did I?

Perhaps, but I did not need her pity. Slowly, I turned back to her. "Go to the council meeting without me. Give Leicester what he asks for: Winchester's life."

"Go without you? I know you are mourning your uncle, but—"

"Without me," I repeated tersely.

"Why?"

"Because if I go, Leicester will harangue me for allowing the king and Despenser to slip away. But he will not defy you. So if he demands Winchester's life, let him know you do not wholeheartedly agree, but tell him you will yield on this and let it be done. Give him what he wants, for now. Let him have this small, singular joy. More important matters will arise soon."

"Like Edward's departure?"

"Such as who shall rule in his place. They will want to name your son Guardian of the Realm. They will demand he have a regent. And that regent should be you, not Leicester."

"Then you will be on the regency council?"

"No."

"But why not?"

"For the same reason I am not going with you today. Because England does not need another Hugh Despenser."

"You are hardly—"

"It is about power, Isabella. Everything is about power. *Everything.* I will not give anyone reason to think that I act on behalf of your son or to accuse me of ambition. No one will ever question your intent. They will see it as a mother's protectiveness. But everything I say or do will be scrutinized, closely. Especially by Leicester, who deems himself a power to be reckoned with already. We must keep him in check, by giving him small victories, never big ones. Better, even, if we could remove him from our midst, although I have as yet to figure out how." I took her by the arms, my grip firm. "It was not enough to land here on England's shores and have the people open their arms to us. We must guard your son's future . . . because ours depends on it. Can you understand that?"

For a very long time she simply stared at me. I was not sure if I had angered or offended her, for I had spoken a brutal truth. What we had done so far was only the beginning. Keeping power would be harder than seizing it. Finally, unable to bear her silence, I let go of her and turned back to my uncle. If she would not answer me, perhaps she would leave me to my grief.

"I'll go," she said softly, "and do as you . . . as you advise. But not because you say so. I will do it to give *you* this one small victory . . . because I will not allow you to be disgraced. And because I love you."

And I you, Isabeau . . . and I would give up everything to keep you.

Her skirts rustled over the flagstones as she went from the chapel.

It was not one small victory that she had given me. It was many.

I had more than survived a death sentence. More than gained my freedom and sent a king running from me.

I had Isabella's heart; I had everything.

Everything but my uncle's forgiveness.

With a stiff hand, I pulled the shroud back over his lifeless features. I could not allow my guilt to consume me. All my sacrifices and struggles— they had *not* been in vain.

One small problem remained, however: Edward was still very much alive, still king and still Isabella's husband.

45

Isabella:

Bristol — October, 1326

THE DOOR GROANED OPEN and a draft invaded the hall of the chapter house. The rusted chain linking Winchester's ankles jerked with each shuffling step he took. Diagonal beams of sunlight stabbed through the long row of cusped windows topped by quatrefoils and reflected starkly against limed walls. Halfway to the dais on which Young Edward and I sat, the earl stumbled to a halt, gazed woefully at the dissecting, oaken beams of the ceiling, then clasped his shackled hands together and raised them to his misshapen lips. A guard butted him in the shoulder blades with the end of a poleax and, with a clink and rattle of iron rings, Winchester inched forward again.

The tribunal sat on benches flanking the central aisle. Smugly, Henry, Earl of Leicester, glared at his prize captive. Eight barons, five bishops and I were to hear the charges and deliver the sentence, although it was a role I would have gladly shriven myself of, had I been able to. Mortimer had not come and no one, as yet, had asked of him. Although his absence spared him much scrutiny, and ultimately blame, it shifted an enormous burden onto my shoulders.

Avoiding Winchester's gaze, I stared at my hands folded in my lap. Today, a man's death would hang on my conscience.

Before the guards could force him down, Winchester dropped in front of me, his knees cracking against the cold tiles. Lord Thomas Wake read the charges: that he had acquired lands rightfully belonging to the Church; that he had illegally appropriated the inheritances of others, diverting them to his own estates; and that he had abetted his son in overtaking the governing powers of England. All tantamount to acting as king.

Deliberations were pointed and precise. The record was clear. He had served as an agent in Edward's misrule. Not a man present would have spoken in defense of him. Even I, in fact, could not. One by one, the men gave their verdicts. Guilty.

Again, I felt Winchester's pleading eyes fix on me. I raised my face to him. His purple-blue lips formed into a sad smile, splitting the dark scab at the corner of his mouth. A fresh line of blood dripped down a wrinkled fold of his face and onto his sullied shirt. His nose, left cheek and jaw were so swollen he wheezed with each shallow breath. His eye on that side was nothing but a red slit above a mottled black bruise.

"My lady," Lord Wake said, "what is your verdict?"

I opened my mouth, but could not draw air fully into my lungs.

"My lady?" Wake prompted again.

A wave of bile burned the back of my tongue. I retched, and then clenched my teeth so I would not vomit onto my gown. Oh, I had not wanted it to be this way. Had not wanted my return to become an invasion the history of which would be written in blood. Yet, how could it be otherwise? Did I so glibly think we would tumble onto England's shores and everything would come to us as easily as plucking dandelions from a meadow in summertime?

When I looked at Bishop Orleton, he nodded to me, as if to say it must be done.

"Let the Earl of Winchester speak first," I uttered.

Wake protested, "But my lady, the——"

"Let him speak," I repeated, no louder than before. If this grim deed could not be avoided, I would at least give it the semblance of extending to him the honor due to an earl.

Leicester burst from his seat and stormed forward, fists swinging at his sides. He blew his cheeks out, as if releasing steam from a boiling pot. His voice began in a low growl, but with each syllable it rose in virulence until it shook the door in its frame and rattled the windows. "My brother was not permitted to speak when King Edward and Hugh Despenser levied a sentence of execution on him at Pontefract. You will not allow it!"

Gripping the arms of my chair, I restrained myself from leaping to my feet and screaming my fury at him for ordering me about. "And you, my lord, will not say what I can or cannot do! The Earl of Winchester was not there when your brother was tried *or* sent to his death. He should be held responsible solely for his own actions, not his son's." But that was far from the truth. Like fires banked to keep the coals burning, grudges often lingered for years, and blood feuds sometimes raged for generations. So it had begun for the Mortimers and Despensers, which made me to wonder if there would ever be any end to this. "So he will speak and then, dear uncle, we will decide what is to become of him."

"I say let him share his final words with a priest."

"I think, Lord Leicester," Young Edward intervened, shoulders pressed against the back of his chair, his hands clasped across his abdomen, "you should listen to the queen. Our Savior, Christ Jesus, preached compassion. My mother only seeks to follow his example. So let Lord Winchester speak." He swept his hand at Leicester to prompt him to return to his bench and I thought, at that moment, how very much like Charles my son was.

Mouth agape, Leicester sputtered. Then, perhaps wisely figuring he should not argue with his future king—and that the choice of regent had yet to be decided—he bowed his head and backed away until he stood before his bench.

"Lord Winchester," I began, my fingers pressed flat in my lap, "you have heard the charges brought against you. Before the final verdict is declared, what have you to say on your own behalf? I urge you, my lord, to beg the mercy of those you have wronged. Say that you committed these crimes and if there is any kindness to be found in this room, some leniency will be granted to you."

"I admit to no wrong," he said. "I regret nothing. And I would give my life ten times over so that my son might live."

Thus, the manner of his death was sealed.

After he was taken away, they went on to proclaim Young Edward as Guardian of the Realm and proposed a gathering at Hereford for the following month to discuss the course of England's future.

To me, the future was an uncertain thing, for Edward and Despenser's disappearance had not been a blessing at all.

THAT EVENING, WHILE A miserably cold rain fell from a pall-black sky, Hugh Despenser the Elder, Earl of Winchester, arrived at the inner ward of Bristol Castle on the back of a cart, his hands tied before him. Before the gibbet stood the Earl of Leicester, Lord Wake, Sir Henry de Beaumont and the earls of Kent and Norfolk. Father Norbert was there, as well, eager to serve as Winchester's confessor.

Through the open shutters of a window of one of the uppermost rooms in the keep, I watched, attended by Mortimer and Bishop Orleton. Mortimer still had little to say, unless delivered in a pithy tone. The timing of his uncle's death, I presumed, had cut deeply to his soul.

The executioner, a man with a neck as thick as an ox's, hooked a hand beneath Winchester's armpit and hoisted him up on a stool and then atop a barrel at the back edge of the cart. The drop from the gibbet was a high one, so that his neck might mercifully break and death come more swiftly. Winchester's knees wobbled with each step. He pitched to the other side and another man there shoved him hard in the ribs to upright him. The executioner clambered up behind him, wood groaning beneath his added weight, and placed the loop around Winchester's neck. As the executioner and his assistant descended from the rear of the cart, the earl lifted his head to gaze up at my window. The rain drove down and the wind gained force. He tottered backward. The rope went taut, gagging him.

A drum throbbed slowly in rhythm with my heart. The jeers of the crowd rose to a deafening clamor. The townspeople were pelting the earl with rotten apples. One thumped squarely against his already bruised jaw, yet he barely flinched. I turned my face from the window, knowing what was next. Orleton moved to stand next to me. A whip cracked, hooves beat on cobbles. I flinched. Although I told myself not to, I looked again. The cart had lurched forward. Winchester twitched and writhed, his face and neck purpling. His neck had not broken. While the crowd lobbed stones at him, he swung in the wind, his body jerking and twirling with each well-aimed strike. A little child, holding a stone as large as his fist, flailed it at the dying man. The earl's legs gave one final, meager kick and then . . . he went limp. In the brisk wind, his body swayed like a plumb at the end of a string. I crossed myself, still unable to take my eyes from the gruesome scene.

"He's dead now," Mortimer stated morosely.

The hinges of the door squealed.

"Mother? There you are! We've been looking everywhere," Eleanor trilled. I jerked my head sideways to see her pulling her little sister along by the hand and coming toward me, both of them wearing bright smiles and new gowns. Eleanor raced past me to stand on tiptoe and peer out the window to see what had captured our interest. "Ida told us there was to be a feast tonight, a big celebration, and we snuck away so we could—" Her jaw dropped open. Immediately, she yanked Joanna to her side and tucked her sister's head against her abdomen.

Bishop Orleton reached out and banged the shutters closed.

Eleanor raised a shaking finger. "Is that Lord Winchester?"

"It was," I said thoughtlessly.

"Is he dead?" Joanna squirmed from beneath her sister's arm, slipping past the bishop. She pressed her eye to the crack between the shutters, then looked up at the bishop and wrinkled her tiny nose in puzzlement. "But he was kind to us. Not like Lady Monthermer and Lady Despenser. They were mean. He wasn't at all."

"I'm so sorry, my little one," I said, aghast, "but he was——"

"A traitor," Mortimer finished.

I cut him a smoldering glare as I drew Joanna to me. In truth, though, he had only said in a more succinct manner the same thing I was about to. Before they could ask what a 'traitor' was, I said to Orleton, "Your grace, will you find Ida and tell her the girls are to stay with her until they are called to the hall?"

The bishop gathered the girls and escorted them out of the room, Eleanor growing more blanched by the moment and Joanna skipping along and humming, her perplexity swept away by the promise of a grand feast. The door closed and I rose to face Mortimer. He narrowed his eyes at me, as if he expected a scathing attack.

"I should thank you," I said, "for returning them to me."

He folded his arms over his chest and leaned back against the wall, looking somewhat relieved. "How could I have done anything else?"

I ran my hand over his forearm, fine cloth beneath my fingertips where only that morning he had been encased in mail. "Roger, I will never forget all that you have done for me."

He scoffed lightly, shaking his head at the sentiment. "One day, Isabeau, we'll tire of each other. I will do or say something to anger you." His eyes, dark and endless, met mine. "And you will forget."

I did not think at that moment that I ever would, or could. It seemed everything was as it should be: my children safe, Edward and Despenser gone from my life, and my gentle Mortimer there to protect me and return my love.

But even when we think everything is right, it is not. Something always changes to destroy that vision of happiness. Like the morning mist, a slight shift in the wind can blow it all away.

46

Isabella:

Hereford — November, 1326

THROUGH A VEIL OF incessant rain we crept slowly north, along the swollen Severn, until our lumbering army could cross the river at Gloucester. There, Lord Henry Percy and a number of Marcher barons who had heard of the king's flight joined us. All of England, it seemed, was eager to embrace the golden-haired Young Edward as their king. His father had abandoned his kingdom—an unpardonable sin, even in the eyes of those few who had been incurably loyal to him.

Now that my daughters were with me, I rode in a carriage, for Joanna had developed a head cold that no remedy could abate. I wiped her nose and wrapped her in my fur-lined mantle to keep her warm and Ida made her a tisane of willow bark and chamomile. Somehow, despite the jostling and rumbling of the carriage and the bitter breath of impending winter, she slept. Along the way I received a letter from my son John in London. It was brief, for he was a boy who preferred riding to writing, but it said that he was well and safe and expected to see us all soon. Knowing John was no longer in harm's way, I would be able to sleep more soundly. Once our business in Hereford was taken care of I could be in London with all my children, long before Christmas.

At Gloucester we stayed two nights—the second only because I insisted on it so Joanna could recover from her nagging illness. She fell asleep in my bed, where it was warm and soft with goose down, and by the third day she was well enough to want to join me in a song. I bundled her in my mantle and Arnaud carried her to the carriage as she squeezed his nose and giggled.

We trundled on toward Hereford with our wagons laden with supplies and our well-honed blades, prepared for a war that was not to be. Behind Young Edward, the long, ever-increasing line of soldiers and camp followers stretched on into the horizon. The rain fell hard and the wind blew cold and wretched, and still we marched on. No one and nothing stood in our way. Even Leicester had cooled his temper, seemingly placated by Winchester's execution.

I marveled how, after so much agonizing, it had all come together. With each day that passed, I grew steadily more believing that everything that was happening was indeed real and I was not dreaming it.

A few days before we were scheduled to reach Hereford, I awoke to a horizon unbroken by clouds. Tents were being taken down, horses saddled, and wagons loaded. Here and there, porridge bubbled in cooking pots over small fires.

Birdsong and the rustle of feathers reached my ears. Above me in a lightening sky, a pair of chaffinches bickered as they swooped and tumbled. I followed their flight a short way into the distance, just beyond camp, where the first light of dawn gilded the yellowing leaves of a hornbeam. There, leaning against the contorting, silver-gray trunk, was Patrice, her mantle parted in front to reveal the flowing scarlet length of her gown. Close before her stood Arnaud, without sword or mail, his tunic hanging unbelted over his leggings, his boots forgotten somewhere amid the meadow grass. Patrice plucked up the bottom corners of her mantle and held them wide. He sank into her inviting warmth and tilted his head to place a kiss in the curve of her neck.

"A fine morning, is it not, my lady?"

Startled, I whirled around to find Father Norbert standing close behind me. He drew back the yawning hood of his black cassock and breathed deeply, his reddened nostrils flaring beneath the pinched bridge of his nose.

"Glorious, Father," I said.

Harsh sunlight reflected white off his bald pate. "Then you are ready for your morning devotions?" His eyes narrowed to slits as he gazed intently toward the hornbeam tree. "Shall I invite your damsel to join us?"

Grabbing the elbow of his sleeve, I turned him away and began to walk with him back to my pavilion. "Come. The girls should be awake by now. Perhaps they would like to ask a few questions of God. They do not quite understand what is happening lately."

"They may ask, my lady, but God will answer as he pleases."

"Of course, Father Norbert," I assured him, although I had every intention of asking God to deliver Hugh Despenser to me. For as long as he yet lived, I was not truly free.

SOON, WE WERE PACKED and traveling along the broad road to Hereford. Around us, gentle hills sprawled. Cattle roamed, grazing on the remnants of dying pastures. To the east rose a bare-topped mound where an ancient fortress once stood. Ringing it were the traces of a defensive ditch that still cleaved the earth. The harvest had been bountiful; the fields cut clean; the tithe barns filled. Wherever we went, we found nothing but peace and contentment, as if England had never suffered strife at all. Three days later, our road joined the River Wye in its course and I knew we were coming close.

"We will reach the town's gates before sunset, my lady," Bishop Orleton told me cheerfully.

We rode side by side near the head of the column, Young Edward and Mortimer leading the way. My son, despite his initial reluctance, if not fond of Mortimer, seemed to have developed an admiration for him. "I will welcome the sight. The castle will be ready, I trust?"

"The castle? Regretfully, no. If it rained while you were there you'd be as wet as if you were standing on the roof. This summer they began to quarry stones from Haye Forest for the needed repairs. If the work continues steadily, you may find it suitable for your next visit. Until then, you may stay at my palace. I've sent word ahead to make certain they prepare it for a queen, no less. That is, if you will agree to be my guest?"

"Happily, your grace. But I'll have need of my closest advisors. You have room for them, as well?" I kept my face forward, although I detected a questioning pause before he spoke.

"How many . . . and who?"

"Only a few: Lord Leicester, Beaumont . . . my children, of course . . . Mortimer, Wake, the other bishops—"

"A dozen, perhaps a few more. I would not wish to crowd anyone," he declared firmly. I doubt I had fooled him by burying Mortimer's name amongst a list of others, but I wanted . . . no, *needed* Mortimer near. A strange unease had settled in the pit of my stomach since learning of Edward's flight and I wished to speak with Mortimer privately about it. "There are two priories and a monastery," he added, "just outside the town walls that can accommodate more."

Further ahead, above the golden crown of a larch, the keep of Hereford's castle rose. At the foot of the hill on which the castle stood, but closer to the river, I could see what I presumed were the rooftops of the church and bishop's palace—both as big and grand as anything I had seen in England, outside London. The sun was touching the rim of the western hills and with its rapid descent came the rush of winter's biting cold.

"Thank you, your grace. Whatever hospitality you can extend will be more than adequate. Simply to be able to rest, fill our bellies and dry our clothes by a warm fire will be a welcome joy."

From the low branch of an oak beside the road, a red squirrel watched the column trudge past with guarded curiosity. It twitched its tufted ears forward and back, turning an acorn nervously in its paws before dropping its treasure to the ground and leaping up to a higher limb.

To the south, a single rider crested a ridge and flew with haste down the slope. As he drew nearer, I could tell he was headed for the front of the column. Mortimer raised a hand and the command went back the lines to halt. Bishop Orleton and I exchanged a look of concern. Without saying a word, we both pressed our mounts into a canter to close the short distance. Leicester, Wake and Beaumont emerged from the rear and followed us forward.

We reached Young Edward and Mortimer in time to see Sir John Maltravers ease to a halt. His mount was lathered, despite the chill, and hung its head, breathing heavily.

"Why did you come from the southern road?" Mortimer said, his voice sharp with suspicion. "You were to go north to Chirk with my sons, to bury my uncle."

Maltravers raised his half-hand to wipe at his brow, then dug into a pouch hanging from his saddle and took out a flask. Before he answered, he wetted his throat. "We were on our way to Chirk when we heard a rumor." He paused to take another drink.

"What rumor?" I asked anxiously. Already, my blood had gone cold.

A faint grimace flickered across his face as Leicester and the others joined us. "That after four days of being tossed about at sea, the king and Lord Despenser were blown back to shore and landed in Cardiff."

"Cardiff?" Young Edward repeated. "My father is in Wales?"

The earth swayed below me. I gripped the cantle of my saddle with both hands to keep myself from falling.

Leicester grumbled in displeasure. "We should have sent a force there after leaving Bristol. We could have had them by now."

Mortimer lifted a hand to silence Leicester, then said to Maltravers, "Where are my sons?"

"They went on to Chirk, to lay your uncle to rest, as you instructed them."

"And you?"

"I rode on toward Glamorgan, to learn what I could. To see if it was true."

A heavy silence settled on the gathering.

"Was it?" Mortimer finally broached.

Maltravers nodded. "The king was in Caerphilly when I turned around to find you."

"And Despenser was with him?"

A light shrug lifted his shoulders. "That much I don't know."

Leicester squinted one eye against the setting sun and swept his steely gaze over everyone. "Going inland, to the hills, where it will be harder for us to track them. Where they still think they can find succor. Where Despenser probably has more money hidden away."

"Gold won't do them any good if no one will take it from them," Mortimer said. "Besides, there's still a reward for capturing Despenser."

"Then we should send someone to find them," Lord Wake proposed. Radiant with the thrill of a hunt, a smile of delight curved his lips.

"But first," I said quietly, thinking aloud, "why not extend an offer? The king, by now, must be desperate. We might be able to get him to come forward. He'll bargain, don't you think?"

"Yes," Bishop Orleton agreed. "They're running out of places to hide, if they haven't already. He still has the Great Seal in his possession."

Leicester shrugged, doubtful. "Who would he heed?"

"His son," I said.

Franticly, Young Edward looked from face to face. I motioned him away. He was slow to follow on his mount, but joined me on a side road where a narrow wooden bridge crossed a dry gully. For a while I said nothing as I let his discomfort ease. "Do you remember," I began, reminiscing, "our last summer at Langley, the day we took the hounds out and they caught a hare?"

His face toward the carmine glow of the setting sun, he nodded. "I remember the day."

"Then you remember when I said you could be king of both England and France? If you don't act, you may be king of neither." He narrowed his eyes at me, as if I had spoken a blasphemy. "Whether Charles will ever name you his heir, should he not have a son, remains to be seen. But he will certainly never do so while England is restive and a wandering king shirks the duties attached to his crown. If your father does not give up that crown willingly, then a council made of men grappling for power will rule here, perhaps until your father dies of old age. You, Edward, can prevent that. You can restore order and ensure peace. You can secure your future by simply asking him to pass his crown on to you."

Unconvinced, he shook his head. "I cannot. It is too much to ask."

"You must, Edward. It is the only way. Promise him his life in return for his crown."

He pulled his chin back. "His life?"

"As long as he remains king, his life is in danger. Without a crown, he is no threat to anyone. They will leave him in peace then." I paused a moment, to let him mull it over, before I added one last condition. "And tell your father he must give up Despenser, as well. If he does not, the barons will hunt them both down. Should it come to that, nothing can be guaranteed. You know there is no other way."

If there was anyone Edward would concede to, it would be his son and heir.

"There is no other way," Young Edward finally said, his head hanging low.

We returned to the gathering. "It will be done," I announced.

We went on through Hereford's wide gates to a heady welcome, but I was only vaguely aware of the cheers that greeted us. My son seemed not to hear them at all.

THAT NIGHT, AFTER I had sat with my son for hours as he labored over every word of the letter he was writing, I retired to my room in Bishop Orleton's palace and summoned Mortimer. As soon as the door closed behind him, I flew into his arms. I pressed my ear to his chest and listened to the strong thumping of his heart and let the warmth of his body spread through me. He lifted my chin with a finger, his breath brushing my cheeks. Then his lips touched mine and my hands wandered around his back and downward until I felt his hips pressing into my belly. With a shower of kisses, all the maddening turmoil of the day was washed away. For a while, I only wanted to know the oneness of lying in his arms and the fleeting fallacy that such bliss could last for an eternity.

Later, we lay in my bed, his lean, scarred body pressed to my back, his arm draped over my waist, our legs entwined. I tried to cling to my happiness, to not allow mere worries of what may or may not come to pass to chase it away, but moment by moment, the brief rush of ecstasy faded, yielding to a shadow, the source of which I did not want to look upon.

Why is the good in life so fragile, shattered by the slightest touch, and the bad so hard to overcome? As if there are forces ever working toward chaos, ready to destroy the steady order and simple pleasures we yearn to hold on to. Father Norbert would say it was the devil at play. But I do not think so. I think that suffering is a disease. Edward had suffered all his life, or rather imagined he did, and so he had infected those around him—most of all me.

Mortimer traced a finger from the curve of my neck to my shoulder. "You do not think Edward will agree to it?"

So long we had lain unspeaking after our lovemaking that the fire in the hearth had dwindled to glowing embers. Cold, I pulled the covers up to my neck. "No, I do." How could he not?

"Then why so troubled, my love?"

"Because we're not in France anymore, Roger. We cannot be alone like this. Not whenever we want to."

"Isabeau, if we truly want—"

"No, Roger, it doesn't matter what we want. Our lives were decided long ago. I have a husband who is king. You have a wife."

"So then, we go back to being as we were—before all this? Living unhappily. Is that what you want?"

"It is what I dread."

"Do not worry about Joan. I will make certain she is well cared for.

But my place is beside you."

"She is your wife."

"And Edward your husband. Does that mean you love him as you do me?"

"Far from it. But what if they make me return to him, stay with him? I am sick at the thought of it."

"With your son as king? I think not. The prince would never allow it to happen if it made you unhappy." His breath curled around in my ear, soothing me. "Nor would I."

"How are we to take Edward's crown from him, Roger? I don't see how it's possible."

"*We* will not do it, Isabeau. If he does not willingly give it up, as his son asked him to, parliament will take it from him. And then, do you think they will allow him to roam freely? Too much danger in that." He withdrew his arm from around me to lie on his back.

His indrawn breath hissed between his teeth. I turned over to see his eyes squeezed tightly shut, his jaw tensed, his whole body rigid, as if he dared not twitch a muscle.

"Roger, what is it?"

A few moments later, he expelled a breath. "It is . . . nothing," he murmured, eyes still closed. "A small pain. It will pass. All things do, my love."

I eased my head back onto the pillow, studying him closely in the dying glow of the hearthfire.

BEFORE THE FIRST SLIVER of dawn rimmed the horizon, Sir John Maltravers departed Hereford. He carried with him the letter in Young Edward's own hand, imploring the king to give himself up peacefully, relinquish his crown in favor of his son and promising that no harm would come to him. It made no promises of sparing Hugh Despenser's life.

While the Herefordshire hills dulled to dun-brown and the sky grew ever thicker with the leaden clouds of winter, I waited for an answer. Barons and great lords, deacons and archbishops, all flocked to Hereford to talk of what would become of England and who would rule it.

Every day, I went to the Lady Chapel of Hereford's church, sank to my knees before the altar and prayed for Edward to come to his senses.

47

Isabella:

Hereford – November, 1326

MY CHIN BRUSHED THE fur lining of my mantle as I turned from the altar. *At last, God answers me.*

Bishop Orleton took the letter from me and moved closer to the row of beeswax candles on the altar. The candlelight played faintly off the two stained glass windows high up on the wall behind him. There, the Virgin Mary, robed in a flowing gown of blue and white, implored Heaven for her son's return. Beside her, St. Ethelbert wore a crown of gold and in his arms he held gifts—gifts for the bride whom he would not live long enough to marry. The bishop held the letter at arm's length, as if to consider the scope of its meaning, and read it aloud:

"My Queen,

Why, Isabella, have you so forsaken me? To what end? I am broken. At your mercy. I have nothing. My sorrows grow by the day.

Take joy in that, if it pleases you.

But can we not have peace between us? I will forgive your betrayal, if that is what you desire, so that we may be as husband and wife again. Let us reconcile then and begin anew. Send me word of where and when. Or send an envoy to speak on your behalf. It matters little. Only, please, let us call an end to this senselessness.

Edwardus Rex
Neath"

"Will you offer him terms, my lady? The Abbot of Neath is waiting at the palace to carry a reply back to King Edward."

The bishop had found me there, in the Lady Chapel of Hereford's church, while I knelt at the altar deep in my evening prayers. I straightened the creases from my loose-fitting, gray gown of fustian. If not for the rich red of my mantle, which I wore only for warmth, I might have been mistaken for a nun. Since my return to England, I had dressed in widow's weeds. So that all would know that Edward of Caernarvon was no longer a husband to me.

"I think he means to offer *me* terms," I said, bewildered by the irony of it. Once, I would have snatched at compromise. However, the time for making amends was long gone. "He says nothing of Hugh Despenser. I am not sure what to make of such a glaring omission."

"Perhaps the king thinks you will overlook that in light of his conciliation?"

"If he believes for even a moment that I might pardon any of Despenser's transgressions, then he is not only arrogant, but deluded. And he comprehends nothing of why I left England." Nothing, indeed. It had cost me my children and earned me the admonishment of the Pope. What woman would suffer such anguish and humiliation if not for good reason?

Orleton returned the letter to me. "They say he tried to raise an army from Gower. No one came to join him."

I cupped my left palm and tapped the letter against it. "Which would explain his desperation, but if . . . if I do as he asks, dear bishop, and send someone to talk with him—what does he expect? If Despenser is still with him, surely he must know that . . ."

Could it be so easy?

I clenched my fingers around the letter until it crimped in the middle. My greatest hope was that Despenser had not abandoned Edward and escaped to Ireland or the continent. I wanted him found and I wanted him brought to me.

Orleton arched a silver eyebrow at me. "Who shall we send back with the Abbot of Neath as our 'envoy'?"

Without hesitation, I answered, "Leicester."

My uncle, Henry, would bring them to me. He had his own matters to settle with Edward and Despenser. The denial of his hereditary titles, for one. His brother's murder another.

Bishop Orleton opened the door and stood aside. A chill draft wrapped around me. I pulled my mantle tight and clutched the letter to my breast.

He offered his arm. "Will you come with me to the hall, my lady? A feast has been prepared in your honor. The guests are waiting." A short walk from the church stood the bishop's palace overlooking the River Wye, where he kept residence and entertained guests. By now the hall would be filled with cries for retribution. "I will offer the Abbot of Neath a room for the night where he can take his supper in private. He is merely the messenger, but I fear there are a few here who might take it upon themselves to prevent his return. In the morning, we will send him on his way. With the earl, of course."

It was inevitable. It would be done. If it was what I had so long wanted, why then did I not feel joy well up inside me, ready to burst in triumph? I searched Orleton's erudite face for solace, some logical reassurance that I had set my feet on the right path; but all I saw in his unclouded eyes was the mounting tally of Edward's wrongs. To falter now, to overlook any of it, was the very weakness that Edward depended on.

I slipped the letter beneath the side opening of my cyclas and tucked it beneath my belt, then hooked my arm inside his. "Revenge, dear bishop—does it ever end?"

He patted my hand. "It ends when we trust in Our Lord and allow Him to deliver—"

"Justice?"

Lightly, he squeezed my hand in correction. "Judgment. God, my child, does not seek justice. That is something he leaves to men."

If justice was the realm of men, then I knew of one man in particular who would be eager to dispense it and without remorse: Roger Mortimer. He would see it done. Just as he had sworn to do.

We walked across the yard in fast falling darkness to the great Norman hall of the bishop's palace and ascended the steps. I lifted the hem of my skirt. Cool November air brushed my ankles. I shivered. The guards bowed, signaled at the door with a knock and it opened. At the threshold, I pulled in a deep breath. So lost in thought I was, that I barely recognized the familiar faces of great lords and knights who rose upon our arrival and smiled at me. We went forward. The torchlight grew brighter, the smells of roasted meats and spiced wine stronger, the sting of smoke sharper, and the sounds of voices louder and louder until all my senses swirled in confusion.

How was it that it had all come to this? How would I ever know that what I was about to do . . . would be right?

I curled my fingernails into the soft flesh of my palm and I remembered . . . everything.

Everything.

THE GREAT SALT WAS carried aloft in a *nef* of pearls and rock-crystal, mounted on a stem of gold. Murmurs of delight and light applause rippled through the great hall of the bishop's palace, as servants bearing silver platters swarmed from table to table. Spit-roasted venison and capons stuffed with breadcrumbs seasoned with rosemary and sage were laid out, sliced and served. Quinces, filled with honey and wrapped in pastries, glowed golden with saffron. I had never known Orleton to be an extravagant man, but on this rare occasion he meant to impress. He straightened in his chair and smoothed the gold-tasseled end of his red silk stole flat against his abdomen.

I laid my hand over Young Edward's, who was seated to my left at the high table. Bishop Stratford, next to him, bestowed me with a welcoming smile and I leaned forward to look further down the table to catch Mortimer's eye, but he was engaged in a lively debate with the Earl of Norfolk.

"Sir Roger," I called above the rising din, but he took no notice. Since returning to England, and particularly since I had reprimanded him on our way to Bristol, Mortimer had been diligent about stepping back into the shadows, so much so that he would not even meet my eyes if I looked at him across a room filled with people. I waved a knife in the air and called his name again, louder.

Stiffly, he turned his head. "My lady?"

"If it is not an inconvenience, I should like to meet briefly with you and Lord Leicester after supper. I have need of your advice regarding a document."

Mortimer arched a skeptical brow at me and nodded. "As you wish, my lady." Then he turned back to Norfolk and said, "I say we hurry no one home, least of all the Hainaulters. It is might in numbers that will keep the peace until—"

"I heard rumor today, my queen," Leicester interposed, as he sawed at his venison, "that the king is making his way to Scotland to throw himself at the Bruce's feet to beg sanctuary there."

"Did you, Lord Henry?" I replied with a small laugh, wishing it were true, for King Robert would have probably locked him up in a dungeon for a very long time, just as he had Edward's cousin, the Earl of Richmond. "Do you think they will join forces and march on York?"

Rumbling with laughter, Leicester elbowed Lord Wake. The ewerer poured wine from a silver-gilt flask into his goblet. Then Leicester hoisted his drink, drained it in a single gulp and slammed it down. Dragging the back of his hand across his mouth, he stifled a belch before imparting more. "I also heard he joined a monastery. That would be more like him, wouldn't it—hiding beneath a cowl?"

I settled back and pressed my right hand to my middle, feeling the crinkle of parchment beneath my clothing. Everything rushed back to me with frightening suddenness: the years I wasted trying to be the loyal, dutiful wife; Edward's constant neglect of me; seeing Despenser hold his face with familiarity and place a tender kiss upon his cheek, then close the door to carry on privately; Despenser tearing my children from my arms and little Joanna crying for me; his knife pressed to my throat . . .

"Mother?" Young Edward turned his hand over, so that my palm was cupped in his. "What troubles you?"

"I'm not troubled," I said, curling my fingers around his and giving his hand a squeeze, "not at all."

"Then anxious? Fatigued? Not ill, I pray?"

I looked down at my right hand, still pressed against the letter, and sighed. "On the contrary—I have never felt better, never more certain of things than I am now."

And strangely, it was true.

"More wine?" I enquired, raising a hand to beckon the ewerer.

Chin lowered, Young Edward nodded. "I was wondering," he began, somewhat shyly, "when Philippa can come to England?"

"I cannot say precisely, my dear." When my cup was filled I sipped from it, its fruity aroma making my head go light. "Certainly you'll want to be able to lavish her with your full attention when she does arrive, yes? And her father will want to see that all the conditions have been fulfilled before he puts his daughter on a ship to England. You understand, don't you? There is so much to do before that can happen."

One day my son would be a king among kings, but he was only a boy. His dreams were simple. He did not understand that to do what was right, what was best—it was not always easy. That was a burden that I took onto my own shoulders, so he would not have to.

Vexed, he wrinkled his forehead. "Such as?"

I set my goblet down and smoothed a stray hair from his temple. "We will talk of it later, my dearest. Until then, you needn't worry yourself. It will all be taken care of."

At that moment, Mortimer reached across his plate, looked my way, and smiled broadly.

BISHOP ORLETON CLOSED THE door of the meeting room behind him, shutting out the lingering clamor of the great hall. One hand shielding the flame of the candle he carried, he crossed the room and placed it on the large oak table there. I drew the letter from beneath my cyclas, opened it and laid it on the table. Mortimer leaned over it, Leicester squinting over his shoulder.

"From Edward," I said, seating myself on a bench at the far end. "You'll find his proposal interesting."

When they finished, neither said a word. Mortimer went to stand closer to the hearth and gazed into its pale blue flames, while Leicester paced, fists braced on his hips.

"Hugh Despenser was at Neath with him," the bishop elaborated, "when the letter was sent, along with Chancellor Robert de Baldock. The king tried again to raise troops, but to no avail."

Leicester swiveled on his heel, stomping his foot thunderously on the tiles. "Did he even receive the prince's letter?"

"Most assuredly, he did." Orleton clasped his hands beneath his sleeves. A pale shine of starlight lit the bishop's features as he drifted toward the only window in the room. The lines on his face, although not numerous, had etched themselves more deeply during the time that I was away. The last few years had been easy for no one, not even a pious and scholarly man such as Adam Orleton. "Maltravers delivered it into the king's hands, saw him open it and read it. The king protested that his son would never have made such a request—that the 'she-wolf', and that 'traitorous bastard Mortimer', put him up to it."

"And he wrote *this* in answer?" Leicester opened his arms wide, incredulous.

"Three days later," Orleton said. "According to the Abbot of Neath, the reason it took so long for the king to reply was that he and Despenser were at odds. An argument, of some sort. He did not hear the full details of it, but he knows that once Lord Despenser learned of his father's fate, figuring his would be the same, he had no wish to parley with the queen. The king, however, rather than submit, since it is obvious even to him that his hold on power has dissolved, seeks to reconcile with the queen."

Mortimer indicated the letter with a tilt of his head. "Does the prince know of this?"

"No," I said, "he does not."

"So, what will you do?" Mortimer stroked at the bristles on his chin and neck. "Call a council meeting? Write back to him?"

"And say what? What is left to be said? Certainly not that I will return to him." My heart racing at the terror of the thought, I tapped a finger heavily on the edge of the table. "No, there is nothing more to be said . . . and if I put this before council, it would only drag on for days." Although I had already laid out my plans, I had avoided recognizing their urgency until that moment. "Time is critical. We have not the luxury of wasting it. I have already decided what is to be done."

For once, Leicester was silent. I returned his penetrating gaze. "Henry, you and Lord Wake are to escort the abbot back to Neath. You will place King Edward, Chancellor Baldock and Lord Despenser under arrest. Lord Wake shall bring Despenser here, to Hereford. I should like to say a few things to Hugh Despenser, before he is sent on to London to stand trial before the people."

The thick line of his eyebrows lifted as he nodded in acceptance, subduing the thrill that must have rushed through his veins at the prospect of hunting down the very man who had decided his brother's fate. "And the king, my lady?"

"You will take him to Kenilworth, my lord, and see to it that there is no way for him to get out, or for anyone to get in. Can you do that?"

It required will, at that moment, not to share a fleeting smile with

Mortimer. For in sending Leicester after the king, I kept him from inter-fering while Mortimer and I laid out my son's future.

As if he were inspecting every angle of my proposition, Leicester took his time answering. Finally, he scoffed. "And you . . . trust *me* to keep watch over the king?"

"There is no one I trust more, Henry."

A mischievous grin curved his lips beneath his full, red mustache. He nodded once and strode from the room.

I gave the letter unto Bishop Orleton's care, with instructions that no one else was to see it until the king was taken into custody. Then the bishop left to return to the great hall to bid his guests a good night. I rose to follow him, but Mortimer placed himself in my way.

The door slightly ajar, he drew me back toward the table and kept his voice low. "Edward's greatest mistake was not in ignoring your beauty; it was in failing to realize your cleverness."

I sank back down onto the bench and rested my elbows on the table as the weight of my decision and what would ensue began to seep into me. "Clever, perhaps. But not without conscience," I confided. "At one time, I thought I would go to any lengths to have my children back. Any length to find happiness." Mortimer laid a gentle hand on my shoulder and I realized that with him I could speak my mind as I never could with Edward. "Now that I have those things, I find it is not all so simple. I fear that what we are doing . . . it will all come back on us—if not immediately, then some day, in some terrible way. God forgive me, but I am not sure, anymore, what is right and what is wrong."

"Do you think anyone does?" He circled the table, until he stood on the other side. Candle-flame danced between us. His eyes intent on me, he leaned forward and spread his fingers on the table. "Do not cling to your guilt, Isabella. It serves no one—least of all you."

When he went from the room, the draft from the door closing snuffed out the candle.

48

Isabella:

Hereford– November, 1326

IN THE DAYS THAT followed, as I waited to learn of Leicester's mission, measures were taken to secure my son's accession to the throne. As much as everyone wanted Edward of Caernarvon shrived of his crown, we flouted law and custom if we took it from him. It would need to be handled delicately, but resolutely. Evidence that Edward had not fulfilled his duties of kingship, however, would not be hard to conjure. Despenser's transgressions even easier. Writs were issued in the prince's name, summoning parliament to Westminster in December. Bishop Stratford, who had been newly named as Treasurer, was dispatched to London. There, Richard de Bethune, who had aided in Mortimer's escape from the Tower, would replace Hamo de Chigwell as mayor.

Then, the day came. The day everything I had planned for, since I first wrote to Charles and begged for his help.

Joanna and I were tucked away in a window seat on a stair landing of the bishop's palace. The light from the afternoon sun was strong, although winter's chill slipped its fingers between the cracks of the window panes to tease at the back of my neck. My daughter was sitting in my lap, copying the letters of the words I had written for her to practice. Distracted, she gouged the clay tablet with the point of her stylus.

"Mother?" She twisted around to look over my shoulder and then wriggled from my hold. The tablet tumbled to the floor. She pressed her fingertips to the frosty glass. "Do you hear trumpets?"

"A hunt, perhaps," I said, as I bent forward to retrieve the tablet. "But that would be far away. You have keen ears, my little one."

"No, down there," she insisted, her small jaw working back and forth. "Who is that?"

Trumpets blared. I peered over her curly head of yellow hair, beyond the low walls of the bishop's palace, where a crowd was rapidly gathering in the market square. What I saw made my heart flame with hatred.

Hugh Despenser rode tied to the back of a nag that was so old and lame it could barely walk. He wobbled side to side, as if too weak to stay upright. From the front of the party, Lord Wake dismounted and strode back to Despenser. He grasped the chain linking Despenser's hands and yanked him down. Despenser's limp body flopped sideways and disappeared below the crowd.

"Ida! Ida!" I called up the stairs as I pulled Joanna away from the window. "Come quickly!"

A few moments later, Ida crabbed sideways down the stairs, muttering to herself. She pressed one hand against her ribs as she gasped from the effort of hurrying and the other hand against the wall to keep her balance. "Yes, my lady?"

"Keep Joanna and her sister in their room. They are not to come out unless I send for them. Do you understand?"

"Something wrong?"

Without answering her, I gathered my skirts up, plunged down the stairs, through the hall, which had already been vacated, and out the gaping outer door. A sharp wind snatched at my breath, reminding me that I was not wearing my mantle. The cry of a trumpet shattered the air again and a drum beat franticly. People poured out of the palace and church. I bunched my skirts in my hands and began to run. Before I reached the object of the crowd's derision, Mortimer caught me by the wrist.

I pulled in a deep breath. A moment passed in which we searched each other's eyes, opened our mouths, and yet remained silent. Then he gave me his hand, turned and guided me through the palace gate, shoving his way through the rising mass of bodies as he shouted to make way for the queen. When we reached the front of the crowd at the market square, he let go of my hand and stepped aside, sweeping his hand outward to encourage me forward. Shouted insults were hurled at the captive, but as they saw me, the noise fell away like the tide breaking on the shore and retreating.

Despenser lay on his side on the cobbles, trying to push himself up on an elbow. He leered back ineffectively at the hostile faces surrounding him. Then, his elbow gave way and he dropped his head, as if he could not hold it up. He drew a shaking hand over his eyes.

Behind him stood Lord Wake, grinning. "Your prisoner, my queen."

I stepped closer to inspect the man who had been the cause of so much turmoil for all of England and personal grief for me. Without his fine trappings and a king's authority to wield, he was nothing. A barely breathing corpse devoid of a soul. He had been stripped bare except for his ragged breeches, which hung so loose on his narrow hips that they did not fully cover those parts they were intended to. The bottoms of his feet were raw to the bone. Blood streamed from his elbows, stomach and knees, the skin dangling by flaps in some places, missing altogether in others, indicating he had been dragged partway through the streets of Hereford.

On his chest, the word '*peccavi*'—Latin for 'I have sinned'—had been carved.

In spite of my loathing for the man, a bolt of disgust shot through me to think of a knife digging at human flesh. I closed my eyes and spread my palms flat against my stomach, stiffening as I recalled the night in the

Tower that Despenser had stolen into my room, pressed his knife to my throat and threatened my children and my life. Then I opened my eyes to meet Lord Wake's gloating gaze.

"An easy catch," he vaunted. "They were gone from Neath long before we got there, but they were not hard to follow. We came upon them near Llantrissant. They tried to run. Didn't get far." Wake nudged at Despenser with the toe of his boot. "He hasn't taken food or water since we began on our way here. Said he'd rather starve to death than be tried for treason."

"And the king?" I asked, my voice sounding small to me. Or perhaps it was that I could not believe that this day had at last arrived. That Hugh Despenser lay sprawled on the ground before me, shackled and gutted of his power.

"Lord Leicester took him directly to Monmouth, my lady. He, too, is weakened from his ordeal at sea and his flight. When the king is fit enough, Leicester will take him on to Kenilworth."

At last, I felt the chill air enveloping me. Became aware of all the ogling faces. Saw the hands clenched in anger, ready to kill. The fingers gripping the hafts of hoes and scythes and butcher's hooks. The snarls of loathing. The enmity, everywhere.

Lord Wake reached into a bag tied to his saddle, took out an object and extended it to me. There in his open palm lay the golden lion pendant, its jeweled eyes dulled by a crust of dried blood and dirt, the fine links of its chain broken. I shook my head, refusing it. "Return it to the king—as a reminder of what becomes of those who have no limitations on their greed and self-interest."

Then I raised my voice to reach even the people crammed into the side alleys who had come to view the spectacle. "A pity, but I doubt this man would survive a journey to London to stand trial there. Indeed, even if he could, some bloodthirsty mob might prevent him from getting so far. Do what you will with him, Lord Wake. If anything more terrible should happen to him . . . I did not get here in time to stop it from happening."

403

As I turned to step back into the crowd, I heard the rattle of metal. A hand—Despenser's—latched around my ankle. I lurched sideways, catching my balance with my other foot. Both Wake and Mortimer started forward, but Despenser's grip was feeble and I jerked my leg forward to tear myself free. He clawed again at me with his scabbed hands. I took one more small step back, holding my hands up to stop anyone from rescuing me. I did not need it. Despenser was too near death already to pose any threat.

"Please," he mewled, raising his grime-covered face to me, his tears mixing with the dirt and blood smeared on his face, "have you no mercy?"

"May Our Lord, at least, have mercy on you," I said to him, "for I have none."

Hugh Despenser was dragged naked behind a quartet of horses to the bailey of Hereford Castle, where a high gallows had already been constructed at Mortimer's instruction. Along with a host of other lords and clerics, Mortimer and I stood atop the wall walk to the rear of the ravenous throng. Before the gallows, logs were piled to the height of men's heads. The fire was kindled with dry hay and rushes and lit, its flames lapping at the sky. Despenser could barely stand without being held up. His wrists were broken; his feet twisted at odd angles; his skin scraped down to sinew in places; blood and dirt clumped on what remained of his flesh. His weak cries were drowned out by the jeering crowd. They looped a rope over his head and—as his long list of crimes were read out—pulled him as high in the air as the castle walls. Thick smoke rolled across my view, but I swear, before his tongue protruded purple from his mouth and his eyes rolled back into his head, he looked straight at me.

When his spirit had left his body, they took him down. Cut his genitals off and flung them into the belching fire for his sodomy. Sliced open his belly, pulled loose his intestines and burned them, too. Then, his heart.

I watched it all as if in a daze, detached from my own horror, unable to feel either compassion or relief, but all too eager to forget the details. It was done.

His head was sent to London. The rest of him to the four corners of England.

Baldock was sent in chains to Newgate prison in London. But before he could stand trial before the clergy, he was murdered by other prisoners.

Edward had been taken on to Kenilworth. Leicester was content to be his keeper.

And only two months since we had landed at the River Orwell in Suffolk.

EPILOGUE

Isabella:

Wallingford – December 24th, 1326

"**B**ITTER COLD OUT HERE," Mortimer complained as he joined me in the garden just outside Wallingford. The cloud of his breath hung in the air and his ears were rimmed in red.

"It *is* winter, my lord," I remarked, watching a robin in the bough of a pear tree fluff its feathers against the chill. "Although my bed was quite warm last night. So warm, in fact, that I had to throw the blankets off."

"I remember." He turned to wander beside me through the orchard. Hoarfrost shimmered on the knobby, bare branches of the apple trees. Icy grass crunched under our feet. "You were feverish. Glistening with sweat."

A smile lifted my cheeks as I slipped my hands free of my mantle and tugged my deerskin gloves on tighter. "As were you."

"Shall I warm your bed again tonight, my love?"

"After vespers. But be gone by midnight."

"Midnight? Why? You'll grow cold long before sunrise. Has the gossip about us sprung anew?" he teased, although the danger of us being discovered was always frighteningly real.

"That," I said, looking at him sideways, "and that I need to sleep *sometime.* Yesterday Joanna was so excited about the prospect of tomorrow's Christmas feast, she came bounding into my chambers when the bells rang prime." I stifled a yawn, my steps dragging as I felt the weariness of my nocturnal ways creeping through my body. Nearly every night since the day of Despenser's death, Mortimer had come to my bed, the result of which had been utter exhaustion for us both come morning. But each night, in the darkness, that exhaustion was drawn from me by his touch, replaced by the promise of rapture. A promise always fulfilled. Indeed, I wondered how long we could go on like this and if on some tomorrow it would all end. Then I would see him, or think of him, my gentle Mortimer, and I would cease to wonder. Because I loved him so completely.

At that moment, with the world sculpted in ice and the distant winter sun climbing in a broad blue sky, there was only now. Only us.

Then, Bishop Orleton appeared at the garden gate, a letter in his hands. Chin thrust forward, his robes flowing behind him, he strode toward us.

"The Great Seal?" I asked. "Did he relinquish it to you?"

"He did," Orleton said. "I gave it over to the prince's care already."

At the good news, I gave Mortimer's arm a light squeeze. "I thank you, your grace. You must have been persuasive. Then he agreed to give up the crown?"

He lowered his eyes, sighing, and held out the letter. "I regret he did not."

My momentary exultation was dashed at the frozen ground. Why did Edward resist the inevitable? I withdrew my hand from Mortimer's arm and took the letter. Bishop Orleton dipped at the waist and backed away, then turned and went from the garden. I fumbled at the seal, which bore Edward's mark, reluctant to remove my gloves and expose my fingers to the cold.

Finally, Mortimer extended his hand to relieve me of the task. When the letter was opened, he laid it in my hands.

My Good Wife and Queen,

My heart is cloaked in winter's cold. Only hope saves it from shattering. But hope of what I do not know. That you will have me back? That the children will send their love in a letter or perhaps even grace me with a visit? That I will one day sit upon my throne, with you again beside me?

In whatever way I have caused offense to you, and you to me, let it be forgotten. For now, I pray to receive Our Lord's forgiveness. He, I know, will be so kind. May He bless both you and our children in abundance. May He take pity on me in my endless shame and enduring grief.

Edwardus Rex
Kenilworth

"He begs forgiveness now," I mused.

"And still thinks he'll be restored to his throne and that you'll have him back. I say he has nothing left but his hope. Let him have it."

Once, it was all I had.

I glanced down at the letter in my hands, remembering everything that had happened and how it had all come around to this day.

Tomorrow, I would sit at the high table, partaking in the Christmas feast. I would watch my children dance merrily and play games until their eyelids grew heavy with sleep. I would listen to the waves of song and the bursts of laughter filling Wallingford's high-raftered hall, as good and loyal friends raised their drinks to me.

My gentle Mortimer would glance at me and a private, knowing smile would pass over his lips.

A hundred times over, I would give thanks that I had never given up hope of this day.

    I had waited so long . . .

Historical Note

The invasion of England by Queen Isabella and Sir Roger Mortimer at the head of a mercenary force began on September 26th, 1326. On the 16th of November, Henry, the Earl of Leicester and later Lancaster, captured King Edward, Lord Hugh Despenser and Chancellor Robert Baldock. The flight of Edward and his companions from London westward and Isabella and Mortimer's pursuit of them have been greatly condensed here and slightly rearranged in their order to fit the telling of this tale.

The eldest son of Edward II and Isabella is referred to in these pages as Young Edward or Lord Edward, to avoid confusion. He was never installed as 'Prince of Wales', as his father before him had been, although he did bear many other prestigious titles, such as Duke of Aquitaine, Count of Ponthieu and Earl of Chester.

Exactly when and where Isabella and Mortimer began conspiring, which one instigated various schemes and when they became intimately involved are the subjects of much conjecture. They first met long before the Mortimers rose in rebellion. There is every reason to believe that Isabella visited Roger at the Tower of London while he was imprisoned there, perhaps even more than once. Clearly, both had motives to eliminate Despenser and remove Edward of Caernarvon from power. Gathering supporters to their cause, especially with Young Edward as their figurehead, was an easy task. King Edward and Despenser had flagrantly abused their power and could garner no sympathy in their most dire hour of need.

Sometimes, however, achieving a desired end is not truly the end. Hugh Despenser may have lost his life in the name of revenge, but the problem remained of what to do with Edward of Caernarvon and how to put his son on the throne in his place.

By the beginning of 1327, Roger Mortimer was the most powerful man in England—king in all but name. He was, however, not the only English noble with ambitions. Henry, Earl of Leicester and Lancaster, was not one to easily yield. And Young Edward would not remain young forever.

Acknowledgments

Many thanks are due to those who kindly offered their time and insight on this story. As always, I am greatly indebted to my critique partners: Lisa Yarde and Mirella Patzer were forever encouraging; Anita Davison is owed much credit for convincing me to be more economical with my words so that their meaning would have greater clarity; and I declare Julie Conner a saint for bravely volunteering to go over the whole thing a second time and helping me better define who my characters are.

I am grateful to the keen eyes of Glenn Kinyon for catching errors that even after several readings and revisions had previously gone undetected. Enormous thanks goes to Greta van der Rol, my writing partner and support system on the other side of the world. Her wisdom shall forever humble me.

My children, Reini and Mitchell (who are no longer truly children), were forever tolerant of my absences while writing, even though I was still in the same house. If I have but one hope for them, it would be that they discover their heart's desire and follow it, as I have.

And to my husband, lifelong love and best friend, Eric Brickson, who has given me the chance to live my dream, a thousand 'thank you's' would not be enough.

About the Author

N. Gemini Sasson holds a M.S. in Biology from Wright State University where she ran cross country on athletic scholarship. She has worked as an aquatic toxicologist, an environmental engineer, a teacher and a cross country coach. A longtime breeder of Australian Shepherds, her articles on bobtail genetics have been translated into seven languages. She lives in rural Ohio with her husband, two nearly grown children and an ever-changing number of sheep and dogs.

Isabeau is her second novel. Her previous work, *The Crown in the Heather*, is the first in a trilogy about Robert the Bruce.

www.ngeminisasson.com

CPSIA information can be obtained at www.ICGtesting.com
Printed in the USA
LVOW122101030212

266935LV00001B/343/P